A MO

Hilary glanc
his long legs spra
tightness of the borrowed shirt emph...
muscled shoulders and that his hair after his bath had
dried in tousled curls. Once again she admitted to herself that he was a disturbingly handsome man, despite
his careless grooming. She said hastily, to distract her
mind from the disturbing feeling, "I can hardly wait to
tell Nate that he has nothing more to fear from the
law."

Turning his head toward her, the duke said, "You
risked a great deal for that man, Hilary. Have you always been a nurturer? In my mind's eye, I can see you
as a child, rescuing injured baby birds. Or feeding beggars at the kitchen door of your father's house."

Hilary blurted, "How did you—?" Then she caught
the glint of amusement in Jon's eyes and began laughing.

"I have the second sight. Some kind of psychic gift,
anyway, so I can see into your mind." He set down his
coffee cup on a table next to the sofa and stretched luxuriously. "It feels so good to be warm and free of mud."

"Oh, that dreadful mud. After today I hope I won't
forget to appreciate the small pleasures of life." She
glanced at her slippers drying on the hearth. "Like dry
shoes." She handed him her empty cup to deposit on
the table next to him.

As their fingers touched, Jon said huskily, "I'd nearly
forgotten another of life's small pleasures." He set the
cup down and lifted her hand to his lips. "Kissing a
beautiful woman's hand, for instance."

ELEGANT LOVE STILL FLOURISHES —
Wrap yourself in a Zebra Regency Romance.

A MATCHMAKER'S MATCH   (3783, $3.50/$4.50)
by Nina Porter
To save herself from a loveless marriage, Lady Psyche Veringham pretends to be a bluestocking. Resigned to spinsterhood at twenty-three, Psyche sets her keen mind to snaring a husband for her young charge, Amanda. She sets her cap for long-time bachelor, Justin St. James. This man of the world has had his fill of frothy-headed debutantes and turns the tables on Psyche. Can a bluestocking and a man about town find true love?

FIRES IN THE SNOW   (3809, $3.99/$4.99)
by Janis Laden
Because of an unhappy occurrence, Diana Ruskin knew that a secure marriage was not in her future. She was content to assist her physician father and follow in his footsteps . . . until now. After meeting Adam, Duke of Marchmaine, Diana's precise world is shattered. She would simply have to avoid the temptation of his gentle touch and stunning physique — and by doing so break her own heart!

FIRST SEASON   (3810, $3.50/$4.50)
by Anne Baldwin
When country heiress Laetitia Biddle arrives in London for the Season, she harbors dreams of triumph and applause. Instead, she becomes the laughingstock of drawing rooms and ballrooms, alike. This headstrong miss blames the rakish Lord Wakeford for her miserable debut, and she vows to rise above her many faux pas. Vowing to become an Original, Letty proves that she's more than a match for this eligible, seasoned Lord.

AN UNCOMMON INTRIGUE   (3701, $3.99/$4.99)
by Georgina Devon
Miss Mary Elizabeth Sinclair was rather startled when the British Home Office employed her as a spy. Posing as "Tasha," an exotic fortune-teller, she expected to encounter unforeseen dangers. However, nothing could have prepared her for Lord Eric Stewart, her dashing and infuriating partner. Giving her heart to this haughty rogue would be the most reckless hazard of all.

A MADDENING MINX   (3702, $3.50/$4.50)
by Mary Kingsley
After a curricle accident, Miss Sarah Chadwick is literally thrust into the arms of Philip Thornton. While other women shy away from Thornton's eyepatch and aloof exterior, Sarah finds herself drawn to discover why this man is physically and emotionally scarred.

Available wherever paperbacks are sold, or order direct from the Publisher. Send cover price plus 50¢ per copy for mailing and handling to Zebra Books, Dept. 4300, 475 Park Avenue South, New York, N.Y. 10016. Residents of New York and Tennessee must include sales tax. DO NOT SEND CASH. For a free Zebra/Pinnacle catalog please write to the above address.

The Duke's Mistress
Lois Stewart

ZEBRA BOOKS
KENSINGTON PUBLISHING CORP.

Chapter I

Northumberland, England, late summer, 1811

Dr. Matthew Vane, late of His Majesty's Anglo-Portugese Army in the Peninsula, limped into the hallway of his new home on the way to his surgery and stopped short at the sight of his sister.

"Good God, what's that thing you've got on your head?" he inquired.

Hilary Vane put her hand up to the towel forming a voluminous turban covering her hair and replied, laughing, "Is it really so dreadful?"

"Yes, it makes you look like a regular man," the doctor retorted. "And why are you wearing what appears to be one of Cook's aprons?"

Glancing down at the enveloping garment that completely concealed her own clothes except for her sleeves, Hilary said, "It *is* one of Cook's aprons. I borrowed it so I could help Sarah clean the house."

"No. I won't have it," snapped Matthew Vane. His normally good-natured expression turned grim. "You didn't come up here to be a maid of all work. You came to open a school."

"And so I will, shortly. But first things first." Hilary gestured to the hallway, lined on both sides with boxes and assorted articles of furniture. The carrier carts had preceded their arrival with the old-fashioned contents of an elderly aunt's house, which the deceased lady had bequeathed to Hilary in her will. The overflow of furniture from the hallway crowded the drawing room.

"Before we can arrange the furniture, the house will have to be cleaned," Hilary went on. "Recall, no one's lived here for over five years. Look." Hilary brushed her feather duster over the door frame of the drawing room. A silent shower of dust fell to the floor.

"Well, but it's not your job to clean the house," said the doctor belligerently. "We have servants—"

Hilary interrupted him. "Matt, we have a staff of exactly three: our indoor maid, Sarah, Cook, and Ephraim, who will take care of the horses and the garden. They all have enough to do. Why shouldn't I work with Sarah if it will help us to get settled more quickly?"

"It's not right. You're the mistress of the house, not the scullery maid," Matt persisted. Suddenly he swayed, grabbing at a set of shelves next to him to support himself. He had turned very pale.

"Matt! Is it your leg? Here, let me help you." Hilary put her arm around her brother's waist and guided him into the drawing room to a chair draped in a Holland cover.

He sat with his head bowed, breathing heavily. After a few moments he muttered, without looking up, "Damned leg. It's left me half a man. I've got no more stamina than a baby. I can't even provide my sister with a proper home, one with enough servants so that she doesn't have to clean her own house."

Hilary looked down at her brother with mingled anxiety and affection. Matt had been wounded three months before at the battle of Fuentes de Oñoro. His fellow military surgeons had just managed to save his leg, but he was left with such a bad limp that he had great difficulty in walking. He decided to leave the Army and establish his own practice in this remote Northumberland village. Hilary knew he still suffered bouts of severe pain, which he ordinarily managed to conceal beneath a sunny, even-tempered facade. But there were times, as now, when dejection at his crippled condition caught up with him.

"I shouldn't have asked you to come to this Godforsaken place," Matt continued, still not looking up. "You were happy in your school at Tunbridge Wells. You were Miss Wiggins's favorite schoolmistress. You told me yourself that she'd hinted she wanted you to take her place as headmistress when she retired. You may have given up a prosperous future when you left Tunbridge Wells. Miss Wiggins's academy is a going concern."

Drawing up another of the Holland-covered chairs, Hilary sat down opposite Matt. "Don't you try to make me out a martyr," she said firmly. "I *wanted* to leave Miss Wiggins's academy. Oh, I was happy enough there. Miss Wiggins was very kind to me, and she allowed me to teach in my own way. But I was still an employee. I always wanted to be independent, to have my own school, and I didn't propose to wait around until Miss Wiggins retired. She won't leave her position as headmistress until she drops in her tracks years from now. I can't wait that long."

Lifting his head at last and leaning back in his chair, Matt grinned sheepishly. "Forgive me for being such a cawker, sister mine. My cursed leg felt as though a squadron of French heavy dragoons were using me for saber practice, and I was feeling sorry for myself. I'll try not to let it happen again." His color had returned to normal, and the pain was evidently less severe. He went on, "Of course, I've known for a long time that you wanted to start your own school ever since Harry Maitland, er, disappointed your hopes."

Her mouth agape, Hilary stared at the brother she thought she knew so well, this tall slender man of twenty-eight, with his regular features, bright blue eyes, and chestnut hair, whom everyone said resembled Hilary so closely they might be twins. How could Matt have misunderstood her actions so completely?

"Harry Maitland? Disappoint my hopes?" she spluttered. "All these years you've actually thought I was casting out lures to Harry and that he didn't come up to scratch?"

Matt looked taken aback. "Well, er—yes. Everybody thought so. Fact is, *Harry* went around hinting that was the case. Oh, he didn't actually say he'd changed his mind about marrying you. He simply said he was sorry that you and he didn't suit, but we all understood he was just being the gentleman, trying to save you from embarrassment."

Hilary ground her teeth. "That man! I refused his offer of marriage as gently as I could. I never told a soul that he'd proposed and that I'd declined his offer for fear of putting his nose out of joint. And this is how he repaid me. Oh, I could cheerfully wring Harry Maitland's neck when I think how the whole county was gossiping about me! Feeling sorry for me!"

After a moment Hilary's anger faded. She smiled at herself for feeling so resentful. It was all so long ago and so unimportant. She'd been eighteen, fresh out of her come-out season, when Harry Maitland courted her.

Now she was twenty-five, and she could hardly remember what he looked like.

Matt looked relieved at his sister's change of mood. "No wish to offend, y'know. I must say I'm glad to learn you haven't been wearing the willow for Maitland. Never liked him. Always thought he was a frippery sort of fellow."

A spark of annoyance reignited in Hilary's heart. "Not only did I *not* wear the willow for Harry Maitland," she retorted, "but, just to relieve your mind, I must tell you I've not been pining away for lack of suitors. I've actually received several eligible offers over the years. I didn't choose to accept any of them."

She glared at her brother for a moment, and then both of them burst out laughing. Wiping his eyes, Matt said, "Oh, Hilary, I missed you so much while I was away in the Peninsula. I didn't have anyone to laugh with or to make me see the ridiculous side of life."

Hilary looked at Matt, feeling a rush of the old affection that had united them so closely when they were growing up. They were the two younger children of an undistinguished Suffolk baronet. As a younger son, Matt had had to find his own way in the world and had elected to become a military surgeon. After her father's death, when she was nineteen, Hilary's older brother Richard, the new baronet, had invited her to stay on in the family home. However, she and Sir Richard's wife had never really liked each other. In any case, Hilary inherited a modest bequest from a favorite aunt and could afford to live independently if she chose. She had always been interested in female education and quickly became one of the most popular teachers at Miss Wiggins's academy. When Matt, invalided out of the Army, invited her to share a home with him in Northumberland, she'd jumped at the offer, especially as it meant she could realize her lifelong dream of opening her own school.

"I hope you won't find it too lonely here," Matt said with a worried frown. "I didn't realize this place was so isolated. We might as well be in the Antipodes as far as civilization is concerned."

"Oh, it's not as bad as that," said Hilary cheerfully. "Look at the bright side. Just because the village is so out of the way and there hasn't been a resident doctor here for over five years, you didn't need a fortune to buy the practice."

"Yes, the Duke of Alverly was apparently glad to obtain a doctor under any circumstances, even a crippled ex-military surgeon." There wasn't a trace of self-pity in Matt's voice, Hilary was relieved to hear. He'd recovered his usual wry, deprecating sense of humor.

Walking to the window, Hilary looked through the grimy panes at the short main street of the village of Wycombe, nestled deep in a valley of the Cheviots, the range of high hills dividing England from Scotland. It was an area of wild and magnificent scenery, consisting of a series of enfolding green hills punctuated by steep plateaus and moorlands, and slashed by a myriad of narrow valleys. It was as Matt had said, also undeniably lonely, a place of widely scattered homesteads, flocks of grazing sheep and herds of cattle and an occasional tiny village.

Hilary stared up at the great castle brooding over the village from atop its steep, nearly perpendicular crag. "Do you suppose we'll see anything of the Duke of Alverly?" she inquired idly. "I'd be interested to meet a modern example of a border lord."

"Border lords? Who are they?"

Hilary smiled. "Not 'are,' Matt. 'Were.' Like a typical schoolmistress, I did some reading about Northumberland before we came here. The border lords were the chieftains, both Scottish and English, who kept the peace by guarding against invading armies and marauding raids from the other side of the border. They were feudal lords, practically kings in their own domains. The Rayners—the Duke of Alverly is a Rayner—have occupied that castle up there since the thirteenth century, acting as 'Wardens of the Middle Marches.' Of course, when England and Scotland united in the early seventeenth century, there was no longer any need for the services of the border lords. Many of their castles were abandoned or pulled down, and the families moved away."

Matt limped up to stand beside Hilary at the window. Gazing intently at the castle for a long moment, he said, "Well, the Rayners are still very much there, at any rate. I've no doubt we'll meet the duke and his family before long." He shook himself. "I must get to work. My surgery is at sixes and sevens."

Hilary watched her brother making his slow and difficult way across the room. It was still so painful for him to walk, and even more painful to watch him. But pity was the last thing he wanted. She could help him most by making the house habitable and by being a cheerful companion. Grabbing her feather duster and a broom and dustpan, she went up the stairs, where Sarah, young and cheerful and red-headed and freckled, was already working industriously. The dust clouds were flying. Hilary wondered ruefully if they were really cleaning the rooms or merely displacing the dust.

"We have our work cut out for us, Sarah," Hilary said, smiling.

11

"Yes, ma'am. But it won't take long, wi' the two o' us working," said the girl shyly. Hilary was becoming familiar with the local accent, which at first she'd found hard to understand, with its lilting cadences and pronounced burr.

The second floor of the large old stone house was bisected by a long corridor from which numerous rooms opened on either side. Hilary had already decided to use all the rooms on the left side of the corridor for her school. There was a large room she could use for dance instruction, and smaller rooms for a library, a music room, and a classroom.

As she and Sarah worked companionably together, depositing dustpans full of debris into a large old barrel, Hilary inquired, "Did the doctor who formerly had the practice have a large family?"

"Oh, yes, ma'am. Thirteen—no, fourteen—children, as I recall. That's why old Dr. Ferris built on the wing for his surgery, so he could have more room for the family."

"As I thought. How lucky for me and my brother," Hilary gloated. "Matt has a separate, private surgery, and I have ample room for my school."

At the end of several hours, Hilary and Sarah had swept and dusted all the second-floor rooms and were beginning to wash the windows. As she worked with Sarah, Hilary chatted pleasantly, partly to gain an insight into the neighborhood, partly to put the maidservant at ease. She had a genuine interest in people, especially young people, and she had always had comfortable relations with her servants.

"Why is the house called Willow Cottage?" Hilary inquired. "There's not a willow to be seen."

Sarah looked bewildered. "Why, I don't know. The

12

house has always been called Willow Cottage as far back as I kin remember." She seemed puzzled by Hilary's curiosity. Clearly she herself had never given a thought to the subject.

Hilary tried again. "Do you ever see the duke?"

"Oh, yes, very often. He rides through the village most days on his way to visit his farms, do y'see. Sometimes he calls on the vicar and his wife, or the headmaster of the grammar school."

Hilary was surprised. She knew the Alverly dukedom was among the oldest and most prestigious in the kingdom, and, without having known one socially, she had always imagined dukes to be distant and standoffish.

"What's the duke like?" she asked Sarah.

"Oh, he's tall, and he has dark hair, and he rides splendid horses. He never talks very much unless he's displeased." Sarah paused, obviously convinced that she'd given an adequate description of the Duke of Alverly.

Hilary sighed, frustrated. Perhaps, one day soon, she would meet the duke and draw her own conclusions about his personality.

She was startled to hear a decisive voice behind her say, "You've made a good start. Before you know it, the house will be ready for occupancy."

Turning away from the window, washing cloth in hand, Hilary observed a tall man standing in the doorway. He had black hair, eyes of a dark slate gray, unsmiling and cool, and a handsome angular face, and appeared to be in his early to middle thirties. He was wearing a rather shabby coat, leather breeches and top boots. He carried in one hand a beaver hat with a low flat crown and a spreading brim.

Before Hilary could reply, the stranger advanced into

the room, gazing about him. He commented with a careless authority, "This seems to be a fair-sized room. I expect the good doctor will use it as the master's bedroom." Giving an abrupt nod, he said curtly, "Carry on," and left the room, but not before Hilary observed Sarah dipping a deep curtsey.

Hilary asked apprehensively, "Sarah, was that—?"

"Yes, ma'am, if you mean was that His Grace. As I was telling ye, he often pops into the village. He likes to know what's happening."

Well! thought Hilary indignantly. His Grace of Alverly might have had the simple courtesy to introduce himself and to greet the sister of his newly appointed surgeon. Then she happened to glance down at her apron, splotched with grime and not a few cobwebs, and groaned. The duke had taken her for a servant, of course. And why shouldn't he? She certainly looked like one. She hurried to the windows in the corner of the room, which overlooked the front of the house. She hadn't yet begun to wash them. She glanced down at her front gate. A large handsome sorrel stallion was tethered there. Perhaps if she hurried . . .

Racing into her bedchamber—she and Matt had sketchily furnished the sleeping quarters as soon as they arrived yesterday—Hilary tore off the offending apron and the towel that covered her hair. Pulling down the sleeves of her sprigged muslin morning gown, she glanced into the cheval glass and groaned again. The gown looked presentable enough, but her hair was hopelessly mussed, and her face wore several streaks of dirt. Hastily she brushed her chestnut curls into a topknot at the crown of her head, wiped her face with a damp cloth, and headed out the door and down the staircase to the foyer.

A quick look out the front door revealed that the duke's mount was still waiting at the gate, but he himself was nowhere in sight. Perhaps he'd gone to introduce himself to Matt. Quickly walking around the side of the house to the surgery, which had its separate entrance at the end of the building, Hilary paused as she observed Ephraim, their man of all work, standing outside the door.

"Good morning, Ephraim. Have you seen—?" Hilary broke off. The man was staring at the door of the surgery, seemingly transfixed. "What is it? Is something wrong?" she asked quickly.

"Well, I don't rightly know, ma'am. A few minutes ago Farmer Dennis's oldest lad brought his father along in a cart. Farmer Dennis was bleeding like a stuck pig, if ye'll excuse me, ma'am. A scythe he was using slipped and cut him something cruel, according to the boy. Well, as it happened, His Grace was jist coming oot the door o' the house. The duke helped the Dennis lad carry his father to the surgery. They're all o' 'em still in there wi' the doctor."

Hilary gently slipped the latch of the surgery door and peered inside. A lad of about seventeen crouched in a corner, his eyes intent on what was happening at the examining table. Matt stood on one side of the patient who was lying on the blood-soaked table. The duke, in his shirt sleeves, stood on the other side of the table, his hands on the crude tourniquet that was tied around the patient's upper leg.

"A little tighter, man," Matt ordered the duke, and a moment later he barked, "Not that tight, you damned fool. D'you want to cut off the patient's blood supply completely? Ease up a bit now—yes, that's it." Moments of hard-breathing silence ticked by. Finally Matt said in a low voice to the duke, "Begin releasing the pressure ever so gradually. . . . That's done it. The bleeding's stopped." He pressed a thick bandage to the ugly-looking cut and tied it securely. Then he stood beside the pale and unconscious patient, observing him closely. Gradually the farmer's eyes opened, and he made an instinctive move to rise. "No, Mr. Dennis, you must stay still," said Matt soothingly.

"My leg," the farmer muttered weakly.

"I believe we've saved your leg, Mr. Dennis, but you must continue to follow doctor's orders. No unnecessary movement, or you may start your wound bleeding again."

The patient's face relaxed, and his eyes slowly closed again.

Turning away from the examining table, Matt clapped the duke on the shoulder, leaving a large bloody mark on the white linen ducal shirt. "Well, sir, I thank you for a good morning's work," he said heartily. "Could I ask you to stay for a bit until I'm sure there's no chance of the bleeding starting again? Mr. Dennis's son will need help in carrying his father out to the cart. I'd not be of much use there. As you've probably noticed, I have a game leg."

"Certainly, doctor," the duke murmured. "I'm happy to be of assistance."

Hilary came out of the semi-trance into which she'd fallen during those tension-filled moments while Matt was trying to save Farmer Dennis's life and leg. She groaned inwardly. She and Matt, each in his or her own way, had just made the worst of initial impressions on the Duke of Alverly. The duke had taken her for her own chambermaid, and Matt had treated him like one of his soldier medical orderlies.

Advancing into the surgery, Hilary said with a deceptive calm, "Duke, may I introduce myself? I'm Hilary Vane, and this is my brother, Dr. Matthew Vane."

The duke's slate gray eyes narrowed as he gave Hilary a long, cool look. He recognizes me, she thought resignedly. However, he merely bowed, saying, "How do you do, Miss Vane, doctor."

Matt's face turned a dull red. "I'm sorry, Duke, I had no idea who you were when I pressed you so cavalierly into service."

"There's no need for an apology," said the duke, as he shrugged himself into his coat. "You had a real emergency on your hands." He smiled slightly. "Actually I was very glad to see you in action, so to speak. Now I know that the village of Wycombe has an excellent resident doctor again."

Matt relaxed at the compliment. Then he chuckled, saying, "Might I ask if you were apprehensive that you'd engaged a butchering incompetent from the Peninsula, sir?"

The duke smiled again. "Not at all. You'll admit, though, that a military surgeon's duties differ from those of a civilian doctor. To be frank, I thought there might be a period of adjustment on your part. I've just been proved wrong. Now then, doctor, when do you wish me to return to help young Alfred"—the duke motioned toward the farmer's son in the corner—"move his father into the cart?"

"No need for that, now I think of it. Ephraim, our outside man, can help Alfred."

"As you will. I'll take my leave, then."

Making an impulsive decision, Hilary said, "Will you take a glass of wine, Duke? Our dining room is reasonably in order, so I can offer you a chair." The duke

17

seemed somewhat surprised at the invitation. After a moment, he said, "Why, yes, thank you."

Matt shook his head. "You'll have to excuse me, I'm afraid. I should stay with Mr. Dennis until he's in stable condition."

The dining room had a more orderly look than the rest of the cluttered house, but it was very bare. The carriers had deposited a table and chairs there, but hadn't laid the carpet, and Hilary hadn't yet had time to rummage through the barrels and assemble her best china and glassware. For immediate use she had only a mismatched jumble of dishes and glasses.

Apparently the duke didn't notice the state of the room. He accepted the wine Hilary offered him and sat back in his chair, eyeing her with an intent look that she found a little unnerving.

Up close he didn't appear especially ducal, she thought. Meeting him without knowing who he was, she might have taken him for a shopkeeper or a not-overly-prosperous farmer, with his shabby coat, his carelessly tied cravat, his rather shaggy hair that brushed his collar in back. But then she met his gaze fully, and she changed her mind. No one encountering the power of those cool, penetrating gray eyes could possibly think of this man as an insignificant tradesman or farmer.

"I hope you won't find Wycombe too dull, Miss Vane," the duke observed. "There's not a great deal of socializing here. In the village, you'll doubtless find the vicar and his wife congenial, and close by in the neighboring valleys there are a number of respectable families, but by and large, we lead very quiet lives here."

"I didn't come here to lead an active social life, Duke. Naturally I'm happy to have the opportunity of making a home with my brother. Matt and I haven't seen very

18

much of each other since he joined the Army. But primarily I came to Wycombe to establish my own school for young ladies."

The duke's slate gray eyes darkened into black. "A school for young ladies? There's no need for such a school in Wycombe, Miss Vane. The children of my tenants are very adequately served by the excellent grammar school my father established in the village many years ago. There the pupils learn to read and write and do their sums and memorize their prayers. What else could they possibly need for their station in life?"

Hilary felt the faint flutterings of disaster. "I'm sure the village grammar school is an excellent one, Duke. What I had in mind to establish is a form of finishing school, in which the daughters of your tenant farmers could acquire the rudiments of good manners, dancing ability, musical skills, an acquaintance with good literature and geography, and a smattering of French and Italian. I taught in such a school in Tunbridge Wells for some years. I believe I'm qualified to establish my own school."

"Doubtless you *are* qualified to operate such a school, and you have my blessing to do so wherever you wish, but not in Wycombe," the duke snapped. "The daughters of my tenant farmers need to know how to run their future households and to please their future husbands, and those duties their mothers can teach them. They certainly don't require any knowledge of French or Italian or the pianoforte."

Hilary bristled. "My teaching would enable these girls to see beyond the narrow confines of the world they live in," she said coldly. "Their lives would be enriched, and they might also acquire such social skills as would allow

19

them to marry above their station. I'm sure their families would welcome *that!*"

The duke rose, setting down his glass. His gaze was glacial. "I'll be frank with you, Miss Vane. I'm very much opposed to your plans to open a finishing school in the Wycombe Valley. I think you'll find that my tenants will agree with me."

"We'll see about that, my lord duke," vowed Hilary silently, as she accompanied her guest to the door and dropped him a chilly curtsey of farewell.

Chapter II

Pulling on her driving gloves, Hilary glanced approvingly into the dining room and drawing room, which were situated opposite each other off the hallway. Several days of hard work on her part and Sarah's had achieved very creditable results. Walls and woodwork, floors and windows, were shining clean, and Aunt Alvenia's substantial, old-fashioned furniture looked perfectly at home in its new surroundings.

Hilary checked the set of her bonnet in the mirror over the table in the hallway. It was a plain bonnet of chip straw, decorated only with a chaste bunch of cherries. Her pelisse, too, was plain, without any elaborate frogging or other trim. Today she was going out to drum up candidates for her school, and it would never do to suggest to her prospective pupils and their families that she was a light-minded female, interested only in a fashionable wardrobe.

Before leaving the house, Hilary delved into her reticule to make sure she had the list of names of tenants in the immediate area and the directions to their farms, a list compiled with the help of Sarah and Ephraim, their man of all work. She went out the front door and around the building to the surgery. Opening the door, she walked through the outer room, occupied by several waiting patients, to whom she gave a smile and a nod, and cautiously poked her head into the examining room. Matt was looking down the throat of a feverish-looking little boy who was attended by his anxious mother. Not even a scant week had elapsed since their arrival, and already he was seeing a fair number of patients.

"Matt? I'm off."

Matt waved. "Good luck. Don't enroll too many pupils," he teased. "Remember you'll be the only schoolmistress. I don't want you to work too hard."

As Hilary rounded the front of the house, a voice called to her: "Miss Vane?"

Hilary looked up to see a young woman approaching her from the gate. A horse was tethered to the fence.

"Yes, I'm Miss Vane," said Hilary, a note of inquiry in her tone.

. The young woman smiled. "I'm Belinda Rayner. My brother Jon told me that the new doctor and his sister had moved into Willow Cottage. I came to introduce myself."

Brother? Rayner? Light dawned. This must be the duke's sister. She was much younger, not more than sixteen or seventeen, but there was a definite resemblance. Dark curling hair, gray eyes—though Belinda's were much warmer than the duke's—and classically handsome features. She was like her brother, too, Hilary thought dryly, in that her riding habit was downright shabby and her dark hair escaped untidily from beneath her hat.

22

"How do you do, Lady Belinda. I'm very pleased to meet you."

"And I you." Belinda's eyes glowed. "It will be so wonderful to have somebody new to talk to." She glanced from Hilary's bonnet and pelisse to the dogcart drawn up before the gate. "You're off for a drive. How clever of you to use a dogcart. The roads in the valley are so dreadful that carriages are practically useless."

Hilary laughed. "I'm afraid my brother and I can't claim credit for being clever. We don't own a carriage. We traveled to Northumberland by mail coach as far as Bridgeton, and then came to Wycombe by hired post chaise. Ephraim, our outdoor man, bought the dogcart and pony for us from a neighboring farmer so we could have some form of transportation."

Lady Belinda nodded approvingly. "The dogcart will do you very well. I like your pony. He looks exactly like the one I learned to ride on! But I mustn't keep you. May I come to call on you another day?"

"Why, of course. My brother and I would be delighted to welcome you at any time." Hilary's heart warmed at the spontaneous friendliness in the girl's manner. So different from her brother's! There was something else in Lady Belinda's voice, too, a wistful note, a hint of loneliness, that Hilary readily recognized from her experiences with homesick young girls entering Miss Wiggins's academy for the first time.

Lady Belinda flashed her a brilliant smile. "We'll meet again soon, then, Miss Vane. Goodbye." A few moments later the girl was galloping pell-mell down the village street. She was obviously an excellent horsewoman.

Hilary climbed into the dogcart and touched the reins

23

gently to the patient pony. In less than a minute she'd traversed the entire main street and emerged into open country. Wycombe didn't really deserve the name of village, she thought. It was more of a hamlet, almost too small to be noted on a map. It consisted only of the doctor's house and surgery at one end, and the church and rectory at the other, with, in between, the grammar school, the headmaster's house, the blacksmith's forge and a tiny shop selling a few necessities and, of course, that most necessary commodity of all, beer.

As she drove slowly beside the little river meandering through the valley, on a narrow, rutted road that could more fairly be called a track, Hilary reflected that the Wycombe Valley was a fitting complement to the lonely little village. On either side of the road soared the rounded green hills and moorlands, empty of any sign of life save for the grazing sheep and cattle. Without the rough map drawn for her by Sarah and Ephraim, she would have found it difficult to find the isolated farmsteads at the ends of their steep driveways.

To her delighted surprise, Hilary found a likely prospect at her very first stop. The entire Grey family surveyed her with a friendly curiosity as they gathered around her in the painfully neat best parlor: Farmer Grey, his wife, his seventeen-year-old daughter Maria, and an assortment of younger brothers and sisters. It wasn't really necessary for Hilary to introduce herself. Obviously the local grapevine had spread the news that the new doctor had brought his sister to live with him. Equally obviously, the novelty of meeting the new doctor's sister was an event in itself, breaking the monotony of an existence in which they rarely saw a stranger from one year's end to the next.

However, Farmer Grey dug in his heels when Hilary described her plans for her school. "A young ladies' academy? A finishing school?" he said dubiously. "That's fer the daughters of the gentry, as I see it, ma'am, not for plain farming folk like we be."

Maria, pretty and bright-eyed and slightly plump, said eagerly, "Oh, Papa, please let me attend Miss Vane's school. You know I've always wanted to learn to play the pianoforte. And Miss Vane could teach me the latest dancing steps and how to behave in polite society and—and how to speak French!" she finished breathlessly.

Mr. Grey gave his daughter a jaundiced look. "And where, pray, would ye find any use fer these grand accomplishments, missy, tell me that!"

Maria's face fell. However, her mother, a mousy-looking woman who up until this point hadn't said a word, now said quietly, with an apparent irrelevance, "Ye'll recall that my Cousin Jane has invited Maria to visit her in Bristol come next spring."

Mr. and Mrs. Grey exchanged long glances. Without knowing any of the circumstances, Hilary's quick, intuitive mind visualized "Cousin Jane" as the wife of a prosperous city tradesman with a grown son following in his father's footsteps in the family business. Mrs. Grey might consider this son as excellent husband material for Maria, provided the girl had acquired a little town polish.

"Weel . . ." Farmer Grey's voice sounded uncertain. After a moment, he asked, "How much would ye be charging fer yer school, Miss Vane? And how many days of the week would ye expect Maria ter attend these fancy classes? Her mother needs her help on the farm, ye know." When Hilary explained her very reasonable terms, he nodded, saying, "I'll think aboot it and let ye know what I decide. That's fair enough, ain't it?"

Ostensibly Hilary left the Grey farmstead with no definite commitment, but she'd seen the smug expressions on the faces of mother and daughter. If Mrs. Grey had anything to say about it, Maria would soon be a pupil in Hilary's school.

At subsequent stops that morning, Hilary had varying degrees of success. One father was downright hostile to the idea of further education for his daughter. Another said he needed his daughter's help in caring for a new baby in the family. A girl in another family already had plans to be married. However, most of the other farmers and their wives and daughters showed at least a tentative interest in the school. By the time Hilary started her drive back through the valley, she had hopes of enrolling five or six pupils. She could make a good start with that many students.

About midway through her drive back to Wycombe, Hilary glanced up the track leading to a farmstead she hadn't visited that morning, because Sarah and Ephraim had informed her that the tenant was a widow without children. Her eyes narrowed as she recognized the rider trotting down the track away from the house. Momentarily distracted, she jerked the reins sharply, causing the dogcart to lurch sideways. One wheel remained on the road, the other sank into a muddy ditch. Hilary clutched at the side of the carriage to avoid sliding down the slanting seat into the ditch.

The Duke of Alverly cantered up, reined in, and dismounted. "Here, let's get you out of there before you sink into the mud," he said briskly. Extending his arms, he lifted her easily from her precarious perch. He looked from her to the cart, shaking his head. "I must apologize to you, Miss Vane."

"Whyever for?" she asked in surprise.

"Well, I fear I'm partially responsible for your accident. I should have warned you about the dreadful state of our local roads. But perhaps you shouldn't attempt to drive yourself. Don't you have a groom who can take you wherever you wish to go?"

His appearance hadn't changed since their first meeting. He wore a shabby coat and breeches and unpolished boots, and his hair still straggled untidily at the nape of his neck. He looks like one of his own grooms, Hilary thought. His effect on her, too, was the same as at their first meeting. She fumed inwardly at the condescension in his tone. Why should he assume, on the basis of this one unfortunate accident, that she was an inept driver?

"I have a groom, yes," she replied frostily. "However, I consider myself perfectly competent to drive myself."

The duke shrugged. "Well, let's see how bad the damage is," he said. He walked around the cart to look closely at the wheel embedded in the mud of the ditch. Placing his hands on the side of the cart, he gave an experimental tug, and then, with a mighty heave, he lifted the vehicle onto the road. Hilary realized that his lithe slenderness was deceptive, concealing a steely strength.

After another close examination of the wheel, the duke turned to her, saying, "I think the wheel's intact. You probably should have a wheelwright inspect it later, but I believe it's safe for you to drive the cart."

27

Reaching out his hand to help her into the vehicle, he pulled back, gazing ruefully at the dirt that encrusted both hands.

"Please don't bother," she said hastily. "I'm used to getting in and out of the cart by myself." Settling herself in the seat, she did her best to sound grateful, saying, "Thank you for coming to my rescue. I don't think I could have ridden the pony bareback, and it's a long walk to the village."

"My pleasure." He paused, his eyes crinkling with a look of secret amusement that puzzled Hilary. "How are your plans for your academy progressing, Miss Vane?"

"Very well, thank you." Hilary gave him a defiant look. "I visited a number of families this morning. I believe I might have as many as five or six excellent prospects. Your tenants seem to think more highly of education for their daughters than you do."

"Indeed. I'm proved wrong, then. My congratulations." The look of secret amusement intensified. The duke touched his hat. "A pleasant day to you, Miss Vane." He mounted and trotted down the road ahead of her.

Hilary returned home without further mishap. As she was putting her bonnet and pelisse away in the wardrobe, the red-headed maid, Sarah, poked her head around the door of the bedchamber. "Ephraim says you had an accident with the dogcart, Miss Hilary," she said anxiously. "You're not hurt?"

Hilary suppressed a smile. She was becoming aware that very little that happened in this house or in the village, for that matter, went unnoticed. "No, I'm not hurt," she told Sarah, "though I'm fortunate the accident happened where it did, opposite the house of—

28

what did you tell me her name was? Oh, yes, I have it—the Widow Frame. The duke was just coming from her house when one wheel of the dogcart slipped into the ditch. He simply lifted the cart out onto the road."

Sarah's cheeks flamed. "Oh, yes, I'm sure His Grace was very helpful," she mumbled, and turned to go.

"Wait, Sarah. Is something wrong? Did I say something to embarrass you?"

"Oh, no, ma'am. It's jist—y'see, me mum says that His Grace often visits the widow, only we're not supposed ter speak of it, o' course." Blushing even more furiously, Sarah fled from the room.

Well! Hilary sat down abruptly. At twenty-five, she was far too mature, unlike the very young Sarah, to be shocked by the duke's peccadillos—wasn't she? But, like Sarah, her cheeks burned. In spite of herself, she was embarrassed to learn she'd been rescued by the Duke of Alverly as he was coming fresh from an assignation with his mistress. In some obscure fashion, Hilary felt insulted.

Lady Belinda Rayner came to visit the next day. Sparkling-eyed and talkative, she sat with Hilary and Matt in the drawing room, consuming vast amounts of tea and biscuits and buttered toast, unheeding of the crumbs that fell on her shabby riding habit. Surveying Belinda's equally shabby riding hat and remembering the duke's usual careless appearance, Hilary wondered: doesn't this wealthy aristocratic family ever buy any new clothes?

In between bites and swallows, Belinda glanced about the drawing room approvingly. "It looks very nice," she said. "In fact, the entire house looks like a completely different place. It was empty for so long that Jon feared it would tumble down in ruins for lack of maintenance."

"Jon?" Matt inquired.

"My brother. Well, actually his name is Jonathan. Jonathan Augustus." Belinda put her hand to her mouth. "Oh, dear. I shouldn't have told you that. Jon *hates* the name Augustus, even though he was named for the great-uncle who left Papa all those coal mines and made us so rich. Jon says he's disowned the name."

If that's not just like our noble duke, Hilary thought crossly. He doesn't like something or somebody, so he proceeds as if they didn't exist.

However, Matt laughed outright at Belinda's remarks about her brother. Without saying very much himself, he'd been watching and listening to her, an appreciative smile on his lips at her vivacity and puppylike friendliness.

"How about you, Lady Belinda?" he asked. "Do you have an obnoxious middle name also?"

"Oh, it's not so very bad, I daresay. It's Rebecca, for my grandmother. But please, Dr. Vane. I hope very much we're going to be friends, so won't you call me just plain Belinda?"

"Just plain Belinda it is," Matt said promptly. He flicked a questioning glance at Hilary, who nodded. They came close, often, to reading each other's minds. "My sister and I don't much care for formality, either. Won't you call us Hilary and Matt?"

Belinda fairly beamed. "I'd like that. Doctor—Matt— are you good with dogs?"

"Dogs?" Matt repeated, nonplussed.

"My hound Sebastian has a sore foot. It doesn't seem to get any better. Could I bring him in to see you?"

Matt laughed. "Of course, bring him in. I've never treated a dog before, but there's always a first time."

"Oh, thank you," exclaimed Belinda with a delighted smile. "I'm sure you can help Sebastian." She turned to Hilary. "I hear you're going to start a school."

"Why, yes, I am. Did your brother tell you about it?"

"Oh, no. Dulcie Cross talked of it when I visited her father's farm yesterday."

"You and Dulcie are friends?" said Hilary, trying to keep the surprise out of her voice. It seemed an unlikely friendship, between a duke's sister and the daughter of one of his tenant farmers.

"Not really. But I ride about the valley a good bit, you know, and I often stop for a chat with Jon's tenants."

Again Hilary detected the wistful tone she'd observed in Belinda's voice at their first meeting. The girl was probably lonely, with no friends of her own rank in the area.

"Perhaps you'd like to enroll in some of my classes, Belinda," Hilary suggested, more in jest than seriously.

The girl made a face. "Not me, Miss V—Hilary. I've been finished with schooling since my governess died two years ago. Oh, I loved Miss Thompson, and I was sorry she died, but she was so boring. She made me memorize lists of all the English kings and all the characters in Shakespeare's plays!" Belinda rose. "I mustn't outwear my welcome, as Miss Thompson used to say. But—may I come back soon?"

"Well, of course," said Matt with a grin. "You'll have to bring Sebastian, won't you?"

After Belinda left, Matt observed, "What a charming girl."

"Yes, but rather a lonely one, I fear."

31

"What is it, Hilary?" Matt inquired several days later, observing the stricken look on his sister's face after she read the note that Sarah brought to her at the luncheon table.

Hilary read the note again. "This is from Farmer Grey," she said on a note of despair. "He's changed his mind about allowing Maria to enroll in my academy. I'm a complete failure, Matt. The Greys were my last hope. During the past few days, I revisited all those families I contacted about the school, and every one of them except the Greys had decided against sending their daughters to me. I can't understand it. Several of those families were definitely interested in the school on my first visit. In any event, just yesterday Mrs. Grey assured me I could count on Maria."

Staring down at the table, Hilary crumbled a piece of bread into crumbs without being aware of what she was doing. "With Maria, I could have made a beginning, at least," she muttered. "Later, perhaps, when Maria's friends saw how much she was enjoying her lessons, they might have persuaded their families to relent. Now, nothing."

Reaching across the table, Matt clasped her hand. "Don't feel so blue-deviled, love," he urged. "It's not the end of the world. Wait a few weeks or months, and talk to these farmers and their families again. They might have a change of heart."

Managing a smile, Hilary returned her brother's hand clasp. Dear Matt. She'd always been able to rely on his affection and sympathy. "I do believe you're right," she told him. "I'll try my luck again in a few months with the farmers."

Matt's face relaxed. Reassured about his sister's state of mind, he quickly finished his lunch. "Sarah tells me I have patients waiting," he said as he limped out of the room. He paused at the door, saying, "Mind, I don't want to find you languishing in a fit of the megrims when I come in from the surgery."

Hilary waved him off with a smile. "I'll be fine," she called after him with a cheerfulness she didn't feel. She lingered at the table, sipping a tasteless cup of tea while she tried to put her thoughts in order.

She was a realist, she hoped, not a Don Quixote-like imitator who kept tilting uselessly at windmills. She had to face it: she would have to give up her dreams of starting a young ladies' academy in Northumberland. From the very beginning, it had been a useless dream. She'd known beforehand how remote the Wycombe Valley was and that it was primarily farming country, but she simply hadn't envisioned the possibility that she would find no tradesmen, professionals, or members of the minor gentry from whose families she might draw her pupils.

Her thoughts drifted back to her last term at Miss Wiggins's academy when a girl in her class, a girl who had seemed hopelessly lacking in scholastic talent when she entered the school, had won the French prize in her final year. Hilary's heart twisted. It was unexpected happenings of that kind that made her career as a schoolmistress so rewarding. For a moment she was tempted to write to Miss Wiggins and ask for her old position back.

Her mouth firming, Hilary put down her teacup with a decisive thump. No, she would not play the coward and retreat from Wycombe with her tail between her legs. It would be too much of a blow for Matt, who had embarked on his new career with such boundless enthusiasm and hope. She couldn't spoil his life for him. Moreover, she was not going to allow herself to wallow in self-pity. She'd find something useful to occupy her time. Perhaps Mrs. Trevor could make a suggestion.

Mrs. Trevor . . . Hilary glanced in dismay at the tiny watch pinned to her bodice. In the turmoil of hearing Farmer Grey's bad news, she'd almost forgotten her engagement to visit the vicar's wife. She raced up to her bedchamber to put on her pelisse and bonnet.

The Reverend Octavius Trevor and his wife lived in a comfortable stone house beside the church. Mrs. Trevor, a sweet-faced, gray-haired lady, had called on Hilary soon after the Vanes' arrival in Wycombe.

"It's so pleasant, actually having an afternoon caller," Mrs. Trevor smilingly exclaimed as her maid served coffee and tiny biscuits. "We see so few people. Sometimes I feel as though I were living at the end of the world, though heaven knows I should be accustomed to it by this time! The vicar and I were naturally delighted to have a resident doctor in Wycombe again. It doubled our social base, so to speak! Oh, very rarely we visit, or are visited by, the rector of St. Boniface in the next valley, and we have several other friends there, but it's difficult to reach them. What roads there are, are impossible, and my husband and I are too old to ride horseback!"

Mrs. Trevor interrupted herself. "But there, I'm feeling sorry for myself. That will never do. Tell me what you've been doing since I visited you."

"Not very much, I fear. My life would have been quite dull, in fact, if Lady Belinda Rayner hadn't called on us several times. She actually persuaded my brother to treat her dog! Successfully, too, I might add. Matt and I are becoming quite fond of her."

Mrs. Trevor nodded. "She's a dear child. We see a great deal of her, too. She's been in and out of the rectory since she first learned to ride. I worry about her a little, now that she's growing up. She's seventeen, I believe. She's had very little supervision since her governess died. Naturally I don't wish to criticize the duke, but I don't think he's aware, much of the time, where the child is or what she's doing. To my knowledge, she spends her days riding about the countryside. She often stops to visit the tenants. They all love her."

"Her mother is dead, then, too?"

"Oh my, no. Belinda's mother is very much alive. Not that anyone in Wycombe, Belinda included, has seen her for many years. She was the late duke's second wife, you know, much younger than her husband. In fact, I believe Elvira—she was Lady Elvira Wright, the daughter of the Earl of Newland—was only nineteen or so when Belinda was born, a few days after the old duke died. Shortly after her husband's death, Elvira left Wycombe for London, and she's never been back."

"She didn't take Belinda with her?"

Mrs. Trevor shook her head. "Jonathan—the present duke—refused to allow his stepmother to take the child."

"But why? Belinda wasn't the heiress to the estate. Why shouldn't she go with her mother?"

Mrs. Trevor shrugged. "It was an open secret in the village that Jonathan violently disliked his stepmother. And, though he was only sixteen when his father died, he *was* the new Duke of Alverly. His father had been ill

35

for many months before he died—he was paralyzed and speechless, in fact—and he hadn't been able to appoint a guardian for his expected child. Jonathan simply assumed the position of guardian, and Elvira didn't—or couldn't—oppose him. Oh, his father had appointed an elderly relative as co-trustee of the estate, but there was never any question about who was in charge. Jonathan always had a very strong will."

Hilary said indignantly, "And so, because he was the duke, he considered he had the right to separate mother and daughter?" She stopped short, biting her lip. "I'm sorry. I shouldn't have said that. What the duke chooses to do is none of my affair."

"I fear I'm at fault, too, my dear," said Mrs. Trevor ruefully. "The vicar would say I'm a sad gossip. My only excuse is that the duke and his family are principal objects of interest here, as you can imagine. In all fairness to Jonathan, however—" Mrs. Trevor paused, looking vexed. "I haven't used the duke's Christian name since he was a boy, before he succeeded to the title. I really must stop doing that. It's not seemly." She continued, "In all fairness to the duke, I think I should tell you that he didn't force Elvira to leave Wycombe. She very much wanted to leave. She always hated the loneliness and isolation of the place. And soon after she arrived in London, she married again. She's the Countess of Lansdale now, the wife of a career diplomat. She and her husband have resided outside of England, in all the capitals of Europe, most of the time since their marriage."

Passing the plate of biscuits to Hilary, Mrs. Trevor said, "That's enough of the duke's affairs for today. How are your plans for your school coming along?"

"There won't be any school, Mrs. Trevor. All my prospective pupils have begged off."

"I'm so sorry. I was afraid that might happen—" The vicar's wife cut herself short, a faint color rising in her plump cheeks.

Hilary stared at her. "What do you mean? Do you know why the families who seemed so interested in my school at first eventually changed their minds?"

Looking visibly flustered, Mrs. Trevor glanced away without answering.

"You do know," said Hilary suddenly. "I know, too. It was the duke's doing, wasn't it?"

"I—" Still looking intensely embarrassed, Mrs. Trevor said, "My dear, I can't tell you anything definite. I did hear rumors that the duke had sent word to his tenants that he saw no need for a young ladies' academy in Wycombe. His opinion would have weighed heavily with them, of course."

"Of course," said Hilary bitterly. "Oh, what a blind fool I've been. His high mightiness told me the first time we met that he was opposed to my school. I should have realized then and there that our border lord had doomed my academy."

"Border lord?" repeated Mrs. Trevor in a puzzled tone.

"According to the history books, the duke's ancestors centuries ago were the border lords guarding the frontier against the Scots and ruling their estates like feudal kings. I don't think their descendants have changed a bit. They still think of themselves as lords of all they survey. I think the Duke of Alverly's word is law in the Wycombe Valley."

Eyeing Mrs. Trevor's troubled face, Hilary said contritely, "I'm sorry. I've no right to embroil you in my problems."

"Perhaps the duke will change his mind later," suggested the vicar's wife, but without any great degree of conviction.

"Yes, perhaps," agreed Hilary, without any conviction at all. She rose, thanking Mrs. Trevor for her hospitality, and took her leave. During the short walk home, her mind was seething with anger. She felt particularly outraged when she recalled her encounter with the duke several days ago when he'd rescued her dogcart from the ditch. She'd been puzzled then by the look of secret amusement in his eyes when he inquired about the progress of her school. Now she understood perfectly. He'd not only been undermining her efforts to enroll pupils, but he was thoroughly enjoying doing it. And she was helpless to thwart him.

Walking slowly, almost lethargically, she opened her front gate and entered the garden. Then she paused, her forehead creased in thought. Abruptly she turned away from the path leading to the door and walked around the house to the small stables at the rear of the surgery, "Ephraim, harness the dogcart, please," she told their man of all work.

Guiding her patient pony up the steep driveway to the ancient castle on its crag above the village, Hilary rehearsed mentally what she was going to say to the castle's owner. She didn't expect to win a battle, let alone a campaign. In all probability, she wouldn't be able to budge the Duke of Alverly from his opposition toward her school. She could, however, make it clear to him that he had no power to destroy her independence of mind. This was especially important to her. She wanted him to know that she would not allow him to dominate her thoughts or her actions during the time she resided in his personal fief, however long that might be.

She drove through the frowning portals of the gatehouse to the wide courtyard of the keep. A groom hastened to hold the pony's reins and help her out of the cart. Ranged around the massively thick walls of the enceinte were various stone buildings that she assumed were stables and other outbuildings. Ahead of her was a long two-storied building constructed against the battlemented walls on the side of the castle overlooking the village. Wycombe Castle, she learned later, was an almost perfect example of a late thirteenth century border castle.

She walked up the staircase to the large two-storied building and was admitted by a liveried footman. As soon as she set foot in the hallway, she realized she'd passed from the medieval period to another epoch entirely. Someone with extravagant tastes—and a great deal of money—had transformed the Great Hall and solar of the original castle into a series of ornately furnished late eighteenth century rooms, with marquetry floors, elaborately coffered ceilings, and classical statues in niches in the walls.

Ushered into the great drawing room, Hilary gazed around her, impressed by the silken covered walls, the gilded ceilings, the jewel-toned Aubusson rugs, the inlaid Italian cabinets with their collection of Chinese porcelains.

"You wanted to see me, Miss Vane?"

Hilary looked up quickly. The duke had entered the room so quietly that she hadn't noticed his arrival. In his shabby coat and indifferently tied cravat, he looked completely out of place in the gracious room.

Rising, she said coldly, "I came to tell you that I consider you a tyrant—and an underhanded one, at that."

The duke raised an eyebrow. He sat down, crossing one leg over the other. "Really? Tell me about it, Miss Vane."

Chapter III

Hilary glared at the duke. It was insufferably rude of him to sit down in the presence of a lady, but then, it was all of a piece with his customary arrogance. No doubt he wanted to put her at a disadvantage by seating himself while she remained standing. Or he intended to emphasize the difference in their ranks. Who could fathom what he had in mind? Well, she wasn't going to give him the satisfaction of indulging himself. She sat down again, eyeing him defiantly.

The duke appeared unimpressed with her sang-froid. "Tell me about it," he said again. "In what way have I been underhanded?"

"Must you be a hypocrite as well?" inquired Hilary frigidly. "I know very well that you instructed all your tenants not to enroll their daughters in my school. How would you describe that, if it wasn't underhanded?"

"That's not true, you know," the duke replied. "I didn't instruct my tenants to do anything. I merely informed them that, in my opinion, there was no need for such an establishment in the Wycombe Valley. I explained that I believed their daughters already had the foundation to become good wives and proper housewives. They had no need for fancy finishing school lessons in French and deportment."

"And your tenants, like a flock of sheep, obediently followed your wishes. How does it feel to be a patriarch, Duke? Don't you ever give your people credit for having minds of their own?"

For the first time, the duke's mask of calm slipped. He said in a nettled voice, "I may appear patriarchal to you, Miss Vane, but I think you'll find that my tenants agree I have their best interests at heart."

"Well, I'm not one of your tenants, and I don't agree that you have *my* best interests at heart," Hilary retorted. "I deeply resent your interference in my affairs, and I thought you should know how I felt. That's all I came to say. Good day, sir." Without giving the duke an opportunity to reply, she stalked out of the drawing room and down the splendid corridor to the door, which a flustered footman hastened to open for her.

By the time she'd passed under the gatehouse and was halfway to the village, the enormity of what she'd done began to dawn on her. Angrier than she could ever remember being in her life, she'd stormed up to the castle with the intention of making the duke aware she knew about his machinations to prevent her school from opening, and also to inform him that she wouldn't allow him to dominate her as he did his tenants. But she'd gone much further than that. Instead of speaking to the duke in a firm, but ladylike manner, she'd lashed out at him, calling him a tyrant and a hypocrite and a conniving patriarch.

With a sinking heart, Hilary knew Matt would be horrified when she told him about her interview with the duke, who might never forgive her for being so outspoken. She should have thought first of Matt and not of herself. In effect, the duke was Matt's patron. He'd invited Matt to become the Wycombe village doctor, and he could as easily banish Matt from his new position, merely by advising the Wycombe tenants not to patronize Dr. Vane. Such behavior would be cutting off the ducal nose to spite his face, of course. Hilary understood the duke had tried for a number of years without success to bring a doctor into this remote area. It would be difficult for him to find a replacement. However, if the duke became sufficiently annoyed with his new doctor's impertinent sister, his anger might well overcome his desire to provide his tenants with proper medical attention.

As Hilary emerged from the last stretch of the castle driveway and entered the village, she observed a small knot of children gathered around her front gate. She recognized them as pupils from the grammar school, the children of the local tenant farmers. She presumed they had just been dismissed from classes. They gazed at her with round, solemn eyes as she reined in the dogcart.

"Is something wrong? Has one of your classmates been hurt?" she inquired.

Electing himself as the speaker for his friends, the tallest urchin replied, "No, ma'am. Not one o' the pupils. It's Lady Belinda. She got thrown from her horse, she did. Sim and me"—he pointed to another boy who nodded with an air of importance at being the center of attention—"we rushed ter her as soon as we saw her fall. Her ladyship was a-laying on the ground at the bridge, scarcely breathing like, ain't that so, Sim?" The other boy nodded again. "Lady Belinda, she's wi' the doctor now. I shouldn't doubt but that she's dead, or anyways dying," the child added with relish.

"Don't be ridiculous," Hilary said sharply. "People

43

don't die from falls from horses." But of course people *did* die from riding accidents, she reminded herself forlornly as she jumped down from the cart. She handed the reins to the tall boy who had been the speaker, saying, "Take the cart and the pony back to the stables, there's a good lad. I must go and see if my brother needs help with Lady Belinda's care."

Hurrying around to the surgery, Hilary found Matt standing beside Belinda as she lay on the examining table. The girl was deeply unconscious, with a livid bruise just above her left temple.

"Is she badly hurt, Matt?" Hilary asked in a low voice.

"I've examined her carefully. She doesn't have any broken bones. This" Matt's long sensitive fingers lightly brushed the ugly contusion on Belinda's temple "this is what concerns me. The bone here is tissue thin. I've known men in battle to die from a blow by a musket butt to this area."

"Matt!" Hilary exclaimed in horror. "You can't mean Belinda's going to die. Not from a mere fall from a horse."

"It wasn't a 'mere' fall," Matt replied grimly. "One of the boys who observed the accident told me he saw a hare dash between the horse's legs just as Belinda started across the bridge, causing the animal to rear and throw her. I think she must have struck her head against the stone coping of the bridge when she fell." He shook his head. "It's been almost an hour since the lads from the grammar school brought her here. She should be recovering consciousness by now unless . . ." Leaving the thought unexpressed, he said, "We can't keep her here on the examining table. Will you tell Sarah to prepare a bed upstairs?"

Glad to have something useful to do, Hilary hurried away to give Sarah instructions. "Is Her Ladyship hurt bad?" anxiously inquired the red-haired maidservant.

"I'm afraid she may be, Sarah," Hilary replied as she helped the servant prepare a spare bedroom for Belinda. Later, after she and Sarah had gently removed Belinda's ripped and dirty riding habit and had drawn the coverlets up around her, a dreary period of waiting began. While Matt sat beside the bed, intently watching his patient, Hilary paced the floor nervously. An hour passed. Belinda hadn't stirred or made any effort to open her eyes.

"I don't like this," Matt muttered. "The longer she remains unconscious, the greater the chance that she'll lapse into a coma. I've treated several cases of patients with head wounds like this who went into comas that lasted for days, weeks, sometimes, before they died."

Hilary gasped. She leaned over the bed, trying to reassure herself by finding some trace of Belinda's normal energy and vivacity and charm in her parchment-pale face. But the still features resembled a waxen mask. Turning away, she said urgently, "Matt, we should have notified the duke immediately about Belinda's accident. If anything should happen to her and he weren't with her, we'd never forgive ourselves."

"Yes, notify him," Matt replied impatiently, without taking his eyes from Belinda. Hilary sensed that his whole being was concentrated on trying to touch the girl's spirit with his own and bring her back from unconsciousness.

In less than half an hour, the duke strode into the bedchamber, which instantly seemed to shrink in size when invaded by the sheer power of his large person and authoritative personality.

45

"How is she?" he demanded.

Matt slowly rose to his feet, favoring his crippled leg. "I can't tell you. I think there's a danger she may slip into a coma, if she hadn't done so already."

The duke frowned. "What would that mean?"

"She might never recover consciousness," said Matt bluntly.

Alverly was silent for a moment. Then he said, "How soon will you know how serious her condition is?"

"I can't tell you that. She may revive at any time. Or she may stay in this state for days, weeks—or forever," Matt replied, with a touch of grimness.

The duke caught his breath. He walked to the bed, bending down to study Belinda's unresponsive face for long moments. Finally he turned to Matt, saying, "I know she's in good hands, Doctor."

"I'll do my best." Matt glanced from his sister to the duke. "There's no need for all of us to stay here. I'll sit with Belinda for a while. I'll call you if there's any change in her condition."

Hilary said to the duke, "I have a small sitting room on this floor. Would you care to wait there?"

"Why—yes. Thank you."

Sitting opposite the duke in the little room she'd fitted out, not so much as a sitting room but as an office for her school and a place to keep her most treasured books and to carry on her correspondence, Hilary felt momentarily tongue-tied, remembering their rancorous scene at the castle earlier in the day. She was glad when Sarah poked her head around the door to inquire if her mistress wanted anything. "Yes, bring up some wine, Sarah, please." Sipping a glass of wine might help to bridge the awkward silence rapidly developing between her and Alverly.

46

A little later, holding his glass absently between his fingers, the duke said abruptly, "The servant you sent to the castle said that Belinda's horse had thrown her. I couldn't believe it. She hasn't fallen from a horse since she was five years old, and I gave her her first pony."

"Oh, I don't think Belinda's fall was caused by poor horsemanship. One of the lads who found her lying by the bridge mentioned he'd seen a hare dart between the horse's legs, causing the animal to shy."

He nodded, a satisfied expression appearing on his face. "I knew it must be something like that. Belinda's the best female rider I've ever seen. I taught her myself." His face softened. "I remember—she couldn't have been more than six or seven years old—when she insisted she was too old for a pony and demanded a full-sized horse. I refused, naturally. She was small for her age then. Next thing I knew, she'd persuaded a groom to saddle one of my own mounts, a young horse I'd just bought and hadn't fully trained. She rode him like a veteran rider, too."

His lips curved in a reminiscent smile. "She had the grace to admit later that she'd barely kept her seat on the animal. I punished her for disobeying me by taking away her riding privileges for a week, and she agreed that was fair. After that, though, I had to allow her to ride a full-sized horse, and she also persuaded me not to give that groom a good hiding, which he richly deserved."

Hilary could hardly believe her ears. Mrs. Trevor, the vicar's wife, had reluctantly criticized the duke for not providing proper supervision for Belinda, and Hilary, from her own observation of the duke's sister, had agreed that Mrs. Trevor's judgment was correct. She'd assumed that Alverly had taken his baby half sister into his care purely out of a sense of duty when her father died—and perhaps also to thwart his stepmother—and that there was probably little affection between brother and sister. Yet, listening to this man who was speaking so wistfully, almost tenderly, about Belinda's childhood pranks, Hilary realized the Duke of Alverly had a heart after all. Apparently he did love his sister, in his own reserved, offhand way.

The duke paused, giving Hilary a faintly embarrassed look. Perhaps realizing he'd betrayed a part of himself that he preferred to keep private, he changed the subject. Glancing about the room at the large tidy desk and the well-stocked bookshelves, he remarked, "This looks more like a library than a sitting room."

"Actually," said Hilary dryly, "I'd intended to use the room as an office for my school."

A leaden silence fell over the sitting room. Hilary wished fervently that she could recall her remark, which evoked so vividly that earlier quarrel, and the duke obviously had no intention of replying to it. He merely looked at her with expressionless dark gray eyes. The seconds and the minutes ticked by with a maddening slowness. An early twilight was setting in when Sarah appeared in the doorway, exclaiming, "Doctor says ter come quick!"

Hilary and the duke rushed down the hallway toward Belinda's sickroom, Hilary with her heart in her mouth, not knowing what to expect and scarcely daring to hope. When she and the duke entered the room, they saw that Belinda, though her eyes were still closed, was moving her head restlessly from side to side. Her face was twisted with pain.

"My head hurts," she moaned.

"I know, love," Matt said soothingly. "Try to lie still

48

while I give you something for the pain." Looking up, he said to the duke, "Raise her shoulders, please." Then, while her brother held her carefully, Matt placed his hand under Belinda's chin to steady her and deftly poured a dose of laudanum mixed with wine into her mouth. The duke gently lowered her to the pillow.

Within a short time, the laudanum began to take effect. The lines of pain slowly faded from Belinda's face. She opened her eyes. "Matt—where am I?" she asked in a puzzled voice.

"You're at Willow Cottage. You hit your head against the bridge coping when your horse threw you. Some of the grammar-school boys brought you here. You'll be all right, but you must be still now."

She smiled drowsily. "I'm glad the lads brought me to you, Matt. You must be the best doctor in the whole world."

"Not quite, but I'm glad you think so," Matt replied with an answering smile, but Belinda's eyes had closed.

"Is she going back into a coma?" Alverly asked Matt in alarm.

"No. It's a natural sleep."

The duke's face relaxed. "She'll recover fully, then?"

"Yes, I think so. But she may have very severe headaches for some time. She took a hard blow to her head, and she probably has at least a slight concussion. I want her to stay in bed, moving her head as little as possible for at least a week."

Alverly nodded. "I'll see to it. The housekeeper and her staff at the castle are reliable. They'll take excellent care of Belinda. You'll be making regular visits, I presume."

Matt stared at Alverly. "Making visits to the castle? Have you gone queer in your attic, man?" he asked rudely. "I won't allow Belinda to be moved from this house until I feel it's safe to do so."

Hilary held her breath. The duke's dark brows had drawn ominously together, and his slate gray eyes had turned almost black. She was beginning to recognize the signs of his displeasure. Doubtless, before her arrival with Matt in the Wycombe Valley, no one in Alverly's semi-feudal domain had dared to cross his will. Now, in the space of one day, both she and Matt had done exactly that, and very impertinently, too. After a long moment, the duke said, obviously reining in his temper, "You're proposing that I leave Belinda here in this house in your care?"

"I am. Until she recovers completely."

Alverly hesitated. "I'm not accustomed to imposing on the hospitality of others. My sister, after all, is a stranger to you. You've no obligation to her or to me."

"She's not a stranger," said Hilary quickly. "She's our friend."

The duke said in surprise, "You know each other, then?"

Hilary nodded. "Belinda has called on us several times. Matt and I found her delightful. We'll be more than happy to take care of her."

"Well . . ." Alverly hesitated. "If you're sure Belinda shouldn't be moved, doctor—"

"I'm sure."

Shrugging, the duke said, "In that case, I thank you." On his way to the door, he paused, saying, "You'll inform me if—"

"Yes, Duke, I will."

Belinda's recovery was slow. The days passed, and she continued to suffer excruciating headaches. Hilary or Matt or the maid Sarah or frequently Mrs. Trevor, the vicar's wife, sat beside her bed at all times, alert to offer her the nirvana of laudanum if she awoke in discomfort. But when the headaches were especially severe, not even the evil-tasting medicine could completely block the pain.

Rather to Hilary's surprise, the duke was a constant visitor, arriving several times a day at Willow Cottage. On the first day after the accident he peered into Belinda's bedchamber as Hilary was trying to coax some gruel down her patient's throat.

"That's nasty stuff," said Belinda mutinously.

Alverly advanced into the room, saying coolly, "Quite right, sister mine. Once when I was very small—"

"That must have been a very long time ago, Jon, probably in the Dark Ages," said Belinda, cocking her head at him with a wicked glint in her eyes. Almost instantly she grimaced with pain at the sudden movement.

"You must keep yourself as still as possible," cautioned Hilary, as she lifted the spoon to Belinda's mouth again.

"As I was about to observe before you interrupted me, infant," said the duke, "once when I was very small and ailing, my old nurse tried to force a bowl of gruel down my throat. I grabbed it from her hands and threw it at her."

"I hope your nurse punished you suitably," said Hilary dryly, before she could stop herself.

The duke looked down at her, smiling faintly. "She did." He stood without speaking at the foot of the bed until Hilary had spooned the last of the gruel into Belinda's mouth. Then, when Hilary rose from her seat to remove the breakfast tray, he sat down in the chair she had vacated. He shook his head reprovingly at his sister. "Well, now, my girl, how do you explain this fall you took? You, the best horsewoman in the county, or so you've always led me to believe. Carelessness, was it, or inattentiveness?"

Careful not to move her head, she gave him a weak smile. "I should have known I wouldn't get any sympathy from you, Jon."

"Not a whit of it. Why, you might have injured the stallion with your poor horsemanship. As it is, he has a graze on his fetlock. The horse's groom isn't best pleased with you."

"I'll have to remind Seymour that he's the horse's groom. *I'm* the owner," Belinda retorted. "And may I remind you, dear brother, who it was who came a cropper over that fence on the home farm last year? Your groom wasn't pleased with *you,* either!"

Listening with a quiet horror, Hilary gradually relaxed as she realized that what she was hearing was not a callous lecture by the duke about his sister's careless riding or a resentful retaliation by Belinda. Hilary suspected that brother and sister found it difficult or embarrassing to express their real emotions. Apparently they covered up their feelings with jibes and quips. Theirs wasn't at all the same kind of relationship she had with Matt, but Belinda and the duke seemed to understand each other perfectly.

When Alverly was about to leave, he clasped Belinda's hand closely. "You make sure you do what the doctor and Miss Vane tell you to do, or I'll beat you," he threatened.

Belinda grinned appreciatively.

At the door, Alverly paused for a word with Hilary. "If you need anything, anything at all, send to me immediately at the castle."

She gazed at his lean, dark face, taut with the concern he wouldn't, or couldn't, acknowledge. "I will," she promised.

Belinda had good days and bad days. On the occasions when the laudanum failed to relieve a headache, those sitting with her could distract her from her discomfort by reading to her or by simply talking to her about anything that came into their heads.

One afternoon, as Hilary was bringing Belinda a tisane, she paused outside the bedchamber door, struck by the soaring, mellifluous sounds she was hearing from inside the room. She recognized the sounds almost instantly, of course. Matt was reciting classical Greek. Ever since he'd been exposed to Homer by his tutor, Matt had been fascinated by the *Iliad* and the *Odyssey*. Hardly a night went by since then that he didn't read at least a few verses from Homer before he went to bed.

When Hilary entered the room with her tray, she was amazed to find Belinda lying with her eyes closed, her face perfectly relaxed, listening intently as Matt declaimed the sonorous verses.

"That was lovely, Matt," Belinda sighed, as he finished. "What did it mean?"

"That was the scene in which Hector says farewell to his wife and son before he goes out to fight Achilles."

"I knew it was something beautiful, even though I couldn't understand a word, of course," Belinda said dreamily. Then, stirring, she said, "Matt, could you teach me Greek? I know I'm ignorant—I don't know a word of Latin, for example—but I'd love to be able to read even a few lines of Homer."

"Teach you Greek?" Matt sounded nonplussed. "Well . . . I daresay I could teach you a smattering. Mind, you'd have to apply yourself," he added severely. "I couldn't waste time on a pupil who wasn't willing to study."

"Oh, I'd study, Matt. Truly I would. I *hated* lessons with my governess. She was so dull, poor thing. But I know you wouldn't be dull."

Matt laughed. "Oh, I'm not so sure about that. You get well, Belinda, completely well, and then you can come here, oh, say twice a week, and we'll study Homer together."

Smiling at the blissful look on Belinda's face, Hilary doubted that the Greek lessons would continue for more than a session or two. Belinda was almost certain to lose interest after a short time. Meanwhile, however, the prospect of studying with Matt was helping to take her mind off her present discomforts.

The day came, finally, when Belinda's headaches ceased and she could sit up and then walk. "You can go home tomorrow, Belinda," Matt announced one evening after he and Hilary had shared supper with her in her bedchamber.

Belinda's face fell. "So soon?"

Hilary said, smiling, "Belinda, you goose, don't you want to go home?"

"Not really." The gamin face, which resembled her brother's so closely in features but not in expression, looked wistful. "I never realized before how—well, lonely—it is up at the castle. Jon and I simply rattle around in that huge pile. And we really don't see much of each other. He's out on the estate early and late every day, and after dinner he goes to his office to work on estate papers. I wish he'd employ a bailiff, but he says he can manage his properties better than any hired employee."

With a pang Hilary reflected that Belinda had summarized exactly the way she and her brother lived. Having inherited the title at such an early age, the duke had apparently thrown himself into his duties to the exclusion of every other interest in life. Perhaps he'd thought he needed to convince the world he wasn't too young to successfully manage his estates. In the process, however, he'd become a near recluse, and he was well on the way to making his sister one, too.

"You and Matt are brother and sister living together, too," Belinda continued. "But you *talk* to each other. And you seem to enjoy being in each other's company."

"Neither of us has as many responsibilities as the duke," Hilary remarked quickly.

Belinda sighed. "Oh, I know. And I shouldn't wish you to think that Jon neglects me or anything of that sort or that we don't—care—for each other, but he's so *busy.*" She added loyally, "Well, I daresay he has to be. He owns half the county of Northumberland or close to it, and then there are all those coal mines in the Tyne Valley."

Matt cut in, "Just because you're going home, Belinda, doesn't mean you won't be seeing me and Hilary. Remember those Greek lessons you wanted to take? I'll expect to see you here on the dot of eleven o'clock every Tuesday and Thursday morning, and if you're late, I'll come up to the castle to fetch you!"

The shadows faded from Belinda's face. Chuckling, she said, "I believe you'd really do that, Matt. I promise you I won't be late for my lessons. I've no taste for being abducted!"

But, though Matt's tongue-in-cheek threat lifted Belinda's spirits momentarily, her eyes filled with tears the following morning when her brother arrived to take her home. Hugging her, Hilary murmured, "Mind, you're welcome here at any time, not just when you come to take your Greek lessons."

Returning Hilary's embrace, Belinda said, "Oh, thank you. That makes me feel so much better because I know you really mean it." Brushing the tears from her eyes, she turned to say goodbye to Matt.

Dressed in his usual shabby coat and breeches, the duke looked his familiar self, down to his characteristically aloof expression. He did manage a wintry smile as he extended his hand, saying, "Thank you for taking such good care of Belinda. I'm very much indebted to you and your brother."

"Please don't feel obligated. It was a pleasure for us to have Belinda here. As I told you, Matt and I think of her as a friend. We're very fond of her."

"Nevertheless, please accept my thanks." Nodding, Alverly swung away to detach his sister from Matt and help her into the waiting carriage. From a quick look at the vehicle, Hilary guessed the carriage was several generations old and was probably never driven on the wickedly rutted local roads unless the duke and his family wanted to make a journey out of the valley. She stood at the gate with Matt, returning Belinda's waves as the girl leaned out of the open window of the carriage, until the vehicle was far up the drive toward the castle.

After dinner that evening, as she and her brother sat companionably in the small room at the rear of the house that Hilary had fitted out as a first-floor sitting room, Matt looked up from his battered copy of the *Iliad* to say in a tone of mild surprise, "I miss Belinda."

"Yes," Hilary agreed. "She was beginning to seem almost like a member of the family."

"Oh, more than that. There are some members of

our family I don't care a fig for! Uncle Adolphus, for example! Cousin Mortimer Slade! No, Belinda is ... Oh, she's just herself. A darling."

As Matt returned to his Homer, Hilary looked at him with a feeling of foreboding. Was it possible he was a little in love with Belinda? No, surely that was impossible. Or, if he did have a *tendre* for Belinda, surely Matt knew quite well that the situation was hopeless. Even if Belinda were to return his regard, nothing could come of it. Matt was over ten years older than Belinda, he had a crippled leg, he had very little money, and his station in life, as the second son of a baronet, was far beneath hers. With a sigh, Hilary fervently hoped she was wrong in her guess about Matt's feelings. She hated the thought of his being hurt, especially since he'd already endured a long and painful recuperation from his Peninsula wound.

The house *did* seem empty without Belinda, Hilary acknowledged during the next several days. Without her constant attendance on their young guest, she had very little to do. Sarah and the cook competently took charge of all the household duties. For the first time in her adult life, Hilary was at loose ends. For a number of years she'd led an active and productive existence as a schoolmistress. Now she felt like a useless drone. Even worse, she could envision little change in her life in the near future.

Then, unexpectedly, her fortunes changed. One morning Farmer Grey came to the house, looking purposeful, if mildly embarrassed. "Miss Vane, ma'am, would ye still be accepting pupils fer yer school?"

"Why, yes, Mr. Grey. Have you changed your mind about enrolling Maria?"

"Weel ... That I have like. Maria and her mother,

57

they both feel right strongly about yer academy. So I've decided to abide by their wishes. I've agreed Maria should have her chance at some o' that fancy schooling ye were telling us aboot."

"I'm glad, Mr. Grey. I'll do my very best to make sure you don't regret your decision." Hilary hesitated. "I must tell you, however, that Maria will be my only pupil, at least for the present."

"Nay, Miss Vane. Jack Waring's girl, Margot, will be enrolling, too, and so I believe will Anna Carson and Betsy Siddons. Never fear, ye'll have more than one pupil."

Hilary gave Farmer Grey an intent glance. She was a realist, and this situation was entirely too pat. There was more to it than appeared on the surface. She said, "Might I ask, Mr. Grey, what caused you to change your mind?"

"Weel, now . . ." Farmer Grey cleared his throat, looking uncomfortable. "Y'see, His Grace came by yesterday. He allowed as how he'd been doing some thinking, and he's now of the opinion that p'raps yer school warn't as useless—begging yer pardon, ma'am—as he'd first believed. So nachurly me and Mistress Grey, we talked aboot it, and since Maria was so partial ter attending an' all . . ."

"I see," said Hilary, putting a merciful end to the farmer's floundering attempt at explanation. "Well, Mr. Grey, I'm very pleased that Maria is to come to me. Pray tell her I'll start classes Monday next."

After Farmer Grey had gone, Hilary paced rapidly back and forth across the room, trying to hold her temper in check. So, His Grace of Alverly had withdrawn his opposition to her school, had he? And his obedient

58

vassals, taking advantage of his implied permission, would now allow their daughters to attend her academy.

Hilary had rarely been so angry. Without being conceited, she knew she was a good teacher, and she was sure she could give her prospective pupils skills and knowledge that would profit them for the rest of their lives. But it galled her to realize that her success was dependent on the whim of one arrogant man. The duke had arbitrarily decided to block the opening of her school in the first place, and now, just as arbitrarily, he'd changed his mind. Did she really want to open a school that she might be obliged to close at a moment's notice if the Duke of Alverly had another change of heart?

Ceasing her restless pacing, Hilary gave her shoulders a determined shake. Well, of course she was going to open her school. She'd take advantage of the capricious ducal good will and let the future take care of itself.

During the next few days, she and Sarah worked hard to prepare her second-floor rooms for the opening of classes the following week. By Saturday, everything was in order. Hilary decided to celebrate her last day of leisure by paying a visit to the vicar's wife.

Beaming, Mrs. Trevor exclaimed, "I'm so happy you're about to realize your dream, my dear. I know how much your school means to you."

"I wish my dream wasn't so dependent on the duke," Hilary replied dryly.

"Why, what do you mean?" Mrs. Trevor sounded a little nervous.

"Oh, come now, I fancy it's an open secret that our resident tyrant gave his consent to Mr. Grey and the other parents to send their daughters to my academy."

Mrs. Trevor looked distressed. "Oh, I did hear something of the sort. . . . But Miss Vane, you really shouldn't speak of the duke like that. Jonathan—oh, dear, I *must* stop calling him that, but it seems only yesterday that he was the high-spirited young lad who came so often to visit at the vicarage. The duke truly isn't the ogre you make him out to be. He was the sweetest little boy. When you get to know him better, I daresay you'll change your mind about him."

"Closer acquaintance might possibly change my opinion of him," Hilary acknowledged, to spare Mrs. Trevor's feelings. The vicar's wife seemed unaccountably to have a tender spot in her heart for Alverly. Well, perhaps he'd been different as a boy. Changing the subject, Hilary plunged into a discussion with Mrs. Trevor about plans for the annual Harvest Festival in the late autumn.

As she was walking from the vicarage to her house, Alverly trotted up the road behind her and dismounted. Bowing slightly, he said, "Good day, Miss Vane. I thought you might like to know the latest news of our invalid."

"Oh? Has something happened since I visited her yesterday?"

"You might say so. She's inveigled me into giving her permission to ride tomorrow."

Hilary laughed. "Now I know Belinda's on the road to full recovery." She hesitated for a moment. "I understand I have you to thank for the fact that I'm opening my school at last."

The duke's face became expressionless. "Why do you say that?"

Somewhat nettled, Hilary retorted, "You'll hardly deny your influence with your tenants. Mr. Grey told me you'd 'come by' to see him and that you mentioned you'd arrived at the conclusion that my school wasn't quite as 'useless' as you'd previously thought. So he acted accordingly. Maria will start classes on Monday."

Alverly didn't seem in the least chagrined by Hilary's remark. He shrugged, saying, "I may have dropped a word or two to several of my tenants."

"Why did you do it, Duke? What made you change your mind about me and my school?"

"Actually I didn't change my mind, Miss Vane," Alverly said coolly. "I still think my tenants' daughters have no need for your fripperies. However, I've never in my life failed to repay a debt. I owe a debt to you and your brother for your care of Belinda."

Never had Hilary been so close to slapping a gentleman's face. "Thank you very much," she said stonily. "Thank you for nothing."

He shot her a sharp, intent look. "If I may say so, that's a rather inscrutable remark."

"You think so? Then let me make it clearer. I deeply resent the fact that I'm to be allowed to manage my own affairs purely on your sufferance, especially since you despise the work I plan to do. However, I have a modicum of common sense. I'm not going to cut off my nose to spite my face. I'll open my school, but don't expect me to be grateful to you for any success I may have."

Hardly had the words left her mouth when Hilary desperately wished them back. Now she'd really gone too far. Alverly wouldn't countenance such insolence.

The duke appeared unruffled. "You're certainly entitled to your opinion as I am to mine," he said calmly. "In any event, I don't want your gratitude any more than you want mine. So we understand each other. Good day, Miss Vane."

In a simmering rage, Hilary watched him ride off.

He'd had the last word as she might have known he would. The Duke of Alverly wasn't accustomed to being crossed. But so, too, had she won, after a fashion. She had her school. That was the important thing.

Chapter IV

Hilary came down the stairs to find Sarah standing transfixed before the door of the sitting room. The red-haired maid turned as Hilary approached her. "Oh, ma'am," Sarah breathed softly, "I never heard the like. It sounds like—like the screech of a rusty axle. What sort of words are the master and Lady Belinda saying to each other?"

Hilary laughed. "That's Classical Greek, Sarah. And don't tell Dr. Vane you think it sounds like a rusty axle. He's very fond of Greek. He's teaching Lady Belinda to read from the works of a famous Greek poet named Homer."

"I dunno how them Greeks can understand sich words. Why don't they learn ter speak proper English?" Shaking her head, Sarah went away.

Smiling at Sarah's remark, Hilary opened the door of the sitting room slightly and stood outside listening to the lesson.

"ειμαι εισαι ειναι—" Belinda broke off. "Matt, I simply can't remember all the parts of the conjugation. I knew them before I left the castle today, but now they've completely escaped my mind."

"Nonsense," said Matt briskly. "Try again. Concentrate."

"ειααι εισμι ειναι—" Belinda hesitated. "ειμεθα εισθε ειναι," she finished triumphantly.

"Splendid, I knew you could do it. Now that you know the present tense of the verb, 'to be,' " we can begin on the aorist."

"Matt!" wailed Belinda. "Must we do more of these dreadful verbs? Can't we begin reading the *Iliad?*"

"No. First you must learn the bare bones of the language. Of course, if you don't wish to study Greek properly, we can discontinue the lessons."

"Beast. Tyrant. I thought you were my friend," Belinda exclaimed feelingly. "Oh, very well, Matt, we'll do it your way. We always do! Now, about this horrible tense you call the aorist . . ."

Smiling, Hilary stole away before Matt and Belinda realized she was there. It was three weeks since Belinda had begun her lessons, and she still seemed enthusiastic, rather to Hilary's surprise. However, Hilary had been relieved to observe that Belinda and Matt apparently hadn't progressed beyond a warm friendship. Affectionate, teasing, confiding, Belinda treated Matt like an older brother or an uncle. And Matt seemed content to have it so.

After Hilary had gone to the kitchen to request Cook to send up tea and biscuits for her pupils' midmorning refreshment, she returned to her classroom where she'd left her students to digest the poems they'd read that morning.

"Oh, Miss Vane, the poem is so beautiful, almost more beautiful than I can bear," exclaimed Maria Grey, her eyes shining. "Listen." She opened her book to read slowly and dreamily, "There was a time when meadow, grove, and stream,/The earth, and every common sight,/To me did seem/Apparelled in celestial light . . ."

Hilary smiled. "Yes, I agree with you about 'Intimations of Immortality.' It's my favorite poem. What a pity that the critics don't appreciate Mr. Wordsworth." Sarah appeared in the door with a tray. "Come along, girls," said Hilary. "We'll have our tea, and then we'll practice the country dance we learned yesterday."

As she watched her students gorging on an incredible amount of Cook's savory biscuits, Hilary reflected that Maria Grey, of all her new pupils, was profiting most from her studies. She was like a sponge, absorbing eagerly everything that Hilary taught her and reaching out for more. The other girls—there were six of them—were typical farmers' daughters, biddable, somewhat stolid, more interested in acquiring ladylike skills than knowledge in the hopes that they might beat out less accomplished damsels for eligible husbands. But Maria was different. Hilary could consider her school a success simply because she'd helped this one young girl to learn that there were wider horizons beyond the Wycombe Valley.

"Time for our dancing lesson," Hilary declared after the last crumb of biscuit had disappeared. She led her pupils into the largest room on the second floor, which she'd cleared of all furniture except for a pianoforte. She arranged the girls in a line.

"First, let's review a bit. Show me your basic foot positions. Remember, the working foot is always at right angles to the supporting foot. Yes, that's right. Now, for the traveling steps we learned the other day: first the chassé on the right foot. Rise on the ball of the left foot, step forward on the right, close the left foot to the rear third position, make a small step forward on the right foot. Very good. What about the hop-one-and-two? Splendid. You haven't forgotten anything. I'm proud of you, girls."

As her students beamed with pride, Hilary went to the pianoforte, saying, "Let's start with a reel." She had the instrument positioned so that she could look over it and direct the dancers as she played.

Absorbed, earnest faces concentrated on their shuffling feet in the quick cadences of the reel. Occasionally Hilary called out, "Betsy, you're off the beat," or "Esther, the ball of your left foot should stay on the floor."

At the end of the reel, Hilary glanced up, observing with surprise that Belinda was standing just inside the door. She came forward, nodding to the other girls as she went. "I didn't mean to intrude, Hilary," she said shyly. "I finished my lesson with Matt, and then I heard music from the second floor, so I came up to see what was happening." She added wistfully, "The dancing looked like such fun. I never learned to dance. Well, I never go to balls, either, so I expect I don't need to know how to dance."

Impulsively Hilary said, "Belinda, would you like to join us for a lesson?"

The dark gray eyes, so like her brother's, lit up. "Could I? You're sure you don't mind?"

That was how Belinda became an unofficial but essentially permanent pupil at Hilary's academy. Soon she began arriving punctually every morning, participating in all the activities. Her Greek sessions with Matt were changed to late afternoons on Tuesdays and Thursdays. Like Maria Grey, Belinda's mind seemed to blossom. One day she remarked after Hilary had described in heartbreaking detail the execution of Anne Boleyn, "Hilary, my old governess never told me any of these in-

66

teresting bits. You make history come alive." Which, all things considered, was the finest compliment Hilary had ever received. Belinda also expressed a desire to learn how to play the pianoforte, so Hilary began giving her lessons several days a week.

The other girls accepted Belinda's presence matter-of-factly or so Hilary thought at first. Gradually, however, she noticed that the farmers' daughters never attempted the slightest familiarity with the duke's sister. To them she was always "Lady Belinda." And, though Belinda used Hilary's Christian name at all times, the other girls never called their teacher anything but "Miss Vane."

The vicar's wife paid a visit one day after Hilary had dismissed her classes. "I hear nothing but good things about you, my dear," said Mrs. Trevor, accepting a cup of tea. "Mrs. Grey came to see me the other morning, positively boasting about Maria's proficiency in French!"

Hilary chuckled. "At this point, Maria can't say much more than, 'How do you do,' and 'I'm enchanted to meet you,' but she's learning. She has a quick mind."

A moment later, Belinda bounced into the drawing room with her usual headlong energy. "I can play the C-Major scale perfectly now, Hilary. I practiced an extra half-hour today. Oh, hullo, Mrs. Trevor," she said, belatedly noticing the presence of the vicar's wife.

"Good afternoon, my dear." Mrs. Trevor added with mock severity, "The vicar is quite hurt because you haven't come to visit us recently."

"Oh, I'm so sorry, Mrs. Trevor. I know it's been a shocking time since I paid you a visit, but I've been so *busy*." She blew hasty kisses to Hilary and Mrs. Trevor. "Pray excuse me. I promised my groom I'd come back early today to begin training a new mare."

After Belinda's whirlwind departure, Mrs. Trevor observed, "The child looks happy. Better than that, contented. I suspect most of that is your doing." She hesitated. "I don't mean to pry, Miss Vane, but I've heard rumors that Belinda is actually attending your school."

"Well, so she is, in a manner of speaking. She hasn't officially enrolled, but she comes here every day. Apparently she enjoys my classes. She's shockingly illeducated, you know. Judging by what Belinda says about her late governess, the woman must have been a very dull teacher who simply couldn't interest Belinda in her studies."

"I knew Miss Thompson, of course. She *was* a rather dull woman." Hesitating again, Mrs. Trevor inquired, "What does Jon—what does the duke think of Belinda's sudden urge toward scholarship?"

"I have no idea. I haven't seen him for some time, and in any case I doubt that we're on speaking terms. On the last occasion we met, we had a mighty set-to."

"Oh, dear."

"I know, Mrs. Trevor. You think it unwise to antagonize the petty ruler of our valley." Hilary sighed. "I know you're right, but I can't seem to curb my wretched tongue."

Mrs. Trevor looked at her sympathetically. Then, changing the subject, she observed, "I do believe today is the first time I've seen Belinda in a gown in—oh, I don't know how long. Usually she wears that dreadfully shabby riding habit. Not that her sprigged muslin is much of an improvement. It is out of date and two inches too short. Belinda has grown taller during the past several years. I'm sure none of her clothes fit anymore."

Hilary nodded. "No one looking into my classroom for the first time would guess that one of the pupils was a duke's sister. Maria and the other girls look like fashion plates in comparison with Belinda. It's a shame."

"It is. And really, the solution to the problem is so simple. In Bridgeton, which, as you know, is the town south of here in the next valley, there's a skilled seamstress who'd be happy to sew Belinda some new clothes." Mrs. Trevor shook her head. "So much for that idea. Since her governess died, there's been no one to take charge of Belinda. What she needs is a female companion, an older woman, perhaps, who could guide her in her choice of clothes and—and other things. I ventured to suggest as much to Jonathan after Miss Thompson died."

"And how was your suggestion received?"

Mrs. Trevor smiled wryly. "Politely but negatively. Jonathan—the duke—said that Belinda didn't want another governess or a companion, and since she was now a young lady, he wouldn't force either on her."

"That must have been the first time in living memory that the Duke of Alverly paid attention to someone else's wishes," Hilary remarked. "And of course he was quite wrong to do so. He should have insisted that Belinda have a companion. Doubtless he didn't care to make the effort to find a suitable candidate."

For a moment Mrs. Trevor looked troubled at this criticism of the duke. Then she said lightly, "Oh, pray give him the benefit of the doubt, Miss Vane." She rose to leave, saying, "Well, unfortunately we can't solve dear Belinda's problems, but I'm very happy that you're doing so well."

Several days later as her pupils were concluding their practice of a lively country dance, Hilary looked up from the pianoforte to observe with a slight shock that

Alverly was standing in the doorway. She left the piano-forte immediately to join him.

"Good day, Miss Vane. I trust you won't think I'm in-truding. I suddenly had the urge to see how your classes were progressing."

That's one way of putting it, my lord duke, Hilary thought with a touch of irritation. What you really mean is that you're on a tour of inspection of your do-main, making sure you know every detail of your sub-jects' lives.

Aloud, she said politely, "You're most welcome, Duke. Would you care to see the girls perform a cotil-lion?"

"No, thank you. I daresay they're most accomplished, but I have other duties—" He broke off, staring fixedly at the pupils, who had continued to practice dance steps by themselves, without benefit of Hilary's accompani-ment. "That's Belinda in the rose-colored dress. What's she doing here?"

"Taking a dancing lesson, of course."

Alverly's brows drew together at the flippant reply. "Does she do that often?"

Lifting her chin, Hilary said coolly, "Yes, as a matter of fact. She takes part in classes every day. I think she enjoys it. She's also taking private Greek lessons from Matt, and I'm teaching her to play the pianoforte."

Alverly's lips tightened. "May I talk to you privately, Miss Vane?"

"Certainly." She called to her students, "Girls, go to the other classroom and practice your French verbs while I talk to His Grace."

Belinda called out to Alverly, "Oh hullo, Jon. Did you see me performing in the country dance? Don't you think I'm becoming quite accomplished!"

70

He replied curtly, "I fear I'm no judge of that, Belinda," and turned away to follow Hilary down the corridor to her office.

"Please sit down, Duke. I'll leave you for just a moment to go downstairs to order some wine for us, or perhaps you'd prefer tea?" Before she could move a step toward the door, Alverly caught her by her arm. "I don't want any wine, Miss Vane. What I want is an explanation."

Gazing up at him, Hilary felt a sudden stab of startled comprehension. Why had she never realized before how attractive he was? Oh, she'd always noticed his austerely handsome classical features and his lithe, powerful figure, neither of which could be overlooked despite his deplorably careless grooming. But not until this moment, standing so close to him with his fingers locked around her arm, had she been conscious of the strong aura of masculinity he exuded.

Her pulse began racing, and for a moment she wondered how it would feel to be clasped close to that taut, hard body. Her cheeks flamed. What a ninnyhammer she was. This was no romantic encounter, nor would she have wanted it to be. The duke could have no personal interest in her. At this moment he was merely angry, toweringly angry. Perhaps it was inevitable. Their mutual hostility had kindled at their very first meeting, and every time they met they clashed again.

She said coldly, "Please release my arm, Duke."

The bemused, almost mesmerized expression faded from his face, and he snatched his hand away so quickly that her arm might have been a burning coal. "I beg your pardon, Miss Vane," he said in a mortified tone.

Sitting down and motioning Alverly to a chair, she

71

said, "I'm quite at your disposal. What did you wish to speak to me about?"

"Your ploy won't succeed, you know."

Bewildered, she stared at him. "What ploy?"

The slate gray eyes were almost black with anger. "You must take me for a real gull," he snapped. "You can stop playing the innocent. I know very well what you're about. You resented the fact that I didn't approve of your school, so you decided to retaliate against me. Somehow you inveigled Belinda into taking part in your classes, thereby convincing the world that I must approve of your school, or why else would I allow my own sister to enroll in it? Well, you've lost this skirmish, Miss Vane. I'm removing Belinda from your clutches immediately. Incidentally I'd considered you a gentlewoman. Now I'm not so sure. Have you no sense of propriety? Don't you realize how improper it is for a duke's daughter to associate on familiar terms with the daughters of her family's tenants?"

Restraining her temper, Hilary said coldly, "You're wrong on all counts, Duke. I did not 'inveigle' Belinda into my school. One day after finishing her Greek lesson with Matt, she heard the sound of the pianoforte and came up here out of curiosity. She looked so wistful as she watched the dancers that I invited her to take part in the lesson. From that day on, she began attending classes every day, entirely on her own. She didn't mention enrolling, nor did I. And there's no question of the other girls becoming familiar with her. They show her nothing but respect. If anything, they're embarrassed and unwilling to have Belinda in their classes. I think they'd much prefer that she wasn't there, so they wouldn't have to watch their tongues and their manners constantly."

72

"Oh." Alverly looked nonplussed. "Well, perhaps I've at least partially misjudged you. I know Belinda can be headstrong. But I trust you'll agree with me that in general it's unwise for young ladies of rank to mingle socially with girls of inferior station?"

"I do. Neither group has anything in common with the other, and certainly in adult life these girls would never have any occasion to associate with each other. But I think this situation is an exception to the rule. Belinda is lonely. If she enjoys mingling with the girls in my school for a few months, I see no harm in it."

"Lonely?" the duke repeated incredulously. "How can Belinda be lonely? She lives with me in a castle full of servants, and she knows everyone on the estate."

"Yes, lonely," said Hilary. She gazed at him defiantly. "What do you know of how she feels, Duke? You spend very little time with her. On any given day I doubt that you know where she is or what she's doing. She has no friends of her own age and rank. I presume that she supervises your domestic establishment through the housekeeper, but other than that she has nothing to occupy her time except to ride about the countryside. Of course she's lonely. She's at a time of life when she needs friends."

Alverly's eyes had turned even darker, and his forehead was furrowed by a deep frown. Hilary resigned herself to an explosion. Probably in all the years since he'd succeeded to the dukedom, no one had ever dared to criticize his relations with his family.

After a long silence, Alverly stirred. His anger had apparently evaporated. He even sounded faintly embarrassed as he said, "You've put me in your debt again, Miss Vane. Belinda has been in my care since she was a baby, but I left her rearing entirely to her governess.

73

Unfortunately Miss Thompson died several years ago. I simply hadn't realized that since then Belinda might be at loose ends." He cleared his throat. "Under the circumstances, I'll allow her to continue in your school. I will insist on paying her fees naturally."

"I have no objection to that at all," Hilary replied coolly. "My academy isn't a charity school. I support myself on the fees I charge my pupils."

Alverly burst out laughing. It was a difficult-sounding laugh, almost rusty, as if he had had little practice in being amused over the years. "That's settled, then," he said at last. "Now, as to another matter, the private tutoring you and Dr. Vane have been giving Belinda. I wish to pay for those lessons also."

"No," Hilary replied immediately. "Matt and I are teaching Belinda Greek and the pianoforte because she's our friend. We don't wish to be paid for acts of friendship."

The slate gray eyes were turning chilly again. "Permit me to inform you, Miss Vane, that I totally disagree with your position. Surely you must know that special tutors—dancing masters, French teachers, the like—who give private lessons are suitably paid. I must insist that you and Dr. Vane accept a fee for teaching Belinda Greek—Greek! How long, pray, do you think she'll remain interested? For however long it is, though, I wish to pay him, and you, too, for your lessons on the pianoforte."

Hilary said stubbornly, "Insist all you like, Duke. Matt and I will refuse to accept a fee for a labor of love." She held her breath. Had she disrupted the fragile truce that had seemed to be developing between her and Alverly?

Apparently not. After a long pause, the duke shrugged, saying, "I can only say thank you, then. I agree with you. Between friends, favors demand no payment."

Hilary eyed him incredulously. This, from the man who'd opposed her at every turn since her arrival in the Wycombe Valley, was total surrender. A vagrant thought sprang into her mind. Did she dare to express it? Without conscious volition, she heard herself saying, "May I ask you a favor, Duke? Would you allow me to take Belinda to Bridgeton to select a new wardrobe for her?"

The dark brows drew ominously together. "A new *wardrobe?* Why does she require a new wardrobe?"

"Have you looked at Belinda of late, Duke? *Really* looked at her? Her riding habit is so shabby that it's threadbare, and her gowns are all too short for her. She's grown several inches since her governess died, you know, and yet she's still wearing the same clothes."

Alverly seemed torn between chagrin and annoyance. "You're not bamming me? You really believe Belinda is shabbily dressed?

"I do. The situation must be self-evident to any female."

Alverly threw up his hands. "Then I suppose I must bow to your superior female taste," he said dryly. "Yes. Take Belinda to Bridgeton to buy a new wardrobe. Have the bills sent to me, and spare no expense. I want her properly dressed as befits a duke's daughter." He added grudgingly, "Thank you for bringing the facts to my attention."

After the duke's departure, Hilary went back to her classes with a singing heart. It was actually possible that she and Alverly might become, if not friends, then friendly adversaries. At the very least, from now on she and Matt should have clear sailing among the shoals of the Duke of Alverly's private lake.

"Hilary? We're risking breaking every bone in our bodies riding in this dogcart," Belinda exclaimed. "We should be going to Bridgeton on horseback."

Hilary retorted, "Granted the road out of the valley is quite dreadful, Belinda, but you forget that I'm not the horsewoman you are. And besides, the dogcart gives us a place to put our purchases on our return journey."

At the mention of the word *purchases,* Belinda's face brightened, and she made no further objection to the dogcart. As soon as they breasted the rise over the gentle mountain to the south of the valley, the road improved.

In a short time they were in Bridgeton, a fair-sized town about seven miles south from Wycombe. It was the terminus of the cross-country post from Newcastle. On their way to Northumberland, Hilary and Matt had traveled via the mail coaches as far as Bridgeton and had then completed their journey to Wycombe by hiring a post chaise. The town boasted a number of shops, mostly catering to the farmers of the surrounding countryside; substantial houses belonging to the local merchants; and even a small assembly hall. In comparison to Wycombe, it was a metropolis.

Madame Arblay's modiste shop was a modest one, but as soon as Hilary inspected the carriage dress in gray Circassian cloth, decorated with bands of white lutestring, which the dressmaker had recently completed for a client, she knew that Belinda was in the right hands.

Belinda pored over copies of *Ackermann's Repository, The*

Lady's Magazine, and *The Lady's Monthly Museum,* concentrating at first, to Hilary's amusement, on models of riding habits. First things first with Belinda, and riding was her passion. At last, pointing a finger at a pictured riding habit with a Hussar jacket and deeply frogged sleeves, she said, "Could you make that for me, madame?"

"But of course, mademoiselle. Would you prefer this dark blue cloth or the green?"

After Belinda had made her selection, Hilary said, "Well, madame, now that we've settled the most pressing question, could we see some samples of muslins for morning and carriage wear?"

Overwhelmed by the necessity of making a choice between Indian muslin, Madras, mull, and nainsook, Belinda finally inquired plaintively, "Do I really need so many gowns, Hilary?"

"Yes, you do," retorted Hilary. "Your brother said to spare no expense. This is the first time in my life that I've been given carte blanche in a modiste shop, and I propose to enjoy it."

Belinda chuckled appreciatively, and the modiste, quick to make the most of a customer with an unlimited purse, asked, "What about evening wear?" She produced a length of delicate French gauze in a coral-colored silk. "This would look lovely on Mademoiselle."

"Yes, it would," said Hilary after a critical look. "And I think you should have another gown for evening, Belinda, perhaps in a pastel shade, like that primrose-colored satin over there."

"An excellent choice," approved the modiste. "Suitable for a formal dinner or to wear to our monthly assembly balls."

"You have monthly assembly balls here?" asked Hilary in surprise. "I would have thought Bridgeton was too small . . ."

"But no, madame," said the modiste with a proprietary air. "Folk attend our balls from all around the countryside. We draw very respectable numbers, I assure you." She smiled slightly. "And I sew many of the ladies' gowns."

"I see," said Hilary thoughtfully, a scheme forming at the back of her mind. Whether it was feasible, only time would tell.

On the return trip to Wycombe, Belinda fairly bubbled with excitement. "That was so much fun. I'll be quite the fashion plate, won't I? Jon won't recognize me in my new finery!" She put out her arm to give Hilary an impulsive hug. "I've just realized how dull the village was before you and Matt arrived. Before you came, each day I'd give instructions for the menus to the housekeeper, go out for a ride, come back to the castle for dinner with Jon, and go to bed. Now my days are overflowing. Maria Grey says the same. She says you've worked miracles in her life."

Secretly glowing with pleasure at the compliment, Hilary patted Belinda's hand, saying quietly, "Thank you, my dear, but don't give me too much credit. I think you and Maria yourselves are the real miracle workers. You've both worked very hard."

"More tea, Matt?" Hilary filled her brother's extended cup and settled back with her letter. In the late afternoons, when her classes had been dismissed and if Matt had no emergency patients, they often enjoyed a quiet cup of tea together.

"What news from brother Richard?" Matt inquired.

"Very little of interest. The weather's been fine, the crops are flourishing—and Felicity is increasing."

Matt put down his newspaper. "Again?"

"Yes, Matt, you're about to become an uncle for the fifth time in as many years. If this child is another girl, you may have to start resigning yourself to becoming the tenth Baronet Vane some day."

"Lord, I hope not. I've never wanted to succeed Richard. I like being a doctor, even more so since I've left the army and we've come to Wycombe. I much prefer seeing patients who don't require their limbs to be amputated or who haven't taken a musket ball to their chests." He gazed at his sister with a faint expression of anxiety. "You like it here, too, don't you, Hilary? Now that your school is going so well and you've succeeded in taming the ogre—"

Hilary flushed. "If you mean the duke, you shouldn't speak of him in that way."

Matt grinned. "Not so long ago, you were used to speak of him in even harsher terms. Tyrant. Despot. Arrogant border lord."

Before Hilary could answer, their maid Sarah appeared at the door of the sitting room. "His Grace and Lady Belinda ter see ye."

"Show them in." Hilary hurried to pick up the pieces of newspaper that Matt had strewn around his chair. She was puzzled. This was the first time Alverly had paid her and Matt a strictly social call. What could he have in mind?

"I know we shouldn't have called at such an unusual hour," Belinda exclaimed as she bounded into the room, followed by her brother. "But I had to show you this—" She pirouetted in front of Matt and Hilary to show off her new riding habit of deep green cloth topped by a dashing small beaver hat decorated with a cordon of gold and a sweeping green ostrich feather at the front. "Do you like it?" she inquired. She flicked a saucy glance at her brother. "Jon says the feather will frighten all our horses."

"Either that or that ridiculous feather will put them off their feed," murmured the duke, straight-faced. So he does have a sense of humor, Hilary thought. What a pity he doesn't show it more often.

Gazing at Belinda admiringly, Matt said, "You're the *dernier cri*, Belinda. What's more important, you look beautiful. And don't worry about your green ostrich feather." He tossed Alverly a look of mock reproach. "Any self-respecting horse will grow to love it."

The duke smiled faintly as he sat down and accepted a cup of tea from Hilary.

"Madame Arblay finished sewing all my gowns in just a week. She must have worked day and night," Belinda explained to Hilary. "She sent them to the castle this afternoon. And that's why Jon and I are here. I want to show off one of my new evening frocks, so Jon and I have come to invite you and Matt to dinner on Saturday. Just a small dinner," she added hastily. "But it will not only give me the opportunity to wear a new frock, I'll also be able to show you how well I've learned the lessons in ladylike deportment, especially the parts about becoming a successful hostess."

"What a splendid idea. Matt and I accept with pleasure." Hilary smiled at her brother. "I presume I can speak for you?"

"Oh, definitely." Matt grinned at Belinda. "I'm looking forward to seeing that new gown, and I'm *especially* interested in viewing your newly acquired 'ladylike deportment.' "

Belinda giggled. "Matt! What an unkind thing to say. You know I've *always* been a lady."

Out of the corner of her eye, Hilary saw Alverly lift his head and glance sharply at Belinda and Matt as they exchanged their bantering remarks. Of course. This was the first time the duke had seen Matt and Belinda together. He had been unaware of the close personal friendship that had developed between them. Did he disapprove? Hilary couldn't tell. The duke's face wore its usual closed expression. He did, however, accept a second cup of tea and another biscuit.

At the door of the sitting room, as he and Belinda were leaving, Alverly gave Hilary one of his stiff little bows and said, "We'll see you and Dr. Vane on Saturday, then. I look forward to it."

Did he really, thought Hilary after he was gone. Or was he merely giving in to Belinda's exuberant desire to show off her new clothes? And did he comprehend yet that his relationship with his sister was changing? He was more in her company these days, and he was making more decisions about her upbringing than he had since she was a baby. But had he realized that Belinda was showing signs of learning how to wind her big brother around her little finger?

Chapter V

Hilary guided the dogcart carefully up the steep slope of the driveway leading to Wycombe Castle. The driveway was very nearly as rutted as the abominable roads in the valley. Why didn't Alverly do something about the roads on his estate, she thought in exasperation. Then she smiled at herself. The duke was a horseman, first and foremost. He rarely used a carriage.

It was a clear, bright early evening in late August. She and Matt were about to attend their first function as guests at the castle.

"You look very fetching tonight, sister mine."

"Thank you, Matt." She knew without his telling her that she looked attractive this evening. She loved pretty clothes, although, as a prim and proper schoolmistress at Miss Wiggins's academy in Tunbridge Wells, she'd never allowed herself to appear too fashionable. The parents of her pupils would have raised their eyebrows. But she hadn't been able to resist buying this gown of deep blue India muslin, the exact color of her eyes, trimmed with delicate gilt spangles. On her tawny curls she wore a blue satin bandeau corded in gilt, and around her shoulders she'd draped her prized Norwich shawl, the gift of the same aunt who'd bequeathed her a houseful of furniture.

Hilary flicked her brother a sideways glance. "You look very dashing yourself, Matt. I can't remember when I last saw you in evening dress."

"Oh, I'm the Top of the Trees, that is, until I stand up and walk," jibed Matt. An instant later, he said, "Sorry. I'm wallowing in self-pity today. My blasted hip hurts infernally."

She looked at him in dismay. "Oh, Matt, why didn't you tell me? Perhaps we shouldn't go to the castle tonight."

"Nonsense. I wouldn't miss Belinda's triumph for a king's ransom." Matt's voice had regained its usual cheerfulness. "And watch your driving, my girl. You almost had us overturned there." He put his hand on her knee. "Hilary, don't mope over me. I want you to enjoy your evening. And I'm feeling better already. I think it was the chilling rain we had last night that triggered this attack. Like most old soldiers with battle wounds, I find that the weather affects how I feel."

Hilary held her tongue. She knew he must have been suffering a great deal of pain from his leg to have occasioned his outburst. Most of the time he concealed any discomfort he might be feeling with a stoic composure, and he hated any display of sympathy. The best thing was to leave the situation alone.

She drove through the long gloomy tunnel under the gatehouse and emerged into the courtyard. A groom rushed to take the reins of the pony. Matt paused for a moment, looking with interest around the enormous cobblestoned expanse of the courtyard. This was his first visit to the castle.

"If these old stones could only speak," he said at last,

"think what they could tell us about sieges and violence and bloodshed over the centuries." He grinned at Hilary. "I'm very glad I wasn't a surgeon during those times. I don't fancy treating patients who've been doused with boiling pitch!"

"Well, thank heavens there's no possibility of those terrible things happening again. The battles at Wycombe Castle are long over."

"Except between you and the duke," Matt retorted.

Hilary gave him a sisterly poke in the ribs. "That's all behind us. The duke and I have declared a truce," she said. "Come along. We don't wish to be late for dinner."

They walked slowly up the staircase leading to the lord's quarters in the large structure built against the outer walls of the castle. As soon as she entered the hallway, she marveled again at the disparity between the ordered elegance and the perfect harmony of furnishings of the interior of the castle and its grim medieval exterior.

"Robert Adam," she heard herself saying aloud as she arrived at the entrance of the drawing room behind the escorting footman.

"Quite right, Miss Vane," said Alverly, bowing as she entered the room. "Shortly after he returned from his Grand Tour and after he married my mother, who had inherited a vast fortune in coal mines in the Tyne Valley, my father employed Robert Adam to renovate the interior of the castle. I believe this was one of Adam's last commissions before he died."

"From what I've seen, I'd say Mr. Adam outdid himself," Hilary murmured politely, as she tried to keep her shock from showing in her face. This was a new Duke of Alverly. He looked quite magnificent in his evening dress. True, his black coat was out-of-date by at least ten years, but it fitted him superbly as did his white breeches and stockings, and someone had surely taken a hand with his cravat, which was tied in an impeccable *Trône d'Amour*. Someone also—it must have been his valet, making a determined stand against his employer's careless grooming—had clipped the duke's shaggy locks into an approximation of the fashionable "Brutus" coiffure.

"Oh, Hilary, you look so pretty," breathed Belinda, standing bright-eyed and flushed with excitement beside her brother. She herself was vividly beautiful in her new gown of clinging primrose satin.

"My dear, I don't hold a candle to you," Hilary said, smiling. "Don't you agree, Matt?"

"At the risk of alienating my sister forever, Belinda, I must agree with her," said Matt solemnly. Belinda burst out laughing at his nonsense. Even the duke smiled slightly.

It was, as Belinda had said when she extended her invitation, a very small dinner party, perhaps the smallest formal dinner Hilary had ever attended. The vicar and his wife were the only other guests.

"If Belinda's gown is a fair sample of your taste, Miss Vane, I'd say her new wardrobe must be a great success," remarked Mrs. Trevor, gazing at Belinda as she sat in laughing conversation with Matt. The duke was chatting gravely with the vicar. "Belinda looks so happy, too," Mrs. Trevor continued. "You've done wonders with the child, Miss Vane."

"You give me too much credit. I think Belinda's like a late blooming flower. The potential was always there."

"Well, perhaps. But what now? She's growing into a beautiful and accomplished young lady, but who will ever see her in this backwater? She's seventeen, you know. She should be making plans for a come-out, if not in London, then in Bath. I believe the duke has an elderly aunt, on his mother's side of the family, who resides in Bath. The aunt could certainly sponsor Belinda. Or Elvira—her mother—may have returned to England and could launch Belinda in London. Lately I've had half a mind to suggest the idea to Jonathan—I mean the duke . . ."

Mrs. Trevor broke off, making a face. "La, I'm becoming an interfering old lady. I've no right to tell the duke how to conduct his family affairs." She gazed about the great drawing room, in which its few occupants appeared almost lost. "I remember this room thronged to overflowing with guests," she said reminiscently. "Jonathan's parents were used to entertain frequently, and Elvira was fond of entertaining, too. Lord, when I think of the shattered axles and other damage to their carriages suffered by the old duke's guests! The roads in the valley were no better then than now, I assure you. But I do believe this is the first time the present duke has entertained since his father died, since Belinda was born. Jonathan has become almost a recluse, I don't know why." The vicar's wife smiled. "Perhaps he'll become less of a hermit, now that you and Dr. Vane have arrived in Wycombe!"

"Oh, I doubt Matt and I will have any influence on the duke," said Hilary, smiling. But as the evening progressed, she had to admit that Alverly, for whatever his reasons, was making a definite attempt to be an affable host. At the dinner table, in the vast dining room with its solid bank of silver pieces on an immense sideboard, Alverly kept the conversation rolling. He chatted with the vicar about parish matters, about which he seemed to know a great deal. More than the vicar himself, probably, thought Hilary in amusement. The duke also politely asked Matt's opinions about the progress of the war in the Peninsula.

"Oh, I daresay it's going as well as can be expected, even without my valuable services," Matt said with a grin. "Can't say I regret not being there. Not that I'd be much use with my game leg. I fancy there'll be more action soon. Wellington's been merely skirmishing on the Coast, but I expect it won't be long before he goes after Ciudad Rodrigo."

A little later Alverly's interest was sparked when Matt inquired about antiquities in the Cheviot Hills. "I did a bit of reading before I came here, Duke. I understand there are a number of prehistoric remains in the area. Stone circles, hill forts, and the like. There's also one quite unusual site called—let me think, now. Yes, I have it—called the 'Devil's Cauldron.' Would you know of it?"

"Oh, indeed," said the duke. "It's our one claim to fame in these parts, though I'm not entirely sure why. The Devil's Cauldron is just a very deep hole in the ground with steep, nearly vertical sides. What intrigues the scholars, apparently, is that they can't imagine what purpose the hole may have served. Some have conjectured it might have been used as a place to corral sheep for shearing, but folk who say that are obviously not farmers! You'd run the risk of breaking the legs of half your flock if you tried to herd them down there. And besides, I doubt that our ancient ancestors cultivated sheep."

His face alive with interest, Matt asked, "Is the Devil's Cauldron far from here? Is it difficult to get there?"

"No, it's not more than three or four miles from Wycombe, but it's very rough riding up the slopes of Devil's Mountain."

"Oh." Matt sighed. "Then I'll not have the opportunity to see it, I still can't sit a horse properly. Hilary, you must go exploring for me and come back with a description of the place."

After dinner while the gentlemen were drinking their port in the dining room, in the drawing room Hilary said smilingly to Belinda, "Congratulations on your first dinner party. You were a great success as a hostess."

"Indeed you were, my dear," Mrs. Trevor agreed. "You were most gracious. One would think you'd been presiding over formal dinner parties for many years."

Belinda glowed. "Thank you. I did everything according to your instructions, Hilary. I supervised our housekeeper's table arrangements and menus very carefully, and I checked to make sure the living quarters were immaculate. As it happened, Mrs. Gardiner—our housekeeper—had everything in hand, but still . . ."

Hilary nodded. "It's always wise for the lady of the house to check the final arrangements. You did well, Belinda."

When the gentlemen came to the drawing room a little later, it developed that Mr. and Mrs. Trevor had a passion for whist, which Matt shared. The trio dragooned Belinda into making a fourth at their table.

"But I don't know how to play whist," Belinda expostulated. "I'll make a perfect idiot of myself."

"No, you won't," Matt assured her. "We'll teach you how to play, won't we, Vicar? Actually, Belinda, we'll be doing you a service. Every young lady of fashion should know how to play a good game of whist."

Laughing, Belinda gave in. "I'm only agreeing to this because I know you're a good teacher, Matt," she said as she sat down at the card table. She called out gaily, "Jon, while I'm learning this game, you must entertain Hilary. You can show her the library and the picture gallery and your conservatory."

"Of course," said Alverly. "Shall we go along, Miss Vane?" His expression was unreadable. It was impossible for Hilary to tell if he resented his sister's peremptory suggestion that he should conduct her on a guided tour of the castle.

As she walked with the duke down the corridor with its elegant coffered ceilings, Hilary spotted a piece of Chinese porcelain on a pedestal in an alcove and paused to admire it. "How lovely," she breathed, eying the luminously beautiful pastel tints in the design.

"That's a *famille verte* eggshell lantern from the K'anghai period," the duke said.

"You sound very knowledgeable," Hilary commented. "I noticed many other pieces of porcelain in the Italian cabinets in the drawing room. Have you been collecting these pieces for a long time?"

"Oh, I'm not the collector. That was my mother. She loved Chinese porcelain. She collected specimens from various periods for many years. This eggshell lantern was her favorite piece."

An amused smile played about his lips. "My mother wasn't an extravagant woman, except when it came to her porcelain collection. My father was used to say, funning, of course, that Mama would send him into low water if she bought one more expensive piece."

There was a softened, almost tender, expression on his face as he gazed at the porcelain. Hilary added a snippet of information to her slender store of knowledge about Alverly's inner personality. It was clear he'd adored his mother.

"The duchess had exquisite taste," Hilary said.

"Yes."

"Did she—did she die young?" Hilary regretted the question the moment she asked it. One didn't put personal questions to the Duke of Alverly.

However, though the softened expression faded, the duke merely replied briefly, "She died when I was twelve years old. My father remarried several years later. If you'll come this way, Miss Vane, we'll go first to the library."

The library was a large room with a gallery running around three of its upper sides. The shelves on both levels had a full complement of books, none of which looked well-thumbed. Hilary suspected that the members of the Rayner family weren't great readers. She spotted a translation of *The Decameron* in a particularly handsome leather binding and took it from the shelves. "I've never seen such a beautiful edition," she murmured as she leafed through the pages.

"If you'd care to read it, I'll send it down to Willow Cottage."

"Oh, thank you, but I don't think I should keep *The Decameron* on the premises," Hilary said demurely. "One of my pupils might chance to open it."

After a puzzled moment, the duke began to laugh. "I see what you mean, *The Decameron* isn't suitable reading for young ladies, is it?"

"My governess once caught me reading it and assured me I was in danger of losing my immortal soul."

The duke laughed again. Was he finding it a little easier to laugh these days?

She was fascinated by the picture gallery. The earlier portraits showed grim-looking men in full armor, bran-

90

dishing swords. The later pictures were of elegant gentlefolk in the wigs and richly laced velvets and taffetas of the sixteenth and seventeenth centuries.

"My parents," said Alverly, indicating two of the last portraits in the long row. He and Belinda showed a strong resemblance to the late duke, a tall figure with gray eyes and straight, regular features. Hilary could see little resemblance between the duke and his sweet-faced mother.

"But where is your portrait, Duke?" Hilary inquired.

"There isn't one. I don't care to look at my own face on the wall," he said curtly, almost rudely. "Nor can I conceive of anyone else being interested."

Hilary stared at him, puzzled by his reaction to her question. Many people would regard it as a family duty for the duke to add his likeness to the long line of ancestors on the wall of the picture gallery. Alverly had not only refused to do so, he seemed angry at the very thought of it.

Shaking her head mentally, she passed on to the last portrait in the gallery, a painting of a beautiful blond woman in a chimney pot hat and a redingote dress in the style of the nineties of the previous century.

"My stepmother," Alverly said briefly. "Belinda's mother." His tone was forbidding. Hilary could well believe Mrs. Trevor's revelation that the duke had disliked his stepmother.

Hastily she changed the subject. "What is the date of your earliest portrait?" she asked, moving to the other end of the room to look at the pictures of the grim-faced men in armor.

"The late fourteenth century, I believe."

"Before then, I daresay, your ancestors were too busy

91

slaughtering Scotsmen to have time to pose for portraits," Hilary remarked with a straight face.

"Slaughtering Scotsmen?" Alverly repeated, as if he hadn't heard correctly.

"Why, yes. Isn't that what the border lords were used to spend most of their time doing?"

"Border lords?" Alverly looked at her sharply as if momentarily he took her remark seriously and was offended by it. Then his face relaxed in one of his rare, difficult smiles. "Yes, I'd say those so-called border lords were very busy, defending the border against the Scottish invader," he retorted. "You were making a joke, Miss Vane, but think about it: perhaps you'd be living under the Scottish crown today if my forebears hadn't done their duty."

Hilary laughed. "Touché." Unable to resist, she said with a teasing smile, "Life must have been so dull for the border lords, both English and Scottish, when the wars between them ended. Think of it: no skirmishes, no bloodshed, no pillaging, no assaults on your neighbor's castle."

Again that fraction of a second of incredulity. Definitely, His Grace the Duke of Alverly was not accustomed to being teased. Then the rare smile appeared again. "Life may have been dull when the wars were over, but it was certainly more comfortable not being exposed to hot pitch and cannonballs," he said dryly. "Shall we visit the conservatory now, Miss Vane?"

A short distance down the corridor, they met with a scene of disaster. Coming toward them was a young footman carrying a tea tray. As he drew abreast of the niche containing the exquisite K'ang-hai eggshell lantern, he unaccountably slipped and fell, dropping tea tray and china with a crash. Worse, his flailing arm

92

glanced off the Chinese porcelain, causing it to topple off its pedestal.

Scrambling to his feet, the footman looked in despair at the fallen tray, the leaking silver teapot, and the fragments of china littering the floor. "I'm so sorry, Your Grace," he gasped. "I dunno how I happened ter fall, me foot jist slipped out from under me . . ."

"I know why you fell," said Alverly grimly. "Lady Belinda ordered all the floors freshly waxed this morning. They're slippery as the devil. Well, Watson, clean up the mess." He bent to pick up several pieces of the broken Chinese porcelain. "Save as many fragments of this Chinese piece as you can find. Perhaps it can be mended."

Suddenly aware of the enormity of his offense, the footman stared in frozen horror at the pieces of the Chinese porcelain. He muttered brokenly, "Your Grace, the housekeeper's warned all the staff these many years ter be careful about cleaning round this 'ere vase, because you prized it so much, and now I've done gone and broke it."

A muscle twitched in Alverly's cheek, but all he said was, "You didn't do it maliciously. It was an accident. As I said, perhaps the piece can be mended." But there was little conviction in his voice.

As she and Alverly walked away from the penitent servant, on his knees carefully collecting the precious fragments of the Chinese lantern, Hilary said quietly. "I admire your forbearance, Duke. I know a number of households in which a servant would have been dismissed out of hand for destroying a family heirloom."

Alverly shrugged. "If this had been a case of sheer carelessness or deliberate spite, I'd have dismissed the footman immediately. But it was an accident. I don't punish people for accidents." He cleared his throat. "The conservatory is this way, Miss Vane."

Hilary had expected to see a modest-sized greenhouse of the kind that many of her father's neighbors in Suffolk possessed. She was unprepared for a soaring glass-enclosed building the size of a small cathedral, with shrubs and flowers and small trees of every description. Nor was she prepared for the change in the duke's personality that took place the moment he crossed the threshold of the conservatory.

"The building was quite small in my father's time," he explained. "He and my mother were mainly interested in growing fruits for the table and flowers for cutting. We still do grow a number of fruits—pineapple and peaches and, at the moment, these grapes." He reached out to snip a small bunch of grapes from a vine entwined on a trellis and handed it to Hilary. "But I've always been more interested in flowers. And I don't like to cut them. I prefer to see them growing."

Alverly bent to stroke gently with his forefinger a small yellow rose. "The Empress Josephine in her gardens at Malmaison has succeeded in crossing the *centifolia* of Provence with the China rose to produce this tea rose, which flowers for weeks. I was very fortunate to obtain a cutting. Wouldn't it be a shame to pick one of these tea roses when otherwise it might bloom for many days?"

Hilary glanced sideways at the duke with a feeling of unreality. Where was the reticent, aloof man she'd first met? Alverly's face had opened up to his feelings, had come alive. His expression had the eager interest of a young boy showing off his most prized possession, Hilary thought, more important to him personally than his wide acres and his coal mines. It was also typical of Alverly's nature to follow an absorbing hobby that didn't require him to associate with other human beings. In his greenhouse he could be as solitary and withdrawn as he wished.

Alverly pointed to several other flowers as they walked slowly along the path. "I have examples of a number of other plant varieties that the Empress Josephine introduced into Europe. The magnolia plant over there to your left, for example. Hibiscus, phlox, Martinique Jasmine. And the camellia." He paused to look with pride at a shrub with thick shiny leaves and large double rose-colored blossoms.

"I've never seen such beautiful camellias," murmured Hilary, somewhat abstractedly. She was truly admiring of the lovely and variegated blooms in the duke's gardens, but she was really more interested in observing a side of Alverly's nature that she would never have dreamed existed.

"Oh, dear," she exclaimed in vexation. The fringe of her Norwich shawl had caught on a trailing vine.

"Stay still. I'll disentangle your shawl."

Hilary watched the duke's long slender fingers at their delicate task. Having freed the fringe, he arranged the shawl over her shoulders. His fingers brushed the sensitive skin of her neck and shoulders, and she felt an electric quiver of sensual arousal. Did she merely imagine that his fingers lingered caressingly on her bare flesh? She glanced surreptitiously at his face, but he looked perfectly calm. Was it possible he didn't feel what she was feeling? Despite herself, she shivered in reaction.

"Are you cold?" the duke quickly inquired. "It's

rather chilly in the conservatory. Perhaps we should return to the drawing room?"

She wouldn't allow him to guess how his touch had affected her. "No, I'm not cold. I'd like to see the rest of the greenhouse."

A gardener at the far end of the conservatory called out, "Your Grace, could I speak ter ye fer a moment? I've been wanting ter tell ye about this here leaky valve."

While Alverly strode off to speak to the gardener, Hilary continued a slow walk along the central path, drinking in the beauty of the fragrant, colorful blooms. A vagrant thought crossed her mind. She guessed that the duke rarely visited the greenhouse while his gardeners were at work. He'd prefer to be alone with his beautiful living playthings, solitary in this as in every other aspect of his life.

"Hilary, will you come up here, please?"

Astonished at his unexpected use of her given name, she walked quickly to the end of the greenhouse where Alverly waited for her, looking ludicrously embarrassed. "Pray excuse me for being so forward," he muttered. "That was a slip of the tongue. You see, I hear Belinda constantly speaking of you or addressing you by your Christian name . . ."

"She does, yes. We're friends, and not *that* far apart in age!" On an impulse, Hilary said daringly, "If you would prefer to call me Hilary . . ."

The duke looked astounded. "Oh. Thank you, I will, Miss—Hilary," he said awkwardly. "Er—my name is Jonathan. Of course, Belinda calls me Jon."

"Yes, I'd noticed—Jon." Unable to resist, Hilary said, "I understand you have another name. Augustus."

The duke's brow darkened. "I'll wring her neck," he muttered. Then he caught Hilary's eye and began to laugh. "So much for my deep, dark secret," he quipped.

Hilary felt flabbergasted. In a moment's time, she and the duke had shifted their relationship to new ground. They could never return to the stiff formality of the past, which, she now realized, had not only kept them at arms' length but had also been a safeguard against intrusion into Alverly's private emotions. Rather to her surprise, she felt comfortable with the change in attitude toward each other. As for the duke . . . She gave him a long look. He still seemed mildly embarrassed, a trifle astonished, but not really displeased.

He cleared his throat. "I wanted you to see this," he said. "This" was obviously the pride and joy of his botanical collection. Climbing a group of nondescript small trees at the end of the conservatory was a rainbow of brilliantly colored and exotically shaped blossoms.

"Oh . . ." breathed Hilary. "They're orchids, aren't they? I've never seen anything so lovely."

The duke said with satisfaction, "I've been collecting these specimens for ten years. Most of them are from the Americas, of course." He pointed to a large, exquisitely beautiful deep purple Cattleya. "That's my latest find." Then he reached out to pluck a tiny, bird-shaped deep yellow bloom. "The Indian moth orchid," he said. "Perhaps you'd like to have it."

"Oh, no, please," she said quickly. "You've told me you prefer to see your flowers growing."

"I'll never miss one, Miss—Hilary," he protested. "I think this specimen would look charming in your coiffure." Slowly, gently, Alverly settled the tiny orchid in the chestnut curls atop Hilary's head. His eyes bemused, he said huskily, "You have beautiful hair. It clings to my fingers, almost as if it had a life of its own."

They were standing very close together in the dimly lit, scented greenhouse. Hilary's heart pounded at the proximity of that tall, powerful body. She had the sensation that they were drawing closer together, although, she realized later, neither of them had moved a fraction of an inch. They stood as if mesmerized, their eyes locked together. The duke's slate gray eyes had turned black, and his breathing was uneven. Slowly he extended groping hands to her shoulders—and dislodged the clinging Norwich shawl. As he bent to pick it up, Hilary came out of her daze. Almost snatching the shawl from him, she wrapped it tightly around her.

"I think you were right, Du—Jon," she said breathlessly. "It *is* rather chilly in here. Perhaps we should return to the drawing room."

"Yes. You mustn't catch a chill," the duke agreed instantly. He sounded breathless, too. He also sounded relieved.

As they walked back together through the long, magnificent corridors to the drawing room, Hilary's thoughts were a chaotic jumble. By suggesting that she and Alverly exchange Christian names, had she placed herself in an impossible situation? Did the duke believe that she'd made a bold overture, expecting him to . . . Her cheeks burned. What might have happened if his awkward fingers hadn't dislodged her Norwich shawl?

Soon, however, she sensed with relief that Alverly apparently didn't suspect her of designs on him. As they neared the drawing room, he slowed, placing his hand on her arm and then removing it hastily. But his eyes were perfectly friendly as he said, "Hilary, I've been remiss. I haven't thanked you properly for taking Belinda to Bridgeton and helping her select a new wardrobe. Her clothes *were* shabby, I can see that now. Her old riding habit was a disgrace."

Hilary smiled. "There's no need for special thanks. I enjoyed shopping with Belinda. I love buying new clothes, for myself or for someone else!" Encouraged by his faintly amused expression, she said without pausing to think, "Will you allow me to make one more suggestion about Belinda?"

Alverly lifted an eyebrow. "Certainly. Your previous suggestions were very helpful."

"Then—have you considered giving Belinda a come-out season?"

Instantly the gray eyes grew chilly. "No. I see no reason for it."

Hilary plunged on. "But why not? A come-out would give her so many opportunities to meet new people."

"I don't believe Belinda has any need to meet new people."

The icy reply failed to deter Hilary. "Oh, I think you're so wrong. She *does* need new friends and acquaintances. And really, her come-out needn't require a great effort or inconvenience on your part. I understand her stepfather is a diplomat, frequently stationed abroad, but supposing he and her mother chanced to be in London at the moment? They could sponsor Belinda's come-out."

Stepping back from her, his hands clenched into fists, Alverly said in a low, deadly voice, "I'll say this only once, Miss Vane, and I trust you'll have the courtesy not to bring up the subject again. Never under any circumstances would I allow Belinda to make a debut in London under the sponsorship of her mother or anyone else. *Especially* not her mother. Do I make myself clear?"

"Yes," said Hilary, almost inaudibly. "I'm sorry," she added after a moment. "I've intruded into your affairs."

"Yes," he snapped. "You have."

Chapter VI

Hilary stepped out of the Bridgeton Assembly Rooms, smiling in satisfaction at the successful outcome of her appointment with the Master of Ceremonies. She paused at the end of the walkway where her pony and dogcart waited, and glanced down the busy main street with a great feeling of pleasure that she was in a bustling town again. Then she laughed at herself. In comparison to Tunbridge Wells, or even to Landview, the village near her brother's estate in Suffolk, Bridgeton was practically a hamlet. Even so, it was definitely superior to Wycombe, and among its amenities was an excellent linen-draper's shop, where this afternoon she proposed to buy some new buttons for her gray pelisse.

As she walked toward the linen-draper's establishment, she noticed a familiar figure proceeding down the street toward her on horseback. She resisted a strong impulse to avoid meeting him by ducking into the nearest shop, and continued on her way.

The Duke of Alverly reined in his mount as he drew abreast of her, and dismounted. "Good day, Miss—Hilary."

"Good day." She hadn't spoken to the duke since

Belinda's triumphant little dinner party several days ago, although she'd observed him riding past Willow Cottage a number of times on his way to visit farms on the outlying part of his estates. Or possibly to visit his accommodating widow, Hilary had thought with a sudden vindictiveness that had surprised and distressed her. It could be nothing to her that the duke kept a mistress.

Today Alverly seemed distinctly ill at ease. He wore his customary nondescript, unfashionable clothes, although, since there hadn't been time for his hair to grow shaggy again since the dinner party at the castle, he looked more presentable than he usually did. And yet, as Hilary noticed the glances directed at him by passersby, she realized that every man, woman, and child in Bridgeton knew quite well that this man was the Duke of Alverly. Despite his shabby dress, his air of authority was unmistakable.

"Er—could I speak to you, Hilary?" The duke glanced around him. "Well, not here on the street, of course. There's an excellent inn a short way from here. Perhaps you'd care for a cup of tea?"

"Why, yes, thank you." Now, what was in Alverly's mind? Hilary wondered. At their last meeting, when he'd accused her of interfering in his affairs by suggesting that Belinda have a come-out, he'd been so angry that she suspected he might never speak to her again. And yet, here he was, not cordial precisely—she doubted that cordiality would ever be a part of his character—but at least he was wishful to talk to her.

The landlord of the Crown Arms leapt to attention when the duke walked into the inn and ushered Alverly and his guest into a private parlor. "Leave the door open, please," said the duke quietly, and Hilary suppressed a smile. She was so accustomed to going about when and where she pleased that it hadn't occurred to her the landlord might suspect her and Alverly of an assignation.

When the tea tray and pastries arrived, the duke played the host to perfection, asking her to pour the tea and passing her the plate of pastries. She noticed, not for the first time, that his graceful hands with their long slender fingers were especially well-kept, in contrast to his otherwise careless grooming. In so many ways, she mused, the man was a curious mixture of contradictions.

Apparently he found it hard to come to the point. After a series of remarks about the weather, the state of the harvest, and the young stallion he'd recently purchased, he blurted, "I owe you an apology. I was rude to you the last time we met, the night you dined at the castle."

He reddened as he spoke, and Hilary reflected that he probably hadn't felt the necessity to apologize to anyone since he succeeded to the title, many years before. She took pity on him. "Thank you. That was generous of you. I daresay I was rude, too."

He shook his head. "It's not the same thing at all. I know you're genuinely fond of Belinda, and you were only trying to be helpful. I shouldn't have barked at you, even though I thought—I knew—you were wrong. You meant well."

"I—" Hilary shut her lips firmly.

The duke shot her a keen look. "But you still think you were right, don't you?"

"Yes, I do," Hilary admitted. She rushed on. "Think about it, D—Jon. Belinda's a beautiful girl of the highest rank and breeding. She should have her chance to spread her wings in the outside world; London, preferably, but Bath would do very well."

"I can't agree with you. Belinda's very young, and she's never been farther from Wycombe Castle than a few brief visits to Newcastle. I don't want her exposed to the pitfalls of London society. She's too young and innocent to cope with the people and the problems she'd encounter there."

Hilary stared at him. Where had he acquired his strange impression of the London social scene? "Perhaps you'd consider a come-out when Belinda is a little older?" she ventured.

"No. Belinda doesn't need to rub elbows with London gallants to be happy. She's content with her life here in the Wycombe Valley. I don't wish to disturb her mind with empty thoughts about the London *ton.*"

"But—what about marriage? If Belinda never leaves the valley, how can she meet a suitable *parti?*"

The duke's brows drew together in his familiar frown. "I've long thought that young women marry much too young. Belinda shouldn't even consider marriage until she's at least twenty-five."

"Twenty-five!" Hilary exclaimed. "By that age, she'll be on the shelf, an unmarriageable spinster. Like me."

"You!" Alverly flushed. "I didn't know how old . . . I didn't mean to suggest . . . How can you say that a young woman is unmarriageable at twenty-five?"

"Because, in the main, it's true," Hilary retorted. "Of course, my case is different from Belinda's. Because I'm a schoolmistress, my chances for marriage have necessarily been limited. For some reason, people don't expect schoolmistresses to marry! But Belinda is a duke's daughter with, I presume, a fortune of her own. Possibly she'd have no difficulty marrying at twenty-five or later. Provided," Hilary added pointedly, "that she had the opportunity to meet an eligible suitor."

She suppressed a wild desire to laugh at Alverly's expression of scowling confusion. He was totally unused to opposition, and he was now so obviously restraining an urge to give her a proper set-down. "I've said everything I wanted to say, Jon," she remarked calmly. "Shall we have a truce?"

His brow cleared in relief. "By all means. I'm happy we've discussed this matter. I believe we understand each other now. Am I correct?"

"Yes, quite correct." That was a lie. Hilary couldn't understand why a wealthy, prominent man of rank would deliberately deprive his only sister of the opportunity to make a debut in society because she was "too young," even though most girls of her age and station were preparing for their come-outs. However, she'd done her best to change the duke's attitude, quite in vain, and now it was useless to argue. If she wished to remain on friendly terms with him, she must learn to keep her opinions to herself.

"Well, now, this is more comfortable," the duke remarked, clearly happy to change the subject. He extended his cup to be refilled. "What brought you to Bridgeton today, Hilary?"

"I had an appointment with the Master of Ceremonies of the Assembly Rooms. I wanted to know if it would be feasible to bring my pupils to the next ball. Suitably chaperoned by Matt and me, naturally. Mr. Armstrong assured me he'd be happy to welcome my girls to the ball."

Alverly considered the matter with the grave deliberation that was so typical of him. "I think it's an excellent scheme," he pronounced. "Most of those attending the ball will be local tradesmen or the more prosperous farmers of the area. The only person of any consequence in Bridgeton is Squire Fenton, and I doubt he'd make an appearance. Your pupils won't feel out of place socially. The situation would be different if you wished to bring your students to an assembly in Stanton, which is the next town of any size south of here. Several families of the gentry reside in Stanton. I fancy they'd look askance if you brought farmer's daughters from Wycombe to their assembly ball."

Hilary felt a twinge of distaste at the duke's air of condescension, although she knew his attitude was shared by most people of his rank. Over the years her own attitude toward class distinctions had somewhat blurred. The city merchants and well-to-do farmers who sent their daughters to Miss Wiggins's Select Academy had seemed little different to her from the county gentry with whom she'd grown up. The parents of her Tunbridge Wells pupils were as ambitious for their daughters and as proud of their respectable station in life as any member of the minor aristocracy.

"Thank you for the tea," she said now. "I must go. Matt will be thinking I've overturned the dogcart on the road over the pass. He doesn't have a high opinion of my skill with the ribbons!"

Alverly rose. Sounding somewhat awkward, he said, "My Martinique Jasmine bloomed this morning. I'd be delighted to show it to you if you care to visit the castle."

Lifting her hands from the keyboard, Hilary said, "That was splendid, girls. You've mastered the pousette step." She added casually, "I think it's time you danced the cotillion in public."

106

Eight pairs of eyes stared at her uncomprehendingly. "What do you mean, Miss Vane?" inquired Maria Grey.

"Oh, just that I've arranged for all of you to attend the Bridgeton Assembly Ball in two weeks time."

"O-h-h," breathed Dulcie Cross. "How wonderful."

Her sister Kate said, "Yes, but, will Papa allow us to go?"

"Don't be a ninnyhammer," said Dulcie scornfully. "He *must* allow us to go."

Hilary wasn't so sure. By this time, she was growing accustomed to the conservatism of her farmer neighbors. During the next few days she made it a special point to visit the parents of each of her pupils, requesting permission for their daughters to attend the ball. Several fathers were reluctant, especially when they learned that a new gown would be required, but their wives and daughters overcame their reluctance.

Farmer Grey's wife was even more enthusiastic than Maria about the ball. Her eyes bright, the buxom, motherly woman said, "I can't thank you enough, Miss Vane. This ball will give Maria just the polish she'll need when she goes to visit her cousins in Bristol next spring." Mrs. Grey added shyly, "May I tell you something in confidence? Mr. Grey and myself are very hopeful that Maria will make a good impression on my cousin's son Alfred. It would be a very good match for Maria. Alfred is an excellent young man, already a partner in his father's business, though he's only twenty-one, and he comes from a very good family, if I say so myself. My cousin Jane and her husband will expect any future daughter-in-law to be a real lady."

"Alfred does indeed sound like a fine young man, Mrs. Grey. If he and Maria should marry, I'm sure they would be very happy."

107

But as Hilary drove back to Wycombe, she found her mind dwelling on a conversation she'd had with Maria Grey the previous week.

"Miss Vane, do you think I might ever become a schoolmistress?" the pretty blue-eyed girl had asked.

Hilary had replied kindly, "Why, with a little more instruction, I think you'd make an excellent teacher, Maria." She hesitated. "Have you talked to your parents about the possibility?"

"Oh, no. I'd never dare. They want me to be married. Mama hopes I'll make a match of it with my Cousin Alfred when I go to visit his family in Bristol next spring."

"And you don't wish to marry Alfred?"

"I've never even met him, Miss Vane! He might be very nice, of course, and perhaps when I'm a little older . . . Before I even think of marrying, though, I'd like to have the opportunity to be a schoolmistress like you." She bit her lip. "Oh, I wish I *could* talk to Mama about it." She'd turned away then, sighing, leaving Hilary vaguely troubled.

On the subject of the ball, Belinda was perhaps the most enthusiastic of all the pupils. She'd hugged Hilary, saying, "You have the most capital ideas! Now, which gown should I wear, my French gauze or my primrose satin? Or should I ask Jon for a new muslin dress like the ones the other girls are having made?"

"Belinda . . ." Hilary looked at the girl helplessly. "I can't take you to the ball. I know your brother would never give his permission."

"You can't mean that. All the other girls are going."

"My dear, that's the point. You aren't simply one of the other girls. You're a duke's daughter."

Belinda looked bewildered. "What difference does

that make? I've been attending classes for weeks now with Maria and the other girls. Nobody's objected to my being here. Jon doesn't object, either. He thinks I'm learning a great deal in your classes."

"I'm happy to hear that your brother approves. On the subject of your fellow pupils, however, have you noticed that they're all very careful to call you 'Lady Belinda'?"

"Well, of course. Everyone on the estate uses my title. Oh. You mean that the other girls don't consider me one of them?"

"Exactly. You *aren't* one of them."

Belinda sounded less sure of herself. "But why should any of this affect whether I should attend the Bridgeton Assembly Ball?"

"Belinda, your brother has more sense of what's due to your rank than you apparently do. Are you aware that I had great difficulty even in persuading him to allow you to enroll in my school? He felt it was unseemly for you to be attending classes with the daughters of his own tenants. Now how do you suppose he'll feel about your presence at a ball attended only by tradesmen and farmers? Bridgeton is a larger place than Wycombe. There might well be gossip if it became known that the sister of the Duke of Alverly took part in such a plebeian affair, *and* in the company of farmers' daughters from her brother's estate!"

Belinda looked thoughtful, but only for a moment. Then she said buoyantly, "You're talking fustian, Hilary. Jon's becoming much more human than he used to be. Haven't you noticed? I can't think he'd turn high in the instep merely because I wanted to go to a village ball. I tell you what: I'll ask him for permission to attend the ball. If he says no, that's an end to it."

"Yes, do that," said Hilary in relief. Alverly was certain to refuse his permission. The matter was out of her hands, and Hilary could hardly be blamed for Belinda's unhappiness and disappointment. The girl had already promised to abide by her brother's decision.

To her intense surprise, Hilary soon learned that Alverly had once again displayed his contradictory nature. "Jon says I can go to the ball," Belinda announced happily when she came a day later for her Greek lesson with Matt. "He said he knows I'll be in good hands with you and Matt. What's more, he says I may stay the night with you—that is, if you'll invite me!—to save you and Matt the trouble of bringing me back to the castle late at night."

"Why, of course you're welcome to stay with us, and I'm glad you can attend the ball," said a rather confused Hilary. She wondered what had caused Alverly to relax his rigid standards, but she was too busy to think about the subject for very long, and she didn't speak to the duke during the next few days.

There were times during the following two weeks when Hilary almost regretted having proposed that her pupils attend the Bridgeton Assembly Ball. She often felt like a mother hen with too many chicks. The heady anticipation of the ball and the excitement of having new gowns were paramount in the minds of her pupils, but Hilary had other concerns. Many of the details that would have been taken care of by the mothers of young ladies about to attend a ball fell to her lot. The girls came to her for approval of their choices of gowns and their styles of coiffures, rather than to their mothers. The question of transportation was a vexing one, also. How were ten adults in evening dress to travel to Bridgeton? Mrs. Trevor came to the rescue with the loan of the vicarage carriage, and Farmer Grey offered the use of a traveling berline so ancient that Hilary suspected it might fall apart before their journey was accomplished.

The great night finally arrived. The carriages made the trip safely, and Hilary's pupils in their pretty pastel-colored muslin and cambric gowns were an instant success. None of them lacked a partner for any dance. Their sparkling eyes and flushed faces revealed quite plainly that this was the most magical evening of their lives. Maria Grey's comment was the most expressive. "Oh, Miss Vane, I feel as if I were living a part in a fairy tale," she said dreamily. "I'm Cinderella, and I'm waiting in dread for the stroke of midnight."

"Perhaps Prince Charming will arrive before then," Hilary said jokingly.

At one point, as he sat with Hilary on the side of the ballroom, Matt observed, "I feel about as useful on this festive occasion as a fifth wheel on your dogcart."

"Of course you're useful. In fact, you're practically essential. The girls and I needed an escort. We must observe the *convenances* at all costs, you know," Hilary said crisply. She noted with a pang how Matt was tapping the floor with his uninjured leg in time to the music. He'd been such a superb dancer before the French bullet had ended his Army medical career and also his social career on the ballroom floor.

Belinda dropped into a chair beside Matt, fanning herself vigorously.

"Don't tell me your partners have tired you out already," Matt teased, after a lively reel had started up and Belinda had smilingly refused to dance with an eager young townsman.

"No, I'm not tired, but the room is a little warm,"

111

Belinda replied. "Besides, I want to hear the end of the story you were telling me in the carriage. About the terrible storm in the Peninsula that caused you to take refuge in a convent. Did you actually evict a poor nun from her bed?"

"Well, I certainly didn't sleep *with* her," Matt retorted, and Belinda collapsed with laughter.

Several times during the evening, Belinda sat out dances to be with Matt, and not just to take pity on his inability to dance, Hilary knew. Belinda and Matt thoroughly enjoyed each other's company.

Since, as a dutiful chaperon, Hilary preferred not to dance herself, she had the opportunity to observe those around her in the ballroom. Gradually she became uncomfortably aware that Belinda was the center of attention at the ball. Repeatedly Hilary heard snatches of comment from passing guests. "The Duke of Alverly's *sister* is here . . ." "Lady Belinda Rayner, fancy that . . ." "Do you think the duke himself might come to our next ball?" If Alverly were here, she knew, he would deeply resent such gossipy attention, and she wondered anew why he'd allowed Belinda to attend the ball. Surely he must have anticipated the amount of attention she would receive.

Hilary had her answer midway through the evening. Glancing at the doorway of the ballroom, she was astounded to see the duke standing with his arms across his chest, watching the dancers. At that same moment, he caught her eye and walked toward her.

"What a pleasant surprise," she said, as he sat down beside her. "Did Belinda know you planned to attend the ball?"

His face was like stone. He said in a low, angry voice, "I make it a practice not to quarrel in public, but in this case it's unavoidable. I demand to know, Miss Vane, how you had the effrontery to drag my sister to this bourgeois affair without consulting me?"

"But . . . Belinda told me you'd given her permission to attend the ball," Hilary faltered.

"I don't believe you. Belinda's flighty, but she's not a deliberate liar. No, this was all your idea, Miss Vane. Imagine how I felt when I heard a woman saying that Lady Belinda Rayner was the most distinguished guest the Assembly rooms had ever seen, and if only they could persuade her to return, they could pack the rooms to overflowing for the next ball!"

Leaning forward from his seat on Hilary's other side, Matt said angrily, "You'll stop dressing down my sister as if she were one of your own scullery maids, Duke, or I'll—"

Hilary said quietly, "Please, Matt, don't make a scene."

But a scene seemed unavoidable when the music stopped and Belinda walked toward them, her face drawn with apprehension. "Jon, how—what are you doing here?" she stammered.

"You may well ask. I stopped at the vicarage this evening to speak to Mr. Trevor. I sat frozen with surprise when Mrs. Trevor twittered on and on about what an enjoyable time you must be having at the Bridgeton ball. Belinda, *did* you tell Miss Vane that I'd given you permission to attend this—this affair?"

"I—yes."

The duke bit his lip. Turning to Hilary, he said, "Pray forgive me. I was quite wrong to accuse you."

"Thank you," Hilary murmured. "But please, don't judge Belinda too harshly."

Ignoring Hilary's plea, the duke glared at Belinda,

saying, "You've never lied to me before, not that I know of. Why did you do it now?"

His tone of cold outrage goaded Belinda into defiance. "Because I knew it was no use asking for your permission, and I *had* to attend this ball. Besides, I didn't think you'd ever find out. Well, you *wouldn't* have found out if you hadn't gone to visit the vicar."

Alverly rose. "So, little sister, you're not only a liar, but you're a very stupid one," he said in a hard voice. "Wycombe's a tiny place, and people talk. Didn't it occur to you that inevitably I'd discover that my sister had been one of the belles of the Bridgeton ball?" He took Belinda's arm. "Where's your shawl or your cloak? You and I are leaving this place immediately."

Rising also, Hilary stepped close to the duke. "Please don't be hasty," she said in a low voice. "If you drag Belinda away from the ball, there'll be gossip. In fact, every eye in the room has been fixed curiously on us since you came into the ballroom and started talking to me. Wouldn't it be better to allow Belinda to stay and to stay on yourself to give the event your stamp of approval?"

He stared at her. "But that's the point, I damned well don't approve!"

"You can pretend, can't you?" Hilary said calmly. "Or would you rather leave the good people of Bridgeton speculating about your private affairs?"

After a long moment's hesitation, Alverly growled, "Very well, Belinda, you can stay." On a threatening note, he added, "I'll talk you to you about this matter when we return to the castle."

With a relieved, surprised smile at her reprieve, Belinda quickly accepted an invitation to dance and went off with her partner.

114

"You did the right thing," said Hilary, as she and the duke sat down next to each other. He glowered at her but said nothing. "Don't be too severe with Belinda," she went on. "Of course she shouldn't have lied to you, but her heart was so set on attending this ball. Her very first ball, Jon! Look at her out on the dance floor. Have you ever seen her so sparkling and happy?"

As he watched his sister dance, Alverly's expression softened. In a few moments, however, he reverted to his most ducal self when the Master of Ceremonies of the Assembly came up to him, bowing deeply.

"Your Grace, permit me to tell you how honored we are to have you and your sister as guests of our ball."

The duke nodded curtly.

"Dare I ask," pursued the Master of Ceremonies, "if we may expect to see you and Lady Belinda on some future occasion?"

"I haven't decided yet, sir," replied Alverly frostily.

"Ah. We may still hope, then." The Master of Ceremonies bowed himself politely away.

Hilary shook her head at the duke. "I hardly think the townsfolk will consider that you've diminished your dignity by appearing at the ball. After all, you Rayners have been doing pretty much what you pleased in this corner of the world for centuries. Why should your conduct be any different now?"

After a moment of frowning silence, Alverly' lips curved in one of his rare smiles. "I'm acting the border lord again, am I?"

Hilary smiled back at him. "Well, aren't you?"

The duke lifted an eyebrow. "Perhaps so. But supposing I enjoy flexing my ducal muscles?"

Hilary burst out laughing. "Be as ducal as you like,

but not at this ball, please. You very nearly sent that poor Master of Ceremonies into a fit of the megrims!"

Alverly chuckled, and for a while they sat companionably together, watching the dancers. Matt murmured behind his hand, "You're not only taming the tiger, you're actually making him human. You have hidden gifts, my dear."

Glancing at Alverly, Hilary said in a sharp whisper, "Matt! He'll hear you."

Grinning, Matt subsided. He did, however, lean across Hilary to say, "Not dancing, Duke? May I suggest that my sister is an excellent dancer?"

"I don't dance," said Alverly curtly. "I never learned."

"Pity," remarked Matt. "Before the Froggies damaged my leg, dancing was one of my greatest pleasures. I recommend it to you."

On an impulse, Hilary said, "Would you like to learn, Jon?" She ignored Matt's faintly astonished expression at her use of the duke's Christian name. "I'm considered a good teacher. We could go to the card room, which was unoccupied the last time I passed it. We'd be quite private."

"Oh, I hardly think so . . ."

"Do take advantage of Hilary's offer, Duke," urged Matt with a mischievous twinkle in his eyes. "She's a dabster on the dance floor."

"Well . . ."

Hilary rose, and the duke, his face bemused, followed her to the card room, which was indeed unoccupied. "Close the door," said Alverly hastily. "If I'm to make a fool of myself, I don't want anyone watching."

Pushing the door shut, Hilary turned, saying, "Now,

then, what would you like to learn? A cotillion step? A country dance?"

Alverly looked blank. "How about a waltz?"

Shaking her head, Hilary said regretfully, "I could teach you the steps, but you'd have no occasion to use them. The waltz isn't performed in polite society. Not in England, at least."

Alverly cocked his head at her. "How is it, then, that you know how to dance the waltz?"

Hilary laughed. "Oh, it's one of my secret vices. Some years ago my cousin George was stationed at the English embassy in Paris, during the Peace of Amiens. He learned to waltz there, and when he came home he taught all his young cousins the steps. Secretly, of course. Our elders would have been terribly shocked to know we were being corrupted by French customs."

"Well, then, you can teach me."

"But what's the point? After you learn the steps, you can't dance the waltz in public."

"Hilary, if I'm to be your pupil tonight, it's the waltz or nothing," said Alverly challengingly.

Throwing up her hands, Hilary replied with a grin, "Very well, then, let the consequences be on your own head." She hummed a few bars of a simple waltz tune. "That's the rhythm. Now, put your right arm around my waist—yes, that's right." Instantly she knew she'd made a mistake. She hadn't been in such close contact with a man on the dance floor since those stolen sessions in the old schoolroom at her father's estate in Landview, when one of her male cousins had romped with her in the forbidden turns of the waltz.

She felt a sudden total physical awareness of the tall powerful man whose arm encircled her waist so lightly and yet so firmly. She was intensely conscious of the

117

faint masculine odor of freshly laundered white linen and scented shaving soap. Clearing her throat, she said briskly, "The waltz steps are really very simple, basically a circling movement to the count of three. Here, let's try it. Left foot first . . ."

Alverly was an apt pupil. He had a natural grace and coordination. Soon he was circling the card room with Hilary as if he'd been dancing the waltz for years. Soon, too, Hilary forgot to hum a tune. She closed her eyes and leaned back against Alverly's arm, dreamily imagining she was floating across a ballroom floor to the strains of an orchestra playing at the court of the Tuileries.

"The music's stopped, Hilary."

She opened her eyes with a start. She and Alverly were standing motionless in the middle of the card room, his arm still round her. "I'm sorry," she murmured. "Did I stop humming?"

"You did," the duke replied, amusement in his gray eyes. "For a while, though, I seemed to hear a melody in my mind. Thought transference, perhaps? In any case, it was very enjoyable. I'm glad you taught me to waltz, Hilary."

"I'm glad, too," said Hilary breathlessly. Their eyes locked together.

The duke's arms suddenly tightened around her. "This will be even more enjoyable," he muttered, as he crushed his lips to hers.

Hilary hadn't lived twenty-five years without being kissed. A few chaste exploring pecks by neighborhood swains when she was growing up. Several more determined efforts by eligible young men during her come-out season. But she'd never experienced anything more than a light pressure on her lips, from which she'd

118

gracefully disengaged. Neither her heart nor her senses had been affected.

This was different. Alverly's mouth claimed hers with a bruising intensity, and he clasped her against him so closely that she could feel the pounding of his heart, and something more as well. Something strange and frightening and enticing, the swelling outline of male arousal that pressed against her through the folds of her gossamer-thin silken gown. Her whole body felt aflame with an unfamiliar fiery desire. Her defenses down, she eagerly responded to Alverly's kiss, reveling in her abandon to the ecstasy of his plundering, insatiable lips and the touch of the long, slender fingers that drifted knowingly across the bare skin of her neck and shoulders.

He lifted his head at last, his slate gray eyes dark with a lambent glow. "I've been wanting to kiss you for weeks," he murmured. "Remember that night in the conservatory? I almost kissed you then."

"I remember," Hilary whispered.

His arms closed around her again with a sudden urgency. "God, Hilary, I want you so much that it hurts," he said huskily. "We can't do anything about it here, tonight, but . . . Look, there's a very pleasant inn, the Angel, in Stanton, the next town south of Bridgeton. The proprietors don't know you, and if they should recognize me, well, they'll be discreet. Will you meet me there one afternoon next week?"

The fiery torrent in Hilary's veins turned to ice water. She pushed hard against his chest, forcing him to release her. "Was that an invitation to sleep with you for one afternoon, or did you have a more permanent affair in mind?" she asked coldly.

Alverly recoiled. "Hilary! You can't think I regard you

119

as a—a common tart? Or that I would ever treat you as such?"

"No? How do you regard me? Surely not as a respectable gentlewoman?"

Biting his lip, the duke said, "We're both of us responsible, mature adults. Neither of us has an attachment to anyone else." He looked at Hilary questioningly. "I never heard, at least, that you were betrothed or had a longtime suitor."

"I don't," said Hilary. "What has that to say to anything?"

"Well, since we're unattached, and we, er, like each other—you do like me at little, don't you?—who would be harmed if we enjoyed a discreet relationship?" His eyes kindled. "And we *would* enjoy it. Don't think I didn't realize that tonight you wanted me as much as I wanted you."

Hilary gasped. Never in her life had she felt as cheapened, as *used*, as she felt at this moment. "Please understand me," she said with a frigid calm. "You're the very last man in the world whose mistress I would care to become. If I should decide to take someone into my bed, I'll choose a gentleman, not a mannerless boor like you. If you want sexual satisfaction, Your Grace, go back to your obliging widow in Wycombe. I'm sure she'll welcome you with open arms!"

Chapter VII

"Hilary? You're not eating your breakfast. Do you feel ill?"

Hilary looked up from her untouched plate of kidneys and sausages. "No, I'm not ill, Matt. A little tired, perhaps. We returned from the Bridgeton Assembly Ball so late last night."

Matt chuckled. "That's an understatement. The small hours of the morning is how I'd put it. I was in mortal fear that Farmer Grey's old carriage would break down before we reached Wycombe. An Irish surgeon I knew in the Army would say that our guardian angels were with us, fortunately. It's a good thing you decided not to hold classes today. I fancy none of your pupils who danced the night away would be much inclined to concentrate on French or deportment lessons."

"No. I'd anticipated that," Hilary replied absently.

Putting down his coffee cup, Matt said, hesitating, "Hilary, don't tell me if you'd rather not, but did you and Alverly quarrel last night? He came out of the card room where you'd been teaching him to dance with a face like a thundercloud, and the moment the assembly was over he snatched Belinda away without even saying good night to the rest of us."

"Oh, we had a slight disagreement," said Hilary lightly. "Nothing of any consequence. It's very easy, you know, to have a disagreement with His Grace the Duke of Alverly if one has an independent thought in her head. Almost inevitable, in fact!"

Inwardly, however, beneath her cool exterior, she was seething over the single most catastrophic event of her life. As the well-bred daughter of a respected, if minor, county family, she'd never contemplated being propositioned so crudely and so baldly by a gentleman of her own class with whom she'd actually been on friendly, social terms. She was furious with the duke for making her feel soiled by putting her on the same level as his longtime mistress, the farmer's widow, but she was even more angry at herself. She writhed in humiliation at the remembrance of how eagerly she'd responded to Alverly's urgent lips and hard embrace. If she hadn't responded to him, if, in fact, she'd refused his advances, he might not have felt encouraged to suggest a lovers' rendezvous in Stanton, the town nearest to Bridgeton, but sufficiently far enough away from Wycombe to allow them to conduct an illicit affair without too much danger of being found out.

Hilary drew a long breath. How could she ever face the duke again? Especially since she couldn't stop reliving the wild abandon of those sensuous moments in his arms.

Sarah appeared in the doorway of the dining room. "Miss Hilary, will ye see—?" Before she could finish her sentence, Belinda burst into the room.

"Hilary, Matt, I must talk to you." Belinda's eyes were puffy and reddened, and her hair, which she'd at-

122

tempted to stuff untidily under her pert riding hat, hung in elflocks around her face.

Matt pushed back his chair with a clatter and limped over to Belinda, putting his arm around her shoulders. "What's the matter, love? You've been crying your eyes out."

"Oh, Matt," she wailed, and burst into a storm of tears, burying her face in his shoulder. He waited patiently until her sobs gradually died away, and then he led her to a chair, thrusting a handkerchief into her hands. Pulling up a chair beside her, he said quietly, "Now, then, tell us what's wrong. Nothing's so bad that it can't be fixed, you know."

Belinda mopped her streaming eyes and blew her nose. "That's not true. My life can't be fixed. Jon's forbidden me to visit you and Hilary ever again. And since he can't trust me to obey him, he says, he'll not allow me to leave the castle without a groom accompanying me to report on where I go and whom I see. Can you imagine that? I've been riding alone about the estate since I was eight years old, and now I'm to have a keeper!"

"Good God," Matt exclaimed. "Why is the duke being so stiff-necked? Oh. I daresay this is your punishment for going to the Bridgeton Assembly Ball without your brother's consent?"

"Oh, of course it is. Jon told me that as long as I was under his care—until I turn twenty-one—he was going to make sure I obeyed his orders." Belinda's forehead wrinkled in a mutinous scowl. "Well, I'll not give Jon the satisfaction of making me a prisoner in my own home. Matt, Hilary, I've come to say goodbye to you."

"Goodbye!" exclaimed brother and sister almost simultaneously.

"Where are you going?" Hilary asked.

"To my Aunt Egeria in Bath. I haven't seen her since I was five or six years old. She came to visit us once many years ago. She was my father's older sister." Belinda paused, her tear-stained face clouding with uncertainty. "It was so long ago, that last time I saw her. She may not even remember me." Belinda squared her shoulders. "But that doesn't matter. She and Papa were close when they were young. Surely she won't turn me away when I tell her how badly Jon has treated me."

Picking her words carefully, Hilary said, "My dear, are you sure you're acting wisely? How will you travel to Bath, for instance?"

"I'll ride to Bridgeton and board the cross-post Mail. I raided Jon's cashbox this morning. I have enough money to pay my shot."

Matt and Hilary exchanged appalled glances. Matt said urgently, "Belinda, won't you go back to the castle and have another talk with your brother? Perhaps you can persuade him to change his mind about all these restrictions."

"Jon?" Belinda scoffed. "He *never* changes his mind!"

Hilary thought quickly. She had no authority whatever to prevent Belinda from running away. Neither could she betray the girl's confidence by reporting her intentions to the duke. But something had to be done. She said, "Belinda, before you ride off to Bridgeton, will you allow me to speak to your brother? As a third party, I'd at least be able to present your case to him more calmly than you probably did."

Belinda looked at her in alarm. "You won't tell him about my plans to go to Bath? If he found out about that, he might lock me up in my bedchamber like a real prisoner."

"No, I won't tell him you're planning to run away."

"Well . . . Go and see him, then. But it won't do any good."

"And you'll stay here with Matt until I return?"

"Yes. I promise."

As Hilary drove the dogcart up the drive to the castle, she felt reluctance fairly oozing out of her pores. She didn't want to see Alverly. She didn't want to talk to him. She had no confidence at all that she could budge him from his decision to punish his sister. But for Belinda's sake, she had to try.

The footman showed her into the drawing room. "I'll inform His Grace that you're here, Miss Vane."

A few minutes later the footman returned to say, "Will you follow me, ma'am? His Grace will receive you in the conservatory."

When Hilary entered the greenhouse, she was surprised to see Alverly in his shirtsleeves. Hardly the proper attire for receiving a female guest, she thought with a shade of resentment. He had a trowel in his hand, and he was obviously busy with the task of repotting plants. Surely this was a menial task that he normally left to his gardeners?

"Pray forgive me for receiving you so informally," he said. The indifference in his tone reinforced Hilary's opinion that he was being deliberately rude.

He looked terrible. His face was pale and haggard, and his eyes were sunk deep in their sockets. Hilary suspected he'd spent a sleepless night. As she certainly had.

"I was quite surprised to hear that you wanted to see me after what happened between us last night," he observed coolly. "Or perhaps you've reconsidered my, er, suggestion and couldn't wait to inform me? If so, I'll reassure you. The offer is still open."

Hilary gasped. She felt the hot color rising to her cheeks. Whatever his arrogance and his libertine tendencies, she'd never before observed in Alverly any sign of gratuitous cruelty. Restraining her temper for Belinda's sake, she said, "My visit has nothing to do with you and me. Belinda came to see us this morning. She's miserably unhappy. I know you feel you must punish her for deceiving you about the ball, but couldn't you be a little more lenient? Perhaps you might restrict her to the castle for a week or so, and then allow her to ride about unescorted. And I realize you're angry with me, so much so that you don't want her to associate with me, but couldn't you at least allow Belinda to continue her Greek lessons with Matt? *He* hasn't offended you."

Alverly's face had changed while she was speaking. Half turning, he struck the hand holding the trowel against a metal upright with such force that the sharp edge of the trowel gashed his hand.

Hilary gazed with alarm at the blood oozing from the wound and dived into her reticule for a handkerchief. "Here, let me help you."

"It's of no consequence," he said, impatiently waving her away.

"It won't do any harm to bandage the cut," she retorted, seizing the hand. "Hold still."

Seconds later he looked down at the handkerchief, neatly folded and finished with a knot, that Hilary had tied around his hand. Then he lifted his head to stare at her with a strained intensity, saying, "Miss Vane, you've told me more than once that I have a tyrannical disposition, that I can't brook dissent. Finally I'm willing to acknowledge that you're right. Last night my conduct was indefensible. I made an improper advance to you at

126

the ball. I apologize for it. I apologize, too, for what I said to you this morning. That was equally indefensible, said in a fit of spite."

He paused, a muscle twitching in his cheek. "I was wrong about Belinda, too. I lashed out at her, not because she deserved punishment, but because I was so furious that you'd refused—" He swallowed hard. "If Belinda is still at your house, please tell her I withdraw all my restrictions on her movements. Tell her she can make up for her behavior about the ball by exercising my new mare for an hour each day this week."

Hilary was in a state of shock. Had she really heard Alverly make his astonishing capitulation? She heard herself saying, "I hardly think Belinda will consider that a punishment. She's horse mad."

Alverly shot her a startled look. Then his rigid lips relaxed in a crooked grin. "Doubtless. Perhaps your brother could assign Belinda an extra hour of drill on her Greek verbs instead?" The smile fading, he said abruptly, "You haven't said that you accept my apology."

Hilary was more in control of herself now. After only a slight hesitation, she said, "Yes. I do accept your apology. I—Thank you."

"Then in that case . . ." Alverly flushed. "Will you allow me to make amends of a sort?"

"Why—what did you have in mind?"

"Do you remember the small dinner party we had here at the castle? Your brother spoke of his interest in our chief local curiosity, the Devil's Cauldron. I realize Dr. Vane's infirmity prevents him from making the excursion, but perhaps you'd care to accompany me on a ride to the Cauldron this afternoon. It's a lovely day. My housekeeper could provide a picnic lunch for us."

Hardly knowing what she was saying, Hilary stammered, "Why . . . Thank you. I'd enjoy visiting the Devil's Cauldron very much."

She drove the dogcart back down the hill from the castle in a kind of daze. What she would have thought inconceivable a few short weeks ago had come about. The Duke of Alverly had admitted he was in the wrong, had apologized, and was trying to make amends. In fact, in Matt's military parlance, the duke had surrendered unconditionally. She didn't know what this augured for the future. Beset by a sudden vivid memory of being locked in the duke's arms, she preferred not to speculate.

Belinda, too, found it hard to understand the duke's change of mind, although she was overjoyed to learn that he'd rescinded all his restrictions. "What did you say to Jon, Hilary? Did you perform a witchcraft spell on him?" she said, not entirely facetiously.

Hilary laughed. "Don't be such a peagoose. The duke is a sensible man, and when I presented him with a reasonable request, he saw the light. Now, my dear, you'd best hurry home and start studying those extra lists of Greek verbs that Matt is about to assign to you."

After Belinda had left, restored to her normal bubbling good humor, Matt shot Hilary a keen glance. "What *did* you say to the duke?"

"Just what I told Belinda. Why do you ask? Don't you believe me?"

"Oh, of course, but . . . Hilary, could the duke be developing a *tendre* for you?"

Hilary said sharply, "Certainly not. Don't talk fustian, Matt. Soon you'll begin to sound like an inquisitive Bow Street Runner."

Shrugging, Matt subsided. But a little later, when a footman arrived from the castle with a vase containing

128

a large bouquet of exquisitely beautiful coral pink camellias, he exclaimed with a rather worried air, "My God, Hilary, I'm no art expert, but if that's not a centuries-old Chinese porcelain vase, then I'm the King of England! You don't suppose Alverly means for you to keep it?"

Gazing at the vase, its colors as luminously beautiful as those of the camellias it contained, Hilary felt her heart constrict, but she managed to say in a matter-of-fact tone, "Of course not, silly. I'll return the vase to the duke as soon as the flowers fade."

The duke had other ideas. As they rode out of the village later in the day, he on his usual sorrel stallion, she on the well-mannered mare he brought with him from the castle, Hilary thanked him for the flowers. "I hope you didn't strip your greenhouse. It's such a large bouquet. And I've told Sarah to be very careful dusting around the vase. I could never hold up my head again if it were damaged before I returned it to you."

Alverly shot her a quick look. "I don't want the vase returned. It was a gift."

"But I can't possibly accept such a valuable item."

"You can if I say so," flashed the duke. There was a moment of silence, and then both of them began laughing. "Was I being the border lord again?" asked Alverly, when their laughter had died away.

"At your most autocratic, my lord duke."

"Well, rank does sometimes have its privileges," retorted Alverly, "and those privileges include presenting a gift if one has a mind to it. I want you to keep the vase."

Feeling weak-willed but curiously pleased, Hilary said, "Well, if you insist ... I'll treasure the vase and keep very good care of it." She added impishly, "Thank you very much, my liege."

He tossed her a quick grin of appreciation at the barbed remark, saying, "I'm glad to see you acknowledge I do retain a bit of feudal authority."

It was a lovely day in early autumn. Hilary had actually seen little of the landscape of the Cheviot Hills except from the vantage point of occasional drives in the dogcart through the valley. Now on horseback she could appreciate the beauty of the rounded hills, clothed in a glorious fall mantel of pink and purple heather and the breathtaking vista of the sharply delineated valleys with their meandering rivers.

"How beautiful," she sighed.

"Yes. I think so."

"Have you always lived here?"

"Yes, except for my school years at Eton. I've never wanted to be anywhere else."

As they rode slowly up one steep hill and down another, Hilary gradually realized she was seeing a side of Alverly that he'd never revealed before, a softer side, more human and accessible. He regaled her with tales of his ancestors' exploits in the border wars; he explained his plans to persuade his tenants to introduce a hardier and more productive breed of sheep. They spoke so naturally together that the passionate scene at the Bridgeton ball might never have happened. A thought crossed Hilary's mind. If Jon had had a circle of friends and acquaintances when he acceded to the title at the tender age of sixteen, would he have become the solitary, self-contained, autocratic man she'd first met?

Finally after a last long steep climb, they reached the Devil's Cauldron. Standing safely away from the precipitously slanting rim, Hilary gazed with awe into the depths of the depression, which seemed to descend far down to the bowels of the earth.

"It's not a natural phenomenon, you know," commented Alverly. "That hole is definitely man-made. But for what? I expect we'll never know." He turned away from the chasm, saying, "My housekeeper has known me since I was two years old. If I come back to the castle with this picnic basket untouched, Mrs. Gardiner will never forgive me."

Hilary thoroughly enjoyed the picnic luncheon on the verge of the Devil's Cauldron, with the September sun slanting down on her face and shoulders and an aromatic breeze blowing off the heather. The meat pies, the roasted capon, the pineapple from Jon's conservatory all tasted more delicious than if she'd consumed them indoors. Sipping the excellent wine that Jon had provided, she smiled at him, saying, "This was an inspired idea. Do you often picnic in the hills?"

He shook his head. "I can't remember the last time I was up here. It was years ago, in any event. Before my father died. After that I was too busy with my duties on the estate."

He was only a boy at the time of his father's death, Hilary reminded herself. She commented, "It must have been difficult for you, assuming such heavy responsibilities when you were so young."

A shadow crossed his face. He said slowly, "It wasn't that difficult. Father had been incapacitated for almost a year before he died, and I'd really been in charge of the estate during that time. What *was* hard was watching him die slowly, a little each day. He was paralyzed by the stroke, you see. He couldn't talk, he couldn't move. It was—it was hell." He jumped to his feet. "Shall we stretch our legs a bit? I need to walk off all that food."

Hilary let Jon go on ahead of her. She knew he was embarrassed because he'd revealed a deeply felt emotion to her. He needed time to recover his composure. After several minutes, she rose and began sauntering slowly along the edge of the Devil's Cauldron. A dark object in the grass caught her attention. A sheep, perhaps, ill or dead? But as she drew closer she saw to her horror that the dark shape was a man. She rushed to him, sinking to her knees beside him.

He was a young man, roughly dressed. His eyes were closed, his face, under a coating of grime, was a pasty white, and an ominous dark stain covered the front of his coat. Hilary was convinced he was dead until he moved slightly and a faint groan escaped from his lips.

"Jon, please come," she called frantically. "There's a wounded man here."

In a few moments, Jon raced to her side. He pulled open the man's bloodstained coat and probed with delicate fingers inside his shirt. "The fellow has a bad knife wound to the chest," Alverly said, resting back on his heels. "See how pale he is? He must have lost a great deal of blood. Your brother should see him immediately."

"But how can we get him down to the village?" Hilary asked. "We could sling him over the back of one of the horses, I suppose, but that might start his wound to bleeding again."

"It's all we can do," said Jon, rising to his feet. "Unfortunately, there's another problem. When you called out to me, I was standing on the other side of the Cauldron, looking down. There's a second body down there. We simply didn't notice him when we first arrived here and took a casual glance into the interior of the Cauldron. I don't know if the man is alive or dead. I'll have to go down there and find out."

"But the sides of the depression are practically vertical," Hilary protested. "You can't go down there alone without ropes or assistance."

Alverly shrugged. "We must know if the man is alive. If he is, I'll have to send a rescue team up here immediately. Otherwise, recovery of the body can wait until morning."

Her heart in her mouth, Hilary watched him pick his way, slowly and precariously, down the steep slopes of the Cauldron toward the indistinct blob that she now recognized was the body of a man. Several times Alverly almost fell, recovering his balance by clutching at a stony outcrop or a clump of vegetation. Finally he reached the body, examined it briefly, and then began his painful climb back up the side of the crater.

When, to Hilary's unutterable relief, he finally pulled himself over the rim of the Cauldron onto the safety of the surface, he said, gasping from his exertion. "The fellow's dead. Another knife wound."

He sank to the ground, mopping his brow and drawing deep breaths to recover from the exertion of his descent into the Cauldron. After a short pause, he said reflectively, "I'd give a monkey to know what really happened here. Perhaps these two men were fighting each other and they knifed each other practically simultaneously. Then perhaps the one man lost his balance and fell into the Cauldron and the other man simply collapsed from the severity of his wound."

Rising from his brief rest, he said, shrugging, "Well, I daresay we'll never know what happened. That fellow on the ground over there is barely alive. I doubt he'll ever be able to tell us his story. Probably he won't survive the journey down to the village, but we must do the best we can for him."

With the controlled, sinewy strength that Hilary had

so often marked in him, Alverly lifted the wounded man from the ground and carefully deposited him crossways over the horse he himself had been riding. Then, turning to Hilary, he said, "Here, let me help you into the saddle." Noticing her glance at the remains of the picnic lunch, he said, "I'll send someone up to fetch the hamper. Don't worry about it."

With Jon leading the horse carrying the injured stranger, and Hilary following behind on her mount, they made an uneventful descent to the village. The duke kept their progress deliberately slow to avoid jarring the patient's wound.

When they arrived at the surgery, Matt took charge. After only a brief interval, he came out to Hilary and Alverly in the waiting room. "It's a hopeless case," he announced, "even though the fellow has a clean chest wound. The knife didn't strike a bone or puncture a lung, as far as I could determine, but I don't think the man will survive."

"Has he recovered consciousness?" asked the duke.

"No, and I don't believe he will. He's lost too much blood, and I suspect he's been lying out in the open, exposed to the elements, for at least twenty-four hours. Hilary, we'll put him to bed in one of our spare bedrooms and let him die in peace."

"Poor fellow," Hilary murmured. "Imagine dying in a strange place without anyone around you knowing who you are."

The duke said thoughtfully, "I wonder who he is. He's not a local man. I know everyone for miles around. Hilary, did you notice the dirt under the man's fingernails and the grime embedded in the skin of his face and hands? The body at the bottom of the Cauldron looked the same. I shouldn't be surprised if both men were coal miners."

"Miners!" repeated Hilary. "But there are no coal mines near here."

Alverly nodded. "Exactly. These fellows have come a long way to die beside the Devil's Cauldron. Well, I'll be off. I know I'm leaving the patient in good hands." He smiled wryly at Hilary. "I'm sorry about our picnic. I didn't expect it to end quite so dramatically."

Chapter VIII

For almost two days, the wounded stranger whom Hilary and the duke had rescued from the Devil's Cauldron remained in a comatose condition in an upstairs bedroom of Willow Cottage. Sarah stayed with him for as long as her duties permitted, and Hilary and Matt, too, slipped in sit with the patient as they could.

The news of the discovery of a dead body and a badly wounded survivor occasioned intense curiosity in the village and among the farmers of the surrounding region. Hilary considered the reaction entirely understandable in people who'd lived their entire lives in a tiny hamlet where nothing exciting ever occurred. Belinda shared the general curiosity. She offered to keep watch over the patient in the afternoons after classes were over, and Hilary reluctantly agreed, suspecting that the duke would disapprove. Jon had mellowed recently, but undoubtedly he still had very strict ideas about what his sister's conduct should be.

In the late afternoon of the second day of the stranger's illness, Belinda came rushing into the schoolroom office where Hilary sat preparing lesson plans for the next day. "Hilary! Come quick! The man's conscious. He asked me for some water."

Putting down her pen, Hilary rose from her desk. "That's a good sign, the patient asking for water. I must go for Matt."

Belinda grabbed her arm. "Don't go, not yet. Come hear what the man's saying." Belinda's eyes were wide with shock.

Hilary hurried down the hallway to the patient's room, pausing in the doorway in dismay. Actually the stranger hadn't recovered consciousness. Rather, he was speaking in a delirium, and his words sent a chill of horror into her heart.

"Kill the duke," the man was muttering. "Yes, kill the duke. He don't deserve ter live, not after wot he's done ter us."

Belinda whispered, "He keeps repeating those words, or something like them, over and over. Hilary, what does it mean?"

"Something terrible, I'm afraid. Belinda, go to the castle and ask your brother to come here."

After Belinda, looking shaken, had left, Hilary hurried to the surgery to ask Matt to come to the sickroom.

"He has a slight fever," Matt reported. "That explains his speaking in a delirium. You say he was lucid for a short time, at least?"

"Yes, I think so. Belinda said he asked her for water."

"He may come out of this shortly, then. We'll just have to wait."

Half an hour later, Belinda and the duke silently entered the sickroom. Together they stood with Matt and Hilary near the bed for over an hour, listening to the injured man's monotonous muttering. "Kill the duke. Kill the duke." Occasionally he paused briefly, only to resume his chant.

Finally the man's eyes fluttered open. "Where am I? Who be ye?" he said in a faint voice.

"I'm Dr. Vane," said Matt soothingly, "and these people are my sister Hilary, the Duke of Alverly, and Lady Belinda Rayner. My sister and the duke found you several days ago, lying wounded at the Devil's Cauldron. They also found another man there, dead at the bottom of the Cauldron."

The man's face twisted. "Danny Wyse. I saw him fall over the rim of that cursed hole. Bill? Did ye find Bill?"

"I don't know any Bill. The duke and my sister found only two men at the Cauldron, you and the dead man."

For the first time, the mention of Alverly's title seemed to penetrate the man's understanding. His expression torn between fear and hatred, he struggled to raise himself. "Ye're the Duke o' Alverly?" he gasped. "Murderer! If I had me way, ye'd be at the bottom o' that infernal Cauldron, instead o' poor Danny Wyse." His sudden burst of energy failed him, and he collapsed like a stone against the pillows. His eyes closed, and in a moment he began again the monotonous chant: "Kill the duke. Kill the duke."

"He's back in a delirium," Matt said in a low voice.

Hilary asked, "Will he come out of it again?"

Matt shrugged.

Belinda moved closer to her brother's side as if for reassurance. "Jon, do you think this man really wants to kill you?" she asked, her pert face drawn with apprehension. "And why does he call you a murderer?"

Alverly shook his head. "I have no idea. We won't know until, or if, the fellow recovers his wits and we can

138

question him." He looked at Matt. "What's your best estimate of this man's chance of survival, doctor?"

Matt shrugged again. "I can only guess. He's survived this long, so it's possible he might recover. Or his fever might become more virulent, in which case he could sink into a deeper delirium and die before ever regaining consciousness."

Alverly thought for a moment. "Well, since the situation is so uncertain, I see no point in remaining here. If the fellow should recover his senses enough to talk, doctor, will you notify me immediately?"

Matt replied with a grim smile, "Indeed I will, Duke. After all, the case does seem to touch you personally."

"Thank you. I think I should notify the magistrates in Wincanton that we have a dead body on our hands here. No doubt they'll wish to investigate. Come along, Belinda."

In the end, it was Hilary who discovered the wounded man's identity and the reason why he had come to the Wycombe Valley. That evening as she sat beside his bed, listening to his disjointed ravings and his constant harsh injunction to "kill the duke," the man suddenly fell silent. Hilary wondered if she was witnessing his final moments. After a short time, however, his eyes opened. They were clear, and when Hilary put her hand to his forehead, his skin felt cool. The fever had broken.

He turned his head slightly to gaze about the room. In a voice that was so weak it was barely a whisper, he said, "Where be I?"

"You're in Dr. Vane's house in Wycombe. No, don't try to talk. Let me give you some water." Hilary slipped her arm under the man's shoulder and held a glass of water to his lips. He drank thirstily. Next, Hilary gave him some milk that she'd kept warming over a spirit lamp. "Thank ye, ma'am," the man murmured when Hilary laid him back against his pillows. His voice sounded stronger. "Ye say I be in Wycombe? How did I get here?"

Hilary said in surprise, "You don't remember talking to Dr. Vane or seeing me earlier today?"

He shook his head. "I don't recall no doctor, and I ain't never seen ye before, so far as I knows, ma'am."

"Well, then, I'll just repeat what my brother, Dr. Vane, told you. The Duke of Alverly and I found you lying, severely wounded, up at the Devil's Cauldron several days ago. After we brought you here, you developed a fever. You went into a delirium, talking about killing the duke—"

As Hilary was talking, a look of sheer horror spread over the injured man's face. With an enormous effort, he tried to sit up, only to fall back, exhausted, against the pillows. He closed his eyes, muttering, "That's torn it, then. The duke, he knows about me. He'll have me on the nubbing cheat afore ye can wink an eye."

"You're afraid the duke will have you hanged? Because of what you said about killing him? But that's ridiculous. You were raving, out of your mind. You weren't responsible for what you were saying. In fact, it sounded as if you were just repeating something you'd heard."

The man looked at her with an expression of utter hopelessness. "But, y'see, ma'am, I *did* plan ter kill the duke."

Hilary gasped.

"That's right, ma'am. Ain't no way of hiding it. So soon as he rounds up Danny Wyse, the duke'll get the truth out o' him. That Danny, he could never keep nothing ter hisself."

"Danny Wyse?" Hilary repeated, frowning in concentration. "That was a name you mentioned earlier, the first time you came out of your delirium. You said you saw this Danny Wyse fall dead into the Devil's Cauldron. Indeed, the duke found the body. And you mentioned another man, someone called Bill."

Complete comprehension dawned in the man's ravaged face. "Oh, God," he whispered. "Now I remember. Bill stabbed poor Danny ter death, and then he turned on me with his knife. And now Bill's out there somewheres, still meaning ter kill the duke. And as soon as he finds out I'm still alive, he'll try ter finish me off, too."

A wave of terror swept over Hilary. Keeping a tight rein on herself, she said quietly, "Would you want to talk to me about it? Perhaps I can help."

After several moments of desolate silence, the man sighed. "Might as well, I reckon. I'm done fer, no matter what."

In a flat monotone, the man began speaking. Her nerves tensed like a tightly coiled watch spring, Hilary let him talk, refraining from interrupting him.

"Well, I guess I should start by saying my name's Nate Derwent," the injured man began. "I'm a coal miner from the Tyne Valley. Ackcherly, I work in the Duke o' Alverly's mines. Everybody I knows works fer the duke. He owns all the mines fer miles around."

Derwent paused for a moment, gazing at Hilary somberly. "I ain't asking fer yer sympathy, ma'am, but I have ter tell ye, mining's not an easy life. Hours an' hours o' hard work fer pennies, barely enough ter keep body and soul together. But me and my family, we did

141

well enough fer a spell so's we had no need ter complain. We was jist glad ter be working. Then, a few years ago, my pa was killed. An explosion in a mine shaft. That meant my mum had ter go down inter the mines too, 'cause I couldn't earn enough ter support her and my baby sister. They set Mum ter hauling loaded carts o' coal. The tunnels, most o' 'em, are too low ter stand up straight, so she had ter haul the carts on her hands and knees."

Hilary drew a sharp breath. "But that's inhuman! I can't believe any employer would allow such a practice."

Derwent shrugged. "Oh, it's true enough, ma'am. All too true." He paused again, staring blindly at the wall opposite him. "Mum's sick now. The lung disease, from all the coal dust. Every day she coughs a little bit o' her life away."

"I'm so sorry."

Derwent spread his hands in a gesture of resignation. "Ah, well, the lung disease happens ter lots o' folk. Why should me and my family be any different?" he said grimly. "What got ter me, though, was what happened ter my baby sister Chrissy. Mum had ter send Chrissy ter the mines when she was only four years old. Some o' the tunnels, y'see, are too low even fer the womenfolk. Two weeks ago, Chrissy was crushed ter death by a runaway cart."

"My God! How horrible," Hilary exclaimed.

Derwent nodded. "That was when I decided ter kill the duke. Tit fer tat, like. My friends, Danny and Bill, promised ter help me. They've lost family in the mines, too, and they've been talking against the duke fer ages. He never comes to the mines hisself, y'know. His manager takes care o' everything. Maybe if the duke re-

142

ally knew how it was in the mines, if he'd ever taken the trouble to come and see what was going on ..." Derwent paused again, looking at Hilary with a mirthless grin. "But that'd be more'n the likes o' us could expect, wouldn't it, ma'am?"

After a moment he continued talking. "So anyways, Bill and Danny and me came up here. We hid out at first near a great big hole in the ground, up in the hills, while we decided how ter go about our plan. Then Bill started talking about killing the duke's sister, too. He said the sister was living off our sweat and hard work jist as much as the duke. But I couldn't see murdering a young girl; I kept thinking o' my baby sister and how she died. And then I began ter change my mind about killing the duke. I didn't hold him any less ter blame, y'understand, but it dawned on me as I was sure ter be caught out, and then what would happen to my mum wi'out my wages whilst I swung a'rotting on the gallows? So I said ter Bill and Danny I was going home. Danny, he said he'd go with me, but Bill turned ugly. He wasn't leaving, he said, wi'out a try at killing the duke. Well, one word led ter another, and before I fair knew what was going on, Bill had stabbed poor Danny and was coming after me. That's the last thing I remember, that terrible pain in my chest."

Hilary was silent for a moment, reflecting on the grisly story that Nate Derwent had told so casually, almost dispassionately. "Do you really think this man Bill is hiding out in the area, still bent on killing the duke?" she asked at last.

"Not a doubt about it, ma'am. Bill ain't never given up on nothing in his whole life."

Her lips set firmly, Hilary rose, saying, "I'm going

143

down to the kitchen to fetch you some broth, perhaps some toast. I won't be gone long."

Hilary had to ring for Sarah. Both the housemaid and the cook had gone to bed long since. When Sarah appeared, Hilary told her to prepare some nourishing beef broth and toast and take it to the injured man's bedchamber. Then, throwing a shawl over her shoulders against the cool autumn night air, Hilary picked her way carefully in the darkness to the stables, where she had to pound for some minutes on the door leading to the handyman's quarters above the floor housing the pony and the dogcart. When the disheveled and drowsy Ephraim finally appeared, Hilary told him to go to the castle with a message for the duke, requesting him to join her immediately.

"Now?" exclaimed the handyman. "I dunno, ma'am. His Grace might not take ter being roused at this hour. Ye couldn't wait until the morning?"

"No. Go at once, Ephraim. Take the dogcart."

Leaving the stables, Hilary returned to the sickroom, where she found that Sarah was competently spooning broth into Nate Derwent. The miner's pasty face was already recovering a little color. After a few minutes, confident she was leaving the injured man in good hands, Hilary told Sarah, "Stay with the patient for a bit. I'll be back shortly."

Hilary had felt too restless and on edge to remain in the sickroom or, for that matter, in the house itself. Bundling herself up again in her fleecy shawl, she wandered out to the front gate, where she stood looking up at the gaunt outline of the castle, visible against the clear light of the rising moon.

Had she done the right thing, sending Ephraim to the castle for the duke in the middle of the night? Naturally

Jon must be warned about the lurking menace of the man Bill, but couldn't the news have waited until morning? After all, if Nate Derwent was right about Bill's tenacity of purpose, the man had been loitering in the vicinity for several days but without making a move against Alverly.

No, Hilary decided, she wasn't sorry she'd sent for the duke. Her nerves were so strained that she wouldn't have slept a wink that night, knowing that Alverly was unaware of his danger.

Continuing to hang on the gate, gazing up at the scowling gatehouse, she eventually heard the sound of pounding hooves, and soon she could make out the figures of a horse and rider galloping down the steep road from the castle. In a minute or two, Alverly reined in his horse in front of the gate. Catching sight of her in the dim light, he hurried over to her. "Hilary! I came as soon as I got your message. Is something wrong?"

Gazing up at him, conscious as always of the controlled tension of his tall powerful body, she said, "Yes. Something's very wrong. The injured man recovered consciousness at last. His name is Nate Derwent. He told me that he and two other men, all workers from your mines in the Tyne Valley, came up here to kill you. Derwent and another man—the one you found at the bottom of the Devil's Cauldron—changed their minds about your murder, but the third man, called Bill, is still out there, still determined to kill you. Perhaps I should have waited until morning to tell you, Jon, but I simply couldn't rest easily until I'd told you about your danger."

In the moonlight, she could see the familiar crooked grin on Alverly's lips. "No, of course you couldn't wait," he said. "You never hold back when it's a question of helping people, do you?" Tucking her hand under his arm, he added, "I'll go back to the house with you, if you don't object. I'd like to talk to this Nate Derwent."

As they turned toward the gate, Hilary caught a flicker of movement out of the corner of her eye. "Jon!" she screamed suddenly. "Watch behind you!"

Whirling about, Alverly instinctively threw up his arm to guard against the knife glinting silver in the moonlight as it slashed down in the hand of his assailant. For the next few minutes, Hilary could only stand helplessly aside while the two men grappled with each other. It was an eerily quiet combat in the half darkness, the silence broken only by the sound of the men's labored breathing and the scraping of their feet against the rough surface of the roadway.

Finally one of the figures broke away, leaving the other motionless on the ground. For a split second Hilary wasn't sure which of the two figures was Alverly. "Jon?" she cried anxiously.

The duke gasped, "I'm all right, but I'm sadly out of condition. I should have put the fellow away much sooner." He bent to pick up an object from the ground. "No need to take any chances," he said grimly, showing Hilary the knife before he pocketed it.

Hilary shuddered. "You could easily have been killed." She stared with fear and distaste at the prostrate figure. "He's not . . . ?"

"No, he's not dead or anything like it, but he won't wake up for a while. I landed a real leveler to his chin."

Drawn by an impulse she was unable to resist, Hilary edged close to the would-be murderer. The man's eyes were closed, but his lips remained curved in an expression of such sheer malevolence that Hilary knew she'd never be able to forget his face.

146

She and Alverly looked up as Ephraim, who had returned from the castle at a much more sedate pace than the duke, rattled the dogcart to a stop in front of the gate and stared with wide startled eyes at the prone figure of the would-be assassin.

The duke said crisply, "Here—what's your name? Ephraim? My good man, do you have a bit of rope you can give me? Good. Fetch it, please."

To Hilary the duke said, "I'll tie the fellow up and take him back to the castle for the night. Tomorrow I'll take him to Justice Albright in Wincanton. The case will be tried at the next Quarter Session, no doubt." His voice softened. "Thank you for your timely warning. If you hadn't called out to me, I'd be lying in the roadway with a knife in my back."

"No thanks to me," Hilary said bleakly. "If I hadn't called you out in the middle of the night, this man Bill wouldn't have had the chance to attack you."

Smiling, Alverly reached out to brush his finger softly against her cheek. "Feel guilty if you must, Hilary. *I* know who saved my life."

Chapter IX

Before her classes began next morning, Hilary looked in on Nate Derwent. Matt was seated beside the bed, concluding his examination. "You're doing splendidly," he told the injured miner. "No fever, no infection. Your wound is healing normally. Frankly, when I first saw you several days ago, I gave you no chance for survival."

"Well, doctor, ye've saved me fer the gallows, right enough," Derwent replied with a bitter smile. Looking up, he saw Hilary in the doorway. He bit his lip. "Sorry, Miss Vane. I didn't mean ter sound ungrateful. Ye and the doctor have been mighty kind ter me."

Advancing into the room, Hilary said, "We've been happy to be of help." She hesitated. "Matt, have you told Nate what happened last night?" Matt shook his head.

Derwent tensed. "Was it something ter do with Bill?"

Quickly Hilary explained about the attack on the duke and how Bill had been captured.

Derwent nodded. "They'll be coming fer me, then," he said in a curiously expressionless tone.

Later, outside the sickroom, Hilary said to Matt with a frown, "The poor fellow seems to think he'll be

148

hanged. That couldn't happen, surely? He didn't really commit a crime, after all."

Matt gave her a straight look. "I'm no expert on the law, but I strongly doubt that Derwent will go scot-free. He may not have actually committed a crime, but he did conspire with two other men to murder the Duke of Alverly. What's more, he confessed to you what he'd intended to do. And you can be sure the other fellow—Bill, is that his name?—won't hesitate to implicate Derwent in an attempt to soften his own punishment." Gazing at his sister's troubled face, Matt patted her shoulder, saying, "Don't fret, love. I could be wrong, you know. And you've done your best for Derwent."

Walking with dragging steps, Hilary went upstairs to her classroom. There she found her pupils standing in a circle, twittering like magpies.

Detaching herself from the group, Belinda came over to Hilary. "They're asking me about the rumor that somebody tried to kill Jon," she said in a low voice. "Of course, they've heard about the body in the Devil's Cauldron, and they also knew that you and Matt were caring for a wounded man in your house. I didn't know how much Jon would want me to tell the girls. Actually I don't know much more than they do. Jon left the castle early this morning before I awakened. The servants told me he was taking a prisoner—or somebody, at any rate, who was trussed up like a Christmas pig—to Wincanton. They also said that your handyman Ephraim came for Jon in the middle of the night. Hilary, did something happen I don't know about?"

"I'll tell you all about it later," Hilary murmured. Raising her voice, she said, "Sit down, girls. I want to see how well you know your fourth conjugation verbs. First, though, I have some news for you."

Her pretty, intelligent face wearing a concerned expression, Maria Grey said hesitantly, "Is it true that somebody tried to kill His Grace?"

Hilary knew the valley must be rife with rumor. In a district where little out of the ordinary ever occurred, an attempt against the life of their duke must be a nine days' wonder. It was better to give the girls some facts, which they would, of course, immediately transmit to their parents, rather than to allow them to speculate. Briefly she told them that a criminal had indeed tried to kill the duke the previous night, but that the miscreant was now safely in custody. "So there's nothing for you to worry about, and now can we get back to the fourth conjugation?"

Late that afternoon Hilary sat with Derwent in the sickroom, helping him to eat his supper. Because of the knife wound in his chest, the miner still found it difficult and painful to use his right arm. While she was sitting with him, Hilary tried to draw him out about his life in the mines. In some obscure fashion, she sensed that the information might be useful. At least she might better understand why Derwent had felt so driven to murder Jon. The man seemed willing enough to talk. Perhaps, she reflected, conversation took his mind off his troubles.

He spoke of the long hours underground and the discomfort of living in the hovels provided by the mine management, and of how the spring and autumn rains sometimes turned the rutted street outside the houses into quagmires.

"I think maybe it's the dirt and grime that bothers Mum the most," he said at one point. "The coal dust settles in yer clothes and inside yer house and on yer skin, and ye can't get it out." He lifted the hand on his uninjured side for Hilary's inspection. "See? Scrub away

150

as ye will, but the dirt's still there. Mum says it will go wi' us ter our graves, and I reckon that's right enough."

He broke off, looking past Hilary. She turned to see Alverly standing in the doorway. There were tired lines in his face, and his breeches and boots were dusty from his long trip over the hills to Wincanton and back again to deliver his prisoner to the magistrates. He walked into the room and stood by the bed, gazing down at Derwent for a long, unnerving moment. The miner's pale, emaciated face reddened.

"Nate," said Hilary hastily, "this is His Grace, the Duke of Alverly. You may not remember that he was here in the room that first time you regained consciousness."

Derwent was silent.

The duke continued to stare down at the miner without speaking. Finally he said coldly, "I thought I might see some differences between the faces of an actual murderer and a would-be assassin. I was wrong, Derwent. You and your friend Bill both look like the thugs you are." He paused, then said in a voice that cut like a whiplash, "However much you hated me, why did you consider it necessary to kill my sister? This Bill tells me it was you who urged him and the other fellow—the one who died—to wipe out the entire Rayner family by murdering my sister, too."

Derwent stammered, "Yer Grace, I swear I never—"

The duke cut him off. "I don't want to hear your lies. Tell them to the court at your trial."

Hilary's heart sank as she heard the note of implacable hostility in Jon's voice. There hadn't been time last night, before the assassin Bill's attack, to tell Alverly all the details of the conspiracy that Nate Derwent had confessed to her, including Bill's proposal to murder

151

Belinda. Bill must have talked—or been made to talk—after he'd been handed over to the authority of the justice of the peace in Wincanton. Otherwise the duke couldn't have known about the scheme to kill Belinda, too.

Rising, Hilary said impulsively, "Jon—" She paused. She mustn't seem overly familiar with the duke in the miner's presence. "Your Grace, I think this fellow Bill may have lied to you. It was his plan, not Nate's, to kill Belinda. In fact, when Bill proposed the idea, Nate and the other man, Danny, refused to go along with him."

Alverly raised an eyebrow. "Or so Derwent told you. A convenient tale. One of his fellow murderers is dead, and it's his word against the other. Not that it matters." He looked down again at the miner, saying with a chilling finality, "Enjoy your convalescence, Derwent, and the kindness of Dr. Vane and Miss Vane. As soon as the good doctor says you're well enough to travel, you'll be off to the gaol in Wincanton to wait for your trial." Nodding to Hilary, he swept out of the room.

Pausing only to give the miner a shakily reassuring smile, she hurried after Alverly, catching up with him at the head of the stairs. "Jon, wait. I must speak to you. It's important."

"Certainly," he said politely. He seemed distant today, much as he'd been in the early days of their acquaintance. It was understandable. His mind must be totally engrossed with the shocking realization that a group of men, complete strangers to him, had tried to kill him.

"We can talk in my office," Hilary said, leading the way down the corridor to the cramped little room she used to plan her lessons and to conduct her correspondence. When she sat down opposite him, she was at a loss for words at first. The duke, grave and intent, sat waiting for her to speak. He'd rarely seemed quite so unapproachable.

At last she blurted, "Jon, is it really necessary to bring Nate Derwent to trial? Couldn't you simply release him and allow him to go back to his home? After all, he hasn't actually done anything wrong . . ."

The duke's gray eyes snapped, darkening to near black as they always did when he was in the grip of a strong emotion. "Not do anything wrong? Have you gone queer in your attic, Hilary? The man conspired to kill me and Belinda. What's more, according to this Bill, Derwent murdered Danny."

"I don't believe it. Bill's lying. The truth is that his suggestion to include Belinda as a victim in the murder plot made Nate and Danny balk against participating in the scheme at all. Nate's baby sister had died as a result of an accident in one of your mines, but he couldn't bring himself to retaliate by killing another innocent female, and Danny agreed with him. However, when they told Bill they were withdrawing from the plot and had decided to go home, he flew into a rage and attacked them. Danny died and Nate was wounded."

"I never thought to see you such a gull, Hilary," Alverly said coldly. "This Derwent has been playing on your sympathy with his show of innocence. Why should we believe his story rather than Bill's? They're both cut out of the same cloth. Well, for instance, what reason did Derwent give for his change of heart about killing me? Did he suddenly feel guilty about breaking one of the Ten Commandments?"

"Well, no," Hilary replied reluctantly. "To be frank, I don't think Nate would grieve at all if you died, provided your death didn't come at his hand. What he told me was that he realized he'd surely be apprehended for your murder, and he feared leaving his mother, who's quite ill, destitute without his wages."

"So much for true contrition," Alverly said dryly. He rose, saying, "I honor you for your warm heart, Hilary, but in this case your sympathies have been grossly misplaced. I intend to make sure that Derwent and his friend stand trial for their crimes."

Hilary asked with stiff lips, "What will happen to Nate if he's convicted?"

Gazing at her worried face, Alverly said impatiently, "Oh, for God's sake, Hilary, you must know that murder's a capital offense. He'll go to the gallows."

"I see." After a moment Hilary said, "Do you know why those three men decided to kill you?"

Alverly smiled bitterly. "That fellow Bill talked about disliking working conditions in my mines. A fine reason to kill your employer, wouldn't you say?"

Hilary didn't return his smile. "What really decided Nate to kill you was his baby sister's death. Chrissy was four years old. She was crushed to death while working in one of your mines."

"Four years old?" Alverly exclaimed incredulously. "Impossible! No mine owner or manager would hire a four-year-old child. There, that proves my point. Derwent is a liar. A very clumsy one. Like as not, he never had a baby sister."

Hilary rose. The duke followed suit. Taking a deep breath, she stepped close to him, placing her hand on his arm. Instantly she could feel his muscles tense. Instantly she was aware of a wave of powerful sensuality flowing between them. Ignoring her feelings, she pleaded, "Jon, I believe that Nate Derwent is telling the truth. Please don't hand him over to the authorities. Let him go free."

Slowly, almost caressingly, Alverly uncurled her hand from his arm. He stepped back, breathing a little unevenly. "I'm sorry. I can't do that. Derwent not only deserves punishment, he needs to be made an object lesson to others who might want to attack their employers." He walked to the door, turning to say, "Please ask your brother to inform me as soon as Derwent can be moved."

She watched him go, wondering bleakly if males—especially powerful aristocratic males—simply had less compassion than women. It seemed grotesque and cruel to nurse Nate Derwent carefully back to health for the sole purpose of putting him on trial for his life. She lingered in her office, cudgeling her brain to discover some way to save the miner from the consequences of his ill-judged actions. Always she came up against the iron resolve of the Duke of Alverly. He'd wrapped himself in the mantle of the border lord again, she reflected. Convinced of the rightness of his position, he'd closed his arrogant mind to any arguments except his own.

Three days later, her brother's announcement at the luncheon table goaded Hilary into action. Matt remarked, "When I examined Derwent this morning, I judged him well enough to travel. In a carriage, of course, and by slow stages. I'll send Ephraim up to the castle today with a message for the duke."

"Don't bother. I'll speak to Ephraim," said Hilary, her tone casual despite the fact that her mind was racing. During a sleepless interval the previous night, she'd hit upon a solution to Nate Derwent's predicament, if only she could execute it properly. When she left the lunch table, she didn't go near Ephraim at the stables. Instead she walked up the village street to the vicarage.

Before she could broach the subject of her visit, naturally, she had to answer Mrs. Trevor's questions about the attack on the duke.

"What a frightful coil, almost too dreadful to bear talking about," gasped the vicar's wife, after Hilary had given her an expurgated version of the attack on the duke. "However, it's good to know the truth. The vicar and I had heard so many rumors, and we were so concerned about the duke's safety. But we didn't quite like to disturb you by calling on you when we'd also heard that you and your brother had your hands full, actually tending one of the criminals in your own house. What good Samaritans you both are. Thank you so much, Miss Vane, for taking the trouble to keep us informed."

Feeling mildly hypocritical, Hilary accepted Mrs. Trevor's thanks and then made her request.

"But of course you may have the use of our carriage, my dear," said Mrs. Trevor with a beaming smile. "The vicar and I use it so seldom, it just sits in the carriage house gathering dust. Are you and dear Belinda planning to go to Bridgeton on another shopping excursion?"

"Well, no. The Bridgeton shops are rather limited, don't you think? I'd prefer to go to Newcastle, if I may keep the carriage for several days."

"Oh, certainly. Keep it as long as you like. And do have a very pleasant journey, Miss Vane."

After arranging with Mrs. Trevor to have the carriage sent around at daybreak the next morning, Hilary walked slowly home. She would have preferred to have the use of the vehicle immediately, but she didn't wish to arouse any curiosity about her plans. Mrs. Trevor would have thought it very odd to set off on a longish journey in the middle of the afternoon.

She broke her news to her brother that evening after supper.

"You're going to do *what?*" he said incredulously.

"I'm taking Nate Derwent away from here before the duke can drag him off to trial," repeated Hilary calmly. "Nate's not really strong enough to travel by himself, or I'd drive him to Bridgeton and put him on the stagecoach. Also, he could too easily be traced on a public vehicle. A private carriage is a much better idea."

Recovering from his shock, Matt expostulated, "Hilary, this is sheer madness. You can't possibly prevent the law from taking its course with Derwent. Why, even before you can get away in the morning, the duke will doubtless arrive to collect Derwent. Actually I'm surprised Alverly hasn't come here this afternoon to make arrangements for tomorrow. He must have received my message shortly after noon."

"He never received your message, Matt. I didn't send it. Before the duke discovers that Nate has escaped, we'll be long gone."

Matt said urgently, "My darling sister, please listen to me. Even if you manage to deliver Derwent to his home in the Tyne Valley, he'll not be safe there. Alverly will know immediately where you've taken the man, and he'll set the authorities onto the fellow. Why persist in this quixotic scheme when you must know in your heart that it will come to nothing in the end?"

"I don't know anything of the sort. For one thing, if I play my cards properly, the duke won't look for Nate in the Tyne Valley."

"But of course he will. Where else would Derwent go?"

"I'll explain later. In any event, even if the duke does suspect that Nate has gone to his home in the Tyne Valley, he won't find him there. I've decided to take Nate to Newcastle, where I'll give him enough money to buy himself a ticket on the stagecoach to some place far enough away so the duke can't catch up to him. Wales, for instance. They have coal mines in Wales, don't they? Nate can find employment there, and then he can send for his mother."

Throwing up his hands, Matt exclaimed, "You *are* mad. You don't expect me to help you, do you?"

"Yes, I do." Walking over to her brother, Hilary perched on the arm of his chair. She placed an arm around his shoulders and rested her cheek against his hair. "You've never failed me yet. I know you won't now."

Matt growled inarticulately in his throat, but after a moment he put up his hand to clasp hers.

Hilary shivered in the dank, chilly early morning air. The sun hadn't yet risen to burn off a heavy fog. Standing with Hilary beside the waiting carriage, Matt held up a lantern to guide Ephraim as he half-supported, half-carried the slight form of Nate Derwent out of the house and helped him into the vicar's carriage. Nate was so bundled in blankets from head to foot that he wasn't recognizable, even if Sarah or Cook or one of the villagers had been awake to see him leave.

While Ephraim climbed up to the coachman's box, Matt extended his hand to Hilary to help her into the carriage. Gazing at her brother's anxious face as he

158

stood beside the steps, Hilary said softly, "Please don't worry. Everything will be all right, I promise you."

"I'm doing my best to believe you," he muttered with a twisted smile. "It's not easy."

She smiled back. "Don't forget, now, to send a message to the duke saying that Nate's condition is improving, but he won't be able to travel for several days."

"I won't forget. However, if despite the message, the duke comes around prematurely today or tomorrow, I'm to tell him that Derwent apparently escaped from his bed in the middle of the night. I'll say the fellow had recovered his strength much faster than I'd thought possible, and obviously he'd been concealing his real condition from me. I'll say I have no idea where he is. Probably out there in the hills somewhere, making for the Scottish border."

Hearing a weak chuckle from the interior of the carriage, Matt waved a hand in acknowledgement at Nate Derwent, and then returned to his conversation with Hilary. "I'm also to send word to Belinda that you've had news of a sick friend in Newcastle and you've decided to visit her for several days. I'm to ask Belinda to kindly notify your other pupils that you'll resume classes when you return. Do I have all your instructions correctly?"

"Yes. You're a darling, Matt. Goodbye. I'll see you again late tomorrow night or some time the next day. With just a bit of luck, nothing will go wrong, you'll see."

The first part of the drive, on the wretched valley road leading over the mountain to Bridgeton, where they would make their first change of horses, was very difficult for Derwent. His near fatal chest wound was barely healed, and the constant swaying and jostling of

159

the carriage on the rutted road caused him acute discomfort. After Bridgeton, however, the turnpike roads were much smoother.

Hilary hadn't wanted, or, indeed, expected, enthusiastic expressions of gratitude from the inarticulate Derwent. However, she was surprised to discover as she chatted with him during the journey that he was somewhat ambivalent about fleeing from the law.

"What if they come after me and catch me?" he said uneasily at one point. "Won't it be the worse fer me? Mayhap if I'd stayed ter face the charge . . ."

Hilary interrupted him, saying quietly, "You do realize, Nate, that murder is a capital offense, no matter what extenuating circumstances there may be? Do you really think you'd have been better off standing trial with Bill testifying against you? Remember, he's now accusing you of killing Danny."

He subsided, muttering, "No, ma'am, I reckon not." A little later, he asked about Wales. "It's a long ways away, ain't it? Do they speak English in those parts, do y'think?"

Hilary looked at him sympathetically. Before his abortive trip into the Cheviot Hills to kill the duke, Derwent had probably never ventured more than a few miles from his home in the Tyne Valley. He was confronting the terror of the unknown, which at the moment seemed to frighten him more than the prospect of the gallows.

She said soothingly, "Yes, Wales is very far from here, and I suspect most Welshmen don't speak English. But you needn't go to Wales, Nate. I've heard there are coal mines in Yorkshire, much closer to your home, and in Lancashire. You can choose where you wish to go."

At Morpeth, some four hours and more than halfway

into their journey, Hilary decided to stop for a late breakfast or nuncheon. She'd been too much on edge to consume more than a cup of tea and a bite of toast before setting out that morning. To avoid exposing Derwent to public attention, she arranged for her coachman, Ephraim, to bring food for the injured miner to the carriage. She herself opted for a meal in the dining room of the inn.

After descending from the carriage, she luxuriously stretched her cramped muscles for a few moments and then headed across the courtyard. At the door of the inn she came to an abrupt halt.

"I want to talk to you," growled a familiar voice.

Hilary's heart lurched despairingly. She raised her eyes from the strong fingers encircling her wrist like a vise to the Duke of Alverly's furious features. His slate gray eyes had turned black with rage.

"Let go my wrist, please. You're hurting me," she said quietly.

Instantly his hand dropped. "Don't think you can avoid talking to me," he said in a low, venomous voice.

"I have no intention of doing so, but could we find a less public place to talk?" Hilary said with a calm she was far from feeling. "People are staring at us. And I'm hungry. Please engage a private dining parlor."

Obviously taken aback by her prosaic request, Alverly stared blankly at her. After a moment he nodded, taking several steps toward the door of the inn. Then he stopped short. "You won't try to get away while I make arrangements with the landlord?" he asked suspiciously.

"Do you take me for a complete idiot? How far could I go before you caught up to me? Besides, I'm starving."

"Oh. Of course."

Hilary was maliciously amused at the frustrated expression on Alverly's face as he turned to enter the inn. At least she'd scored one point against his armor of male arrogance. It was likely to be the last one, she thought, as her brief spurt of amusement faded. She'd lost her gamble to save Derwent unless she could somehow miraculously think of a fresh argument to change Alverly's mind. Which was highly unlikely.

She walked slowly into the entrance hall of the inn, where she found the duke talking to a harassed-looking individual whom she took to be the proprietor of the establishment. The two men appeared to be arguing. After a brief interval Alverly broke off the conversation and walked over to her.

"We can't be accommodated immediately," he said curtly. "Both private dining parlors are engaged. I've paid the landlord to evict the occupants from one of the parlors, but it will be a few minutes before the room can be cleared."

Hilary stared at him in outrage. "Jon! You've no right to force the landlord to treat his guests in that fashion!"

Alverly gave her a stony look. "Force? You overestimate the delicacy of the fellow's sensibilities. He was willing enough to toss his guests out of their quarters for a suitable price. Why are you complaining? You said you wanted a private dining parlor." As Hilary opened her mouth to reply, he added savagely, "And don't you say one word about border lords!"

"You must have been reading my mind," she retorted, and then lapsed into a stubborn silence, ignoring the duke's presence. In a few minutes the landlord, looking more harassed than ever, ushered them into a private parlor. "I'll send a servant to take your order," he informed them.

As soon as the door closed behind the proprietor, Alverly said, "Now, Hilary, we'll have this out—"

Hilary shook her head. "Not now we won't. I don't intend to have my nuncheon spoiled."

She removed her pelisse, laying it over a chair, and sat down at a small table before the fireplace, looking calmly up at the duke. Tossing her a baffled glance, he clamped his lips firmly together, betraying his impatience only by a restless pacing back and forth across the room. When the servant arrived, Hilary deliberately lingered over the menu, finally settling on ham and buttered eggs. "I'll have the same," snapped Alverly when the waiter turned to him.

Hilary made a leisurely meal, ostentatiously enjoying every bite of ham. Maintaining a grim silence, the duke merely pushed his food around his plate. When at last she put down her napkin, he leaned back in his chair, saying morosely, "Well? Can we talk now?"

"Certainly."

Hilary sensed that the enforced wait had taken the edge off the duke's temper. He sounded almost more disillusioned than angry. She'd hoped for that. She'd even counted on it. It was her one chance to make Jon see reason.

She boldly took the initiative. "How is it that you came after us so quickly?" she asked out of real interest. "I told Matt to send you a message that Nate wasn't ready to travel yet, so I counted on a full day, perhaps two, of freedom from pursuit. In fact, I thought there was a chance I might get back to Wycombe before you even realized Nate Derwent was missing."

He gave her a sour look. "You were too clever. Your brother's message made me suspicious. It seemed so unnecessary for him to be sending me a bulletin about

163

Derwent's heath, when all I wanted to know was when the fellow could travel. And then Belinda told me about your plan to visit your 'sick friend.' *That* rang a bell! I went straight around to Willow Cottage, where, of course, Dr. Vane couldn't produce his patient. It wouldn't have been difficult for a five-year-old to deduce that you'd spirited Derwent away, and the most logical place for you to go was the Tyne Valley."

After a pause, Alverly added, "I confess I was curious about your mode of transport. Somehow, I couldn't envision you and a critically wounded man starting out on a long journey in a dogcart! Naturally your loyal brother wouldn't open his mouth about the matter. So I paid a visit to the vicarage, where I learned from Mrs. Trevor that you'd borrowed her carriage for a 'shopping excursion' to Newcastle."

Hilary sighed. "You were incorrect to call me clever, Jon. Matt was right when he said my plan was a mad scheme."

His temper rising again, Alverly said roughly, "Why did you do it? Don't you realize you yourself could be accused of being an accessory to a capital offense by helping a murderer to escape punishment?"

Raising an eyebrow, Hilary inquired, "Are you going to charge me before the magistrates?"

He reddened. "Don't be ridiculous. I'll take Derwent to Wincanton and turn him over to the justices, and that will be the end of your connection with the case."

"Jon, will you try to listen to me with an open mind? I decided to help Nate Derwent because I thought he was innocent of any real crime. No, wait," she added, as the duke opened his mouth to object. "I know you believe Bill's story that Nate and the man Danny were willing collaborators to murder. But why, in that case, did the three men fight? Why did Bill kill Danny and attempt to kill Nate? And don't tell me that Nate killed Danny. That doesn't make sense. There's only one logical answer to this puzzle: Bill simply went berserk when Nate and Danny told him they'd changed their minds about taking part in your murder."

Alverly's expression changed. Hilary knew she'd struck a nerve. But he wasn't willing to concede defeat. "Even if what you say is true," he burst out, "Derwent hated me enough to plan to kill me. For that he deserves some punishment. Perhaps you don't realize there's a spirit of unrest abroad in this country. I hear that gangs in the Midlands have been smashing hosiery frames and burning houses and barns belonging to their employers. We can't allow the lower classes to conspire against the persons and possessions of property owners."

Hilary said quietly, "Nate hated you enough to want to murder you because he believed the inhumane practices in your mines caused the deaths of his father and his sister and the current illness of his mother."

Alverly turned white. "Are you saying I myself am responsible for the fact that Derwent tried to kill me? You've accused me of many faults in the past, Hilary. Are you now accusing me of being a monster of inhumanity? Of deliberately ignoring the health and welfare of the people who work for me?"

"No. I know you're not a monster."

"Well?"

"Jon, will you do something for me? Will you go with me and Nate to the Tyne Valley and inspect the condition of your mines? And then, if you believe Nate had the slightest justification for hating you and wanting to kill you, will you let him go free? For my sake, if not for his own?"

165

Alverly's eyes bored into hers. After a long, difficult pause, he said in a low voice, "Yes. I'll do it. For your sake."

Chapter X

Nate Derwent said plaintively, "Please, ma'am, cain't I go wi' ye? We're so close ter home here. I'd like ter see my mum."

"You're too exhausted to travel any more today," Hilary replied, standing beside the miner's bed as she tucked the coverlets up around his chin. They were in a bedchamber of an unprepossessing inn in the equally unprepossessing village of Midvale, on the edge of the Tyne Valley coal fields. Though it verged on the primitive, the establishment was quite clean, and the proprietor anxious to please. Which was fortunate, Hilary thought, because she and Nate and Jon would be obliged to spend the night in Midvale.

"I promise you'll have the opportunity to see your mother, whether or not . . ." Hilary broke off.

"Whether or not the duke decides ter hand me over ter the magistrates ter stand trial," Derwent finished. "Don't ye feel bad, ma'am. Ye've done yer best, but I know it ain't likely His Grace will change his mind about me jist by inspecting his coal mines. His mind is made up."

"Don't give up hope, Nate," Hilary said with a smile

of encouragement. However, she knew her voice lacked conviction. As she left the room and walked down the stairs to the ground floor, she reflected that Nate was probably right. She knew from experience that it was enormously difficult to change Alverly's inflexible mind.

He was waiting for her in the entrance hall. "Derwent settled in?" he inquired. He cleared his throat. "You don't think he'll try to escape while we're gone? After all, we're very close to his home ground."

"Nate's much too weak to attempt to escape," Hilary said sharply. "Nine hours in that carriage almost finished him."

"Oh. Yes, I daresay." The duke pulled the end of his riding crop between his fingers. "Hilary, it's not necessary for you to go with me to the mines. It would serve no useful purpose."

She lifted her chin. "I want to see your mines. I want to see the conditions Nate described to me."

Alverly's eyes glinted with anger. "So you've already prejudged me, have you?" He paused, biting off his words. "As you wish. Shall we go? It's midafternoon. At this time of year it will soon be dark."

They walked in silence out of the inn to the courtyard, where Mrs. Trevor's carriage and Alverly's mount—one of several that he'd exchanged for his own horse on his journey from Wycombe—awaited them.

"Will you ride with me, Jon?"

After a brief hesitation, the duke said coolly, "Why not? Your coachman can tether my horse to the rear of your carriage in the event I wish to go off by myself."

In less than ten minutes after leaving the outskirts of Midvale, they entered the area surrounding the coal fields. Hilary stared out the window of the carriage, growing steadily more appalled. She glanced surreptitiously at Alverly, wondering if his reactions mirrored her own. This place was more like one of the lower levels of hell than a corner of rural England. No greater contrast could be imagined than that between the austere, lonely beauty of the Cheviot Hills and this desolate landscape with its nearly lifeless vegetation, consisting of a few blackened and stunted trees and shrubs. Great heaps of tailings reared like small mountains across the landscape, and the little streams ran dark with mine waste.

Alverly's face registered no expression as he gazed out the window of the carriage, but when they reached a jumble of buildings grouped around the entrance to the mine, he said abruptly, "I think you should stay in the carriage. This is no place for you."

"I told you, I came here to see your mines."

He shot her an unfriendly look but did not reply. When the carriage stopped, he took her hand to help her down the steps. A sense of shock set in immediately. It had rained heavily earlier in the day, and the single narrow street, if one could call the rough track a street, was a river of mud. Before Hilary had taken more than a few steps, her thin slippers and the hem of her skirt were sodden with a viscous moisture.

Alverly caught her arm as she slipped into a deep depression in the roadway and lost her balance. "I told you this was no place for you, Hilary. Do you want to return to the carriage?"

"No," she replied defiantly. "A little mud won't hurt me."

He shrugged. "As you wish."

She stared at him resentfully. His boots were splashed with mud almost to the knee, but undoubtedly his feet, unlike hers, were still warm and dry.

She walked on, picking her way cautiously. What must it be like to live here, she wondered, as she gazed around her at the blackened, ill-built hovels clustered on the hillside above the entrance to the mine. Some of them leaned at a crazy angle, as if they might tumble down the hill during the next storm. She saw very few people. No adults, except for several aged men sitting apathetically on their doorsteps. The able-bodied men and women of the community must be below, toiling in the mine shafts. Hilary saw no children either, save for a few babies, some of whom might be as old as three years. Dirty and half naked, they were playing in the mud outside their hovels, where their mothers had apparently been forced to leave them unattended when they reported for work.

Hilary gasped as one child, possibly two years of age, slipped down the embankment and fell into a muddy pool of water in the roadway. Before she could make a move to help him—it was easy to tell he was a boy because he wore virtually no clothing—the duke strode forward and plucked the tiny boy from the water, depositing him on a safe ledge above the roadway.

"He might have drowned," Hilary said in a shaking voice.

"Yes, very easily," Alverly replied. His mouth was set in a grim line.

"Your Grace, is that really you?" a voice called. Hilary and the duke looked up to see a figure racing toward them from a small but substantial building near the mine entrance. The man skidded to a stop in front of them. His eyes wide with shock, he gasped, "It *is* you, Your Grace. I couldn't believe my eyes. What—?"

"What am I doing here?" The duke gave the short, stout, modestly dressed man a measuring look. "I thought it was time I actually visited my properties here. It will save you at least one long uncomfortable journey to confer with me in Wycombe." He glanced at Hilary. "Miss Vane, may I present my mine manager, Horace Latham?" To Latham, he added, "I trust you're prepared to give me a guided tour?"

"You mean—go down into the shafts?"

"Certainly," Alverly replied curtly. "I wish to see the entire operation." To Hilary he said as she opened her mouth, "The answer is no. You are *not* going down into the mine. I suggest you return to the inn. I'll join you there for supper this evening."

Hearing the finality in the duke's voice, Hilary knew there was no point in arguing with him. Nor, to tell the truth, did she really wish to descend into the bowels of the earth. Seeing the misery and the dirt above ground had been quite sufficient for her. "I'll say goodbye then," she told him, and walked to the carriage. As the vehicle moved off, she sank back against the squabs, grateful to be leaving the depressing vicinity of the Midvale mine.

Several hours later, Hilary sat, half dozing, on a sofa in front of a blazing fire in a private dining parlor of the inn. She'd long since finished a reviving pot of tea, and she felt warm and relaxed. Returning to the inn from the mine, she'd first checked on Nate Derwent to see that he was comfortable, and had then changed into a fresh gown and stockings. Her slippers, wiped clean of mud, were drying in front of the fire. As she gazed into the flames, she speculated apprehensively about what the duke was thinking and feeling as he toured one of his mines for the first time. Would the results of the tour be favorable or unfavorable for Nate Derwent? She sat up abruptly at the sound of the door opening. She must have fallen completely asleep, she realized.

"I'm sorry to be late," said the duke. "I decided to visit two other mines belonging to me in the area. Shall we order supper? I'm famished."

She gazed at him in astonishment. He wore a shirt that was too tight for him across the shoulders while his breeches were much too loose. His feet and legs were encased in serviceable homespun stockings. He wore no boots.

He gave her a twisted smile. "What do you think of my new wardrobe? Don't I look like a real Dandy? Our landlord generously offered me the use of some of his own clothes while he, or one of his minions, tries to clean my coat and breeches and boots and washes my shirt and hose. I've had a bath, too. Mines are filthy places." He made a face. "Pity my mine manager. Poor Latham, I don't think he'd climbed down a mine shaft in many years. When we came to the surface he looked like a blackened henchman of the devil, fresh from tending one of the furnaces of hell."

A discreet knock sounded at the door and their landlord appeared, beaming with pleasure when he observed the duke's appearance in the borrowed clothes. "A very fine fit, wouldn't you say, Your Grace?"

"Very fine indeed," said Alverly dryly. "What really concerns me, however, is food. What do you have to offer us tonight?"

The landlord mentioned a haunch of roast venison, boiled beef, a steak and kidney pie, a broiled salmon. "We'll have some of everything," said Alverly, to the landlord's gratification.

Soon Hilary and the duke were seated in front of a bountifully laden table. It suddenly occurred to Hilary that it felt strange, even a trifle alarming, to be sharing a meal with Jon in such intimate surroundings. In their acquaintance to date, they'd never been so alone or so far from the Wycombe Valley.

The duke was in an abstracted mood. Though he ate heartily, Hilary doubted that he really tasted his food or that he could have described later what he'd eaten. And he was unusually taciturn. At one point, she ventured to ask, "What did you learn from your tour of the mines?"

He hunched his shoulders, saying curtly, "A great deal, all things considered." But he didn't volunteer any information. He seemed on edge, frequently glancing at the door of the dining parlor. At last, as the maidservant was clearing the table, the landlord ushered into the room the mine manager, Horace Latham. He, too, had obviously bathed and changed his clothes.

"Well, here I am, Your Grace. I came as soon as I could." The man was clearly nervous, turning the rim of his hat around and around between his fingers.

Turning in his chair to face the mine manager, Alverly didn't ask Latham to be seated. The discourtesy puzzled Hilary. Jon was often curt to the point of arrogance, but he was rarely rude, especially to his subordinates. Later she realized that his failure to invite the mine manager to sit down was a deliberate omission, meant to keep Latham off balance and to emphasize what he had to say.

Measuring the mine manager with a long, unnerving glance, Alverly said in a hard voice, "I'm sorry to tell you that I'm displeased with the conditions in my mining properties."

Latham tensed. "In what respect, Your Grace?"

"In virtually every respect. Let's start with the hovels my workers live in. I wouldn't allow my livestock to be

173

housed in such squalor. All those houses must be torn down and replaced, and all roads within the area of the mines must be surfaced so folk can walk without sinking to their ankles in mud. And I want you to build a grammar school in each community. These children are growing up totally uneducated."

"But Your Grace—"

The duke cut him off. "As to the mines themselves, they're a disgrace to humanity. Recall, I talked to workers in all three of the mines. They told me about the frequent flooding in the shafts, the explosions, the landslides that killed whole companies of colliers. I saw for myself the women and children pulling loaded carts like beasts of burden. I want changes made immediately. First, you're to improve safety precautions in all areas of the mines. One suggestion: reinforce supports in the tunnels so that the miners won't live in fear of being crushed to death. Next, you're to assign women workers to lighter jobs. No more pulling loaded carts of coal on their hands and knees. And above all, you're not to hire children under the age of ten—no, twelve years would be better." The duke gave Latham a challenging look. "Well? Do you understand what I want you to do?"

Looking aggrieved and angry, the mine manager burst out, "Your Grace, I must protest the implication of your remarks. Your mines are as efficiently managed as any in the Tyne Valley. Ask anyone. Not a soul will say I'm a bad manager."

Jon put up his hand. "I'm not accusing you of inefficiency. I simply want you to perform your duties differently in the future."

Growing even more agitated, Latham exclaimed, "If I carry out your instructions, half your profits will go whistling down the wind. Do you understand that?

174

What's more, I—you—will be the laughingstock of the valley for treating your workers like cosseted children."

The duke snapped, "Do *you* understand, Latham, that I don't care a damn what people think of me? I'll do with my property as I see fit. And my employees will obey my orders or they'll be dismissed."

Suddenly deflated, Latham muttered, "Yes, Your Grace. I'll do whatever you ask to the best of my ability."

"Good. Oh, one more thing. Not long ago I encountered a man who until very recently was a collier in our Midvale mine. Nate Derwent is his name. He's too ill to work at the present time, but as soon as he's fit I want you to give him back his job at a substantial increase in his wages. He needs the extra money to support his mother who's too ill to work in the mines anymore."

Latham flashed an incredulous look at the duke, but made no objection. "Very well, Your Grace. I'll take care of the matter. Er—you won't object if I conceal the amount of Derwent's wages from the other colliers and ask him to do the same? It will prevent discontent among the workers."

"Not at all. Do as you think best. Well, then, I believe we've covered all the points I wished to make. You may go, Latham."

The mine manager bowed to the duke, made an extra bow to Hilary, and left the room with the relieved air of a man who'd escaped from mortal danger.

Hilary had been listening, mesmerized, to the conversation. As soon as Latham had gone, she said wonderingly, "Jon, do you realize just what you've done?"

"Cut my income in half, most likely." He cocked his head at her. "Do you consider me a candidate for the nearest lunatic asylum? I'm sure Latham thinks so, if only he dared to tell me."

"Of course not," she said impatiently. "What does it matter if you lose half your income from the mines? According to Belinda, you already have more money than you'll ever need."

"Does Belinda tell you all my secrets?" the duke said, raising an eyebrow.

"Why no, of course not. Belinda would never . . . That is, I didn't mean to imply—" Hilary paused, helplessly floundering.

Jon smiled faintly. "Don't worry about it. I know what you meant." He gave her a direct look. "Then you approve of the reforms I'm putting into effect in my mines?"

"Approve?" Hilary's eyes shone. "Oh, yes, I approve. What you've done will change the lives of all your workers for the good for years to come. Perhaps you'll even persuade other mine owners to follow your example." She shook her head. "Frankly when I asked you to look into the conditions at your mines, I never really believed—" She broke off.

He said mockingly, "You never really believed a border lord could change his stubborn mind?"

Hilary bit her lip. "I'm sorry, Jon. I was wrong."

"No, I think you were almost right. If it hadn't been for one thing, I might have been able to shrug off everything else I saw in the mines."

"What was that?"

"The baby who nearly drowned in that muddy street. I couldn't ignore that."

"No, you couldn't." Hilary smiled at him. "Well, as a result of the reforms you've just initiated, that baby will probably never be at risk of drowning again." She rose.

TAKE ADVANTAGE OF THIS SPECIAL OFFER, AVAILABLE *ONLY* TO ZEBRA REGENCY ROMANCE READERS.

You are a reader who enjoys the very special kind of love story that can only be found in Zebra Regency Romances. You adore the fashionable English settings, the sparkling wit, the captivating intrigue, and the heart-stirring romance that are the hallmarks of each Zebra Regency Romance novel.

Now, you can have these delightful novels delivered right to your door each month and never have to worry about missing a new book. Zebra has made arrangements through its Home Subscription Service for you to preview the three latest Zebra Regency Romances as soon as they are published.

3 **FREE** REGENCIES TO GET STARTED!

To get your subscription started, we will send your first 3 books ABSOLUTELY FREE, as our introductory gift to you. NO OBLIGATION. We're sure that you will enjoy these books so much that you will want to read more of the very best romantic fiction published today.

SUBSCRIBERS SAVE EACH MONTH

Zebra Regency Home Subscribers will save money each month as they enjoy their latest Regencies. As a subscriber you will receive the 3 newest titles to preview FREE for ten days. Each shipment will be at least a $11.97 value (publisher's price). But home subscribers will be billed only $9.90 for all three books. You'll save over $2.00 each month. Of course, if you're not satisfied with any book, just return it for full credit.

FREE HOME DELIVERY

Zebra Home Subscribers get free home delivery. There are never any postage, shipping or handling charges. No hidden charges. What's more, there is no minimum number to buy and you can cancel your subscription at any time. No obligation and no questions asked.

TO GET YOUR 3 FREE BOOKS
ILL OUT AND MAIL THE COUPON BELOW

FREE BOOKS

Mail to: Zebra Regency Home Subscription Service
120 Brighton Road
P.O. Box 5214
Clifton, New Jersey 07015-5214

YES! Start my Regency Romance Home Subscription and send me my 3 FREE BOOKS as my introductory gift. Then each month, I'll receive the 3 newest Zebra Regency Romances to preview FREE for ten days. I understand that if I'm not satisfied, I may return them and owe nothing. Otherwise, I'll pay the low members' price of just $9.90 for all 3 books and save over $2.00 off the publisher's price (a $11.97 value). There are no shipping, handling or other hidden charges. I may cancel my subscription at any time and there is no minimum number to buy. In any case, the 3 FREE books are mine to keep regardless of what I decide.

NAME _____

ADDRESS _____ APT NO. _____

CITY _____ STATE _____ ZIP _____

TELEPHONE ( ) _____

SIGNATURE _____
(if under 18 parent or guardian must sign)

RG0993

Terms and prices subject to change. Orders subject to acceptance by Zebra Home Subscription Service, Inc.

ZEBRA HOME SUBSCRIPTION SERVICE, INC.
120 BRIGHTON ROAD
P.O. BOX 5214
CLIFTON, NEW JERSEY 07015-5214

AFFIX
STAMP
HERE

"Shall we have our coffee in front of the fire? The sofa is reasonably comfortable, and you must be exhausted from climbing in and out of mine shafts all afternoon."

A little later, as she and Jon sat companionably side by side on the sofa, drinking their coffee, Hilary marveled at the dramatic ups and downs of the long day that was coming to a close. She'd started off at dawn, confident that she could spirit Nate Derwent to safety. Then Jon had caught up to her, and she was equally sure she'd failed. Now, some seventeen hours later, Nate Derwent was safe, and Jon had completely overturned all her previous negative ideas about his flexibility of mind and his empathy for those outside his class.

She glanced sideways at him as he lounged on the sofa, his long legs sprawled toward the fire. She noted that the tightness of the borrowed shirt emphasized his powerful muscled shoulders and that his hair after his bath had dried in tousled curls. Once again she admitted to herself that he was a disturbingly handsome man, despite his careless grooming. She had to resist a sudden erratic impulse to run her fingers through those springy black curls. She felt an unfamiliar sensation of heat in her groin and said hastily, to distract her mind from the disturbing feeling, "I can hardly wait to tell Nate that he has nothing more to fear from the law."

Turning his head toward her, the duke said, "You risked a great deal for Derwent, Hilary. Have you always been a nurturer? In my mind's eye, I can see you as a child, rescuing injured baby birds. Or feeding beggars at the kitchen door of your father's house. Or later, taking the blame for something one of your brothers did, so he could avoid a hiding."

Hilary blurted, "How did you—?" Then she caught

177

the glint of amusement in Jon's eyes and began laughing.

"I have the second sight. Some kind of psychic gift, anyway, so I can see into your mind," said Alverly facetiously. He set down his coffee cup on a table next to the sofa and stretched luxuriously. "It feels so good to be warm and free of mud."

Hilary shuddered. "Oh, that dreadful mud. After today I hope I won't forget to appreciate the small pleasures of life." She glanced at her slippers drying on the hearth. "Like dry shoes." She handed him her empty cup to deposit on the table next to him.

As their fingers touched, Jon said huskily, "I'd nearly forgotten another of life's small pleasures." He set the cup down and lifted her hand to his lips. "Kissing a beautiful woman's hand, for instance."

Hilary tried to ignore the shiver of electric excitement that swept through her. "Jon, please don't . . ."

Paying no attention to her halfhearted protest, he slipped his arm around her and pressed his mouth to hers in a gentle, undemanding kiss. "You taste like honey," he whispered against her lips. "And your skin is like cream," he added softly as his mouth traced a warm, clinging path along her cheek and neck into the delicate hollow at the base of her throat.

Fighting against the mindless desire that threatened to engulf her, Hilary pushed against Alverly. "Jon, stop . . ."

"I can't stop," he said hoarsely, his fingers biting into her shoulders. "If I so much as touch you, I can't let you go." His arms tightened around her until she could feel the buttons on his shirt pressing into her flesh. His mouth crushed hers in a fierce, insatiable kiss that emptied her of thought and logic and prudence, everything

178

except the overwhelming urge to meld her body against his. With an inarticulate cry, she wound her arms around his neck, pressing against him as she eagerly responded to him with a hunger that matched his own.

He left her gasping when he wrenched his mouth from hers and pushed her away from him. "God, what are we doing?" he said, his eyes dazed with passion. "We can't make love here. There's no lock on the door. Someone could come in at any time." He reached out his hand to pull her to her feet. "Hilary, come to my bedchamber. I want you so much I'm dying of it."

But the respite, slight as it was, had been enough to enable Hilary to recover her sanity. She tugged her hand free. "No, Jon, I won't come to your bedchamber. I won't make love with you."

He stared at her. "You can't mean that. You responded to me. You put your arms around my neck; you returned my kisses. I *know* you want me as much as I want you." He took a quick step toward her.

She moved backward, her face flaming scarlet. "I'm sorry, Jon. You're justified in what you're saying. I *did* respond to you. I—I enjoyed kissing you. But . . ."

"But?"

"I told you how I felt at the Bridgeton ball. I don't want to have an affair with you. I don't want to be your mistress. Call me prudish, old-fashioned, whatever you like. No matter how much I might be physically attracted to a man, I couldn't allow myself to love him without a commitment."

Alverly froze. "You're talking about marriage."

She met his gaze steadily. "Yes. Are you proposing marriage, Jon?"

"No!" The answer was explosive. "I don't believe in marriage. I don't intend to be married."

179

Hilary felt as if a fiery arrow had transfixed her heart. Forcing herself to sound calm, she said, "So you've decided against marriage. Temporarily or permanently?"

"Permanently. Hilary—"

She interrupted him. "You're the heir to an ancient title. If you don't marry, how will you carry on your line?"

He shot her an impatient glance. "I have an heir, my cousin Wilfred. He can 'carry on the line,' if he's so inclined. So, as you see, I've no need to be married."

The indifference in Jon's voice chilled Hilary and at the same time stiffened her backbone. "I've no need to be married either," she told him coolly. "Nor do I need to take a lover who won't marry me. Good night, Jon."

As she swept out of the dining parlor, she heard Jon's voice protesting, "Wait, Hilary, let me talk to you." Ignoring him, she hurried up the stairs to her bedchamber. In the upper hallway, passing Nate Derwent's door, she paused. If he were still awake, waiting anxiously to learn his fate after the duke's tour of inspection of the mines, she couldn't leave him in suspense. Cautiously she opened his door. In the moonlight streaming in through his window, she could make out his quiet form. He seemed to be sleeping peacefully.

She slipped the door shut and walked swiftly down the hallway to her bedchamber. A maidservant had left a lamp burning and had turned down her bed. She closed and bolted her door and sank into a chair, burying her face in her hands. Now she could give in to her mangled feelings of pain and humiliation and loss. Until she met Alverly, it had never occurred to her to break the rules of convention governing the proper romantic deportment of young women. But tonight ... Tonight she'd felt tempted as never before to bury her scruples and surrender herself completely to Jon's tempestuous lovemaking. If he'd murmured one word of real affection, if he'd given her one reason, however inadequate, to explain his reluctance to marry, she might not have been able to resist him. But he hadn't. And she hadn't succumbed, though she'd come very close to allowing physical passion to dull her sense of pride and self-worth.

Someone knocked at her door. She froze momentarily, then got up from her chair to stand beside the door. "Yes?" she said in a low voice.

"Hilary, I must talk to you. We can't leave the—the situation as it is," Jon said, so softly that he was barely audible through the thick door panels. But she could still hear the tension in his voice. "Please, can't I come in? Just for a few moments?"

"No. There's nothing more to say. Please go away, Jon, before you embarrass both of us. I'm sure you don't wish either the inn servants or our fellow guests to eavesdrop on our personal affairs."

After several moments of silence, she heard his footsteps moving slowly away.

The carriage stopped, and Hilary sat still for a moment, gazing glumly out of the window. The area around the mine head at Midvale looked even more depressing than it had the day before. It had again rained heavily during the night, and the mud was deeper than ever. Ephraim opened the door of the carriage and helped her down the steps. She'd had the forethought to borrow a pair of patterns from one of the maids at the inn, which she now wore instead of her slippers, but even so, she suspected her feet and skirts would soon become mired in mud. Dismounting quickly from his horse, Jon put a steadying hand beneath her arm as she waited for Ephraim to help Nate Derwent from the carriage. Without looking at Jon, Hilary pulled her arm free.

Nate Derwent, pale, emaciated, unsteady on his feet, looked about him with an air of wondering joy. "The old place ain't changed a bit," he murmured, as if he'd been gone for years, rather than days. "I never thought ter see it again." Blinking his eyes against sudden tears, he said to Hilary, "I never would have seen Midvale again, Miss Vane, if it weren't fer ye, yes, and yer brother. I'd be dead by now or sitting in a cell at Wincanton gaol. My thanks ter ye from the bottom o' my heart."

"I was glad to help, Nate." Hilary patted the miner's shoulder. "I wish you health and happiness in the future."

"Thank'ee, ma'am." Derwent turned to the duke, standing quietly to the side. "Well I know, Yer Grace, that I owe ye a share o' my life, too. Miss Vane and the doctor, they did everything they could fer me, more'n I ever deserved, but if ye hadn't come all the way ter Midvale ter have a look at yer mines and then ter give me my job back, and at such wages—"

Alverly cut off the miner's floundering attempt to express his gratitude. "No need to thank me," he said curtly. "I made a mistake, and I owed it to myself to correct it." He flicked Derwent a wintry smile. "The next time you feel the urge to kill me, however, don't give in to it."

The miner recoiled in a sort of horror. "Oh, no, Yer Grace, how can ye think I'd ever do sich a thing again?" He looked up at the cluster of hovels on the ridge, say-

182

ing with a restrained eagerness, "If ye don't mind, Yer Grace, Miss Vane, I'll be going on home now."

The duke glanced at the steep embankment, glistening with mud, that led to the miners' hovels. "Ephraim and I will help you up to your house. In your condition you could easily fall and break a leg, if not your neck."

"Oh, no, Yer Grace, I cain't let ye . . ."

"No arguments. I don't want your death on my hands, not after all the trouble you've put me to already," snapped Alverly with a grim humor. The miner grinned weakly and ceased protesting.

For a few moments Hilary stood watching the three men as they made their laborious way up the slippery embankment, the slighter figure of Nate Derwent walking between the duke and Ephraim. A few old men and a handful of small children looked at the trio curiously. Hilary wondered if they realized that one of the men supporting Nate up the hill was the all-powerful duke who controlled the destinies of everyone who lived here.

Her movements awkward in the clumsy pattens, she climbed back into the carriage. Soon Alverly strode up to the open door of the vehicle. "Derwent's snug and happy in that hellish place he calls home," he reported. "Shall we be off?"

His dark face was aloof, his voice even more so. Their passionate interval might never have taken place, Hilary reflected. She hadn't been alone with Jon since last night. To avoid seeing him this morning, she'd had breakfast sent to her bedchamber, and after that she'd helped Ephraim prepare Nate Derwent for his return to Midvale. She'd exchanged formal greetings with Jon, and that was all.

"You needn't accompany the carriage," she said now. "Ephraim is quite capable of driving me home safely.

Actually it would be better if we weren't seen together. I don't want people suspecting we traveled to and from Wycombe in each other's company. I presume you agree with me."

"Quite. However, you won't object if I ride along with you as far as Morpeth? From there it's an easy drive to Bridgeton."

"No, not at all. Thank you."

Nodding, Alverly put up the steps and closed the carriage door. As the vehicle moved off, Hilary felt rather proud of herself. She considered that she'd conducted her exchange with Jon with the proper dignity. She'd concealed from him any hint of hurt or humiliation. At the same time she was glad he was accompanying her during the first, unfamiliar part of the journey home. Since he'd be on horseback, she wouldn't have to be in contact with him in any way. Because it wasn't usual, or even proper, for a gentlewoman to travel alone, Jon's escort would lend her journey a comforting respectability. When they approached familiar territory near Bridgeton, it would be time enough to separate.

Hilary settled back against the squabs, allowing herself to relax for the first time since she'd set off from Wycombe yesterday morning. She felt deliciously drowsy, which wasn't surprising. She'd had very little sleep for the past two nights. Last night sleep had stubbornly refused to come as she unwillingly experienced, over and over again, those searing moments in Jon's arms.

Despite the jolting motion of the carriage, she repeatedly nodded off. She would jerk herself awake, only to doze off again. Finally she abandoned the attempt to stay awake, yielding to the overwhelming desire for sleep. She woke briefly at each stage stop, where they changed horses, and promptly went back to sleep again.

Finally as the carriage rumbled into the courtyard of yet another inn, Hilary sat up, yawning, and peered at the watch pinned to the collar of her pelisse. Six o'clock. They'd left the Midvale mine in the middle of the morning. This must be the last, or almost the last, stage stop before Bridgeton. She'd be home with Matt in Wycombe by early evening.

The carriage door opened and Jon looked in. "I thought you might like to rest a bit and have a cup of tea. It's been a long day, and we didn't stop for lunch."

"I'd like that. Thank you." Suddenly Hilary's stomach felt hollow, and she longed to stretch her legs after her long hours in the carriage. She took Jon's hand and stepped down into the courtyard. "Where are we?" she inquired, looking around. "Did we stop here on our journey south? I don't recognize the place."

"We're at the Albatross Inn at Bewick-on-the-Bay."

"Bewick-on-the . . ." Hilary threw back her head and sniffed the air. The tangy smell of seaweed and fish was unmistakable. She rounded on Alverly. "Where is this place exactly?"

He faced her down. "Bewick is a little seaport about four miles from Alnick."

"But that's . . ." Hilary made a quick calculation. "Alnick is northeast of Newcastle, when we should have been going northwest. We've gone miles out of our way. Why, Jon?"

He said quietly, "We have unsettled business between us, Hilary. You wouldn't talk to me last night, and you avoided being alone with me this morning. So I decided to delay returning to Wycombe for another day."

"You're planning to spend the night here?"

185

"Yes. We'll have time to talk."

Hilary's eyes blazed with anger. "No, we won't, my lord duke. I'll not stay here another minute. I'm going to order Ephraim to drive me to Wycombe, starting immediately. We can travel through the night." She turned back to the carriage and paused in dismay. Ephraim was nowhere in sight, and a pair of ostlers was leading away the team to the stables.

"Ephraim thinks you ordered the change in itinerary," Alverly said calmly. "He's gone off for a well-deserved rest and supper."

"He'll have to change his plans, then," Hilary snapped. She wheeled and set off in the direction of the stables. In several long strides Alverly caught up to her and grabbed her arm.

"Let go of me," Hilary gasped in affronted surprise. She tugged frantically to release her arm, but Jon's grasp was like iron.

"Hilary, listen to me. Do you want to make a public spectacle of yourself? Several ostlers are staring at us already. Come into the inn. I'll engage a private parlor. We can discuss this in a civilized way."

"Civilized?" Hilary exclaimed bitterly. "Only a border lord like you would dare to use the word *civilized* about this situation." But she ceased struggling. She had no wish to create a public scandal. She allowed Jon to lead her into the inn.

He ordered a lavish high tea. At first Hilary merely stared at the food, unwilling to cooperate with him in any way. Then hunger won out. She made a leisurely meal, ignoring Jon's attempts at conversation. Draining her second glass of wine, she wiped her mouth and set down her napkin. "Well?" she inquired. "What's the next step? Rape at twelve paces?" The moment the words were out of her mouth, she felt a sense of acute shock. Gentlewomen weren't supposed to know about such subjects as rape, let alone speak of them in mixed company.

Alverly turned a dull red. "Hilary! You must know I'd never force you . . ."

"No, I don't know. You've already used force today, bringing me to this place, refusing to let me go."

With a sudden lithe movement, he rose from his chair and lunged toward her, pulling her to her feet. "Tell the truth, Hilary," he muttered. "You know I don't need to use force for this." He wrapped his arms around her, bending his head to devour her mouth in a kiss that destroyed her defenses. Her treacherous body responded against her will. She melted into his hard embrace.

He released her, holding her loosely as he looked down at her, his breath coming in long, uneven gasps. "Admit it," he urged. "You want me to make love to you as much as I want to do it. We're here in a place tonight where no one knows us. I've given the landlord a false name for both of us. What's the harm if we enjoy each other's company for the night? No one will ever know. And afterwards . . . Afterwards we can continue to meet without any scandal. I swear I'll never compromise your reputation, I swear I'll never allow any other woman to come between us . . ."

Hilary said coldly, "You mean you're going to dismiss the farmer's widow?"

Jon turned away. "There's nothing between us," he muttered. "I started sleeping with her because I was lonely and she was lonely. I swear to you, Hilary, I'll never go to her again."

Hilary cut him off. "You're swearing a great deal too much, Jon. Be honest. What you feel for me is lust. And

187

yes, what I feel for you is lust, heaven help me. The difference between us is that I have no intention of giving in to my desires. Not unless you force me into your bed tonight. Is that what you have in mind?"

He curbed an angry, instinctive move toward her. After a long moment, he said heavily, "No. I want you willingly or not at all. You've won, Hilary. I'll tell the landlord to prepare an extra bedchamber."

Chapter XI

An early dusk was falling as Hilary's borrowed carriage stopped in front of the gate of Willow Cottage. She'd left Bewick-on-the-Bay early that morning, accompanied only by Ephraim. The landlord of the inn at Bewick, obviously puzzled by the strange doings of the gentry, had informed Hilary that her gentleman escort had left the inn some hours previously. On the whole, Hilary hadn't resented Jon's premature departure, even though it meant she would have to continue on to Wycombe alone. After what had happened between them, it was better for her and Jon to avoid each other's company.

Hilary stepped out of the carriage, turning her head to stare at the smart traveling berline that had been following close behind her since she left Bridgeton for the final stage of her journey to Wycombe and home. In the weeks she'd been living in Wycombe, this was the first time she'd seen an outsider's carriage. Instead of proceeding through the village, the berline turned off to go up the driveway leading to the castle. This was the first time, too, that Hilary had observed a visitor arriving at the castle.

Tamping down her curiosity, Hilary refused to allow herself to speculate about the identity of the occupants of the berline. Jon's visitors were certainly no concern of hers. She turned to speak to Ephraim, who had just retrieved her portmanteau from the luggage basket.

"Thank you for taking such good care of me, Ephraim."

The handyman's craggy face expressed a mingled embarrassment and gratification. "My pleasure, ma'am. Ye and Dr. Vane have been right good ter me. I was glad ter do a little something in return. And don't ye worry about—well, ye know what I mean."

The door of Willow Cottage opened and Matt limped out. "Lord, Hilary, I'm glad to see you. I was beginning to worry—" He broke off, glancing at Sarah, hovering in the doorway behind him. Matt cleared his throat. "When you didn't return yesterday, I began to worry that your friend had taken a turn for the worse. How is, er, Tabitha?"

For a moment Hilary's mind went blank. Then she remembered she'd ostensibly traveled to Newcastle to comfort her imaginary friend, Tabitha, on her sickbed. "Tabitha is much improved in health," she assured Matt.

As they walked into the house together, Matt murmured, "I'm sorry. I almost gave the game away. I forgot that Sarah didn't know about your plans to help Nate Derwent to escape. I told her, as I told everyone else, that Nate had miraculously recovered his strength and disappeared from his bedchamber during the night." In a louder voice he added, "I'm agog to hear all about your journey, but first you must have a cup of tea and something to eat. You look exhausted."

A little later, as brother and sister sat opposite each

other at the dining-room table, Matt waited with visible impatience while Sarah served a simple meal. As soon as the maidservant left the room, he burst out, "Well? What happened? I've been nearly out of my mind with worry since the duke descended on me and guessed you'd spirited Nate derwent out of Wycombe. Did Alverly intercept you before you could reach the Tyne Valley?"

Hilary drained her teacup and set it down. Briefly she described how Jon had caught up with her and had then agreed to go with her to the mines. "My God," Matt exclaimed wonderingly as Hilary finished her tale. "I can't really comprehend it. Nate Derwent's a free man. And the duke has ordered his manager to reform conditions in his mines." Matt looked curiously at Hilary. "How did you do it? Belinda once suggested—remember?—that you were able to cast some sort of magic spell on Alverly to persuade him to change his opinion. But of course I don't believe in magic. So I repeat, Hilary. How did you do it? How did you succeed in taming the tiger once again and make him realize he's a human being as well as a duke?"

"I didn't really do anything," said Hilary slowly, "and you're not being fair, Matt." She thought back over the past three days, trying to separate her personal feelings from the events that had occurred. Then, experiencing a faint sense of shock that she was actually defending Jon, she went on, "Give the duke some credit. He may be narrow-minded, but I think he has a strong sense of justice. At my request, he agreed to look into Nate's account of the terrible conditions in the mines. As soon as he realized Nate hadn't exaggerated, he decided to correct the situation. It was as simple as that."

"You make Alverly sound like a paragon."

191

"No, he's not a paragon," said Hilary sharply. "Far from it. Sometimes I'd like to wring—" She cut herself off. After a moment she said, "No, he's not a paragon, but in this case he's done the right thing, and I think I should give him his due."

Matt looked at Hilary with the clear-eyed brotherly gaze that always made her uneasy. "Well, then, if Nate's free and Alverly's mine workers are going to have a better life, why don't you look happier? Hilary, did something happen to overset you on this journey? Something you aren't telling me about?"

Hilary put down her napkin and rose from the table. "Don't be silly. Nothing is wrong. I'm just tired. Today was a very long day. Good night, Matt."

He caught her arm as she passed by his side of the table. "I'm sorry, love. I know I shouldn't pry. But there is one thing: what about Ephraim? Will he talk? Oh, I know he'd already agreed to help you in Nate's escape and to keep the scheme a secret. I think he had a sneaking feeling of sympathy for Nate. But that was before Alverly entered the picture. Will Ephraim also keep secret the fact that you and Alverly spent two nights in each other's company?"

Hilary nodded. "I talked to Ephraim this morning. He feels a great loyalty to us, you know, for giving him the first secure job he's had for many years. He was aghast to think I might suspect him of gossip. In fact, he said, 'Ain't no reason why the folk in the valley should know anything aboot yer affairs, Miss Vane, nor the duke's neither.' Don't worry about Ephraim, Matt. I trust him completely."

* * *

As Hilary came down the stairs next morning, she stepped slowly, without the purposeful energy with which she usually began each day. She felt tired and sluggish, despite the fact that she'd slept soundly for many hours. She suspected that, beneath the surface of sleep, her unconscious mind had been busily active through the night, reviewing each moment of her romantic entanglement with Jon during the trip to the Midvale mines.

Listlessly she wandered into the drawing room and sat down, staring across the room without seeing her surroundings. Her lacerated nerves shrieked at her to condemn Jon for the emotional turmoil she was experiencing, but her sense of fairness wouldn't allow her to do that. Jon had a right to live his life as he saw fit. He hadn't tried to deceive her. He'd told her exactly what he wanted. He wanted to sleep with her. He didn't wish to be married. He'd accepted her decision not to become his mistress. She couldn't accuse him of coercion or false pretenses. So why, then, did she feel this aching void in her heart?

She realized suddenly that her eyes had been transfixed for an indefinite time on the Chinese porcelain vase Jon had sent to her on the day they'd discovered Nate Derwent's wounded body at the Devil's Cauldron. The vase occupied the place of honor on the mantel. Sarah had been dusting it with meticulous care since it arrived. Abruptly Hilary rose and removed the vase from the mantel. She walked into the hallway, where Sarah had begun her morning dusting.

"Find a piece of old blanket or a clean bit of rag and wrap this vase in it," Hilary told Sarah. "Then tell Ephraim to deliver it to the duke at the castle. After that he can take a message to my pupils' families that classes will start again tomorrow."

Leaving the puzzled Sarah to gape at her, Hilary went upstairs to her little office, feeling curiously liberated. It was almost as if, by returning Jon's priceless vase, she was severing any lingering ties of regret or disappointment that still connected her to him.

Feeling relaxed, almost lighthearted, she immersed herself in preparations for the following day's lessons. Several hours later she glanced up from her desk to find Sarah standing in the doorway, looking thoroughly bewildered. The maidservant clutched with both hands the Chinese porcelain vase, now filled with feathery ferns and a profusion of exotic orchids.

"One o' the duke's footmen just delivered this from the castle, ma'am," said Sarah nervously. "Where shall I put it? On the mantel in the drawing room like before?"

Hilary took a deep breath. "No, put the vase on my desk, Sarah. Thank you."

After the maidservant had left, Hilary sat staring grimly at the vase. Its brilliant beauty was almost obscured by the breathtaking loveliness of the fragile blooms it contained. She put out a gentle finger to stroke the silken cup of an Indian moth orchid. Damn Jon. He must have stripped his greenhouse of the gorgeous specimens he'd been cultivating lovingly for years. Why had he done it? Out of frustrated anger and an arrogant refusal to be bested? Or to remind her that he was still a force in her life and that he wouldn't allow her to ignore him? She shook her head. Whatever his reason, she couldn't allow him to shake her newfound sense of serenity. She'd enjoy the dazzling beauty of the magnificent orchids he'd sent her and try not to think about the donor.

Belinda arrived at Willow Cottage in midafternoon for her Greek lesson with Matt. She bounced into Hilary's office, exclaiming joyously, "I'm so glad to see you! Matt told me you were back." She pulled up a chair next to Hilary's desk and sat down. "But that's all Matt did tell me, just that you came home last night," she said reproachfully. "He wouldn't give me a scrap of real information." She lowered her voice to a conspiratorial pitch. "Hilary, I can put two and two together. Jon came home last night, too. You were both gone for three days, at the same time that Nate Derwent made his escape. There must be some connection. Please tell me about it."

Hilary shook her head. "If you're so sure a mystery is involved here, why don't you ask your brother about it?"

"I *did* ask him," exclaimed Belinda indignantly. "That is, I mentioned what a coincidence it was that you and he had left Wycombe at the same time. He was already in a foul mood, though, so he practically snapped my head off and refused to talk to me. And then he went off to the stables, still in a huff, and wouldn't let his groom take sufficient time to tighten his saddle girth properly. And *then*, would you believe it, he fell off his horse and twisted his ankle. Jon! He hasn't fallen of a horse since he was in leading strings!"

Well! thought Hilary. Something had obviously occurred to disrupt Jon's usual aloof, self-contained facade and throw him into a rage. She wondered if the arrival of the Chinese porcelain vase was responsible. She hoped it was.

195

Glancing at Hilary's desk, Belinda spotted the Chinese vase. Her eyes widened. "Those flowers look like Jon's prize collection of orchids."

"I believe they are. The duke sent the orchids this morning," said Hilary coolly. "It was kind of him, don't you think?"

"Oh, yes, very." Belinda gave Hilary a long speculative look. Clearly she would have liked to ask some questions about this interesting new development, but instead she returned to her original inquiry. "Hilary, I know you and Jon are hiding something from me. Were you two together during the time you were both gone from the valley? Was Nate with you? I didn't believe Matt for a moment when he said Nate had escaped from Willow Cottage in the dark of night. I knew how weak the man was. He couldn't have walked more than a few feet on his own. Won't you tell me what happened? I swear I won't repeat what you say to a living soul."

Hilary shrugged. What harm could it do, after all, to tell the duke's sister about Nate's escape? She gave Belinda an expurgated version of her journey to the Tyne Valley. "But mind, you must keep your word not to tell anyone about this," she warned as she finished. "I'm sure you don't wish to see your brother and me in the dock, accused of being accessories to a criminal's escape."

"I swear," Belinda repeated. Her gamin face glowed with delight. "Oh, I'm so happy you and Jon helped Nate to escape. I felt so sorry for the poor fellow. I never thought he should hang just for *planning* to kill Jon! Thank you so much for confiding in me." Belinda leaned from her chair to give Hilary a quick hug.

"Thanks especially for trusting me." She rose, picking up her riding whip. "I must get back. Mama will—" She interrupted herself. "Oh, Hilary, I almost forgot to tell you. My mother has come to visit us. My cousin Wilfred Rayner, too. He's Jon's heir, you know. It was such a surprise to see them. They arrived completely unexpectedly early yesterday evening."

A minor mystery solved, Hilary reflected. The occupants of the elegant berline that had followed her into Wycombe yesterday were Belinda's mother and the heir to the dukedom of Alverly.

"What a wonderful surprise for you, Belinda," Hilary remarked. "You and your mother must be having a grand reunion."

"Oh, of course. In a way, though, it's almost like meeting a stranger. Mama and I haven't seen each other since I was a tiny baby."

Hilary shot Belinda a searching glance. The girl sounded so casual, so matter-of-fact, with no hint of the poignancy one might expect after the first meeting of a mother and daughter separated for so many years. Remembering what the vicar's wife had told her about the Rayner family history, however, Hilary wasn't entirely surprised at Belinda's attitude. In all the time she'd known Belinda, the girl had never once mentioned her mother. Hilary had sometimes wondered if this silence sprang from Belinda's resentment at being left by her mother in the care of a much older brother almost from the moment of her birth.

"Mrs. Trevor once told me your mother lived on the Continent," Hilary remarked now. "Has she recently returned to England?"

"Yes. Her husband—well, her second husband, you

know, not my father—was a diplomat who served in many embassies abroad. He was the Earl of Lansdale. He was a very distinguished man, I believe. He died several months ago in Vienna, and Mama came home to England. After she'd recovered a little from her grief, she decided to come and see me and Jon. My cousin Wilfred kindly offered to escort her."

"How long will she stay?"

"Lord, I don't know. Some weeks, I expect. Hilary, you and Matt must come to the castle tomorrow to drink tea with us." Belinda giggled. "It will be another opportunity for me to show off my skills as a hostess!"

On the following afternoon, Hilary drove with her usual care up the rutted driveway leading to the castle gatehouse.

"Belinda doesn't seem particularly excited about her mother's arrival. Odd, don't you think?" Matt commented from his seat by Hilary's side.

"Not really. She simply doesn't know Lady Lansdale very well," Hilary replied absently. She was thinking ahead to the visit, and her attitude toward it was strongly ambivalent. On the one hand, she was curious to make the acquaintance of Belinda's long-absent mother. On the other hand, she dreaded meeting Jon so soon after their last uncomfortable encounter at the inn in Bewick-on-the-Bay.

Almost immediately after Hilary stepped from the vast courtyard of the castle into the family living quarters, she was conscious of a different atmosphere in the building. Perhaps it was her imagination, but she didn't think so. The servants seemed more alert, the very air seemed charged with a heightened electricity, as if the arrival of the newcomers at the castle had already

made changes in the living arrangements of the household.

As she entered the drawing room with Matt, Hilary
found her impression confirmed. The room no longer
seemed overly large and empty as it had on previous visits. Now it served as a fittingly ornate frame for the
larger-than-life presence of the Countess of Lansdale.

Hilary hadn't quite known what to expect of Elvira,
Lady Lansdale. Mrs. Trevor had described Belinda's
mother as a very beautiful woman, but the reality
made the description pale by comparison. Elvira was
an ethereally lovely creature with spun-gold hair, sparkling violet eyes, a flawless creamy complexion, and a
slender lissome figure, clad now in deepest mourning
black.

Belinda made the introductions with her newfound elegance of manner. "Mama, Cousin Wilfred, allow me to
present to you my good friends, Miss Hilary Vane and
Doctor Matthew Vane. My mother, Lady Lansdale, and
Mr. Wilfred Rayner."

"I'm delighted to meet you, Miss Vane, Dr. Vane.
Belinda has talked so much of you," said the countess
graciously. Even close up, Hilary couldn't detect the
faintest line or shadow in the lovely face. As a matter of
fact, Elvira appeared very little older than Belinda. But
then, Hilary reflected, Elvira was still a comparatively
young woman, some years short of forty. She'd given
birth to Belinda when she was still little more than a girl
herself.

Wilfred Rayner bowed with a consummate grace. "A
great pleasure," he murmured, with a thoroughly appreciative glance at Hilary. He was a tall, handsome man
in his late twenties, with dark hair and gray eyes. In fact,

199

he was a true Rayner, with a strong resemblance to both Jon and Belinda. But Hilary decided the resemblance was purely physical. With his exquisitely tailored clothes, fashionable coiffure, and smiling ease of manner, Wilfred was totally unlike Jon in every other respect.

Footmen appeared with heavily laden trays, and Belinda poured tea and offered refreshments to her guests with an ease and a grace of which she would have been incapable short weeks ago.

The countess, sitting beside Hilary on a settee, looked across at her daughter and said in a low voice, "Such a lovely girl, don't you agree, Miss Vane? Such charming manners. She must have had an excellent governess."

"Yes, I believe Miss Thompson was a fine person," Hilary replied, hoping that she wouldn't forget to repeat Elvira's remark to Belinda, who would, of course, go into gales of laughter, recalling the ineptitudes of her old governess.

"May I offer my condolences on your recent bereavement, Lady Lansdale?" Hilary said after a moment.

The countess touched a wisp of black lace to her eyes, though Hilary hadn't noticed a trace of tears. "Thank you, my dear," Elvira said with a brave smile. "It does seem hard to be widowed twice, but one must keep up one's spirits. At least Osbert—my second husband—and I had many years of happiness together. I have those memories to comfort me."

Elvira's violet eyes assumed a faraway look. "I had little to comfort me during my first widowhood," she mused. "I was so young, you see, barely nineteen, carrying my first child while my dear husband lay paralyzed, dying by inches, unable even to speak. And then when Belinda was born, mere days after her father died, I had to leave her here while I went on to London alone. My stepson preferred to keep Belinda here at Wycombe, and because he was now the head of the family, I had to agree. But as a result of my long separation from Belinda, I really lost my daughter. Would you believe it? This is the first time she and I have been together since shortly after she was born."

Elvira touched her eyes again with her black lace handkerchief. "It seems such a dreadful waste. What does one have in the end, after all, but one's family?"

Elvira's account of her first husband's last illness was very similar to Jon's version of his father's death as he'd related it to Hilary on the day of their excursion to the Devil's Cauldron. But while it had been evident that Jon's grief was still raw so many years later, Hilary wasn't impressed by the pathos in the countess's voice. Admittedly she was prejudiced, Hilary reflected, because of her affection for Belinda, but Elvira's comments sounded to her more like a ploy to gain her new acquaintance's sympathy than an expression of genuine sadness.

Lady Lansdale said with a pensive air, "I do have one consolation in my grief, Miss Vane. I've lost my dear Osbert, but now at last I have the opportunity to be reunited with my child. Belinda and I can be mother and daughter again."

"It must be a great comfort, both to you and Belinda," said Hilary politely. Privately, however, she questioned the genuineness of Elvira's maternal instincts. Surely at least once in the years since Belinda's birth, she might have made the effort to come to Northumberland to visit her little daughter. It was unlikely that the Earl of Lansdale had been posted to the Continent uninterruptedly for seventeen years, thereby depriving his wife of any opportunity to return to England.

"I'm so happy I could come to Wycombe, not just for my own sake but for Wilfred's," Elvira went on, glancing at the young man as he sat close by, deep in conversation with Belinda and Matt. "Wilfred is my stepson's heir, you know, and it's only right that he should see something of the estate he may inherit, especially since Jonathan apparently has no plans to marry." The countess added severely, "Actually I consider Jonathan quite thoughtless in neglecting to provide for the succession. Why, he must be all of thirty-five . . ." She frowned thoughtfully. "No, I believe he was sixteen when Belinda was born. He's thirty-three, well of an age to marry and sire a family, don't you agree?"

The countess couldn't know she'd hit a tender nerve. Hilary said calmly, "Come now, Lady Lansdale, you wouldn't wish me to speculate about the duke's matrimonial plans. He'd have no reason to confide in me."

"Oh. Well, of course." Elvira appeared mildly flustered. She looked up as Belinda erupted in a shriek of laughter. She said in a pained voice, "My dear child, what on earth—?"

Chuckling, Wilfred Rayner said, "She's laughing at my Greek pronunciation, Elvira. It seems Belinda is taking lessons in Classical Greek from Dr. Vane."

"Greek?" repeated the countess in a bewildered tone.

"Why, yes, Mama. I'm making excellent progress, too. Listen to this." Lifting her chin, Belinda dramatically recited a short passage in Greek.

"Belinda, those are the opening lines of the *Iliad*," exclaimed Hilary in surprise. "I had no idea you were doing so well in your studies. You've been hiding your light under a basket."

"Actually those are the only lines I know from the *Iliad*," confessed Belinda. "Matt is still drilling me on my Greek verbs. He says they're shaky."

"Well, no matter that your verbs are shaky, Belinda, you're still my favorite pupil," said Matt with a grin.

"But I don't understand, my dear child," said Elvira. "Why Greek? In my day it wasn't considered necessary for young ladies to study Classical Greek."

"Oh, but I'm studying other subjects, too, Mama. Hilary is teaching us French and literature and music and—oh yes, deportment." Belinda smiled saucily at her mother. "Didn't you notice how gracefully I poured the tea?"

"Did you say 'us'? Do you mean that you're attending Miss Vane's school?"

"Why, yes, Mama."

"But didn't you tell me that Miss Vane's pupils are all farmers' daughters from the estate?"

"Yes, Mama, and very nice girls they are, too."

Elvira frowned. "Really, Miss Vane, I cannot think it suitable for Belinda to be associating with the daughters of her brother's tenants. I wonder that my stepson allows it."

Leaping to Hilary's defense, Belinda declared indignantly, "On the contrary, Mama, Jon thinks Hilary's school is a splendid one!"

Elvira looked visibly ruffled at her daughter's remark, and Wilfred Rayner quickly intervened with a change of subject. He said to Belinda, "Tell me, how do you occupy your time when you're not attending school?"

"Oh, I ride a great deal, and I like to dance, that is, when I have the opportunity." Belinda turned to Hilary, her eyes sparkling. "I talked to Maria Grey today," she said excitedly. "Maria said you were considering taking

203

the class to the next Assembly Ball in Bridgeton. Please do, Hilary. We had such a lovely time at the last one."

The frown between Elvira's eyebrows grew deeper. "In my day, only farmers and merchants and their families attended the Bridgeton Assembly Balls." She broke off as Alverly entered the drawing room, walking with a distinct limp and supporting himself with a cane.

"So you've decided to honor us with your company, my dear Jonathan," said Elvira with a sugary smile. "I vow, I was beginning to think that Wilfred and I had offended you."

"Not at all," replied Alverly curtly. "However, should you give me any cause for offense, I'll inform you immediately."

The smile faded from Elvira's lips. Hilary winced inwardly. This was Jon at his very worst: cold, aloof, barely civil. She remembered what Mrs. Trevor had told her, that Jon had always disliked his stepmother intensely. Apparently the years hadn't softened his attitude.

Jon nodded to Wilfred and bowed to Hilary and Matt before easing himself rather gingerly into a chair.

Hilary couldn't resist saying with a show of solicitude, "I'm sorry to see you've injured your leg, Duke. How did it happen?"

They could almost read each other's minds by now. Jon shot her a look that told her he knew she was making secret fun of him. "I fell off a horse, thereby making myself the laughingstock of the countryside," he replied coolly. "I'm surprised Belinda hasn't told you about it. She tells you about everything that happens at the castle."

Hilary felt a stab of annoyance. His remark implied a degree of intimacy between them that she didn't wish to acknowledge publicly. Before she could stop herself, she retorted. "You're exaggerating, Jon. Belinda doesn't tell me *all* your secrets!" She knew immediately she'd made a mistake. Beside her, Lady Lansdale made a quick, involuntary movement. Elvira hadn't missed the interplay, it was clear, especially Hilary's use of Jon's Christian name.

Apparently unaware of any underground tension, Belinda giggled, saying, "Lord, Hilary, I don't *know* any of Jon's secrets."

"And a good thing, too. You talk too much," Jon said with a faint smile that belied the severity of his words. "If you're playing the lady of the manor today, Belinda, could you pour your brother a cup of tea?"

A few moments later, Wilfred Rayner remarked with the easy charm that Hilary was beginning to realize was an integral part of his personality, "I say, Miss Vane, Belinda makes your school sound so interesting that I'd rather like to enroll as a pupil myself. Do you accept adult males?"

Hilary laughed, shaking her head. Elvira, however, pounced on the subject. "My dear Jonathan," she began, "I daresay Miss Vane's school is excellent, but do you think it wise for Belinda to mingle so freely with the daughters of your tenants? Isn't it possible these girls might presume on their acquaintance with Belinda? There is such a thing as class distinctions, after all! However, far be it from me to interfere, and of course I'm quite aware that, as head of the family, you've assumed the position of Belinda's guardian . . ."

For a moment Hilary was puzzled by Elvira's use of the phrase, "assumed the position of Belinda's guardian." Of course Jon was Belinda's guardian. Then Hilary understood. Shortly after Belinda's conception, the

205

old duke had suffered a stroke which left him paralyzed and unable to speak. He'd been unable to provide for his unborn child. Jon, as heir and new head of the estate, had indeed "assumed" the post of Belinda's guardian without any written authorization in a will.

Jon drawled, "I'm glad you haven't forgotten, Elvira, that I am indeed Belinda's guardian. Her sole guardian. As such, I'm happy to entrust her to Miss Vane's excellent care." He put down his cup and turned to Hilary. "I have bad news for you, I fear. The assizes are being held in Wincanton early next week, and you and I have been summoned as witnesses in Bill Syncott's trial. I received my notice a few minutes ago. Doubtless you'll find your summons waiting for you when you arrive home."

"Syncott?" Hilary's forehead creased in a bewildered frown.

"We've been calling him simply Bill," Jon explained. "His surname is Syncott."

"The fellow who tried to kill you?" Matt inquired. "See here, Duke, why are they asking Hilary to testify?"

Jon shrugged. "She's the only witness, besides myself, of course, to Syncott's attempt to murder me. From Nate Derwent's confession to Hilary, we know Syncott killed Danny Wyse, but Nate has disappeared. Without his testimony, there's no proof that Syncott committed murder. Hilary and I are the only witnesses who can testify that Syncott attempted to commit a capital crime."

Observing the bewildered expressions on the faces of her mother and Wilfred Rayner, Belinda quickly explained about the plot of the three miners to kill Jon. "Hilary saved Jon's life," Belinda said proudly. "She glimpsed the murderer creeping up behind Jon and warned him."

206

"Good heavens," said Elvira, shuddering. "My dear Miss Vane, I assure you that violent events of this nature simply didn't occur while I was living in Wycombe." She flicked a faintly spiteful look at Jon. "In fact, I've been telling everyone for years that the most exciting thing that ever happened in the Wycombe Valley was the changing of the seasons!"

His face alive with interest, Wilfred said, "Belinda mentioned three plotters. What happened to the other two?"

"One's dead, another escaped," Jon replied. "The man who escaped is beyond our reach as a witness unfortunately. We think he probably succeeded in reaching Scotland." He exchanged a blandly innocent glance with Hilary. After a moment he said to her, "I'm sorry you've been called as a witness. It will be distressing for you. Naturally I'll be happy to escort you to Wincanton."

Before Hilary could reply, Elvira exclaimed, "Jon, you're not thinking of traveling alone with Miss Vane to Wincanton, I trust. You must think of her reputation."

"I have no intention of endangering Miss Vane's reputation by traveling with her unchaperoned," Jon told his stepmother. Hilary thought she detected the faintest tremor of sardonic amusement in his voice. He didn't look at her, but she had no doubt he was thinking of their two days and nights alone together during their journey to the Midvale mines. She wondered resentfully if Jon was going to continue this unnerving under-the-surface byplay, in which every word and every glance between them had an added meaning.

"I'm relieved to hear you're observing the conventions," Elvira said approvingly. "Who will you ask to be chaperon—" She paused, as if struck by a sudden idea.

"Jon, Miss Vane, I'll be most happy to offer my services."

For a moment Hilary panicked. Whether or not she was justified in her opinion, she already disliked Lady Lansdale. She had a sinking feeling at the thought of being in intimate contact with the woman for several days.

Jon forestalled his stepmother. "Elvira!" he exclaimed reproachfully. "What about Belinda? If you accompany Miss Vane, you'll leave Belinda at the castle in the company of an unmarried gentleman. Most improper, I'm sure you'll agree, even though Wilfred *is* a distant relative. We must think of Belinda's reputation, too."

As Elvira gaped at him in sheer surprise, Jon remarked to Hilary, "Perhaps you could ask Mrs. Trevor to accompany us."

"Oh, yes," agreed Hilary in relief. "I daresay she'd be happy to oblige us. She's always been most kind."

A little later, under cover of the general goodbyes, Jon maneuvered Hilary slightly apart from the others. "You'll speak to Mrs. Trevor, then?"

"Yes. I'll go and see her tomorrow." With a quick side glance, to make sure she couldn't be overheard, Hilary said in a low voice, "Why did you send back the Chinese vase filled with all those orchids? I've seen your greenhouse, remember. You must have decimated your orchid collection."

Jon's dark face was expressionless. "I can grow more orchids."

"But why, Jon? Why did you destroy the work of years in one meaningless gesture?"

The slate gray eyes blazed. "Meaningless? Gesture? What do you call what you did, Hilary? You sent back in a fit of childish pique the vase I'd given you. I don't allow my gifts to be returned. I wanted to make that clear to you."

"Hence the orchids."

"Yes," said the duke coldly. "Hence the orchids."

Chapter XII

Looking down the short village street through her drawing-room window, Hilary saw the Rayner carriage drive away from the vicarage with Jon riding beside it. She picked up her portmanteau and hurried into the hallway and out the door of Willow Cottage. Before she could reach the gate, Jon had trotted up in front of the house. He dismounted quickly and strode up the path to take the portmanteau from her.

"You're very prompt as I anticipated you'd be," he said pleasantly.

"Thank you, but I don't think I deserve any special credit. I fancy schoolmistresses are born with an ingrained sense of time," she replied, equally pleasantly. As she followed him to the carriage, where he handed her portmanteau to his coachman to place in the luggage basket and gave her his hand to help her up the steps, Hilary marveled at the peculiarities of human nature. Here she and Jon were exchanging impersonal civilities quite as if, a few short days ago, he hadn't been trying his determined best to seduce her. Mrs. Trevor was sitting with her abigail on the forward facing seat of the carriage, and Hilary sat down opposite them. Jon closed the door and remounted his horse. The coach lumbered slowly down the street.

"Well, Miss Vane, we're starting off on a real adventure," twittered the vicar's wife in a tone of mingled excitement and apprehension. "I declare, I can't remember the exact date of the last occasion when I traveled out of the valley. It was at least two years ago, that I know." She clutched at her abigail as the carriage plunged with a bone-shattering bounce into a large pothole. They were driving out of the village in the opposite direction from Bridgeton, but the road was equally bad.

"I'm so sorry to put you to such discomfort, Mrs. Trevor," said Hilary remorsefully. "I know you dislike traveling by carriage."

"Nonsense, my dear. It's not the carriage, it's the road. And I know quite well that as soon as we're over the mountain the road will improve. It's only in the Wycombe Valley that we take our lives in our hands when we enter a carriage! In any case, I couldn't allow you to accompany Jonathan—the duke—to the Wincanton assizes without a chaperon."

Flicking a glance at her silent abigail, Mrs. Trevor cleared her throat, saying, "Lady Lansdale called on me the other day. I was most pleased by the attention. I wasn't sure she would even remember me. She told me that she, too, had offered to chaperon you and Jonathan."

"Indeed she did. It was most kind of her," said Hilary insincerely. "But then the duke reminded her she'd be leaving Belinda without a chaperon. Because of Mr. Wilfred Rayner's presence, of course."

"Very proper, too." Giving her abigail another faintly

admonitory look, Mrs. Trevor said, "And what were your, er, impressions of Elvira?"

"Lady Lansdale is the most ravishingly beautiful creature I've ever met. Charming, too, and most gracious. And, all things considered, surprisingly uncondescending."

The vicar's wife nodded. "Elvira always had great charm." She fidgeted with the strings of her reticule. "Have you—ah—been much in Elvira's company when the duke was present?"

Hilary understood the question behind Mrs. Trevor's elliptical remark perfectly and was amused by it. The unexpected visit to the castle by Lady Lansdale and Wilfred Rayner was undoubtedly a chief topic of conversation throughout the entire Wycombe Valley, and the vicar's wife wasn't immune to the curiosity. At the same time, her breeding wouldn't allow her to gossip in front of a servant, so she'd taken a roundabout way of asking Hilary about Jon's relations with his stepmother.

Hilary had to disappoint her. "I've only met the countess once, Mrs. Trevor. The duke joined us for tea, but he was preoccupied by his summons to testify at the assizes. He had little to say to Lady Lansdale."

Looking somewhat dissatisfied, Mrs. Trevor soon had another topic to engage her attention. While the road had improved after they passed the summit of the mountain into the next valley, the weather had not. The overcast autumn sky had gradually darkened. Now a deafening crack of thunder ripped the air and a torrential rain began pouring down. Mrs. Trevor hastily lowered the glass. "Jonathan—Duke—stop the coach and come inside with us before you catch your death of cold," she called against the roar of the wind.

The carriage continued on for several minutes. Probably, thought Hilary wryly, the duke was pondering whether he'd weaken his masculine image by seeking shelter from the elements. Finally, however, the coach did stop. Through the slanting sheets of rain Hilary glimpsed Jon as he dismounted and tied his horse to the back of the carriage. He climbed into the coach to sit beside Hilary on the backward facing seat, splattering his fellow passengers with a flurry of raindrops as he removed his hat and managed to wrestle himself out of his sodden greatcoat in the restricted space.

"Sorry to drench you," he apologized, as he took out his handkerchief and mopped his face and neck. "The water's coming down in a deluge out there." He smiled at the vicar's wife. "I'm glad you insisted I come in out of the rain."

"Well, Jonathan—I mean Duke—I learned long ago that men must be coaxed into admitting they're poor fallible creatures like us females."

The duke laughed. "How long have you known me, Mrs. Trevor?"

"Why—ever since you were born. I came to your christening."

"And what were you used to call me?"

Mrs. Trevor looked confused. "You remember. I called you Jonathan, or plain Jon, when you were a child. Then, when you became duke . . ."

"When I inherited the dukedom, you suddenly started behaving very formally. It was 'Duke' this and 'Duke' that." Jon cocked his head at the vicar's wife, his eyes twinkling. "That is, unless you forgot to use my title, which was most of the time! So in the future, to save you the trouble of taxing your memory, I think you should always use my given name."

213

Mrs. Trevor's lips curved in a tremulous smile. "I will, Jonathan. And thank you. It brings back old times."

Hilary caught her breath. She would have found it impossible to believe, when she first met Jon, that he was capable of such a tender, considerate gesture to his vicar's wife.

Just then the carriage lurched around a curve and she was thrown against Jon on the seat. She felt the hard pressure of his thigh against hers, and immediately a familiar sensation of sensuality stirred within her. When she first met Jon, she would also have found it impossible to believe that a casual physical contact with him could arouse such intensely erotic feelings in her. She bit her lip. She and Jon had ended any romantic entanglement between them at their last meeting in Bewick-on-the-Bay. Why, then, did she feel like a wanton whenever he came near her? And would she be able to maintain her composure during the next few days when she and Jon would be in such close quarters at the assizes? She cast a quick sideways glance at him. His dark, expressionless face showed nothing of what he was thinking or feeling.

Mrs. Trevor's chatter brought her out of her brooding thoughts. "My dear Jonathan, I fear my memory isn't what it was," the vicar's wife was saying. "For the life of me, I can't remember exactly what Mr. Wilfred Rayner's relationship is to you. I know he can't be your first cousin. The late duke didn't have a brother."

Alverly frowned. "Let's see. The connection is quite distant . . . I have it. Wilfred is the son of my father's second cousin once removed."

"A distant connection indeed. Do you like Mr. Rayner, Jonathan? Or perhaps I'm being too inquisitive."

Jon shrugged. "I don't know him at all, actually. I believe we met when we were very young, though I don't remember the occasion. He seems a fine enough fellow. In any case, what I think of him doesn't matter. He's my heir. I can't change that."

"Your heir presumptive only, Jonathan," Mrs. Trevor reminded him with a smile. "Mr. Rayner will lose his standing when you have children of your own."

Hilary felt a sudden convulsive tightening of the muscles in Jon's arm. His voice, however, was calm as he said, "I hardly think Wilfred has anything to worry about. As you should know better than most people, Mrs. Trevor, man proposes, but God disposes."

"But . . ." The vicar's wife opened her mouth to speak, then thought better of it. But her expression remained vaguely troubled as if she sensed a glimmering of the truth that Hilary already knew, Jon's iron determination not to marry.

Peering out the window, Jon changed the subject by announcing, "The rain's slackening, and we're just coming into Branstead. That's the last stage before Wincanton."

Forty-five minutes later the rain had stopped completely, the sun had come out, and they had reached the end of their long four-hour journey. They drove into Wincanton, a town about twice the size of Bridgeton, its buildings clustered on the banks of a rushing little river in a valley of the rounded Cheviot Hills.

"Oh, look," exclaimed Mrs. Trevor. "Gypsies. They're holding a carnival of some sort." She added wistfully, "My word, I remember how I was used to enjoy carnivals and fairs when I was a young girl."

Glancing out the window at the gypsies in their gaudy costumes, Jon commented, "They'll probably do good business now that the weather has cleared. With the huge crowds of people attending the assizes, the population of the town must be double its normal size." He smiled suddenly. "Would you like to attend the carnival, Mrs. Trevor?"

"Oh, could we?" Mrs. Trevor's face fell. "But I wouldn't wish to impose. You and Miss Vane have come here on legal business."

"Nonsense. Miss Vane and I aren't scheduled to testify until tomorrow. It's still only a little past noon. We'll get settled in at the inn and have some lunch, and then we'll go to the carnival. You don't object, Miss Vane?"

"Not at all." Hilary squeezed Mrs. Trevor's hand. "Dear ma'am, you deserve some reward for making this long and uncomfortable journey for our sakes."

Wincanton was not only bigger than Bridgeton, it was much older. Originally it had been the site of a large and famous Cistercian Abbey, secularized during the Dissolution and now reduced to a group of ruins near the town center. The town itself had flourished, boasting a street of prosperous shops and several inns, all of them crowded, as it turned out, because of the influx of visitors into the town for the assizes.

Shortly after she walked with Jon and Mrs. Trevor into the hallway of the Crown and Rose Inn, Hilary witnessed again the power of the inborn authority that Jon projected so effortlessly despite his customary shabby appearance.

"I require three bedchambers," Jon told the proprietor of the Crown and Rose when that gentleman appeared after the party had been waiting for several minutes in the hallway.

"Impossible, sir, we're full up," said the landlord impatiently, beginning to turn away.

Without raising his voice, Jon continued, "I'd prefer that the rooms be to the rear of the building away from street noises. And of course I also require a private dining parlor for nuncheons and suppers."

As if an invisible hand had seized him by the throat, the landlord jerked to a stop. He turned, saying doubtfully, "Well, p'raps I could find ye something, sir . . ."

"I believe you might prefer to call me 'Your Grace,'" said Jon pleasantly. "I'm the Duke of Alverly."

"Oh. To be sure, Your Grace. If ye'll wait fer jist a few minutes, I'll have yer rooms ready, quicker'n the cat can lick behind its ears, I swear."

Dukes! thought Hilary in amusement. They conducted their affairs by standards different from those of other people. As he was making plans to visit Wincanton during the assizes, an ordinary citizen might have considered it prudent to reserve accommodations in advance.

Jon drained his wineglass and put down his napkin. "I'm at your disposal, ladies. Shall we go to the carnival?"

The landlord had kept his word. Three comfortable bedchambers—all to the rear of the building—had materialized in short order, as had the private dining parlor where the duke's party was finishing an excellent lunch.

As they emerged from the door of the inn, Jon with Hilary on one arm and Mrs. Trevor on the other, Hilary said pensively, "I keep wondering if the landlord evicted some of his previous tenants in order to accommodate us. He did say he had no vacant rooms."

Mrs. Trevor said, distressed, "Oh, surely not. I'd feel so guilty."

217

Jon flashed Hilary a look that told her he was remembering another inn and another landlord who *had* ousted guests from a private dining parlor. "I have no idea," he said coolly. "That's the landlord's problem, is it not?"

The streets of Wincanton were very crowded, much more so than usual, Hilary guessed, because of the great numbers of people attending the assizes. The pavements, too, were still somewhat muddy and slippery from the recent rains. She was glad to have the support of Jon's strong arm, especially since it soon became evident that many men among the lower elements in the crowd had been drinking heavily.

One burly individual, his breath reeking of gin, accosted Hilary, saying with a leering smile, "I kin pleasure ye better than that there swell ye're with, lass."

Instantly Jon detached his arm from Hilary's hand and planted his stick firmly against the drunkard's Adam's apple. "Move on, my man, unless you want this stick shoved all the way down your gullet."

"No harm meant, guv," said the man hastily, and wheeled away.

"Oh, dear. Perhaps we should return to the hotel," said Mrs. Trevor with a nervous glance around her.

"Now, don't tell me you don't trust me to take care of you," said Jon lightly, and the vicar's wife relaxed. But Hilary noticed that Jon kept a vigilant eye on any man who ventured near them.

The carnival was being held on a large cleared space within what had been the grounds of the old abbey. Jon pointed out to Hilary the one intact building remaining from monastic times. "That's the monks' refectory. The town uses it as the assize court. I fancy you'll see more of it than you care to before Bill Syncott's trial is over."

The carnival was a rather unprepossessing affair,

nothing like as elaborate as the large fairs at Peckham and Deptford that Hilary had occasionally attended in the London area. Among the attractions were booths selling cheap ornaments and toys, others offering games of chance, a Punch and Judy show and, most intriguing to the children in the crowd, a rather moth-eaten and sad-looking tame bear that performed a few simple tricks in exchange for coins.

Mrs. Trevor enjoyed it all with the uncritical enthusiasm of a child. She clapped her hands in glee at the antics of Punch and Judy, she watched the bear and laughingly tossed its keeper several coins, she bought a knot of ribbons for her abigail, she shook her head wonderingly at the little pony whose owner had taught it to "count."

When she lingered in front of a booth where frustrated marksmen were attempting to win prizes by throwing balls at a string of mechanical ducks, Jon said, half in jest, "Shall I try to win a prize for you, Mrs. Trevor?"

She laughed. "Well, I do think my cook's little boy would like that carved wooden horse."

Jon handed the proprietor of the booth several coins and hurled the small wooden ball at the line of painted ducks. He missed. He missed again. His third throw hit the mark. One of the ducks collapsed. He handed the crude carving to Mrs. Trevor. Tucking it into her reticule, she said, "Thank you, Jonathan. Little Jeremy will love the horse." She gave Jon a teasing smile. "Come now, I'm sure you don't mean to overlook Miss Vane. You must win a prize for her."

With an expert shot, Jon hit his second duck. "Well, Miss Vane? Which prize do you fancy?"

Hilary studied the prizes arranged behind the ducks.

They were a sorry lot. "What about the bracelet?" she said finally.

"A fine choice, lady," the proprietor of the booth assured her as he handed her the bracelet, composed of crudely fashioned metal links set with several chunks of glass.

As they moved away from the booth, Hilary examined the bracelet. She said, smiling, "I thank you for this unusual piece of jewelry, Duke, but if you don't object, I won't wear it. I fear my skin would turn green."

"A wise decision." Jon took the bracelet from her. "If I may?" Glancing about him, he spotted a small girl accompanied by her mother. Bowing to the woman, he bent down to the child's level, showing her the bracelet. "Would you care to have this, my dear?" The little girl nodded shyly, then reached for the gaudy bauble with wide-eyed pleasure.

"You should have been a diplomat, Duke," Hilary murmured. "Thank you." He tossed her a faint, amused smile.

"Tell yer fortune, lady?"

Mrs. Trevor gazed with a half-frightened fascination at the speaker, a gypsy woman in flowing skirts and a colorful bodice draped with ropes of beads.

The gypsy went on in a coaxing voice, "I kin read yer palm lady, or if ye like, I have a crystal ball in that tent over there."

Mrs. Trevor said in a flustered voice, "Oh, I don't think I should. I'm sure Octavius wouldn't approve. He'd say fortunetelling was rank superstition or even that it smacked of dealing with the devil."

Hearing the note of regret in Mrs. Trevor's voice, Hilary said laughingly, "The vicar isn't here to disapprove, and certainly neither the duke nor I will tattle on you! Do have your palm read. What's the harm? It's just funning, you know. Nobody really believes in it."

"Well . . ." Slowly Mrs. Trevor extended her hand. The gypsy examined it closely, then said with a beaming smile. "I see only good things, lady. Health and long life and happiness wi' yer man."

Her face glowing, the vicar's wife reached into her reticule for a coin and deposited it in the gypsy's rather grimy palm. She turned to Hilary, saying, "It's your turn, Miss Vane."

Shrugging, Hilary allowed the gypsy to take her hand. The reading took a little longer than Mrs. Trevor's had done and was even more favorable. Fixing her dark liquid eyes on Hilary, the gypsy said dramatically, "Ye have problems o' the heart now, lady, but ye mustn't despair. Soon ye'll have a great place in the world. I see ye as a princess, mayhap, or a—a duchess!"

Carefully avoiding Jon's eyes, Hilary paid the gypsy woman and turned to Mrs. Trevor, saying, "There, what did I tell you? This fortunetelling is all nonsense. Me, a princess! Did you ever hear the like?"

"Will ye no' let me read yer palm, too, Yer Honor?"

Jon shook his head at the gypsy. "No. I don't care to know the future," he told her curtly. He reached for his purse. "But here's something for your trouble."

Mrs. Trevor teased him. "La, Jonathan, you should have allowed the gypsy to read your palm. I'm sure she'd have told you that you'd be a king one day or even an emperor!"

She gasped as Jon wheeled abruptly and slammed his fist into the jaw of a man standing next to him, sending him crashing to the ground. "Fellow tried to pick my pocket," Jon explained. "I think we should go. This crowd is growing unruly. It's the drink, I expect."

At the inn, Mrs. Trevor excused herself from supper. "I'm a little tired. I'll ask my abigail to bring something to my bedchamber." She put her hand on the duke's arm. "Thank you, Jonathan, for a lovely afternoon. I hadn't been to a carnival for so many years. It brought back so many pleasant memories."

Standing with Jon in the hallway after the vicar's wife left them to go up the stairs, Hilary said, "That was kind of you, Jon. You gave Mrs. Trevor a great deal of pleasure."

"I'm fond of the lady," said the duke quietly.

A waiter approached. "Your dining parlor is ready, Your Grace."

Hilary said quickly, "Jon, I'd prefer to dine in the common room tonight."

Jon waved the waiter away. Giving Hilary an intent, not altogether friendly look, he said, "May I ask why you want to have supper in the common room? It will be crowded and noisy, and there could easily be unpleasantness. Virtually every male in Wincanton has been swilling beer or gin for most of the day."

Clearing her throat, Hilary replied, "I only thought . . . It might cause talk if we dined together in a private dining parlor in Mrs. Trevor's absence."

A muscle twitched in his jaw. He said in a hard voice, "If you're so concerned about dining unchaperoned, I believe I can satisfy your qualms. I'll tell the waiter to leave the door of the dining parlor open. I'll also request that a servant remain in the room at all times until the meal is over."

She met his angry gaze. Their minds were meshing again. He knew she was thinking about the private dining parlor at Midvale and what had almost happened there and that she didn't trust him to keep his distance.

"Thank you," she said stiffly. She turned to go to the private dining parlor just as a drunken guest entered the hallway and lurched against her. She would have fallen if Jon hadn't reached out a long arm to help her keep her balance. Jon then seized the man by his cravat and dragged him down the hallway to the door, where, with a final vigorous kick, he forced the volubly protesting culprit to leave the inn.

When Jon returned, apparently unperturbed by the episode, Hilary said, "When I'm wrong, I admit it. The common room of this inn is not the place for a lady to dine this evening. Thank you for insisting on the private parlor."

Chapter XIII

Shortly before ten o'clock the next morning, Hilary and Jon and Mrs. Trevor joined the throng of people entering the former refectory of the Cistercian monks. The building was well over a hundred feet long with a high vaulted ceiling and a long central aisle. It betrayed its monastic origins in the lovely rose window on its east wall and the perfectly preserved wall pulpit with its arcaded staircase. Now, however, the refectory was a hall of justice.

At the front of the hall were places for jurors, witnesses, turnkeys, solicitors, and prosecutors for the Crown. Behind this area were several rows of seats reserved for members of the local gentry who wished to observe the proceedings. Ordinary spectators filled the rest of the hall.

Jon and Hilary took their places in the seats reserved for witnesses, and Mrs. Trevor sat immediately behind them. Hilary was quite calm, even though she knew she would shortly be called upon to testify. She was, in fact, genuinely interested in learning about the trial procedure. She'd never attended a criminal trial before.

After a short delay, the clerk of the court hammered

down his gavel, and Mr. Justice Petrie, in red velvet and ermine and a rather marvelous wig, took his place as presiding judge.

Turnkeys led a group of prisoners into the dock. One of them turned his head to stare at the witnesses. Hilary felt chilled. She'd had only a brief look at Bill Syncott in the moments after Jon had foiled the man's attempt to kill him, but she remembered perfectly that long, narrow face, badly pitted with smallpox scars, and those malevolent slitted eyes. Obviously Syncott recognized her and Jon, also. He continued to stare at them until a turnkey roughly pushed him into line with the other prisoners.

Jury selection began. Hilary noticed that the men being considered for duty, without exception, appeared to be sober, respectable citizens of the town. After the jury selection was complete, the turnkeys removed the prisoners from the court and the day's proceedings began.

The first three cases were disposed of in short order. The offenses were all minor: petty theft, vagrancy, soliciting. The jury brought in quick verdicts, not even bothering to retire, and the judge pronounced equally quick sentences. Hilary winced as she watched a young woman being led away to be stripped and flogged publicly for prostitution.

The next case was very different. In "the Crown versus Samantha Pointer," the prisoner in the dock seemed little more than a child. She was fifteen, it developed later. She was a thin, pale girl with unkempt hair and soiled clothes, so apathetic that she appeared scarcely aware she was in the dock. As the clerk of arraigns droned out the indictment in a rapid, near unintelligible monotone, Hilary realized with horror that Samantha Pointer was being tried for murder.

A particularly distressing murder. Samantha Pointer had been a maidservant in the home of one Joseph Wade, a prominent Wincanton merchant. Led through her testimony by the prosecuting solicitor, she related that she had been seduced by her employer and had become impregnated by him. In order to conceal his philandering from his wife, Joseph Wade had forced Samantha to go to an abortionist and had then thrown the girl out on the streets without any means of support. Speaking in a flat, expressionless voice, Samantha admitted that she'd crept into her employer's bedchamber, as he lay sleeping beside his wife, and had hacked him to bits with an axe.

The jury pronounced Samantha guilty without retiring to consider their verdict, and the judge sentenced her to the gallows. At this point she suddenly emerged from the dull, uncaring apathy that had enveloped her while she testified. Jumping to her feet in the dock, she screamed at the judge, "My lord, ye can't let me be hanged. I saw a feller hanged oncet. The hangman, he didn't know his business, and the feller's neck wasn't broke when they sprung the trapdoor. He dangled at the end o' that rope, a-clawing at his neck, choking to death, it seemed like fer hours, afore he finally died. Please, ye can't let that happen ter me. Joe Wade, *he* should ha' swung on the gallows. He told me he loved me, and then he made me kill my baby and left me ter starve."

Collapsing in hysterics, Samantha Pointer had to be forcibly dragged from the dock, still screaming her terror-filled entreaties. Hilary felt almost physically flayed by this exhibition of visceral emotion. Trying to contain her feelings, she dug her fingers spasmodically into Jon's arm. Instantly his hand closed around hers in a warm, comforting grasp. "Steady," he murmured.

She looked at him gratefully, but his attention was already diverted. Releasing her hand, he vaulted over his seat to the row behind him, where Mrs. Trevor sat slumped in a dead faint. He lifted her into his arms and edged his way out of the row of spectators. Hilary did the same, following him out of the hall. By the time she reached the portico, Mrs. Trevor was on her feet, looking wan but in command of herself.

"I'm so sorry to cause you all this trouble, Jonathan," she began. "The fact is, I can't bear to witness any more of these—these sordid proceedings. I never realized before what Octavius meant when he spoke about 'man's fallen nature' in his sermons. I shall go back to the inn. You certainly won't need a chaperon during your testimony."

"We'll go with you," said Jon, eyeing Mrs. Trevor's pinched face with disquiet. "You're not well."

"Nonsense. Your case may be called next. I shall be quite all right. The inn is only a few steps from the hall."

Jon caught the attention of a turnkey who was about to enter the hall. Handing the man some coins, Jon said peremptorily, "Pray escort the lady to the Crown and Rose Inn."

Mrs. Trevor smiled at the duke. "That wasn't necessary, Jonathan, but thank you."

As he and Hilary walked back into the hall of justice, Jon said in a low voice, "Are you all right?"

"Yes." Hilary swallowed hard. "It's just that I wasn't prepared to hear about a fifteen-year-old axe murderess." She looked up at him, trying to smile, "After dealing with schoolgirls for so many years, I think I should be better prepared than Mrs. Trevor to cope with the manifestations of 'man's fallen nature.' "

The duke flashed her a quick grin of appreciation.

They arrived back in their seats in time to witness a rather dull case of assault and battery. Then, in late afternoon, it was Bill Syncott's opportunity to plead his case before the assizes.

Syncott practically swaggered into the dock. He showed no signs of fear or apprehension. He listened with a sneering half smile to the indictment read by the clerk of arraigns: ". . . William Syncott, of Midvale, of the County of Northumberland . . . feloniously, willfully, and with malice aforethought did attempt to murder Jonathan Rayner, Duke of Alverly . . ." After the clerk had finished reading the indictment, Syncott glared at the judge, the prosecutor, and Jon and Hilary with an impartial cold ferocity.

The prosecutor, Sir Roderick Dyson, presented his case with a calm certainty. He related how Syncott, with two fellow coal miners, Danny Wyse and Nate Derwent, had conspired to assassinate their employer, the Duke of Alverly, and how Syncott, when Derwent and Wyse had withdrawn from the scheme, had decided to carry out the murder on his own. The prosecutor called on Hilary and Jon to confirm his opening remarks.

"Miss Vane, I understand that during an excursion to a place of local interest called"—the prosecutor consulted his notes—"the Devil's Cauldron, you and the Duke of Alverly discovered two bodies, one alive, but wounded and unconscious, the other dead. At the time did you or the duke know the identity of either man or what their purpose had been in coming to the Devil's Cauldron?"

"No, we did not."

"I believe you and the duke then brought the wounded man to your brother's surgery in the village of Wycombe, where Dr. Vane succeeded in saving the man's life. You and your brother then cared for the patient in your own home."

"Yes."

Sir Roderick said respectfully, "May I say, Miss Vane, that you deserve great credit for acting with such Christian charity toward a man who, it later transpired, was a criminal."

"Thank you, sir, but my brother and I could hardly leave a wounded man uncared for."

The prosecutor gave Hilary another look of smiling admiration before continuing. "Now, then, on one occasion when you were attending on the wounded man as his nurse, he recovered consciousness and spoke to you. Will you tell the court what he said?"

"The man told me his name was Nate Derwent, that he and two other men who were, like him, employed in the Duke of Alverly's mines, had come to the Wycombe Valley with the intention of killing the duke. Nate Derwent and a second man, Danny Wyse, changed their minds about taking part in the murder, whereupon the third man, Bill Syncott, attacked them, killing Danny and injuring Nate Derwent. Nate Derwent told me he was positive Syncott wouldn't rest until he had killed the duke. At that point, even though it was late in the evening, I sent for the duke to warn him about his danger."

"Thank you, Miss Vane. That will be all for the present. Your Grace, please tell the court what happened when you answered Miss Vane's summons."

Jon rose to give a brief account of Syncott's attack on him at the front gate of Willow Cottage.

The prosecutor pointed to Syncott. "Is this the man who attempted to kill you?"

"He is."

"Jist a minute, *Yer Grace,*" called Syncott from the dock, with a surly emphasis on Jon's title. "Ye say I attacked ye. Did ye hear me threaten ye? Did ye receive one scratch during the time ye say I was trying ter kill ye? Wasn't *I* the feller who landed flat on his back wi' his chin almost broke?"

"When a man jumps at me from the rear with a knife in his hand, I think I'm justified in assuming he wants to injure me," snapped the duke. "Unfortunately for you, Syncott, you're a very inept murderer."

Turning a dull red, Syncott snarled, "If I'd really tried ter kill ye, and I ain't saying I did, mind, ye'd be a dead man, *Yer Grace.*" He turned his attention to Hilary. "Tell me this, missy: ye say Nate Derwent told ye I knifed him and killed Danny Wyse. Where's yer proof? Where's Nate Derwent? Why ain't he here ter testify agin me?"

Before Hilary could answer, Mr. Justice Petrie, peering at the prosecutor through the spectacles perched precariously on the end of his nose, remarked, "That's a good question, Sir Roderick. Where is this man Derwent? He should be in the dock with the prisoner. It would seem he's equally guilty of conspiring to kill the duke."

Sir Roderick looked at Hilary. "Miss Vane?"

She rose, clasping her hands closely together to hide her nervousness. "Nate Derwent escaped. My brother, Dr. Vane, considered the man was too weak to walk unaided more than a few feet, so we didn't keep a close watch on him. One morning the servants discovered his bed was empty." In one part of her mind, Hilary marveled at how easily one could conceal the actual facts

230

without telling a lie and breaking a sworn oath to testify truthfully.

Addressing the judge, the prosecutor said, "Under the circumstances, my lord, in the absence of this fellow Derwent, I believe Miss Vane's testimony is sufficient."

The judge nodded. "I understand. Pray proceed, Sir Roderick."

Smoothly, concisely, the prosecutor summed up the evidence against Syncott. Obviously he thought the Crown's case was conclusive. So did the jury. In less than five minutes they pronounced Syncott guilty of the murder of Danny Wyse and the attempted murder of the Duke of Alverly. The judge promptly sentenced the prisoner to the gallows.

But Bill Syncott didn't go meekly to his fate. Jumping up in the dock, he shook his fist, shouting, "Ye call this justice? Ye've convicted me o' murder wi'out a speck o' real evidence, jist on the word o' that lying devil, the Duke o' Alverly, and his doxy." He pointed at Jon. *"There's"* the one who ought ter go ter the nubbing cheat. He's a murderer scores o' times over. Fer years, he's been sending men and women and chilern ter their deaths in those mines o' his, and nobody ter say him nay."

Syncott glared at Jon with a look of such venomous hatred that Hilary shuddered. "When I swing on the gallows, Yer Grace, wi' every last breath I take, I'll be asking the devil ter roast ye in the hottest fires o' hell fer all eternity."

Alverly stared back at Syncott without a shade of expression on his impassive face.

The judge said sharply, "That's quite enough, prisoner. Turnkey, take him away."

Another trial was to follow Syncott's, but for Hilary

and Jon the day was over. With a vast feeling of relief, Hilary walked with the duke out of the hall of justice and into the crisp air of the late October afternoon.

"You're a little pale," said Alverly with a searching look. "Are you feeling ill?"

"No," said Hilary, breathing deeply. "It's just that it was so stuffy in the hall." But as they walked the short distance to the inn she burst out, "Jon, I've never seen such pure hate on a man's face before. Given the slightest opportunity, Syncott would kill you with no more compunction than he'd swat a fly."

Shrugging, Jon said, "I daresay you're right. But the point is moot. Syncott isn't a factor in our lives anymore. He'll soon be dangling at the end of a rope."

At the inn they found Mrs. Trevor fully recovered. "I had a nice long nap," she announced happily as she sat down with her companions in the private dining parlor for supper. "Then I drank a huge pot of tea and ate some perfectly delicious biscuits. I must have my abigail get the recipe from the kitchen." She glanced from Jon to Hilary. "Is the trial over? Must you give any more testimony?"

"Yes, the trial is over, thank God," Jon replied. "Syncott was convicted of murder and attempted murder. He'll hang shortly."

Hilary shivered. "Hanging is such a dreadful way to die. I keep thinking of what that girl Samantha Pointer said about watching a man slowly choke to death on the gallows . . ."

Mrs. Trevor interrupted her. "I don't wish to be rude, my dear," she said with an uncharacteristic firmness, "but I must ask you not to speak of such things. I'm afraid I'll become ill if I hear one more word about trials and criminals and hangings."

"I'm sorry, Mrs. Trevor. Of course we'll talk of something else," Hilary replied quietly. Jon shot her a swift, questioning look but said nothing.

The rest of the meal was subdued and almost silent. The only conversation concerned preparations for their journey back to Wycombe on the following day. The two women retired to their bedchambers after drinking their coffee, leaving Jon to his solitary glass of port.

Hilary was too restless to prepare for bed. Scenes from Samantha Pointer's trial, and Bill Syncott's, also, kept revolving in her mind. She tried to read, but she couldn't concentrate. Finally she squared her shoulders and left her bedchamber to walk a short distance down the hallway to Jon's door.

He answered her knock immediately. "Hilary! What—?" He glanced up and down the corridor, which was empty. "You'd best come in before someone sees you." As he closed the door behind them she noticed for the first time that he was only half dressed, in shirt and breeches and without boots.

"What is it, Hilary?"

She said in a rush, "I can't stop thinking about that girl Samantha Pointer and how she'll suffer on the gallows. Jon, she must have been half out of her mind when she murdered the man who betrayed her. Even Bill Syncott couldn't have been quite rational when he committed his crimes. He was in a blind rage when he killed Danny Wyse and when he tried to kill you."

He was looking at her intently, his face puzzled. "Hilary, you're trying to tell me something, but I don't understand what it is."

Trying to formulate her thoughts, she spoke slowly and haltingly. "Until today, I never thought about what happened to criminals after they were convicted. Now I know something of what it's like to die on the gallows, and I can't believe anyone deserves a horrible death like that. Jon, can't you go to the judge and ask him to commute Samantha Pointer's sentence, at least, and maybe Bill Syncott's as well? Perhaps the judge could order them both transported to Australia for life."

Jon stared at her incredulously. "Good God, have you gone queer in your attic?" he asked roughly.

Hilary clenched her hands together in an attempt to control her feelings. In a shaking voice, she said, "I was only asking you to show a little compassion."

Jon's expression changed. Taking a step forward, he placed his hands on her shoulders. "I'm sorry I snapped at you," he said gently. "You were really affected by Samantha Pointer's trial, weren't you? You found it hard to believe she actually hacked a man to bits with an axe, but that's what she did, you know. She's a murderess, just as Bill Syncott is a murderer. They both got fair trials, and in my opinion they got fair sentences. In any case, even if I wanted to, and I admit that I don't, I couldn't persuade the judge to change his sentence. You must see that."

Hilary drew a deep breath. "Yes, I do see it," she said after a long painful pause. "Samantha *is* a murderess. I simply couldn't bear the thought of a fifteen-year-old girl—a *fifteen-year-old*, Jon—going to the gallows. But I shouldn't have asked you to intercede with the judge."

Jon's hands tightened on her shoulders. "I wish I could say yes to all your requests," he said huskily.

The gray eyes kindled, and an answering spark ignited in Hilary's heart. It would have been so easy to succumb to the powerful lure of Jon's masculinity, and it was so hard to resist. She twisted away from him as he slowly bent his head toward her mouth. "I thought we

234

understood each other," she said breathlessly. "I told you at that inn in Bewick-on-the-Bay that I don't wish to become your mistress, and you apparently accepted my decision."

"Oh, I've accepted it," he said savagely, "but that doesn't mean I've stopped wanting you. You're a fire in my blood. When I see you or come near you, I can scarcely keep my hands away from you. When I touch you, my heart pounds and my entire body is aware of you in every fiber of my being . . ." He broke off, his mouth working. "Don't worry," he said into the hard-breathing silence. "I'll manage to keep my impulses under control."

Hilary met his angry, desolate eyes without answering him, and started for the door.

"Wait," he said, and thrust a velvet-covered box into her hand. "I bought this for you. You may as well have it. I've no use for it."

She looked at him without speaking and then walked slowly from the room. Inside her bedchamber, she sank into a chair, where, after a dazed moment, she opened the velvet-covered box with clumsy fingers. The magnificent gold bracelet, set with large diamonds, bore only the remotest resemblance to the clumsily fashioned trinket that the duke had won for her at the gypsy carnival, but she immediately understood its significance. For some obscure reason, Jon had decided to replace the crude, cheap bauble with the real thing.

She closed the box and put it down. Shivering, she folded her arms closely across her chest as if to protect herself from the frightening truth she'd just discovered.

Now she knew why she'd tried so hard to deny, and then to resist, the physical attraction that existed between her and Jon. He knew it for what it was: a consuming lust that wouldn't be satisfied until he'd finally succeeded in possessing her body. She could no longer deceive herself. What she felt for Jon was sensual desire, yes, but it was more than that. Slowly, insidiously, without her knowledge or volition, she'd fallen in love with her border lord.

Now she must guard every thought, every word, whenever she was with him. She was sure that if he ever found out she loved him he could destroy her.

Chapter XIV

Hilary hung her dressing gown in the wardrobe and was about to close the door when her eye fell on the velvet-covered box on the top shelf. She stared at it for a moment, and then reluctantly, as if drawn by a magnet, she removed the box and opened it. The diamonds winked up at her from the golden links of the bracelet.

Why had Jon given it to her? He surely couldn't have expected that the exquisite gift would persuade her to change her mind about sleeping with him. Nor could he have seriously believed she would consent to keep the bracelet. Hilary sighed as she closed the box and put it back on the shelf.

There'd been no opportunity to return the beautiful glittering thing to Jon on the return journey from the Wincanton assizes without unleashing Mrs. Trevor's curiosity. Nor, during the two days she'd been home in Wycombe, had she considered it wise to send the bracelet to Jon by a servant's hand. At the castle the slightest mischance—a glimpse of the bracelet by a servant or a member of the family, for example—might reveal that the Duke of Alverly had been presenting valuable jewelry to the village schoolmistress. No, her only recourse was to return the bracelet in person to the duke.

Hilary hurried down the stairs. The time she'd wasted on brooding over the bracelet had made her late for breakfast. In the dining room she found Matt finishing his kidneys and bacon. As she entered the room he looked up with a teasing grin, saying, "Sleepyhead! You got out of the habit of early rising on your trip to Wincanton."

"I'm ten minutes later than usual, which hardly makes me a sybarite, my good doctor," she retorted, pouring herself a cup of tea.

He laughed and extended his cup for a refill. "I missed you while you were gone," he said after a moment. He added wistfully, "You've been away a good bit of late."

She smiled at him. "I don't see any more trips in my future. You and I will grow old gracefully together in Willow Cottage."

Sarah appeared in the doorway. "His Grace is here ter see ye, ma'am. I told him ye was at breakfast, and he said he'd come back later, but I thought as how ye'd prob'ly wish ter see him."

Recovering from her initial surprise, Hilary said hastily, "You were right, Sarah. Of course I'll see the duke."

She hurried to the drawing room, where Jon stood before the fireplace, absently slapping at his boots with his riding whip. He was carelessly dressed as usual, in worn leather breeches and a shabby coat. Hilary noticed that his dark curling hair had grown too long again. What on earth was Jon paying his valet for?

"I'm sorry to disturb you so early," he apologized. "Your maid said you were at breakfast."

His aloof face and clipped voice betrayed no trace of

the passionate lover who'd cried out to her so recently at the inn in Wincanton: "... I want you ... you're a fire in my blood ... when I'm near you I can scarcely keep my hands from you ..."

Hilary realized that her fingernails were digging into her palms, but she managed to say calmly, "You're not inconveniencing me. What did you wish to see me about?"

"I came to tell you I've found a new pupil for your school."

"You *what?*"

Ignoring her look of astonishment, Alverly replied, "Jane Earnshaw will be your new pupil. I talked to her father yesterday. He said you'd contacted him about your school when you first arrived in the valley, and he and his daughter were interested, but—"

"But he couldn't afford the fees," Hilary finished. "I told Mr. Earnshaw he could pay the fees over a long period of time, as he felt able to do so, but he refused. He's a man of great pride, I think."

"Yes, he is. I told him he was too stiff-necked. I came to an arrangement with him. You'll send Jane Earnshaw's school account to me, and Earnshaw will repay me. You needn't even discuss the matter with him."

Drawing a deep breath, Hilary asked, "Jon, I don't understand why you've done this. You fought me tooth and nail over my school in the beginning—"

He interrupted her. "I may be stubborn, as you've so often pointed out, but I'm not stupid. I thought you knew that I've long since recognized the value of your academy. I'd like to see all my tenants send their daughters to you." He paused, clearing his throat and looking uncomfortable. "I have something else to say to you."

239

"Yes?" Hilary was in a daze. Would she ever be able to understand this bewildering, infuriating man?

"I want to apologize." He smiled ruefully. "I know, it must seem to you that I've done little but apologize to you since we first met. At any rate, I want to say that I embarrassed you by what I said to you that last night in my bedchamber at the inn in Wincanton. I should have kept my thoughts and my feelings to myself."

In control of herself now, Hilary gave him a calm look. "I think we both made remarks on that occasion that we'd rather not recall. Shall we mutually agree to forget?"

"Yes. Thank you." He hesitated, looking at her under drawn brows. "I'll be honest. I don't regret the feelings I have for you, only that I expressed myself so crudely." Moving toward the door, he said, "Goodbye, Hilary. Again, I regret calling on you today so early."

Hilary bit her lip. The man was incorrigible. Well, she wasn't going to allow him to have the last word in everything. She called, "Jon, wait."

He paused, looking at her inquiringly.

"It's the bracelet, Jon. You know I can't accept it. If you'll wait for a moment, I'll go upstairs to get it."

"Don't bother," he said flatly. "Give it away, throw it in the fire. Do anything you like with it. I won't take it."

"Throw it away?" she gasped. "That beautiful thing?"

"Do you remember what I told you when you tried to give back the Chinese porcelain?" He glanced at the glowingly beautiful vase in its place of honor on the mantelpiece. "I said then that when I gave a gift it was irrevocable. I still mean that. Goodbye, Hilary."

She remained in the middle of the room, staring numbly at the door for several moments after he left. Then, shaking her head, she went upstairs to her office.

Her pupils would be arriving soon. She had to shut Jon out of her thoughts, prevent his disturbing influence from encroaching into her professional life. At the least, she thought with satisfaction, she'd been able to keep to her resolution to conceal from Jon her newly discovered love for him. On the whole, considering his latest disconcerting action in obtaining a new pupil for her, she'd kept her composure very well.

But what on earth was she to do with a valuable diamond bracelet she couldn't wear without raising eyebrows or worse? Continue to keep it safely hidden away, she thought glumly. Damn Jon. He was developing a genius for throwing her off balance. Which may have been why he'd given her the bracelet in the first place, of course.

As she sat in her office turning the pages of a French grammar book, she heard the sound of running footsteps in the hallway. Belinda burst into the room. She was much more suitably dressed than she used to be, before Hilary had helped her to select a new wardrobe, but she showed signs of having pulled on her clothes with her brother's careless inattention to grooming.

"Well! I'm flattered," said Hilary with a smile. "Here I was gone only a few days and you missed me so much you can't wait to start classes. Or is it something else that brings you here so early?"

Belinda grinned at her. "Oh, I missed you, of course, but I came early to give you some news before the other girls arrived. Hilary! I have a suitor!"

Hilary stared. "A suitor? Who?"

Obviously enjoying Hilary's surprise, Belinda declared dramatically, "Wilfred Rayner, that's who! Last night he asked Jon for my hand."

"Good heavens. This is so—so sudden. You and Mr.

Rayner have known each other for such a short time. No more than three weeks, if I remember correctly."

"Oh, well, it wouldn't have made any difference if I'd known Wilfred for months or years. Jon refused his offer."

"I'm glad," Hilary exclaimed impulsively. "I shouldn't like to see you betrothed to someone you've known for only a few weeks. Of course, if Mr. Rayner were to wait a suitable interval before renewing his addresses, that would be a different matter entirely. You and he would know each other much better by then."

"Well, Wilfred tells me he still wants to marry me and has every intention of pressing his suit, but I don't think he realizes yet that Jon always means what he says. Jon informed Wilfred that the match was totally unsuitable and that he wouldn't consider giving his consent under any circumstances."

"Oh," said Hilary blankly. The remark sounded like Jon at his most inflexible. She looked closely a Belinda. "Are you disappointed?"

Belinda giggled. "Lord, no. I don't wish to marry Wilfred. I'm grateful to Jon for saving me the embarrassment of refusing him."

"You don't like Mr. Rayner?"

"Oh, yes, I like him well enough. In fact, I'm enjoying his company. He's a bruising rider, you know. While you and Jon were in Wincanton, Wilfred and I had some glorious gallops. He plays a good game of draughts, too. And he has a fine singing voice. I've actually accompanied him on the pianoforte."

"Well, then?"

"Well, what? I may enjoy his company, Hilary, but I certainly can't see myself spending the rest of my life with Wilfred Rayner!"

Before Hilary could say any more, the other pupils began trailing in. As she conducted her classes, however, Hilary had to make a real effort to keep her mind from wandering off to the latest Rayner family puzzle. She'd have expected Belinda to be more excited about her first offer of marriage. Not only excited, but intrigued, perhaps half inclined to accept the proposal of this handsome, charming young man with his polished manners and the aura of a hundred fashionable London drawing rooms.

And Jon. Why was he so adamantly opposed to the marriage of his only sister and his heir? To most people, the match would seem to have everything to commend it. If Jon never married, Belinda would become the next Duchess of Alverly, and the two branches of the family would be reunited.

After the day's classes were over, Belinda departed with her customary flurry of energy to have luncheon with her mother and Wilfred at the castle, and the other girls trailed out to the stable to mount their ponies for their return to their homes. Maria Grey lingered behind.

"Can I help you, Maria?"

The girl's pretty plump face was troubled. "Could I talk to you for a few minutes, Miss Vane?"

"Of course. Is something wrong?"

"No. Yes. Do you remember I talked to you about the possibility of becoming a teacher like you? Well, the other day I mentioned the idea to Mama, just to see how she would react to it, you know."

"What did she say?"

"She was furious to think that I would even consider becoming a schoolmistress."

243

"I see," said Hilary slowly. "Your mother's mind is still set on you marrying your cousin in Bristol?"

"Yes, My cousin Alfred. Mama is convinced that when I go to Bristol next spring to visit my cousins, Alfred will fall in love with me and propose to me. Apparently Alfred's parents have hinted to Mama that they wouldn't be averse to the match."

"Maria, have you actually told your mother that you don't wish to be married at this time?"

The girl's expression became even more troubled. "I tried to tell her the other day. I was afraid she'd have a heart spasm. You see, the problem is that Mama thinks marriage will keep me safe. She worries that I'll go bad like my sister Jane."

"I didn't realize you had a sister named Jane."

"We never speak of her. Jane ran off with a discharged soldier she met in Bridgeton. He never married her, and she died in childbirth. That was five years ago, but to Mama and Papa it's as if it were yesterday."

"I'm sorry. Maria, if you think it would help, I'd be happy to talk to your parents about my work. Perhaps I could persuade them that teaching is a very respectable profession."

"Thank you, Miss Vane. I don't think it would help actually. Mama and Papa wouldn't really listen to you. It has helped me so much to talk to you, however. I feel ever so much better." Shyly Maria gave Hilary a brief hug and slipped from the room. Watching her go, Hilary felt torn between concern for Maria and frustration over her inability to help her.

At luncheon Hilary sat for so long before her untouched plate that Matt inquired, "Feeling peckish, love?"

"What? Oh, no. The steak and kidney pie smells delicious. No, I was just thinking about the unexpected turns life can take."

"My word, Hilary, you're waxing philosophical today."

"No, really, think about it. Don't you remember when we first came here, how we regarded Wycombe as a dull, sleepy little place where nothing was ever likely to happen? And now—!"

Matt laughed. "Oh, you mean all the excitement about the attempt to murder the duke and your trip to Wincanton to testify at the assizes and even Lady Lansdale's visit to the castle. Yes, I'd have to admit that Wycombe is livelier than I would ever have thought possible a month ago."

And Matt didn't know the half of it, Hilary mused as she popped a bit of steak into her mouth. She couldn't tell him about Wilfred Rayner's proposal to Belinda or Maria Grey's struggle with her mother over her desire to become a schoolmistress because both girls had talked to her in confidence. And how would Matt react if he had even an inkling of the passionate secret byplay between his sister and the Duke of Alverly?

After luncheon Hilary went back to her office to choose music for the next day's dancing class. Absorbed in her task, she jumped at the sound of a strange voice.

"I beg your pardon, Miss Vane," said Wilfred Rayner, strolling into the room. "I didn't mean to startle you. Your maidservant wanted to announce me, but I told her I could find my own way up here."

Again Hilary noticed the family resemblance between Wilfred's dark handsome features and Jon's, but the contrast between Rayner's turnout—superbly tailored coat, skintight breeches, highly polished boots—and Jon's usually slapdash appearance was almost ludicrous.

"I thought I'd like to have a look at your establishment since Belinda talks of you constantly," said Wilfred, gazing about Hilary's office. "Could you give me a short tour?"

Hilary smiled. "I'd be happy to do so, Mr. Rayner, but there's very little to see. My girls are the school, not the rooms. I fear you'll consider your visit here a waste of time."

"I'm sure I'll do no such thing. In any case, Elvira and I came here primarily to see you and your brother."

"Lady Lansdale is here? Oh, I mustn't keep her waiting."

"No need to hurry. Dr. Vane and Belinda are entertaining her. And you still haven't given me that guided tour."

A little later, having inspected the classroom with its slateboard and desk and neat circle of chairs, Wilfred stood at the pianoforte in the large bare room that Hilary used for her dancing lessons. He idly picked out a simple tune with one hand. Looking up, he said, "You and Belinda have become very close, I believe."

"Yes. We're fond of each other."

He hesitated. "I'll be frank with you, Miss Vane. I've fallen in love with Belinda. I want to marry her. Unfortunately, to date she appears to regard me only as a friend. You know her so well. Could you tell me if she has any other, er, heart interest? I confess it seems unlikely. This is such an isolated community. I haven't met any members of the gentry since I arrived here."

Hilary gave him a level look. "I'm afraid I can't help you. I don't know anything about Belinda's possible 'heart interests.' Nor, quite frankly, would I tell you if I did!"

Wilfred smiled, apparently taking no offense. "No, of

course you wouldn't. I know you're a loyal friend." He glanced out the window at the vista of hills rising into the distance from the valley floor. "The longer I stay here, the more I realize what a lonely place the Wycombe Valley is." Looking back at her, he said, "Much as you enjoy your work here, I fancy you must feel rather cut off from civilization at times. Do you ever visit London? Do call on me if you should come. I'd be delighted to take you to the Opera or to a showing at Somerset House."

"Thank you. That's very kind of you. I'll certainly keep your offer in mind. And now I wouldn't wish to be remiss in my attentions to Lady Lansdale. Shall we go to her?"

As she walked down the stairs with Wilfred Rayner, Hilary fought to keep her temper. She was beginning to dislike Mr. Rayner intensely. She was sure she hadn't mistaken his intentions. The flirtatious invitation in the man's voice had been veiled but very real. Somehow, Rayner's polite, guarded overtures infuriated her more than Jon's bold, open attempts to seduce her had ever done. At least Jon made no bones about what he wanted! And she hated hypocrisy. Wilfred was so transparent. He had no interest in her school. He'd come to visit her classrooms to pick her brain. Piqued because Belinda apparently had no romantic interest in him, Wilfred had taken this underhanded approach to Hilary in order to find out if he had an unknown rival for Belinda's hand.

Lady Lansdale sat in almost regal splendor in the most comfortable armchair in the drawing room. "Good day, Miss Vane. I thought it was time, and more than time, to return your call," she said graciously.

Rising, Matt said, "If you'll excuse us, Lady Lansdale, it's time for Belinda's Greek lesson."

Wilfred smiled, saying. "Can I help? No, don't laugh, Belinda. I won the Greek prize my last year at Eton, I'll have you know."

Matt was firm, "Thank you, Mr. Rayner. Belinda and I do very well by ourselves. Come along, my girl."

As she watched them leave, Elvira shook her head, saying, "I vow, I simply cannot understand that child's interest in ancient Greek."

"Perhaps it's not the subject, but the teacher," Wilfred observed. His tone was light, but Hilary thought she detected a faintly resentful undercurrent.

Hilary laughed. "That's probably true, Mr. Rayner. I think Belinda rather hero-worships Matt. He not only saved her life, you know, he cured her dog!"

"Saved Belinda's life?" Elvira exclaimed. "Whatever do you mean?"

While Hilary was explaining to Elvira about Belinda's riding accident and resulting severe concussion, Wilfred appeared to listen with only half his attention. At one point, he got up to examine closely the Chinese porcelain on the mantel. "I say, Elvira," he remarked, "this vase looks just like those Chinese things that Jonathan dotes on."

"So it does," said Lady Lansdale thoughtfully. "Perhaps the vase is a family heirloom, Miss Vane?"

"No, not at all. It was a gift." There, thought Hilary defiantly, make what you like of that!

After a few more minutes, in which he joined only desultorily in the conversation, Wilfred rose, saying, "I know you ladies will have a much more comfortable coze without me. I'll be off. Miss Vane, please tell

Belinda I'll return after her Greek lesson to go riding with her."

After he had gone, Elvira remarked, "Wilfred and Belinda enjoy riding together so much. They make such a charming pair. In fact, they would make a very charming *permanent* pair, in my opinion. Imagine! Belinda the next Duchess of Alverly!"

Hilary pretended to be puzzled. "Belinda a duchess? The Duchess of Alverly? Dear Lady Lansdale, how——?"

Elvira lowered her voice, looking around as if to make sure no eavesdroppers were present. "You sound surprised. You'll be even more surprised, then, to learn that last night Wilfred asked my stepson for Belinda's hand. Jonathan refused."

Hilary assumed an innocent look. "Poor Mr. Rayner," she said with an air of sympathy. "I thought he looked a trifle blue-deviled today. I daresay the duke considered Belinda too young to be betrothed? Or possibly that she and Mr. Rayner had known each other for too short a time?"

"If those were Jonathan's reasons, he didn't mention them," declared Elvira indignantly. "He simply said the match was unsuitable. Unsuitable! A marriage between *my* daughter and *his* heir! No, Miss Vane. My stepson is simply acting in character. From the time I first knew him, Jonathan has been a surly, selfish, unfriendly person, caring for nobody except himself. Why, I'm convinced he spends more time in that outlandish conservatory of his than he does with his own sister! As a matter of fact, I believe you've had personal experience with his bad temper and selfishness. Belinda's told me Jonathan was opposed to your school at first, going to the lengths of urging his tenants not to send their daughters here."

249

Hilary was astounded to hear Elvira's denunciation of Jon. Of course, it was evident to anyone with half an eye that Jon disliked Elvira and that she resented his cavalier treatment of her. But surely a sophisticated woman like Elvira must realize how impolitic it was to criticize her stepson to a stranger?

"Whatever the duke may have thought originally, he's now very supportive of my academy," said Hilary hastily. "And forgive me for saying so, but I hardly think we should be discussing him in this fashion."

"My dear, I'm so sorry. I wasn't thinking. I see I'm putting you in an awkward position. You and your brother are dependent on my stepson for your positions here in Wycombe. Although . . ." She shot Hilary an oddly speculative look. "Belinda's also told me you've occasionally been able to persuade Jonathan to change his opinion. But I really couldn't ask you to . . ." Elvira's voice trailed away.

An idea had begun to form in Hilary's mind. She waited for Lady Lansdale's next remarks.

"You're quite right, Miss Vane, I shouldn't be criticizing my stepson to a person outside the family. However, the fact is that I'm becoming quite desperate about my daughter, and I must talk to someone who has her interests at heart. Jonathan's selfish, solitary ways are injuring Belinda. Here she is, shut up in that castle with a man who can't be bothered to consider her welfare. She's seventeen years old, an age when most girls are preparing for their come-outs, or at least are mingling with other young people of their own class and rank. If Jonathan doesn't wish Belinda to marry at this time—and she *is* rather young, I admit that—then he should allow me to take her to London, where I could introduce her to society and make sure that she enjoys the opportunities befitting her rank and fortune. Surely you must agree with me."

"Well, it's true I've always thought Belinda should have a more normal social life," said Hilary cautiously. "She seems contented enough now, living with her brother, but one day she may wish to marry, and it's clear she'll have no chance at all to meet an eligible suitor unless she leaves Wycombe. So yes, I agree she should have a come-out of some kind, if not in London, then in Bath, where I believe she has an elderly relative, or even in Newcastle."

Noting Elvira's pleased smile, Hilary added, "But my opinion is of no consequence, Lady Lansdale. The duke is Belinda's guardian."

"No consequence! You're far too modest, my dear. Your opinion, as Belinda's loving, devoted friend, must always be of consequence. In fact, since Belinda tells me you have a certain—er—influence with my stepson, you might care to suggest to him—"

Hilary cut her off. "You're quite mistaken. I have no influence with the duke. I wouldn't dream of making any suggestion to him about his sister's future."

Elvira looked flustered. "You must forgive me. . . . I had no intention of embarrassing you in any way. It's just that I'm so concerned about Belinda . . ." She sat for a moment, her head bowed. Then she rose, a tremulous smile on her lips. "I've intruded on you far too long, keeping you from your work. But I'm very grateful to you, Miss Vane. It's helped me so much, just having a sympathetic listener. And it's comforting, too, to know that you agree with me about dear Belinda's problems."

Quivering with fury, Hilary stood at the drawing room window, watching Lady Lansdale's smart carriage making its laborious way up the rutted driveway to the castle. She'd just been used as a pawn by two experts in the game. Neither Wilfred Rayner nor Elvira had come to Willow Cottage out of friendship or good will.

Wilfred had come to elicit information and—possibly—sympathy for his courtship of Belinda. Given any encouragement, he might also have chosen to start a full-fledged flirtation with Hilary.

Elvira had been a little less direct. Obviously she wanted Belinda to marry Wilfred. Failing that, she wanted to take her daughter away from Wycombe and launch her on a come-out in London. On the surface, both objectives had merit. Wilfred might be a worm and a libertine, which Hilary was beginning to suspect, and of which Elvira might be unaware, but he was still a matrimonial catch as the next Duke of Alverly. And it *was* a good idea to give Belinda a chance to spread her wings in society.

But was Elvira the proper person to launch Belinda on a social career? Hilary had her doubts in light of the countess's devious behavior here this afternoon. Clearly Elvira expected opposition from Jon in her plan to take her daughter to London, so she'd first blackened her stepson's reputation to Hilary and then attempted to persuade Hilary to plead her case with Jon. Well, reflected Hilary with satisfaction, she'd squelched that scheme. Then, as she continued to gaze up at the castle from the drawing-room windows, an unwelcome thought intruded. She'd agreed with Elvira that Belinda should have a come-out. Now Elvira could go back to the castle and buttress her arguments by reporting to Jon that Hilary, too, was of the opinion that Belinda should leave Wycombe for a season in London.

Hilary sighed. Elvira couldn't know that Hilary had already suggested to Jon that Belinda have a come-out, with disastrous results. Jon had lost his temper and accused her of meddling in his affairs. If Elvira did go to Jon, he'd undoubtedly accuse Hilary again of meddling. She squared her shoulders. There was nothing she could do about Elvira's loose tongue. Meanwhile, she had work to do.

Late that afternoon she went to the vicarage to confer with Mrs. Trevor about the Harvest Festival, the date of which was drawing near. They walked to the parish hall, a large barnlike building behind the church.

"Oh, dear, it rather looks as if lightning has struck, doesn't it," said Mrs. Trevor in distress as she surveyed the collection of oddments that cluttered the interior of the hall—several pieces of furniture in need of repair, two old desks and a slateboard, obviously from the village grammar school, some sacks of grain and assorted bits of harness, a farm cart with one wheel. "I've allowed our own servants and a number of the villagers to store objects here because the hall is weathertight and is so seldom in use, and now look at it."

"The place needs a great deal of work before we can use it for the Harvest Festival," Hilary agreed.

"Good afternoon, ladies." Jon strolled into the hall. After bowing to Hilary and depositing a light kiss on Mrs. Trevor's cheek, which caused her to blush like a girl, he gazed around the room with raised eyebrows. "Do I gather that these objects will be exhibits at the festival?"

"Oh, Jon, doesn't the place look dreadful?" Mrs. Trevor exclaimed. "It's all my fault. I *would* allow people to use the hall as a storeroom."

He nudged a large hollow wooden trough with his foot. "What in the fiend's name is this thing?"

"I think it's a contraption our farmhand uses to dip

253

pigs into in order to remove their bristles. He says it can be mended."

"The man's daft."

"I daresay." Mrs. Trevor sighed. "I don't quite know what to do about this mess. Unfortunately young Simon Gillis, our outdoor man who usually cleans the hall for the festival, has come down with the mumps. He won't be able to do any work."

"Don't worry your head about it. I'll send some men down from the castle. Half my servants don't have enough to do."

"Oh, Jonathan, thank you. I might have known I could depend on you," said Mrs. Trevor gratefully. A maidservant appeared in the door of the hall, beckoning to her. "Great heavens, I expect Cook has burned the roast of venison. Octavius will be so disappointed. Excuse me for a moment." She hurried away.

The duke said, "I understand you and my stepmother have been making great plans for Belinda's future."

Hilary gritted her teeth. She'd been sure that Elvira would make mischief, but not quite so soon.

Without waiting for her to reply, the duke continued. "Yes, this afternoon Elvira asked me for permission to take Belinda to London in order to introduce her to society. I refused naturally. Well, you know my views on the subject. Then Elvira told me that you agreed with her plans. She seemed to think your approval would induce me to change my mind."

"I hope you disabused her of that notion," said Hilary dryly.

"I told her nothing of the sort. I speak to my stepmother as little as possible." He studied her expression. "You look a trifle fussed."

"It's just . . . Jon, I want you to know that I did *not*

254

conspire with Lady Lansdale to persuade you to allow Belinda to go to London for a come-out."

"Of course you didn't."

She stared at him.

"You're not underhanded, Hilary. If you wanted something from me, you'd tell me to my face." He gave her a twisted smile. "Although, recently, it's what you *don't* want from me that you choose to tell me about."

Mrs. Trevor returned with an invitation to join her in a cup of tea and some of Cook's marvelous cakes. As she sat opposite Jon in the cheerful vicarage parlor, Hilary covertly studied his face. He was becoming more and more inscrutable to her. He obviously cared for her in some fashion. He believed in her integrity, he admired her work, or at least he said he did, he was strongly attracted to her physically. Why, then, did he so strenuously refuse to commit himself in marriage?

Desolately Hilary answered her own question. He wanted her, but he didn't love her.

Chapter XV

Several days later, as she so often did, Belinda lingered after classes in the afternoon to chat with Hilary. "Mama and I are having quite a to-do about the Harvest Festival Ball," she observed. "Mama says I mustn't dance with anybody except Jon or Wilfred, and I keep insisting I want to dance with everybody so I won't waste all that wonderful instruction you've been giving us. I wonder if she thinks I'll be contaminated, or something of the sort, if I dance with a farmer's son?" Belinda sighed. "I'm afraid Mama is overset with me."

"Lady Lansdale is planning to attend the parish Harvest Festival?" asked Hilary in surprise.

"Oh, yes. Well, she can hardly *not* attend. Jon says those of us who live at the castle have an obligation to make an appearance at the festivities."

"The border lord. *Noblesse oblige,*" Hilary murmured.

"What?"

"Nothing. A private joke," Hilary said hastily.

Belinda's eyes twinkled. "You were talking about Jon, weren't you? You're right, of course. Border lord. It suits him. Sometimes he does act very medieval and lord-of-the-manor. Only no one except you would dare to say so."

"Don't you dare repeat what I said, you minx."

Belinda laughed. "I won't say a word, I promise. It will be entirely *entre nous*. There, see how well I can use those French phrases you've taught us!" She glanced at the clock over Hilary's desk. "Heavens. I'm late for lunch with Mama and Wilfred. I'll be off." She made for the door with her usual ebullient energy, turning to wave a saucy goodbye.

Smiling at Belinda's nonsense, Hilary walked to her office, where she found Maria Grey waiting for her. There were shadows under the girl's eyes, and her figure was stiff with tension. Hilary remembered that Maria had arrived at Willow Cottage much earlier than usual that morning and that she had seemed uncharacteristically quiet and inattentive during classes. "What is it, Maria?"

Involuntarily the girl flicked a glance toward a corner of the room. For the first time, Hilary noticed a small valise wedged beside the door.

"I've left home, Miss Vane. I need your help."

Sitting down, Hilary motioned Maria to a chair near her. "Tell me about it."

"I told Papa last night I wanted to become a schoolmistress. Somehow I couldn't keep it to myself any longer. He was so angry, even angrier than Mama had been. 'I'll make sure you stop thinking about such foolishness,' he told me. He's going to send me off to my cousins in Bristol as soon as he can make the arrangements. I simply can't go to Bristol. If I do, I know both families will pressure me and my cousin Alfred so much that we'll end up getting married despite ourselves. Can

257

I—will you allow me to stay here with you? I know it's asking a great deal . . ."

Feeling hopelessly inadequate, Hilary said, "Maria, I want to help. I think your family is wrong to force you into a marriage that's distasteful to you. But you're only seventeen years old. You're not of legal age. I can't allow you to stay here against your father's wishes."

The slow tears glided down Maria's cheeks. She whispered, "I was so sure you'd help. You're so strong and independent. I thought you'd want me to be like you."

Against all logic, iron bit into Hilary's soul. "Yes, you can stay here, Maria. I don't quite know how I'll manage the situation, but I'll do my best to cope."

Coping was extremely difficult. Even good-natured Matt remonstrated, "Sheltering wounded criminals is one thing, Hilary. Giving refuge to the daughter of a respectable yeoman farmer is quite another. Farmer Grey isn't going to like this one bit."

He didn't. Late that afternoon Farmer Grey pounded at the door of Willow Cottage. Hilary confronted him in the drawing room, which seemed dwarfed by him, not so much because of his size, although he was a large man, but because of the sheer magnitude of his anger.

"Is it true, Miss Vane, what it says in this here note my Maria left in her bedchamber afore she went oot o' our house ter come ter school this morning?" His eyes bulging in a barely controlled rage, Farmer Grey waved a sheet of paper in Hilary's general direction. "Has my girl run away from her home ter stay wi' ye?"

"Maria is certainly here, Mr. Grey."

"Ah. Then please ter fetch her here this minute. I've come ter take her home."

Hilary rang the bell. When Sarah appeared, she said, "Ask Maria Grey to come here, please."

258

Her eyes cast down, Maria entered the drawing room with dragging steps several minutes later.

"There ye are, my girl," Farmer Grey said gruffly. "Yer mother says ye took a valise wi' ye this morning. Go fetch it, and then we'll be off."

Maria looked up. "Do you still intend to send me to Bristol, Papa?"

"I do. I'd be failing in my duty if I didn't take ye away from this place that's filling yer head wi' such outlandish notions." Farmer Grey flashed Hilary a look of pure hostility.

Clenching her hands tightly together, Maria said in a tremulous voice, "Then I won't go with you, Papa. I don't wish to go to Bristol. Miss Vane is allowing me to stay at Willow Cottage with her."

The farmer burst out, "Ye're doing me a great wrong, Miss Vane. Maria's just seventeen. Until she's twenty-one she should be in the care of her family."

Hilary was torn. On the one hand she felt a certain sympathy for Farmer Grey. He sincerely believed he had Maria's best interests at heart, and certainly he had the law on his side. But she couldn't bring herself to abandon Maria.

"I'm sorry, Mr. Grey. I've given my word to Maria. I won't force her from my house. Maria, I think it would be better if you left your father and me to talk privately."

As Maria scuttled out of the room, her father took an impulsive step after her. Hilary calmly moved in front of him. "I'd like to have that talk, Mr. Grey. Let's begin at the beginning. Do you understand why Maria doesn't wish to go to Bristol?"

"It's because o' that fool notion o' hers aboot being a schoolmistress, that's what," growled the farmer.

"That's part of it, yes. She's also afraid she may be forced into an unwelcome marriage."

Farmer Grey reacted as if stung. "If ye're talking aboot young Alfred, there's no way her mother and me would force Maria ter take him if'n she didn't like the lad."

"Well, perhaps I should have said the use of too much persuasion, rather than force. Maria's told me how strongly both families favor the match. Well, Mr. Grey, now you know Maria's reasons for leaving home. I suggest you go now. Leave Maria with me for a few days until you've all had a chance to think more calmly."

Standing for several moments in hard-breathing silence, the farmer exclaimed finally, "If ye think I'll change my mind, ye're wrong. I'll go now, but don't think ye've heard the last from me. If ye don't give my girl back, I'll have the law on ye."

After Farmer Grey had gone, slamming the front door so hard that the sound reverberated through the house, Hilary climbed the stairs slowly to her office. Had she bitten off more than she could chew this time? Farmer Grey had spoken of "having the law" on her, and she suspected he was probably a man of his word. On the other hand, what did he mean by "the law"? Strictly speaking, there was no law in Wycombe. The nearest authority was the justices of the peace in Wincanton. Unless . . .

She wasn't really surprised to find Jon standing on the threshold of her office an hour later. "Sarah told me to come up," he said.

She pushed aside the pile of examination papers she'd been correcting. "Shall I guess why you've come?"

"I fancy there's no need for you to guess," he said coolly, seating himself opposite her. "I think you know why I'm here. Ebenezer Grey just paid me a visit, breathing fire and brimstone. He claims you've abducted his daughter, and he demands that I force you to give her up." He added with a dangerous glint in his eyes, "And I don't wish to hear a word about border lords or lingering vestiges of the feudal system. My tenants have always come to me with their problems. Now then, is it true, Hilary? Have you kidnapped Maria Grey?"

"No, but I've given her permission to stay at Willow Cottage. She doesn't want to return to her parents."

"Oh? And why is that? Grey babbled something about Maria wanting to become a schoolmistress."

Hilary explained briefly.

For a few moments, Jon sat in frowning silence, absently slapping his palm with the butt of his riding whip. "I trust you realize you're in an untenable position," he said at last. "Maria Grey is a minor. She has no right to leave the protection of her father's roof if he refuses her permission to do so. And another thing: if the farmers of the valley suspect that you're encouraging their daughters to be disobedient, they'll turn against you and against your school."

Hilary nodded. "Yes, that had occurred to me." She shrugged. "I'm afraid it's an impossible situation. I gave my word to Maria. And besides, I think she's in the right."

"Perhaps I can help. I suggest we ride out to the Grey farm together. I brought a mount for you from the castle stables. If we work in cooperation, we might be able to arrange some kind of compromise—persuade Ebenezer Grey to postpone Maria's visit to Bristol, for example, or even to consider seriously her wish to become a teacher."

"You mean you'll give us our marching orders, tell us all what to do," Hilary blurted, before she could stop herself.

He shot her an exasperated look. "My only object was to be helpful," he said coldly.

"I know. I'm sorry, Jon. I think your idea is an excellent one. As long as Mr. Grey and I keep talking to each other, that's surely an advantage."

A little later, riding beside Jon out of the village, Hilary mused on the changes in the duke's personality since their first meeting. Oh, he was still the border lord, and probably always would be. Authority was ingrained in his character. But now, at least occasionally, he was willing to consider someone else's opinion. She speculated that his narrowness of mind might have been caused by the fact that for so many years he'd lived a life of unrelieved monotony, with no one of his own rank to talk to except a much younger sister and occasionally the vicar and his wife. Then Hilary and Matt entered his life, and after that his daily routine had been disturbed by the drama of the murder plot against him and his realization that his mines had been mismanaged. Jon had certainly mellowed. In every area save one. He still had an animus against marriage.

Mr. and Mrs. Grey greeted their guests stiffly in their equally stiff, neat-as-a-pin parlor. Hilary suspected that they would have refused to admit her to their home if she hadn't been accompanied by their all-powerful duke. Mrs. Grey, her plump motherly face pinched, silently served her homemade mulberry wine and biscuits while she looked to her husband to direct the conversation.

Jon said pleasantly, "Mr. Grey, I'm distressed that you and Miss Vane are at odds. She and I have come here today to see if we can't resolve the situation. Perhaps, to start, you might allow her to tell you something about the teaching profession."

Inwardly quailing at Ebenezer Grey's expression of granite-hard hostility, Hilary began nervously. She described her daily routine at Miss Wiggins's academy. She told the Greys about the prosperous merchants and farmers from whose families her pupils came and how highly respected Miss Wiggins and her staff had been in the community of Tunbridge Wells. She even mentioned the amount of her yearly salary, which caused Mrs. Grey to widen her eyes in surprise.

"So I think it's clear that being a schoolmistress is an entirely respectable, even honorable profession." Hilary finished.

"I won't have my Maria going off among strangers," muttered Mrs. Grey, and Hilary realized that this was the sticking point. The Greys were mortally afraid that Maria would share the fate of her older sister who had indeed gone off among strangers and had become a fallen woman.

Groping for a solution, Hilary said, "Supposing I were to write a letter to Miss Wiggins, introducing Maria, and asking Miss Wiggins to give her a trial as an assistant mistress? Under those circumstances, Maria wouldn't feel she was among strangers."

Ebenezer Grey exploded. "I see what it is. Ye want ter git Maria so far away from us that me and my wife will nevermore be able to reach her or guide her. Ye're a wicked woman, Miss Vane. Ye're corrupting as good a girl as ever was."

"That's enough, Grey," snapped the Juke 'I an'' al-low you to speak to Miss Vane in that fashion."

But Grey was beyond reason. "I ain't surprised ye've

263

been siding wi' this woman," he snarled. "She's one o' yer own class, after all. I warn ye, Yer Grace. If ye won't help me, I'll git my girl back on my own, and hang the consequences."

The duke rose. "And I'll warn you, Grey," he said in a voice that cracked like a whiplash. "If you try to harm Miss Vane or if you start a whispering campaign against her in the valley, you're finished on the Rayner estate. I won't renew your lease."

Grey stared open-mouthed at the duke. "Yer Grace, ye can't mean that. My family has farmed these here acres for generations past," he faltered.

"So they have. But just remember those acres belong to me. I can do as I like with them. Come along, Miss Vane." Jon stalked out of the room without a backward glance. Staring helplessly for several moments at the Greys, who both appeared in a state of shock, Hilary also left the room.

In the stableyard, a grim-faced Jon extended his hand to help Hilary into the saddle. As they rode down the driveway toward the road, he remarked, "I fancy you'll have no further difficulties with Ebenezer Grey about Maria's stay in your house."

Hilary burst out. "Jon, did you have to be so cruel?"

The duke stared at her incredulously. "Cruel? Me?"

"Yes, you," replied Hilary hotly. "Mr. Grey only wants what's best for his daughter. He's mistaken about me. I'm not trying to alienate his daughter. I only want what's best for Maria, too, but you had no right to threaten his livelihood when he didn't agree with your opinion."

They had reached the juncture of the driveway with the valley road. Jon reined in his horse and reached across to grasp Hilary's bridle. "It's the same old story,

264

isn't it?" he said. The slate gray eyes had turned a dangerous black. "I'm the lord of the manor, and therefore I'm automatically wrong. I came here to help you, Hilary. Frankly I don't care about Maria Grey. If you want to know what I think, I side with her father. I think she should obey him. But I don't want you hurt, and I won't tolerate any attempt by one of my tenants to injure you."

Hilary said stubbornly, "I realize you're trying to help, and I'm grateful, but still you had no right to use your position to bully Mr. Grey."

"I've never been called a bully before, but you're entitled to your opinion," said Jon coldly. "Since you don't care for my approach, what do you suggest that we do?"

"I think we should wait a few days to allow Mr. Grey's temper to cool. Then he might agree to allow Maria to stay with me at Willow Cottage until the end of next term. By that time he may have mellowed."

"That, if I may say so, is an idiotic assumption," retorted the duke. "Trust me to know my tenants better than you do. Ebenezer Grey will never give up until he's gotten his daughter back." His hand tightened on her bridle. "Use the brains God gave you. Didn't you hear Grey threaten you? You can't reason with him as if he were a gentleman. Soft words won't convince him. A threat to his purse might. So let me handle the situation as I see fit."

Hilary stared at him resentfully. "Please don't talk to me as if I were an addlebrained female who can't manage her own affairs," she flared.

"Well, what else am I to think—?" He broke off as he spied Wilfred Rayner trotting down the road toward them.

265

"Hallo, you two," called Rayner cheerfully. "May I join you?"

Hilary gritted her teeth. "By all means, Mr. Rayner, please join us," she said resignedly. She hardly knew whether to be glad or sorry for the interruption. Certainly Wilfred's presence would prevent her quarrel with Jon from escalating, at least for the moment.

"I'm passing the time with a leisurely ride until Belinda finishes her Greek lesson," Wilfred remarked. "As you're well aware, Jonathan, there's not a great deal to occupy one's attention in these parts."

Jon flicked his cousin a sour look. "I marvel that you stay here, then, if the social amenities are so boring."

"Now you're putting words in my mouth," said Wilfred good-naturedly. "I'm staying in the valley to become better acquainted with you and Belinda, of course." Stealing a glance at Jon's hand, still firmly grasping Hilary's bridle, he added casually, "If you're going to Willow Cottage, I'll ride along with you, if I may."

During the ride to the village, Wilfred kept up an easy chatter, which served to obscure Jon's studied silence. However, as he dismounted in front of Willow Cottage and helped Hilary from her horse, Jon muttered, "If anything untoward happens, send me word." He jerked a bow to Hilary, nodded to Wilfred, and rode off toward the castle, leading Hilary's mount.

Wilfred tethered his horse to the gate and walked up the path to the house with Hilary. In the foyer Sarah greeted Wilfred with a smile, saying, "Lady Belinda and the doctor aren't finished with their lesson, Mr. Rayner."

"Thank you, Sarah, I'll wait."

266

Though she had no desire for Wilfred's company, Hilary felt obliged to invite him to take tea with her.

"Do you often ride with the duke?" he inquired as he finished one of Cook's little cakes. The remark was quite casual, but Hilary thought she detected a sharp note of curiosity in the tone.

"No, not at all," she replied, keeping the irritation from her voice with an effort. "As a matter of fact, the duke and I called on Farmer Grey today on business connected with my school."

"Really?" Wilfred cocked his head at her. "It's odd, but I had the distinct impression that you and Jonathan were having a very private meeting." He rose abruptly and crossed the room in several long strides. Pulling the dumbfounded Hilary to her feet, he looked down at her with an unpleasant smirk. "In fact, I thought you and my cousin were uncommonly friendly." The clasp of his fingers on her arms tightened. "So I did wonder, my dear, if you'd like to be friendly with me, too."

"I'd rather be friendly with the devil," Hilary retorted, recovering her wits. She kicked Wilfred's shins as hard as she could, inflicting little damage, since she was wearing soft slippers and he was wearing riding boots. However, the unexpectedness of the attack made him release his hold on her. Glancing quickly around her for a weapon, Hilary seized the plate of teacakes and smashed it down on Wilfred's head, reflecting in one distant corner of her mind that she'd just sacrificed a piece of Great-aunt Alvenia's favorite tea set.

"Damnation, you vixen, you've cut me," Wilfred complained, snatching up a napkin to mop at a slender stream of blood trickling down his forehead.

"Serves you right. Next time perhaps you'll think

267

twice before inflicting your favors on a woman who doesn't want them!"

"Good God. What's this, then?"

At the sound of Matt's voice, Hilary and Wilfred turned toward the door, where Matt and Belinda stood staring at the shards of china and bits of cake littering the floor around Wilfred's feet.

"Don't embarrass Mr. Rayner, Matt," said Hilary with a specious sympathy. "He dropped the cake plate and has already apologized profusely."

"Ah. And how did you cut your head, Rayner? Here, let's have a look at it," said Matt, advancing toward Wilfred while whipping a handkerchief from his pocket.

"Cut myself with my signet ring," muttered Wilfred.

After a quick glance at the wound, which was superficial, Matt wrapped his handkerchief around Wilfred's head and tied an expert knot. "A mere scratch, Rayner. Nothing to worry about."

"Come along then, Wilfred," said Belinda. "We're late for our ride."

After the two had left, Matt gave Hilary a hard look. "Signet ring be damned," he growled. "What did he do, hit his head in an absent-minded gesture? Do you know what I think? I think you bashed Rayner over the head with that cake plate. Was he casting out lures to you?"

"Yes. But don't concern yourself about it. I fancy he'll keep his hands to himself in the future."

"He'd better. If he doesn't, the next thing that lands on his head will be more substantial than that plate."

"I think the comb will look lovely just here, Miss Vane," said Maria Grey as her skillful fingers fastened the pearl-studded comb into the glossy coil of chestnut-colored hair on the crown of Hilary's head.

The comb did look well, Hilary decided, looking into the mirror of her dressing table. The gleam of the pearls in the comb was repeated in the tiny seed pearls embroidered on the bodice and abbreviated sleeves of her rose-colored gown of gauze silk.

"You look lovely, Miss Vane," said Maria, standing back to admire her handiwork. "I'm sure you'll enjoy yourself at the Harvest Festival Ball tonight."

Turning away from the dressing table, Hilary looked up at Maria. "I'm sorry you won't be going to the ball, my dear. I don't like to think of you alone in this empty house tonight."

Maria's face clouded over. "It's all for the best," she said quietly. Hilary's visit to the Grey farm had occurred three days previously. During that time Maria's father had made no gesture of reconciliation. Hilary had suggested to Maria that she should defuse the situation by staying away from the ball, thereby avoiding a possible hostile encounter with her father, and Maria had agreed.

"Could I ask you something?" said Maria hesitantly. "Those men at the front and back of the house—who are they? When we first noticed them late this afternoon, Sarah went out to ask them what they were doing there. They said to ask you, Miss Vane, or the doctor."

Hilary's lips tightened. Jon! She could cheerfully strangle him for this latest interference in her life.

She'd spent the greater part of the day at the parish festival, turning her hand to any task that needed attending to. She and Belinda had organized the children's games, which she thought Belinda had enjoyed even more than the boisterous urchins from farm and

269

village. Certainly Belinda had come away from the apple bobbing with a wide grin on her face and a thoroughly drenched gown.

Hilary had also supervised the tables displaying the entries in the various agricultural and handicraft competitions, and she'd stood beside Mrs. Trevor as part of the appreciative audience who watched the duke gravely award prizes of gaily colored ribbons for the largest marrow, the most perfect ears of maize, the most tasty pastry, and the most attractively knit shawl.

During the day, Hilary hadn't really spoken to Jon. For one thing, she'd been too busy assisting Mrs. Trevor with the details of the festival. For another, Jon was at his most aloof and unapproachable. Doubtless he was still annoyed by her refusal to allow him to manage Maria's difficulties with her father.

It wasn't until she returned home at the end of the day that she realized Jon had simply taken matters into his own hands. Turning in at the front gate of Willow Cottage, she'd heard a rustle of movement in the shrubbery and stopped short. "Is someone there?" she called out sharply.

A tall man emerged slowly from the shrubbery. Touching his hand to his hat, he said politely, "Miss Vane? His Grace sent me and t'other feller at the back o' the house. We've already spoken ter the doctor."

Hilary looked closely at the man. He wasn't wearing the Rayner livery. Rather, he wore a nondescript dark coat and breeches and serviceable boots, and he carried a stout cudgel. "Why did the duke send you here?" she inquired.

The man's face turned impassive. "Well, now, ma'am, ye must ask His Grace aboot that," he mumbled.

"That's not good enough. I'm asking *you*," declared

Hilary with asperity, but she was talking to empty space. The man had ducked back into the shrubbery.

Hilary left her dressing table to take one last look at herself in the cheval glass. "I'm not sure what those men are doing out in the garden, Maria," she said over her shoulder, "but I intend to find out!" She picked up a fringed silk shawl, draped it around her shoulders, and headed for the door of her bedchamber.

"Good night, Miss Vane. I hope you enjoy the ball," called Maria wistfully.

A little later, as he walked with Hilary along the pathway to the front gate in the gathering twilight, Matt glanced to both sides, saying, "I don't see either of those fellows, but I daresay they're both still out there." He added grimly, "Alverly has a deal to answer for, let me tell you. The gall of the man, invading our property! He may be a duke and I may be a country doctor, but a man's house is his castle! You say Alverly will be at this ball tonight?"

"Let me speak to him, Matt," said Hilary in alarm. She had a vision of her brother quarreling with Jon in sight of the entire population of the Wycombe Valley assembled in the parish hall. Then, as she continued to walk with Matt down the village street, keeping pace with his slow, halting steps, she smiled ruefully at herself. Judging by her past experiences with Jon, she was as likely to quarrel with him as her brother. More so, perhaps!

The Harvest Festival Ball of St. Bride's parish, Wycombe, was not, properly speaking, a ball. It was a country dance, in the true sense of the word, an occasion when the people of the valley gathered to enjoy

271

themselves with music, food, and—in Mrs. Trevor's dark suspicions—illicit liquor.

When Matt and Hilary entered the parish hall, it was already crowded, but the dancing hadn't yet begun. Two fiddlers were tuning up their instruments on the sidelines. Obviously watching for them, Belinda rushed up, her eyes glowing with excitement. "You look beautiful, Hilary."

Gazing with admiration at Belinda's primrose satin, Matt exclaimed, "I've been favored by fortune tonight. Here I am in the company of the two most beautiful ladies in the ballroom."

"No, no, Matt, you're sadly out," Belinda said, laughing. "Mama outshines us all. Look at her."

Elvira sat at the side of the room talking to Mrs. Trevor and the vicar. Even from a distance, Hilary could tell that the countess's robe of silver and violet tissue made her look as ethereal as an angel and as enticingly beautiful as Circe.

"Astounding," murmured Matt as he looked at Lady Lansdale. "Your mother doesn't look a day over twenty-five."

"Come and say hello to Mama before the dancing starts," urged Belinda, taking Matt's hand.

Before Hilary could follow them, Wilfred Rayner appeared beside her. "I must talk to you," he muttered.

"Not here. Not now."

"It won't take a moment." Wilfred seized her wrist. "We can talk over there by the door. It's not so crowded there."

Hilary unobtrusively tried to release her wrist. "I don't want to talk to you, Mr. Rayner."

"We must talk." Rayner tightened his grip. "You completely misunderstood me the other day. I hope you're not considering discussing the matter with Jonathan—"

"What matter would that be?" said Jon coldly, coming up to stand beside Wilfred.

"Nothing—nothing at all, Jonathan," stammered Rayner, hastily releasing Hilary's wrist. "A misunderstanding only, as I was explaining to Miss Vane."

"I believe we can consider the matter closed, Mr. Rayner," said Hilary with an icy politeness.

"Oh. Yes. Of course. Thank you, Miss Vane." As he walked away, Rayner took out his handkerchief to mop his forehead.

"Was he playing the loose fish?" Jon asked abruptly. The gray eyes were turning dark.

"Very inexpertly. I'd have expected more finesse from a London libertine," replied Hilary flippantly.

"See, here, Hilary, if my cousin's been annoying you . . ."

"I can take care of Mr. Rayner. I *have* taken care of Mr. Rayner. Don't concern yourself, Jon. This is my affair—" Hilary broke off, her eyes widening as she looked more closely at Jon. Since she'd seen him earlier in the day, someone had clipped his unruly dark curls, which now were arranged in a fashionable Brutus. "You're wearing new clothes," she said, in a tone that was almost accusatory.

Reddening, Jon glanced down at his coat and waistcoat and breeches, which, if not up to the sartorial splendor of Wilfred Rayner's evening dress, were a vast improvement on his former outmoded garments. "My valet ordered these from my tailor in Newcastle," he said morosely. "He seemed to think I needed a new wardrobe."

Hilary guessed that Jon's valet—that shadowy figure

273

whose very existence she had merely surmised—had taken it upon himself to order a new wardrobe for his master as a result of the arrival at the castle of a genuine London Pink of the *ton*. Perhaps Wilfred's valet had made slighting remarks about the duke's unfashionable clothes.

"Well?" Jon inquired with a faintly defensive air. "Do I pass muster?"

Hilary studied him deliberately from head to toe. "Yes," she said. "You look very—very ducal."

His lips tightened, and Hilary belatedly realized that by being provocative she was in danger of quarreling publicly with him. She said in a low voice, "Jon, I want to know about those men lurking in my shrubbery. One of them told me you'd sent him."

"I did, yes. I think you need protection. Those men are my gamekeepers."

Hilary blinked. She couldn't have heard correctly. "Protection against what, in heaven's name?"

"Against Ebenezer Grey. I went out to see him early today, hoping to make him see reason, and he refused to talk to me. In fact he slammed the door in my face. Now, clearly, if Grey chooses to treat *me* in that rude fashion . . ."

Jon paused, shaking his head in obvious disbelief. Hilary thought it likely that never, in all the years since he'd succeeded to the dukedom, had one of his tenants treated him so cavalierly.

"Well, at any rate," Jon resumed, "Grey's behavior, in the face of my warning that I might refuse to renew his lease, leads me to think he must be a little unbalanced. He may be capable of anything, including violence."

Still keeping her voice low and controlling her resentment with a real effort, Hilary said, "Jon, I ask you once more. Please allow me to settle this affair with Mr. Grey in my own way. And remove your watchdogs before they arouse the very gossip I'm trying to avoid."

"No," said Jon bluntly. "I don't trust Grey, nor your ability to manage him. And there needn't be any gossip. My men won't open their mouths. If you and your brother don't talk, who will know about the guards I've posted at your house?"

"You're impossible, utterly impossible," muttered Hilary beneath her breath. However, she pasted a bright smile on her lips, saying aloud, "It's been so pleasant talking to you, Duke, but I really should pay my respects to Mr. and Mrs. Trevor and Lady Lansdale."

The music was striking up as she sank into a chair beside Elvira. Mrs. Trevor greeted her with a beaming smile, thanking her for her help with the children's games earlier in the day. The vicar, his kindly face troubled, was talking to Matt about the case of a grammar school youngster who had a deformed foot.

"Well, Miss Vane, you look perfectly charming tonight," said Elvira graciously.

"And you, Lady Lansdale. What a beautiful gown."

Elvira nodded complacently, taking the compliment as her due. Glancing about her, to make sure she wasn't being overheard, she said, "Of course, our finery is wasted on an affair like this. I shouldn't have come at all tonight if my stepson hadn't insisted." She motioned to the dancers on the floor. "Look at them. No decorum at all. It's all of a piece with what you and I were discussing the other day. Belinda should not be taking part in such a vulgar gathering."

Hilary suppressed a retort. It was quite true that the local people, dancing a lively reel, lacked the finesse and mannered deportment of a group of dancers at Almack's

Assembly Rooms in London, but they were clearly enjoying themselves. So, too, was Belinda, who came off the floor, her eyes sparkling with excitement, on the arm of a farmer's son and sat down next to her mother. "That was lovely," she sighed, ignoring Lady Lansdale's disapproving frown. A conspiratorial note in her voice, she said to Hilary, "Later on we have a little surprise for you."

The "little surprise," toward the middle of the evening, turned out to be a special quadrille performed by Belinda and three of her fellow pupils. The girls were partnered by four young men who were strangers to Hilary but who she guessed were probably the brothers or cousins of her pupils. The eight young people danced the five intricate movements of the quadrille with a fluid grace worthy of a more cosmopolitan ballroom.

Flushed and smiling, Belinda walked off the floor to receive the congratulations of her friends and family. Jon, who had been standing with his arms crossed on his chest as he watched the dancers closely, patted his sister's shoulder, saying, "Well done, Belinda."

Her mother agreed, albeit somewhat grudgingly. "Yes, you danced very well, my love."

Hilary hugged Belinda. "You wretch, you deceived me," she exclaimed, laughing. "Those were all brand-new steps."

"We practiced secretly," acknowledged Belinda with a grin. "We wanted to surprise you. Betsy Siddons rounded up our partners—her brother Tom, a cousin, and two of Dulcie Cross's brothers. We practiced at Betsy's house in the late afternoons after the daily chores were finished."

Elvira exclaimed in horror-stricken accents, "You went repeatedly to the home of one of Jonathan's tenant farmers to practice *dancing?* What could you have been thinking of?"

His lip curling, Jon said, "I fancy Belinda will suffer no permanent harm from the experience, Elvira."

Lady Lansdale flushed at the implied rebuke. Hilary reflected that, when she first met Jon, his reaction to Belinda's visits to Betsy's home for dancing practice would have been exactly the same as Elvira's. It was another indication of how much he'd changed.

Belinda tried to cover an awkward pause by turning to her brother, saying gaily. "Well, Jon, now that I've demonstrated my dancing skills, you must do the same. Why don't you dance the next country dance with Hilary?"

"Jonathan can't dance. He could never be bothered to learn. It was very disappointing for his father," remarked Elvira in a voice dripping with venom.

Ignoring his stepmother's jibe, Jon said to Belinda, "That's a capital notion. I'd be delighted to dance if Miss Vane is willing to oblige me. Not a country dance, however."

He beckoned to the two fiddlers, who, though about to strike up for the next dance, started obediently across the room at his summons. Jon walked to meet them. The three men conferred for several minutes in the middle of the floor. Mystified, Hilary noted that Jon appeared to be moving his hand rhythmically up and down. Finally the fiddlers retired to their former position on the opposite side of the room. Jon walked over to Hilary. Bowing, he said, "May I have the pleasure, Miss Vane?"

The fiddlers began playing a waltz tune, the same tune, Hilary recognized with a catch in her throat, that she'd hummed to Jon at the Bridgeton Assembly Ball on

277

the disastrous night when she'd attempted to teach him how to dance.

She rose from her chair, saying urgently to Jon in a low voice, "I can't dance the waltz with you. I told you, it isn't danced in polite society in England. Surely you couldn't have forgotten that."

Smiling faintly, he put out his hand, and her resistance evaporated. As if mesmerized, she allowed him to encircle her waist and sweep her into the middle of the floor to the lilting strains of that simple little waltz tune.

"Jon, you know we shouldn't be doing this," she murmured a moment later in a belated protest.

"Well, Belinda told me to dance with you, and this is the only dance I know how to do. You taught me, remember?"

Unwillingly she recalled the passion-drugged moments in his arms during that dancing lesson. Shaking her head to clear it, she glanced around her and gasped. "Jon, we're the only couple on the floor!"

He smiled down at her. "Why does that surprise you? We're the only people here who know how to dance the waltz. Well, except Elvira, I daresay. She probably danced it on the Continent." He tightened his arm around her waist and held her closer as he guided her through the graceful circling pattern of the dance. As if under the spell of a magic potion, she surrendered to the music and to the enticing nearness of Jon's body and his faint clean masculine scent. It was only when the sound of the fiddles died away that she became aware again of the possibly scandalous consequences of Jon's imperious decision to dance the waltz with her.

As she walked off the floor with him, she could almost feel the curious eyes of the villagers and farmers boring into their backs. The local people had undoubtedly never witnessed what they would consider intimate touching during a public dance. More especially, they'd never previously had cause to link their duke personally with the new schoolmistress. Hilary gritted her teeth. God knows what might be going through their heads now, she thought.

Nor was the reaction among the gentry appreciably different. As she approached their chairs at the side of the room, Hilary noted that Mrs. Trevor and the vicar appeared somewhat scandalized, Matt looked faintly concerned, Belinda was flushed with excitement. Of them all, Elvira seemed the most composed.

"Well, Miss Vane, you and Jon quite surprised me," Lady Lansdale said coolly. "I had no idea the waltz had come to the North Country. In London, it's still considered as much as a young lady's reputation is worth for her to dance the waltz at Almack's."

Conscious of a hot color rising in her cheeks, Hilary said, "Matt, I'm feeling very warm. Will you walk outside with me?"

"Allow me," said Jon, and took her arm.

Outside the doors of the parish hall, Hilary turned on Jon, saying angrily, "How could you do such a thing? You've embarrassed me in front of your family and friends and tenants, and you've very possibly called attention to the fact that there's some kind of—connection between us."

"There *is* a connection between us."

Hilary clenched her hands together. "Jon, you promised—"

"I agreed to stop pressuring you to become my lover. I never promised to stay away from you or to cease reminding you that what I feel, you feel, too." He put out his hand, gliding it slowly, caressingly, over the silken skin of her throat and shoulders.

"Oh, stop!" Hilary cried, and turned her back on him. Trying for composure, she walked back into the ballroom.

Chapter XVI

Hilary shivered in her pelisse. She'd discovered that autumn temperatures in the Cheviot Hills were downright chilly, especially in the very early hours. She and Maria Grey had left Willow Cottage this morning before sunrise to drive to Bridgeton in the dogcart. The sun was only now beginning to rise above the horizon.

Hilary glanced at her watch. "The stagecoach is late," she fretted. "I can't stay with you much longer if I'm to get back to Wycombe in time for classes."

"Do go on home, Miss Vane," urged Maria. "There's no need to wait with me. I'll be perfectly safe here until the stage arrives."

Hilary glanced around her. They were standing in the courtyard of the Prince's Arms, waiting for the arrival of the stagecoach from Berwick. While Maria was the only ticketed passenger for this stop, a number of inn servants and stable hands were passing in and out of the courtyard. Maria would have company if Hilary left her alone to wait for the stagecoach.

"I believe I will go, then, Maria." Hilary added, "You're sure you have your ticket and your money and the letter to Miss Wiggins?"

Maria nodded, then looked uncertain. "Well, perhaps I should just check my reticule again."

Hilary smiled at herself. She was as nervous and uncertain as Maria about this early morning escapade. She'd asked Maria about money and tickets and letters several times, and each time Maria had obediently checked the contents of her reticule.

"Be sure to write to me as soon as you get to Tunbridge Wells, so I'll know you arrived safely," said Hilary.

"I will, Miss Vane."

"And write to your parents, too."

"Yes." Maria's eyes brimmed with tears.

Hilary said quickly, "Maria, you *are* sure you want to go to Miss Wiggins's academy? You can still change your mind."

Maria brushed the tears from her eyes. "I'll not change my mind." She clasped Hilary's hand. "I can never thank you enough for all you've done for me."

"I don't want any thanks. Just do well, that's all I ask." Hilary kissed Maria's cheek. "Remember, if you find you don't like being a schoolmistress, write to me. I'll arrange the matter with Miss Wiggins. Goodbye, Maria." She kissed the girl again and walked to the waiting dogcart.

As Hilary drove out of Bridgeton and over the rutted mountain road to the Wycombe Valley, the eastern sky began to brighten. She should be back at Willow Cottage before her classes were scheduled to begin.

Actually, she arrived home in time for breakfast. She entered the dining room as Matt was sitting down at the table with a laden plate.

"There you are," he said. He looked worried. "Where

have you been, Hilary? Sarah told me you left the house with Maria in the dogcart before dawn this morning."

Hilary helped herself to buttered eggs and bacon, poured a cup of tea, and sat down opposite Matt. "I went to Bridgeton to put Maria on the stagecoach for Tunbridge Wells."

Matt stared at her. "Tunbridge Wells? You've sent Maria to Miss Wiggins's academy?"

Hilary nodded. "I wrote to Miss Wiggins a week ago. She replied yesterday, agreeing to accept Maria provisionally as an assistant mistress. I don't think Maria will have any difficulty. She was a very bright pupil."

"But—my God, Hilary. You've practically kidnapped the girl. At least that's what her father will probably think. The duke, too."

Shrugging, Hilary said, "I felt I had to get Maria away before something dreadful happened. Do you remember the night of the Harvest Festival Ball? When we returned to the house we didn't see anybody in the grounds, not even our watchdogs, who always keep themselves well hidden. But later that night, when I looked out my bedchamber window, I saw Farmer Grey on the opposite side of the road, looking up at the house from the shadow of some bushes. He didn't dare approach the gate, of course. The duke's watchdogs would have swarmed all over him, and he knew it. I could see his face quite clearly in the moonlight, and his expression was—it was ghastly. I think the duke is right. Mr. Grey isn't quite normal anymore. I decided I should get Maria away before he lost all control and harmed her."

"Lord!" Matt shook his head. "What now?"

"I'll send the Greys a message explaining what I've done. They don't know the exact location of Miss Wiggins's academy, and in any case I can't see Mr. Grey

283

chasing all the way down to Kent to retrieve Maria. I hope he'll now accept the situation. What's important is that Maria is safe from being harassed or molested, at least for the time being."

Matt looked dubious, but all he said was, "I hope so, love."

"Where's Maria?" asked Belinda after classes started that morning.

"She's gone away for a spell," said Hilary noncommittally.

"Where—?" Belinda subsided in the face of Hilary's straight, unsmiling stare.

None of the other pupils asked after Maria, which Hilary found both disquieting and unsurprising. There was no need for the girls to inquire about Maria. They knew something was amiss. Gossip had begun to spread in the valley. She and Matt hadn't said a word to anyone about her quarrel with the Greys or about the presence of their ghostly watchdogs in the shrubbery. She guessed that Farmer Grey, warned by Jon not to start a vindictive whispering campaign against Hilary, had refrained from discussing his family problems with his neighbors. But Hilary suspected that rumors had begun circulating along the grapevine almost from the moment Maria came to stay at Willow Cottage. Nor had Jon's imprudent behavior at the Harvest Festival Ball done anything to squelch the rumors.

Gazing at her pupils' faces, which looked rather guarded and withdrawn in contrast to their normal cheerful expressions, Hilary was glad that she'd sent not one, but two, messages to Miss Wiggins in Tunbridge Wells. The first message she'd told Matt about; that was the request to give Maria a trial as an assistant mistress. The second message she'd kept from her brother. She'd asked Miss Wiggins for her old position back, beginning with the autumn term the following year.

It wasn't that Hilary really wanted to leave the Wycombe Valley. She knew her departure would sadden Matt and might even cause him to give up his practice in the village. But she feared that her life here might soon become untenable. More likely than not with Maria Grey gone, the parents of her remaining pupils would eventually conclude that she'd separated a daughter from her family, and they'd condemn her for it. It would be impossible to conduct her school under those circumstances.

Hilary's mind was only half on the lesson as she began drilling the class in French verbs. The other half of her mind was fixed on Jon. She admitted to herself that a possible censure by the parents of her pupils wasn't her prime reason for leaving the valley. Quite simply she doubted her ability to keep resisting Jon's overtures. He'd made it plain the night of the parish Harvest Festival Ball that he wanted her as much as ever—without benefit of matrimony, naturally—and that he had no intention of staying away from her. It would be much better for her peace of mind to live in a place where she wouldn't be subjected to his devastating physical magnetism.

Suddenly Hilary was struck by an astounding thought that caused her to stop in mid-sentence and stare straight ahead of her, oblivious to her surroundings. What if Jon were opposed to marriage because he already had a wife? What if he'd secretly married some unsuitable girl from the lower classes who'd then become insane or incurably ill? He'd be effectually barred from marrying anyone else until his first wife died.

285

She heard Dulcie Cross's voice saying uncertainly, "Miss Vane? We've finished the preterite of 'to be.'"

Confused and embarrassed, Hilary said quickly, "Thank you, Dulcie. I'm afraid I was woolgathering. Will you repeat the drill, please?"

Although she tried her best to concentrate, Hilary found her mind wandering again. What an idiot she was! She'd been so eager to explain Jon's unwillingness to marry her that she'd actually invented an imaginary wife for him! Indeed it *was* time for her to leave the Wycombe Valley!

Never had a morning's classes seemed to drag by so slowly. Hilary was glad to see her pupils leave, and they seemed equally glad to go. Only Belinda appeared unaware of any strain in the atmosphere. She lingered behind as she so often did to chat.

"Look, Hilary, aren't they pretty?" she said, dangling an object between the thumb and forefinger of each hand.

"They" were unusually beautiful earrings set with sapphires and diamonds. "How lovely," Hilary murmured. "A gift from your mother?"

"No. Wilfred gave them to me. He says they belonged to *his* mother." Belinda raised the earrings to eye level, swinging them slowly to and fro. "The only thing is, Wilfred doesn't want me to mention them to Jon. He says Jon might consider the gift inappropriate, since Wilfred and I aren't betrothed."

"Mr. Rayner is quite correct. I'm sure your brother *would* consider the earrings an inappropriate gift from a young man to a young unmarried female."

"Oh. I was afraid you'd say that," Belinda sighed. She eyed the earrings longingly. "They're so beautiful, though." She cocked her head at Hilary. "I asked

286

Mama's opinion. She said the earrings were merely an expression of cousinly affection, and I shouldn't hesitate to accept them."

"Lady Lansdale isn't your guardian, is she? Your brother is," Hilary retorted. She had a shrewd suspicion that both Wilfred and Elvira regarded the earrings as a reinforcement to tempt Belinda into favoring Wilfred's suit.

"Oh, very well. I daresay you're right," Belinda grumbled. She tucked the earrings into her pocket. As she rose to go, she said, "You haven't forgotten about my dinner party tonight, have you?"

"Of course not. Matt is looking forward to it. He says you promised him you'd ask your cook to prepare his favorite *gâteau* for him."

Belinda laughed. "That pig, Matt. Thinks only of his stomach. I'm so glad you're coming. Mama is beginning to look quite blue-deviled. She wants company. She says this must be the most boring place in all of England. If it weren't that I live here, she says, she'd have left for London long ago."

Early that evening as he drove with Hilary in the dog-cart up the drive to the castle, Matt consulted his watch and said in surprise, "Didn't we leave much too early?"

"No. I wanted to arrive early so that I could have a word with the duke. I thought I should tell him about sending Maria Grey to Tunbridge Wells before he found out for himself."

"Won't the watchdogs have told him? They surely saw you leave with Maria this morning and come back without her."

"No, I don't think so. I believe they change watches around midnight."

The footman showed Hilary into the library, promising to inform His Grace that she was waiting for him there. She wandered for a few minutes around the great room with its two-story gallery, gazing at the rows of unused-looking books. Belinda was no great reader, and Hilary guessed that Jon seldom used the room except as an office. Presently she sat down on the large sofa facing the fireplace, enjoying the welcome warmth of the flames. November evenings in the Cheviots were brisk.

She must have dozed briefly, waking with a start at the sound of voices. About to make herself known, she stiffened suddenly and huddled deeper into the sofa. She recognized the voices. More important, she grasped immediately the tenor of what was being said, and the knowledge chilled and repelled her.

The voices, though low-pitched, were perfectly audible in the stillness of the room.

"My God, Elvira, I'm growing weary of this hole-in-the-corner business," growled Wilfred. "I practically have to make an appointment to make love to you. Look at us—we're like two callow youths, sneaking into an empty room so we can kiss each other without being observed. It's hell, I tell you!"

"Oh, I know, darling. I'm so sorry," came Elvira's sighing voice. "But a least we have this moment. Oh-h-h-h ... That was wonderful. Kiss me again, hold me even tighter ..."

The brief silence that followed was broken by the sounds of heavy breathing and a whimpering cry of ecstasy from Elvira. Then Wilfred said urgently, "There's a perfectly good sofa in front of the fireplace. Why don't we use it? Nobody will come into the library. That oaf Jonathan never opens a book, nor anyone else in this cursed household."

"Darling, we can't risk it. You know Belinda's invited guests for dinner. Someone *might* wander in here."

"God, yes. The doddering vicar or that sanctimonious brother and sister team ... Then let me come to your bedchamber tonight. I can't hold out too much longer, my love. I must have you soon."

Elvira said doubtfully, "It's so dangerous. What if someone should see you leaving my room?" She drew a hard breath and said huskily, "But yes. I can't wait any longer either. Come very late, when there's no chance that Jonathan or Belinda or the servants will still be prowling about the house." Elvira's voice lost its tremulous quality and became more normal. "We must go now, though. Belinda's guests will be arriving soon. She'll be wondering where we are."

As the door of the library clicked shut behind Wilfred and Elvira, Hilary began to tremble so hard that she had to clench her hands tightly together to keep them steady. She was twenty-five years old, and until now she'd considered herself reasonably sophisticated. She knew quite well that people, even in her own social milieu, occasionally succumbed to the lure of illicit passion. All she had to do was to consider her own case and how close she'd come to surrendering to Jon. Ordinarily she wouldn't have been especially shocked by anything Wilfred Rayner and the Countess of Lansdale chose to do in their private lives. But this ... This was different, monstrously different.

She heard the door open and Jon's voice saying, "Hilary? Are you in here?" He walked into the room and around the sofa, stopping abruptly when he saw her. "What is it?" he demanded, reaching down to grasp her hands and pull her to her feet. "What's happened? Are you ill?"

She stared up into his eyes, trying to speak, but she couldn't form the words. She was shivering violently as if she had the ague. Finally she managed to say, "No, I'm not ill. I wish I were ill, it would be so much better than this . . ."

He swore under his breath. "We can't talk here," he muttered. "Someone might come in." Taking her arm, half supporting her, he walked her to the door of the library. After making sure the hallway was clear, he proceeded down the long corridor to the conservatory, which was dimly lit by a few hanging lamps. None of the gardeners was present.

"Now, then, what's the matter?" Jon said grimly, placing his hands on her shoulders and swinging her around to face him.

Swallowing hard, she said, "While I was waiting for you in the library, Wilfred Rayner and your stepmother came in. They didn't realize I was there. I overheard them talking . . . Jon, they're lovers."

"What?" Jon spat the word out. Even in the dim light from the hanging lamps she could see that he'd turned a pasty white.

"They're lovers," she repeated. "I couldn't have been mistaken. They were quite explicit. Jon, Wilfred says he wants to marry Belinda, and he's also been propositioning me, and now we find out he's been sleeping with Lady Lansdale. It's—it's almost incestuous, wouldn't you say?"

"Oh, my God," Jon burst out. He released Hilary and turned away, clenching his hands around one of the posts supporting the conservatory roof and resting his head on his hands. He remained in that position, rigid and silent, while Hilary looked at him helplessly.

She hadn't felt she could keep her hideous discovery

from Jon. He had a right to know that his heir, a guest in his house and a suitor for his sister's hand, was also cohabiting with his sister's mother. She'd expected him to be shocked and angry, perhaps murderously so. She really wouldn't have been surprised if Jon had physically attacked Wilfred. She hadn't expected this reaction. Jon seemed crushed, lifeless as if the vital juices had been sucked from his body. Finally he turned back from the post, straightening himself with an obvious effort. His face looked drained and tired, but he was in command of himself again.

"I'm sorry to make such an exhibition of myself," he said curtly. "I was in a state of shock, I suppose. Certainly I never expected to learn that my heir was courting both my sister *and* her mother."

"The news must have been a dreadful blow to you. But I didn't think I should keep it from you."

"No. You did the right thing. I had to know." He added savagely, "I wonder if Wilfred planned to live in a *ménage à trois,* sleeping on alternate nights with Belinda and then with Elvira?" He broke off. "Excuse me for speaking so crudely."

"There's no need to be sorry. You haven't shocked me. How else could you talk about this horrible situation?" Hilary shook her head. "I could believe anything of Wilfred. I think he's quite capable of courting both mother and daughter without letting either of them know about the other. But Jon, it's so hard for me to believe your stepmother could be a party to this."

"I don't find it hard to believe," Jon said grimly.

"What makes the whole terrible situation even worse is that Elvira has been actively encouraging Belinda to marry Wilfred," said Hilary, her forehead furrowed with distress. "How could she do a thing like that? She must know it smacks of the incestuous."

Flinching at the word, Jon seemed to bury himself in his dark thoughts. At last he said slowly, "I can think of one good reason why Elvira might wish Belinda to marry Wilfred. I don't know how Lord Lansdale left Elvira financially. However, I well remember how extravagant she's always been. I wouldn't be surprised to learn she'd run through Lansdale's money before he died. On the other hand, Belinda will come into a handsome fortune *when she marries*. Wilfred and Elvira may be scheming to spend that fortune on themselves."

"Jon!" Hilary gasped. "No mother could be so—so loathsome."

"Believe it. Elvira's capable of anything." Frowning, Jon fell silent again. At last he said, "The question is, what's to be done about the situation?"

"Done? Why, I presume you'll ask both Lady Lansdale and Mr. Rayner to leave Wycombe Castle at once, of course. Oh . . ." Hilary's voice trailed off. "You're thinking of Belinda's feelings. You don't want her to know about her mother and Wilfred Rayner."

Jon nodded. "I don't believe Belinda feels any deep affection for her mother. Well, why should she after all those years of neglect? But Elvira *is* her mother, and Belinda would be crushed to find out what sort of woman Elvira really is. I don't know how Belinda feels about Wilfred. When I refused his offer for her, she didn't seem especially unhappy." He flicked a sudden guilty look at Hilary. "I know what you're thinking," he mumbled. "I *should* know how Belinda feels about Wilfred. I should have discussed his proposal with her before I dismissed it out of hand."

Hilary forbore to rub salt into Jon's wounds. The border lord was learning, that was enough. She said comfortingly, "Belinda told me she had no desire to spend the rest of her life with Mr. Rayner. She enjoys his company, that's all."

Looking both relieved and chastened, Jon went on, "I can't very well ask Elvira and Wilfred to leave at a moment's notice without causing Belinda to suspect that something's wrong. You see, lately Elvira's been hinting that she'd like to stay at the castle indefinitely 'to become better acquainted with her long-lost daughter.' Belinda's an intelligent girl. After listening to such expressions of devotion from her mother, she's hardly likely to believe a manufactured tale that Elvira had dashed off to London to sit at the bedside of a sick friend, or some such thing."

"Yes. I see the problem." Hilary thought for a moment. "Jon, I know you have an aunt living in Bath. Why don't you tell Lady Lansdale that you've arranged to take Belinda to Bath at Christmastide to visit your aunt? You could say you've been keeping the visit a secret from Belinda. It's to be your surprise Christmas gift to her. So . . ."

"So naturally there'd be no reason for Elvira to remain at Wycombe in Belinda's absence." Jon gave Hilary a twisted smile. "What a splendid, diabolical plot. As a last resort, I could actually take Belinda to Bath. Let's see, now. It's almost December. We need only put up with Elvira's presence for a few more weeks, and then we'll be rid of her. Thank you, Hilary."

"It was a pleasure." She returned his smile. "If I could suggest one more thing . . ."

"What's that?"

"Well, I think it would be better if you didn't indicate to Lady Lansdale and Mr. Rayner that you know about their liaison. You'll avoid a good deal of unpleasantness."

"Or something worse," said Jon, his face darkening. "If Elvira is really desperate about money . . ." He shrugged. "Thank you again. Well that's settled, then. Shall we join the others?" He paused. "Wait. You wanted to talk to me in the library."

"Oh, that. I've done something you won't like, Jon. This time I've really kidnapped Maria Grey, or that's what her father will think. Early this morning I put her on the stagecoach to Tunbridge Wells to stay with my old headmistress Miss Wiggins."

Jon's brows drew together. "Why did you do that?"

"Because on the night of the parish ball, I saw Ebenezer Grey loitering across the road from Willow Cottage. He frightened me. I knew I had to get Maria away so that her father couldn't reach her."

His lips tightening, Jon said, "You've made matters worse, you know. Ebenezer Grey doesn't give up easily. You've merely given him another reason to nurse a grievance against you." He squared his shoulders. "Well, we can't solve the problem here and now. Belinda will be wondering where we are."

The dinner party that followed was the most awkward social event that Hilary could ever remember attending. Initially every eye in the drawing room fastened curiously on her and Jon as they entered the room, self-consciously late. In particular Matt's shrewd gaze bored into Hilary, probing for an explanation of the heightened emotion he could sense in her but didn't understand.

Conversation at the dinner table was a near disaster. Hilary couldn't bring herself to speak to Elvira or Wilfred. Even to meet their eyes made her feel vaguely unclean. She addressed jerky remarks to Matt and Belinda and to the vicar and Mrs. Trevor. She realized she was making very little sense when she caught Belinda staring at her with a bewildered frown. Jon spoke hardly at all. He appeared to be in a brown study, replying to direct questions but otherwise saying nothing.

When the ladies retired to the drawing room, leaving the gentlemen to their port, Belinda drew Hilary aside. "What's the matter with Jon?" she murmured. "I haven't seen him so—so unfriendly in ages. Why, Wilfred asked him a question and Jon didn't answer."

Hilary smiled brightly. "You're imagining things, Belinda. The duke is never very chatty, I think you'll agree."

Belinda looked unsatisfied. "Well, if you say so . . ."

Elvira called out. "Do come and talk to me and Mrs. Trevor, Miss Vane. You and Jonathan were so late coming in to dinner that we suspect the two of you of nursing deep, dark secrets together. We're dying to pick your brains!"

Hilary walked over to sit between Elvira and Mrs. Trevor on a settee. The vicar's wife, who looked miserably embarrassed, said with a forced smile, "Lady Lansdale is teasing you, Miss Vane. Of course we don't suspect you of 'deep, dark secrets.' The idea!"

"Indeed. The very idea!" said Hilary cheerfully. She gave Elvira a direct look. "My dear Lady Lansdale, what on earth do you imagine those secrets to be? Perhaps you suspect the duke of confiding in me that he plans to buy a new variety of sheep?" She lowered her voice. "Actually, we *were* discussing something rather private. I'm sure I needn't ask you not to mention what I'm about to say. The duke, who's always so generous, has agreed to pay the school fees for the daughter of one of his tenants. Naturally we'd prefer that this information not be widely known in order to spare the family embarrassment."

Mrs. Trevor's face glowed. "Oh, what a splendid thing to do! It's so like Jonathan!"

Hilary felt mildly ashamed of her mixture of fact and fiction.

For a moment Elvira's face registered a strong discomfiture. Then she said with a brittle smile, "I was just funning, Miss Vane. Of course I don't believe you and Jonathan have secrets together. Good heavens, you have nothing in common except that you live in the same village!"

"Exactly," agreed Hilary, refusing to give Elvira the satisfaction of knowing that her bolt had struck home.

The gentlemen entered the drawing room now after a brief stay over their port. Belinda immediately pounced on Hilary, dragging her off to the pianoforte. "Wilfred's promised to teach me how to waltz," she giggled, "but of course we haven't been able to practice without an accompanist. You'll play for us, won't you, Hilary?"

"Indeed I won't. Well-bred young females don't dance the waltz. Not yet. Not in England."

"But Hilary . . . You and Jon danced the waltz at the Harvest Festival Ball."

"Yes, we did. We were very foolish. As you'll recall, Mrs. Trevor was quite horrified."

"Oh, come now, Miss Vane, aren't you being the least bit missish?" Wilfred asked as he strolled up to them. "The most gently bred females all over Europe dance the waltz. Elvira is a real dabster at it, I'm told. It's only a matter of time before the waltz is allowed at

Almack's, you know. In the meanwhile, how can it possibly cause scandal for Belinda to learn the steps in the privacy of her own drawing room?"

Hilary gazed at Belinda's eager face and gave in. "Oh, I daresay you won't ruin your reputation if Mr. Rayner teaches you to waltz in private."

Belinda was a natural dancer. Under Wilfred's expert tutelage, she quickly learned the movements of the waltz. Flushed and laughing, she swooped, clasped in Wilfred's arms, around the area in front of the pianoforte in graceful, widening circles. Hilary noted with a growing sense of disquietude how easy and natural the relationship between Belinda and Wilfred appeared to be. Could it be that Belinda, gradually and insensibly, was beginning to care for Wilfred?

She stopped playing, and Belinda, leaning forward, kissed Wilfred lightly on the cheek. "Thank you. I enjoyed that so much." Then she opened the tiny reticule hanging from her wrist and handed Wilfred an object or objects that Hilary couldn't see. "Thank you for these, too, but I can't accept them."

Wilfred stared down at the objects on his palm. "But Belinda, why? You said you loved the earrings."

"I did. I do. But I talked to Hilary, and she told me it wasn't proper for me to accept such a gift from a gentleman to whom I wasn't closely related, such as a father or a brother. She said, too, that I shouldn't conceal such a gift from Jon."

After a long moment, Wilfred turned to Hilary, leaning over the pianoforte to speak to her in a tight-lipped rage. "You're taking a great deal upon yourself, Miss Vane. I'm Belinda's cousin, as you doubtless know. Why shouldn't I give her a gift? And what right do you have to interfere in her affairs?"

Belinda gasped. "Wilfred! Don't speak to Hilary in that fashion. She's my dearest friend. Whatever she told me was for my good. What's more, perhaps you've forgotten you once told me the relationship between us was so distant, we were hardly cousins at all?"

Taking a deep breath, Wilfred tried to smile. "Good lord, Belinda, don't you ever forget anything?" He turned to Hilary. "I apologize. I spoke out of turn. It's just that I was so disappointed when Belinda returned the earrings. I so wanted to give her a gift that would tell her how much I—how much I value her."

"It's all right, Wilfred," Belinda said forgivingly. "I'm sure Hilary understands."

"Oh, I do, Belinda. I understand Mr. Rayner perfectly."

Too late, Hilary realized she'd failed to keep an edge of disdain out of her voice. Wilfred shot her a sharp glance. Apparently Belinda wasn't aware of anything amiss. Seeming satisfied that her friend and her cousin had patched up their slight difference, she responded with alacrity to Matt's call to make a fourth at whist.

"Matt and I are going to win tonight," she gaily informed the Trevors. "I'm a *much* better player than I was used to be. Wilfred and I have been practicing two-handed whist."

"Don't be too sure of yourself," Matt said with a grin. "Pride goeth before destruction, eh, Vicar?"

Released from the pianoforte, Hilary poured herself a cup of coffee and sat down to enjoy it. Still enveloped in the aloofness that had made him such a taciturn figure at the dinner table, Jon leaned against the fireplace, drinking his coffee away from his guests. Wilfred sat down beside Elvira on the settee, speaking to her for several minutes before abruptly jumping to his feet and leaving the drawing room.

Her face cold and distant, Elvira came over to take a chair beside Hilary. "Well, Miss Vane, I see you've enlarged your sphere of responsibilities," she began. "Not content to be a schoolmistress, you've appointed yourself an expert in the etiquette."

Hilary stared blankly at Elvira.

"Oh, come now, don't play the innocent," snapped Elvira. "You told Belinda to return the earrings Wilfred gave her, and this after I'd already informed her that it was quite permissible to accept a cousinly gift. I should like to know by what authority you saw fit to advise my daughter."

Restraining her temper with an effort, Hilary retorted, "I have *no* authority over Belinda as you're well aware. However, she asked me for my advice, and I told her what I believe to be true. Mr. Rayner is a very distant relative, and as such it was improper for him to present such an elaborate gift to a young unmarried female." Hilary couldn't resist adding, "It was also exceedingly improper for Mr. Rayner to suggest to Belinda that she conceal the gift from her guardian!"

Turning a bright red, Elvira appeared to swell with anger. "Aren't you the fine one to speak of improper behavior when it's obvious you're carrying on a scandalous relationship with my stepson!"

At Hilary's gasp of pure astonishment, Elvira's lip curled. "Did you think nobody would notice? Just in the few weeks that I've been here, the signs have been increasingly clear. That disgraceful dance you performed with Jonathan at the village ball, for instance. That was certainly public enough. And tonight, on a more private level: even Mrs. Trevor, an innocent of the first water, took notice of your *tête-à-tête* with Jonathan before dinner tonight when you kept all of us waiting for fully fifteen minutes."

Hilary interrupted her. "You've no right to criticize my conduct, and I'm under no obligation to listen to you. Pray excuse me." She started to rise.

"I'm not finished yet." Elvira put out a rough hand to restrain Hilary from getting up. Hilary was so petrified with astonishment that she made no move to free herself.

Continuing her tirade, Elvira said spitefully, "Then there was that Chinese vase on your mantel. Did you really think I wouldn't realize it came from Jonathan's collection? That vase proved to me that you're carrying on a love affair with my stepson. I suspect you haven't yet realized that it will never be more than that, a furtive little affair. I know who you are. You're the daughter of an insignificant country baronet. And Jonathan has his faults, too many of them, but he'd never pollute the Rayner heritage by marrying a nobody like you."

Jon's voice cut in. "Who gave you permission to speak for me, Elvira?" Both women looked up in surprise to find Jon standing in front of them. His face was rigid with anger.

Hilary drew a sharp breath. Already enraged almost beyond endurance by his discovery of Elvira's affair with Wilfred, would he now, under this further provocation, confront his stepmother with his knowledge?

But Jon had his anger under control. "I've never hidden my dislike for you, Elvira," he said, a cutting edge to his voice. "If you weren't Belinda's mother, I wouldn't have allowed you to visit Wycombe Castle. If, however, I ever again hear you insulting an invited guest

300

in my home, I'll ask you to leave. And I insist you apologize to Miss Vane."

Elvira's thoughts were quite transparent. At all costs, if she were to carry out her schemes, she had to remain at the castle. Swallowing her vindictiveness, she said, "Pray accept my apologies, Miss Vane. I see now I must have misinterpreted your situation."

Chapter XVII

On the day after the dinner party at the castle, Sarah walked into the classroom where Hilary was conducting a literature class and whispered urgently in her ear, "You'd best come down right away, ma'am."

Narrowing her eyes at the obvious signs of strain in Sarah's face, Hilary got up from her desk immediately. "Belinda, continue reciting from 'Love's Last Adieu' and go on to the 'Elegy on Newstead Abbey.' I'll return in a moment."

As she hurried down the stairs with Sarah, Hilary inquired, "What's the matter?"

"It's Farmer Grey, ma'am. Before I knew what was happening, he'd burst inter the door, demanding ter see ye. Right after him inter the house came one o' them guards the duke sent here, and the guard, he grabbed Farmer Grey and sent me fer the other feller at the back of the house. And Dr. Vane heard all the commotion while I was calling the other guard and *he* came inter the house, too, and told me ter fetch ye downstairs."

Bewildered by Sarah's confused and breathless account, Hilary hardly knew what to expect when she rounded the curve of the staircase into the lower hall.

There she found Ebenezer Grey in the clutches of the duke's bodyguards, one on either side of him, truncheons at the ready, and Matt facing the trio warily.

"There ye be," Grey shouted when he saw Hilary. He struggled desperately to release himself. His face was so livid with anger that Hilary feared he might have a heart attack.

"Let Mr. Grey go," she said quietly to the guards.

"Careful, Hilary," Matt warned her.

"There are four of us to Mr. Grey's one," she reminded him. "And two of us have clubs."

The guards reluctantly released Grey but remained very much on the alert. Ignoring the men, Grey brandished a crumpled piece of paper at Hilary. "Be this true, wot ye wrote?" he said in a choked voice. "Ye've sent my girl away, clean ter the opposite corner o' the kingdom?"

"Yes, Maria is staying at the school where I taught for so many years. I wrote to you because I thought you should know the news as soon as possible. Maria will also be writing to you shortly."

The veins in Grey's temples swelled alarmingly, and his voice rose to a shriek. "Ye evil woman, ye've taken away my child. Ye've sent her away ter the ends o' the earth where ye means fer me ne'er ter see her again."

"That's not true at all, Mr. Grey . . ."

"Then tell me where ye've sent her so's I can go fetch her from that den o' iniquity ye calls a school."

"I can't do that. I promised Maria she should have her chance to find out if she really wished to be a schoolmistress."

Making a sudden lunge toward Hilary, Grey growled, "Then I'll make ye tell me." But before he could take more than a step, the two watchdogs had grasped his arms, doubling them behind his back so tightly that he uttered a groan of pain.

"Don't hurt him," Hilary exclaimed.

After several hard-breathing moments, Grey muttered, "I'm finished fer now. Ye can let me go."

Hilary nodded to the guards, who released their grip while continuing to keep a hard eye on their quarry. Grey turned immediately and made for the door without a backward look.

"Wait," said Hilary to the guards as they turned to go. "Will it be necessary for you to report to the duke about this incident?"

Both men gazed at her with the polite but totally blank expressions that informed her as clearly as words that they had no intention of telling her anything. She sighed. "Very well. You can go."

After the men left Matt observed, "The duke isn't going to like the fact that Farmer Grey succeeded in getting into the house before the guards caught up to him."

"No. It will simply confirm Jon—the duke—in his opinion that I was wrong to spirit Maria out of the valley."

Matt gave her a quick look at her use of the duke's Christian name, but he made no comment. Instead he said, "I don't like the situation either. It's going from bad to worse. Ebenezer Grey may be becoming queer in his attic."

Hilary shook her head. "He's just concerned about Maria. He's pinned all his hopes on her, and now she's gone. I can't blame him for feeling angry and troubled."

"I'm worried about your safety, Hilary."

She smiled wryly. "Don't be. Our watchdogs seem quite efficient." As she went back up to her classroom, however, her smile faded. She could see no real solution to the problem. Ebenezer Grey appeared to be growing more bitter and obdurate.

Hilary had a vague expectation that Jon would pay her a visit the following day after his guards had reported to him about the latest incident concerning Farmer Grey, if only to say, "I told you so." He didn't come, but she received news of him from Belinda during their customary daily chat.

"Mama's forgotten how to talk to Jon, if she ever knew how," Belinda remarked with a grin.

"Oh? Why do you say that?"

"Well, this morning at breakfast he mentioned that he planned to go off on a short business trip. He was in one of his moods, so I knew better than to question him. At best he really doesn't like to talk about his affairs. But Mama was curious and pressed him about where he was going and why. He just looked at her with that gimlet-eyed stare of his and said, 'My business is personal and private, Elvira.' Poor Mama. She looked quite crushed."

Her forehead wrinkling in thought, Belinda added, "There was one odd thing. The stable boys told me that Jon went off in the carriage. He hates being driven. I've never known him to take the carriage when he could ride." She got up, jamming her hat on her head and retrieving her riding whip as she prepared to go. "*I'm* curious, too," she admitted. "Where do you suppose Jon went? Oh, well, perhaps he'll tell you all about it when he returns."

"Me!" Hilary exclaimed.

"Well, he seems to tell you things he doesn't tell anyone else," Belinda retorted as she went out the door.

It was almost a week later before Hilary discovered the secret of Jon's mysterious errand. She and Matt were enjoying their usual companionable late afternoon cup of tea in the sitting room when Sarah came into the room to announce, "His Grace is here ter see ye, ma'am." The maidservant's voice registered a hint of incredulity as she added, "He's got Mrs. Grey wi' him."

Exchanging a quick, mystified glance with Matt, Hilary hurried out the door and down the hallway to the drawing room. Mrs. Grey sat stiffly upright in an armchair, looking as though she felt out of place. In a position Hilary had often seen him assume, Jon stood at the fireplace, leaning an arm on the mantel.

"Duke, what a pleasure," said Hilary politely. "Mrs. Grey, how nice to see you."

Mrs. Grey stood up, her hands clasped tightly to her breast. "God bless ye, Miss Vane," she said in a tremulous voice. "I've seen my Maria, and now I know she's safe and happy."

"You've seen Maria? How—?"

Jon stepped forward. "I took Mrs. Grey to Tunbridge Wells to visit Maria at Miss Wiggins's academy," he said quietly. "I thought she'd be easier in her mind if she could actually see where Maria was living."

Mrs. Grey's face flushed pink with delight. "The academy is such a lovely place, Miss Vane. A beautiful great building set in a park full of trees and shrubbery, just outside the town. But of course you know all that. You were used to be a schoolmistress there. That Miss Wiggins is such a lovely lady, not the least bit high in the instep, even though Maria told me she's the daughter of a viscount. Imagine that! Miss Wiggins, she greeted me so kindly, I felt right at home wi' her. She said she thought that Maria might well turn out to be one of the most accomplished assistant mistresses she'd ever engaged. And would you believe who is sharing a bedchamber with Maria? A young lady named Lavinia

Marston, the daughter, I'll have you know, of the mayor of Tunbridge Wells himself!"

Feeling somewhat dazed, Hilary said, "I gather you approve of Maria's new position, then."

"Approve? Oh, my, yes. I'm that pleased to see Maria so well-established. And I'll tell you something else, Miss Vane." Mrs. Grey lowered her voice confidentially. "On our last day in Tunbridge Wells—it was a Sunday—Miss Lavinia's brother, the mayor's son, you know, came to visit his sister, and he seemed so taken with my Maria."

In a sudden burst of insight, Hilary realized that Mrs. Grey was already thinking of the mayor's son as a possible substitute for Maria's Cousin Alfred in Bristol, whom her parents had for so long schemed for her to marry.

Hilary asked cautiously, "What do you suppose your husband will think about your visit to Miss Wiggins's academy? Mr. Grey was so opposed to Maria's employment there."

Mrs. Grey set her mouth in a stubborn line. "Well, I won't lie ter ye. Ebenezer will likely need some argufying with, but he'll come around in the end, I promise ye that. Fact is, I can't wait ter tell him aboot my journey to Tunbridge Wells." She glanced at Jon rather anxiously.

"You want to get home, Mrs. Grey. Come along, then," he said.

"I did want ter thank ye, Miss Vane, but now I really should get home ter Ebenezer." Mrs. Grey hurried to the door.

As Jon prepared to follow her, Hilary said in a low voice, "Can you wait a moment, Jon?" He paused, and she rushed to say, "That was a stroke of genius. The

Greys' great concern was always for Maria's future. Her sister had disgraced them by having a child out of wedlock, so above all they wanted Maria to be respectable, preferably in an arranged marriage with her cousin. By taking Mrs. Grey to see with her own eyes Miss Wiggins's eminently respectable establishment, you relieved all her worries. As I said, a stroke of genius!"

Jon shrugged. "Thank you, but it was more a stroke of last resort. Grey's anger and suspicion were growing worse with each passing day. I felt I had to do something."

"Well, you certainly won over Mrs. Grey."

Jon smiled faintly. "Actually I think it was the visit of the mayor's son that finally convinced her."

"Did you arrange that?" The words slipped out before Hilary could recall them.

After a moment of blank silence, Jon laughed outright. "No, I had nothing to do with the young man's visit, word of honor. I'm unacquainted with the mayor of Tunbridge Wells." He raised an eyebrow. "Outside the Wycombe Valley, I have no authority, you know." Hilary felt mildly rebuked. Almost automatically she'd once again accused him of manipulating matters to suit himself, but in this case he hadn't been guilty. "Well, I thank you, Jon, for going to the trouble of taking Mrs. Grey all the way to Tunbridge Wells. I think—I hope— that my problems with the Greys will soon be over."

He gave her a quizzical look. "Do you realize this is the very first time you've ever approved of my 'interference' in your affairs?" His eyes slowly kindled with a spark of the familiar fiery desire, and he took several involuntary steps toward her. Then restraining his impulses with an obvious effort, he touched his hat and

308

walked to the door. "Mrs. Grey will be growing impatient. Goodbye, Hilary."

As she walked to the sitting room to rejoin Matt, Hilary felt her heart twist painfully as she reflected that she'd just uncovered still another facet of Jon's complicated character. Apparently he had no compunctions about his attempts to seduce her, but he refused to demand sexual favors from her in return for rendering her a service. If she were ever to give in to him, he wanted the surrender to be voluntary.

The quarrel with the Greys came to a complete end several days later when Sarah ushered Ebenezer Gray into Hilary's drawing room. He was unaccompanied by either of Jon's watchdogs. Noticing Hilary's quick glance behind him, Grey smiled grimly. "Ye don't need guards anymore, Miss Vane. I've come ter make it up wi' ye. I was wrong ter blame ye fer encouraging my Maria ter be a schoolmistress. My wife says my girl's living in a grand place among folk who treats her like one o' their own and that she's happier 'n she's ever been in her life. I'm satisfied. I want ter apologize ter ye fer the trouble I've caused."

"There's no need to apologize, Mr. Grey." Hilary held out her hand. "I'd just like to be friends again."

Grey enclosed her hand in his huge work-worn paw. "Friends we are, right enough," he said, looking mildly embarrassed. He added, "I'm glad I came. His Grace, he said I'd feel better if I talked ter ye face ter face, and he was right."

Hilary suppressed her amusement until after Grey had left the room. So Jon had suggested to the farmer that he finally mend his quarrel with Hilary by coming to see her. What a meddler Jon was. He could no more

309

control his impulse to arrange other people's affairs than the sun could control its rising and setting.

During the next few days Belinda was the only source of news from the castle. She attended classes every day and arrived twice a week to take her Greek lessons with Matt. Hilary glimpsed Jon often as he rode through the village on his way to visit his outlying farms, but he didn't call at Willow Cottage. He was biding his time, no doubt, until his next onslaught on her virtue, she thought ironically. That was all right. Life was easier for her when she wasn't obliged to confront him.

Life at Willow Cottage, as a matter of fact, was more peaceful and uneventful these days than it had been for a long time, she was thinking one afternoon as she passed the door of the sitting room where Belinda was taking her Greek lesson with Matt. The door flew open and Belinda, sobbing bitterly, caromed into Hilary.

"In heaven's name, what's the matter?" Hilary exclaimed, catching Belinda's arm as the girl tried to race away from her toward the front door.

"Let me go. I can't stay here," sobbed Belinda.

Out of the corner of her eye Hilary saw Matt standing in the doorway of the sitting room, his face twisted with pain.

"Matt, what is it—?"

To Hilary's astonishment, Matt shook his head and went back into the sitting room. He closed the door behind him.

Hilary took a deep breath. Matt could wait until later. Now she must deal with Belinda. "Come, love," Hilary said gently. She put her arm around Belinda's waist and half-led, half-supported the weeping girl to the drawing room. Seating herself beside Belinda on the sofa, she said, "Now, then, what's wrong?"

310

Belinda shook her head, unable to speak through a fresh paroxysm of tears. Finally she said in a choked voice, "Oh, Hilary, Matt doesn't love me."

"What on earth do you mean? Of course he loves you. That is to say, he's immensely fond of you. You must know that."

"Fond!" The word temporarily stemmed Belinda's weeping. "Fond of me as he would be of a child, you mean? Or because I'm his favorite pupil? I wanted him to love me as a woman!" The tears began flowing again.

Hilary placed her hands on Belinda's shoulders and gave her a little shake. "Stop crying and tell me what happened," she said. She handed the girl a handkerchief.

The note of authority in Hilary's voice apparently reached Belinda. She mopped her streaming face with the handkerchief. "Well, we were just finishing our lesson today, and Matt said he'd miss teaching me when I left the valley. So I said I had no intention of leaving Wycombe, and he said of course I'd be leaving some time to get married. And then—I don't know what came over me, Hilary—I said I wouldn't marry anybody but him. And he said that was the most ridiculous idea he'd ever heard in his life. He said he wasn't a marrying man, but if he were, he certainly wouldn't marry a harum-scarum schoolgirl who would bore him to death in six months." Belinda began to cry again. "Hilary, it's not like Matt to say such cruel things," she exclaimed between muffled sobs.

"No. No, it isn't." Hilary took the handkerchief and carefully wiped Belinda's face. "Go home now, love. I'll talk to Matt. I'm sure he never meant to hurt you."

"Perhaps not. He made it very clear, though, that he didn't love me," said Belinda desolately. She squared her shoulders, trying for composure. "Well, there's nothing to be done about it, is there? You can't *make* somebody love you, can you? Thank you for trying to help, Hilary." She trailed out of the drawing room with slow, dragging steps.

Waiting until she heard the front door closing, Hilary marched down the hall to the sitting room. Matt was sitting back in his favorite chair, his eyes closed, his hands clenched tensely on the arms of the chair.

"Well, Matt, what have you been up to? You've made Belinda very unhappy."

Matt opened his eyes. He said dully, "No more unhappy than I've made myself. In her case, though, she'll recover. I doubt I ever will."

Hilary sat down in her usual chair opposite him, eyeing him sympathetically. "You seem to be in as bad a case as Belinda. She told me she asked you to marry her and you refused her."

"Yes." Matt swallowed hard. "It was so completely unexpected. I simply said, joking, you know, that I'd miss her when she left the valley to get married. And she said she planned to stay here and marry me."

"And you told her you wouldn't dream of marrying a schoolgirl who would bore you to death in six months. Do you realize how much that hurt Belinda?"

"Hilary, I had to say something that would shock Belinda out of this insane notion that she's in love with me and wants to marry me."

"Is it so insane?"

Matt gave his sister a disbelieving look. "You know it is! I'm years older than Belinda. I'm a hopeless cripple. I'm penniless. And I'm the village doctor. Can you imagine for one moment that the Duke of Alverly would allow his sister to marry the village sawbones? He'd be right, too. I'm the last man in the world Belinda should consider marrying."

A great feeling of sadness washed over Hilary. She knew Matt was right. He was saying no more than she herself had thought some time ago when she'd begun to suspect that he cared for Belinda. A marriage between Matt and Belinda would simply be too unequal in almost every respect. And yet . . .

"You love Belinda, don't you, Matt?" she said softly.

The knuckles of his clenched hands showed white. "Love her? I adore her. She's the most—" He broke off. "That doesn't matter. It's Belinda's welfare that's important." He looked at Hilary with a worried frown. "She'll be all right, won't she? She's so young . . . What she feels for me is a sort of calf's love, I think. She'll soon be over it—won't she?"

Hilary tried to give Matt reassurance. "Belinda has a strong character. And she's grown up so much in these past few months." But inwardly she wasn't so sure. Losing one's first love was such a hurtful experience, and Belinda had no one in whom to confide. Jon loved her, but he and Belinda had never shared their inmost thoughts. Elvira? Hilary would have staked her life on her belief that Belinda would never take her troubles to the mother who'd neglected her all her life.

When Belinda didn't appear for classes for several days, Hilary became increasingly concerned. She told herself that Belinda might be avoiding the school because she was fearful of an embarrassing encounter with Matt, but that was a frail argument. Normally Belinda didn't even catch a glimpse of Matt on her visits to the house unless she sought him out. His surgery hours kept him to his duties until well after Hilary had dismissed her classes.

313

Finally, on the fourth day after Belinda's disastrous proposal of marriage to Matt, Hilary could contain her apprehensions no longer. She had Ephraim harness the pony to the dogcart and drove up to the castle. A footman reported to her that Lady Belinda was indisposed and not up to receiving visitors. After scribbling a note to Belinda and leaving it in the care of the footman, Hilary returned to the courtyard, where the dogcart was waiting. As she climbed into the driver's seat, Jon cantered into the courtyard.

"Hilary," he said in evident surprise. "Did you wish to see me? Can I help you?"

"I came to see Belinda. She hasn't been in class for several days. I was afraid she was ill."

His brows drawing together, Jon said slowly, "She's been keeping to her bedchamber complaining of the headache and a chill. It's not like Belinda to be indisposed, not for days at a time like this and not for such trifling ailments. She *hates* staying in bed. It was all we could do to keep her in bed when she had the measles some years ago. Perhaps your brother should examine her."

Oh, *Lord,* Hilary groaned inwardly. Aloud, she said, "I'm sure Matt will be happy to visit Belinda if she doesn't improve soon. Please give her my love, and tell her I'll call again."

Driving back to Willow Cottage, Hilary was more concerned than ever. She quickly refuted the favorite plot device of romantic novelists: at seventeen, Belinda was certainly not going into a decline because of a broken heart. On the other hand, it wasn't natural or healthy for her to immure herself in her bedchamber for days on end, brooding about her doomed love for Matt.

Inquiring eagerly about Hilary's visit to the castle,

Matt fell into a funk when he learned that Belinda had taken to her bed. "If she becomes ill, it will all be my fault," he groaned. "But what else could I have done, Hilary? I had to tell her there was no possibility of a marriage between us."

Hilary sighed. "Don't blame yourself too much. You acted for the best."

Another week passed. Belinda didn't return to classes, nor did she reply to the several notes that Hilary sent to her. Hilary decided to take matters into her own hands. Today after she dismissed her classes, she would go up to the castle and refuse to leave the premises until Belinda agreed to see her.

When she arrived at the castle, however, she discovered there was no need for her to do battle to see Belinda. The footman informed her that Belinda wasn't at home. "Her Ladyship's gone riding with Mr. Rayner."

Hilary felt a surge of relief. If Belinda was out enjoying her favorite form of recreation, she must be on the road to recovery. Still, Hilary wanted to judge for herself. "When did Lady Belinda go out for her ride?" she asked the footman.

"Oh, several hours ago it was, ma'am. Round about one o'clock, I'd say."

Hilary glanced at her watch. "Her Ladyship will return soon, then, no doubt. I'll wait."

Trying to curb her impatience, Hilary sat in the vast drawing room of the castle, hoping that Belinda would come back shortly, hoping she wouldn't encounter Jon, hoping that a long, intimate talk with Belinda would restore their old close relationship.

"Miss Vane. I didn't realize you were here. The servants didn't inform me." Lady Lansdale advanced into the room.

Hilary suppressed the wave of instant hostility she felt at the sight of Elvira's beautiful face. She got up from her chair, saying, "Actually I came to see Belinda."

"I believe she went riding with Wilfred."

"Yes, I know. I told the footman I'd wait for her. I'm especially eager to talk to her. It's been a number of days since she last attended classes, and I've been somewhat concerned about her."

A note of smug satisfaction sounded in Elvira's voice as she said, "Oh, as to that, Miss Vane, you're aware, I think, that I never approved of Belinda's participation in classes attended by the daughters of her own brother's tenants. I rather fancy that Belinda has been converted to my way of thinking."

"If you don't object, I should like to hear that opinion from Belinda herself."

"Oh, well, of course. I'm sure Belinda meant to tell you about her change of mind. Meanwhile, though, there's no reason for you to waste your time waiting for her to return. Why, she might not be back for hours. You know how she is when she goes off on one of those long leisurely rides! I'll tell her you called."

Hilary gave Elvira a hard look. There was satisfaction in the woman's voice, yes, but there was something more. What was it? Triumph, that was it. Elvira was reveling in a secret triumph. She was fairly bursting with it.

Consulting her watch, Hilary said, "It's well after four. I really doubt that Belinda will be gone much longer. I believe I'll wait."

Two bright spots of angry color appeared on Elvira's cheeks, eclipsing the artfully applied rouge. "You force me to be impolite, Miss Vane. I tried to convey delicately that you are not welcome to remain here. When Belinda returns, I will inform her that you called. She will then contact you if she so chooses."

Hilary said suddenly, "You're hiding something. What is it?"

Elvira gasped. "How dare you speak to me like that?"

Groping her way through her chaotic thoughts, Hilary said slowly, "You don't expect Belinda back here this afternoon. That's why you don't want me to wait for her. That's the truth, isn't it?"

Elvira turned pale. Sweeping past Hilary, she walked toward the bell rope. "I'll have the footman show you to the door. We have nothing more to say to each other."

Before the older woman could reach the bell rope, Hilary seized her arm, bringing her to a stop. "I don't intend to leave this room until I have the truth," Hilary said. *"Where is Belinda?"*

"Let me go, or I'll scream for the servants," said Elvira in a trembling voice. "I've never been treated so shamefully in my entire life."

"There's always a first time," Hilary retorted. She grabbed Elvira's shoulders and shook her, not gently. "Tell me where Belinda's gone."

A voice said from behind them, "What the devil is going on here?"

Taking advantage of Hilary's momentary inattention, Elvira tore herself loose and ran to her stepson's side. Clutching at his arm, she exclaimed, "Jonathan, this woman has attacked me for no reason at all. I think she's mad. Call the servants and have her thrown out. And don't allow her to come here again, ever."

Eyeing Elvira's clutching fingers with acute distaste, Jon removed her hand from his arm. Addressing Hilary directly, he said, "Well, did you attack Elvira? If so, I daresay you had good reason. I'd like to hear it."

Elvira swelled with anger. "I might have guessed you'd side with this creature against me."

Jon ignored her, keeping his eyes fixed on Hilary.

Her brows knit in intense thought, she didn't reply immediately. Then her eyes widened in horror. "Jon, I think Belinda has eloped with Wilfred Rayner and her mother is trying to keep it from you until it's too late to do anything about it."

A muscle twitched in Jon's cheek. "What makes you think that?"

"Belinda went riding with Mr. Rayner hours ago, but Lady Lansdale refuses to allow me to wait for Belinda's return. So obviously Lady Lansdale doesn't expect your sister back today. If Belinda has gone off for the night with Mr. Rayner, what am I to think, other than the obvious conclusion that they've eloped?"

Jon gave her an incredulous look. "You must be mistaken. Only days ago you told me yourself that Belinda had no romantic feelings for Wilfred."

"I still think that's true. But . . ." Reluctantly Hilary told Jon about Belinda's ill-fated proposal of marriage to Matt. "Belinda was so unhappy about what she considered Matt's rejection that she may have turned to Mr. Rayner for reassurance and affection. He, at least, was a man who wanted to marry her, unlike Matt."

"My daughter marry the village doctor?" Elvira erupted in tones of pure outrage. "Your brother, Miss Vane, had the insolence to look so high above his station?"

She broke off as Jon turned on her, his face hardening. "I don't wish to discuss Dr. Vane. What I want from you, Elvira, is the truth. Has Belinda eloped with Wilfred?"

After a long moment's hesitation, Elvira declared defiantly, "Yes, she has, my dear Jonathan. She's married by now, I'm sure, and beyond your selfish influence. At last I have the comfort of knowing my little girl will take her rightful place in society."

Clenching his fists until the knuckles showed white in an effort to keep himself under control, Jon exclaimed, "You mean Belinda will take her place in a *ménage à trois* with you and your lover, don't you?" At Elvira's sudden expression of shock, he nodded, saying, "Oh, yes, I know all about your affair with Wilfred. You came to Castle Wycombe with the express intention of marrying Belinda off to Wilfred because, unless I miss my guess, the pair of you are in low water. You needed Belinda's fortune to survive in the social swim. Well, Stepmother, neither you nor Wilfred will profit from this scheme, I'll see to that."

Quailing before Jon's angry, contemptuous stare, Elvira said with stiff lips, "It's too late for you to interfere. Belinda and Wilfred left for Scotland early this afternoon. Before you can possibly catch up to them, they'll be safely married."

"Married or no, it makes no difference. I'm going after them, Elvira. If they're already married, I'll bring Belinda back here and apply for an annulment immediately. If Wilfred won't cooperate, I'll have him up before the magistrates for abduction and rape. Or I'll kill him. I'd as lief kill him, actually, and rid the world of a piece of vermin. Now, where in Scotland did they elope?"

"I don't know," said Elvira. Her face was sullen.

"You mean you won't tell me. Well, I'll find Belinda without any help from you. By the way, I'll expect to find you gone by the time I return with her. What's more, if you ever try to contact Belinda in the future, I'll make sure she knows about your affair with Wilfred."

With this parting shot, Jon swung on his heel and headed for the door. Ignoring a white-faced Elvira, Hilary raced past her to follow Jon. She caught up with him in the hallway outside the drawing room. "Jon, wait. I'm going with you."

"Like hell you are." Without so much as turning his head to look at her, he continued down the hallway.

Half running to match his long strides, Hilary succeeded in cutting ahead of him to plant herself against the massive door leading to the courtyard, blocking his exit. "Jon, listen to me. When you come up to them, you'll need a woman with you to comfort Belinda. Whatever happens, whether Belinda is married or not, the situation will be very difficult for her. Please, Jon. You know I'm right." Hilary neglected to state her main reason for her urgent desire to accompany Jon. Above all, she had to prevent him from killing Wilfred.

Jon stared down at her, his face bleak. "I hadn't thought of Belinda's feelings. I only knew I couldn't allow her to remain for one minute longer than necessary in Wilfred's company. You're right, of course. She'll be devastated with humiliation, grief, God knows what other emotions when I snatch her away from that swine. You could help her so much." His brows knit together. "But I can't let you become involved. Think of the gossip if folk in the valley found out you'd gone across the border with me, unchaperoned."

"I don't care about gossip. And I'm already involved, just because I love Belinda." Moving closer to him, Hilary placed her hand on his arm. Immediately she was aware of the tremor that went through his body at her

320

touch. Hastily she said, "You'll be riding, won't you? Bring a mount for me to Willow Cottage. I'll change into riding dress and be waiting for you."

Jon shook his head. "I can't—"

"I can always follow you in the dogcart, you know. Of course, I might lose my way when darkness falls. Or drive the cart into a ditch. Or a thug might attack me. Or . . ."

"Hold on." Some of the strain faded from Jon's face. Giving her a twisted, reluctant smile, he said, "I give up. I can't be worrying about your safety while I'm chasing off after Belinda and Wilfred. Can you be ready to leave in fifteen minutes? That's all the time I'll allow you."

"I'll be waiting at the gate of Willow Cottage with time to spare."

Chapter XVIII

After a headlong dash down the driveway of the castle, Hilary drove the dogcart at even greater speed into the stable yard of Willow Cottage and reined in the pony with a jerk. As she jumped down from the driver's seat, the little animal turned his head to gaze at her with an expression that said quite plainly he was unaccustomed to such inconsiderate treatment. Hilary gave the pony a hasty remorseful pat, tossed the reins to Ephraim, who had emerged from the stable to take charge of the dogcart, and raced into the house. She ran down the hallway to the morning room, where Matt sat in his favorite chair, drinking his customary late afternoon cup of tea.

He looked up at her hurried entrance into the room. "You're late. Your tea is getting cold," he observed. After a moment he added, a strained note in his voice, "Sarah told me you went up to the castle this afternoon. Did—did you see Belinda?"

"Matt, I have bad news. Belinda's eloped with Wilfred Rayner."

He put down his cup with a clatter of china. "She

can't have married Rayner. She didn't love him. He amused her, that was all. She told me once, laughing, that he was a 'Bond Street Lounger'—now, where on earth did she learn that term? She's never been to London. Well, no matter. She thought Rayner's main interests in life were the style of his cravat or the set of his coat." Matt cut himself short. He turned white. "Hilary, she didn't . . . She couldn't have married Rayner because of me? Because of what I said to her?"

"Matt, all I know is that she eloped to Scotland with Wilfred Rayner. Her mother admitted it. I thought you should know that much, but I can't stay to talk about it. In a few minutes from now—" Hilary glanced at the clock on the mantel—"in less than five minutes the duke will be here with a mount for me. He's riding across the border to find Belinda. Whether or not she's married, he intends to bring her home. And I'm going with him. Belinda will need me. I'll be back as soon as I can."

As she turned to leave the room, Matt pulled himself up from his chair and took several hobbling steps after her, saying urgently, "You can't run the risk of compromising yourself by going off like that with Alverly. It will be well after nightfall when you reach Scotland. You might not return until tomorrow. In any case it's not your responsibility. It's mine. Let me go with the duke . . ." His voice faded away. "I know," he muttered. "I can't ride. Even if I *could* ride, what use would I be to Alverly with this game leg of mine?"

"Matt, I'm sorry, I can't talk any more." Hilary ran up the stairs to her bedchamber. She tore off her pelisse and gown and changed hurriedly into her riding habit. As she dressed, a wave of guilt flooded over her because she hadn't taken the time to comfort Matt. His physical limitations must be more galling to him than ever in this emergency, when, as a whole man, he might have helped to rescue Belinda. But Hilary knew she couldn't delay even a moment longer to speak to her brother. After all these weeks in Wycombe, she knew His Grace the Duke of Alverly through and through. If she weren't ready on time, he would go on without her.

She was waiting at her front gate, breathless after a dash down the stairs and out the door, when Jon, leading a horse behind him, emerged from the driveway of the castle and cantered up to Willow Cottage. He dismounted and walked over to her. "You're ready on the minute."

"You didn't think I would be?"

He shook his head. "Oh, I knew you'd be standing at the gate, waiting for me. But Hilary, please think again. If accompanying me should prove a cause for scandal—"

"Scandal be damned," she said calmly. "Let's be going."

He gave a short, unwilling bark of laughter. "Very well. So be it." He extended his hand. "Let me help you mount." As she settled herself into the saddle, a sharp gust of chilling wind caused Hilary to clap her hand to her riding hat.

"I'm glad to see you're warmly dressed," Jon said, eyeing approvingly her long thick woolen cape. "It will be very cold once the sun goes down." He himself was wearing a long, ankle-length caped greatcoat. The garment was decidedly not of the latest cut, but it was made out of some bulky woolen material that looked very warm.

"I absconded with Matt's campaign cloak," Hilary explained with a laugh. "He's been telling me tales for years about the many occasions in the Peninsula when he spent the night sleeping on the ground, cozily warm in his campaign cloak."

"Thank the good Lord for Dr. Vane's cloak. It may save you from freezing to death. Shall we start?" Jon mounted his own horse.

As they headed out of the village toward the pass in the hills leading to the town of Bridgeton, they passed an urchin with a stick over his shoulder, trailing a line with a solitary small fish dangling from the end of it. Hilary recognized the boy as the son of the headmaster of the village grammar school. She sighed resignedly. By the next day the residents of the village and the farmers in the valley would know that the duke and Miss Vane had ridden together out of Wycombe in the direction of Bridgeton as dusk was falling. Well, it couldn't be helped. Belinda's welfare was all that counted now.

As they cantered briskly up the steep rutted road leading over the pass into the town, it quickly became apparent to Hilary that Jon was reining in his anger with an almost superhuman control. At one point he muttered, "I know Wilfred Rayner is a poltroon and a libertine, but I can't understand how even a man like that could take advantage of a defenseless, grief-stricken girl by persuading her into a marriage she'd never consider if she were in her right mind."

"She felt rejected," Hilary said. "She wanted to be valued by a man, and Wilfred was very much there."

He tossed her a quick, questioning glance. "I knew Belinda and Dr. Vane had become close friends, but I never suspected any romantic attachment between them. How was it that Belinda came to feel that your brother had rejected her?"

"It was sheer happenstance. Matt teasingly said he'd miss his favorite pupil when she married and went off to London or wherever, and Belinda blurted out that she had no intention of leaving Wycombe. All she wanted was to stay here and marry Matt. He was dumbfounded. So much so that he probably wasn't very diplomatic when he told Belinda that such a marriage was impossible. He gave all the correct reasons—he's years older than Belinda, he's crippled, he has no money, he ranks far below her socially—but Belinda couldn't accept any of them. She simply thought that Matt didn't love her."

"And does he?"

"Well, of course he does. He adores Belinda. But what has love to say to anything in a situation like this?"

"Nothing, I suppose. And yet . . ."

Raising an eyebrow, Hilary said, "Surely you agree with Matt that a marriage to Belinda would be unsuitable on all counts? You'd never allow Belinda to marry him?"

"Oh. Well, no. I daresay I wouldn't."

Jon's tone was so lacking in conviction that Hilary stared at him in surprise. If she weren't so aware of his pride in his rank and family heritage, she might almost suspect that he wouldn't object too strenuously to Belinda's marriage to Matt. But no, she must be mistaken. His attitude, or what she thought to be his attitude, was simply another aspect of the enigmatic riddle of personality that Jonathan Rayner, Duke of Alverly, presented to the world.

Jon lapsed into a silence that lasted until they crested

the pass in the mountain and descended into Bridgeton. It was now past five o'clock and the November sun was low on the horizon, but there were still pedestrians on the main street who recognized Jon and respectfully doffed their hats to him. Hilary devoutly hoped that no one would recognize her from her sporadic shopping expeditions into the town and her one appearance at the local assembly ball.

Leaving Bridgeton, they rode faster, traversing the narrow valley in which the town was situated, crossed another line of hills, and emerged into the turnpike leading north from Morpeth and Newcastle.

It was past seven o'clock by now. Dusk had fallen. Still wrapped in his cloak of brooding silence, Jon increased their pace to a fast canter when they joined the turnpike. At first Hilary had to concentrate all her attention on guiding her horse over the unfamiliar route in the darkness until the rising full moon cast its light on the road. Then she was able to relax a little and to indulge her growing curiosity.

"It just occurs to me that Scotland is a very large country," she observed. "Do you have a definite destination in mind?"

Jon roused himself from his dark thoughts. "Yes, though I'm guessing, naturally, since Elvira refused to tell me where Wilfred was going. Carter Bar is the nearest pass into Scotland from Wycombe, but I decided Wilfred would probably head for the border crossing at Coldstream, which happens to be one of the major marriage mills in Scotland. He'll want to marry Belinda as soon as possible. He knows me. He knows I'll come after him. However, he probably believes that if he and Belinda are already married when I reach them, I'll drop the matter." Jon gave a short ugly laugh. "He doesn't know me as well as he thinks he does."

Hilary shivered. Lord, she prayed silently, help me to prevent Jon from doing bodily harm to Wilfred Rayner. She never wanted to endure the agony of seeing Jon in the dock, sentenced to hang for murder, as she'd observed Samantha Pointer and Bill Syncott at the assize trials in Wincanton. But of course, Jon, as a peer, would be tried in the House of Lords. Small comfort that was. His fellow peers could condemn Jon to death as easily as could the justices in Wincanton. Refusing to allow herself to dwell on such horrors, she said aloud, "How far is it to Coldstream?"

"About fifteen miles. We should be there in under two hours." Jon went on talking, more to himself than to her, Hilary thought. He seemed almost to be sorting out his thoughts by speaking them aloud. "I know Wilfred has a long head start," he muttered, "but it will have taken him a certain amount of time to find a suitable place to be married and to arrange for the ceremony. And I daresay he wouldn't omit a festive wedding supper. So if we reach him and Belinda between nine and ten o'clock, we may be in time to—to . . ."

His voice trailed away. Hilary was grateful that the moonlight wasn't bright enough to reveal her embarrassed blush. She'd grasped immediately what Jon had in mind. He hoped to catch up to Belinda before Wilfred could bed her. Hilary hoped so, too. She believed that Wilfred Rayner's only chance of survival lay in Jon's discovery that his sister was still a virgin.

An hour and a half later, as the horses were showing signs of weariness from the steady, relentless pace Jon had set, he pointed ahead to a glimmer of moonlight on water. "The River Tweed," he said. "The border between England and Scotland. We're here, Hilary."

They trotted across the bridge to the Scottish side of the river. A man carrying a lantern emerged from the tollhouse to collect the toll. "Would ye be after getting married, sir?" he asked Jon hopefully. "I could perform the ceremony fer ye right in the tollhouse."

"No, thank you. The lady and I aren't eloping." Jon tossed the tollkeeper a coin. "Tell me, though, have you married many couples today?"

The man shook his head. "Nay, sir. Ane couple only," he said mournfully. "Round aboot noontime, it were. Weel, it be getting on fer winter, ye ken. Summer's the time fer weddings, forbye."

Jon reached into his pocket for another coin. "Do you recall seeing a young couple on horseback crossing the bridge in late afternoon? A fashionably dressed man and a very pretty girl of about eighteen?"

The keeper pocketed the second coin so swiftly he might have been a conjurer, and wrinkled his brow thoughtfully. Hilary intervened, saying, "The young lady was probably wearing a green riding habit and a hat trimmed with an ostrich feather."

The tollkeeper's face cleared. "*That* young couple. Aye, I remember them. A grand gentleman and a verra bonnie lassie, they were. Wanted tae know which was the best inn in the town."

"Which is?" Jon prompted him.

"Weel, noo, I canna rightly say. There be *twa* verra guid inns in Coldstream. The Crown and Anchor, and the Coldstream Arms. And I wouldna take it amiss if ye were tae mention tae the landlords that I recommended their establishments."

Jon burst out laughing, his amusement momentarily easing the lines of strain in his dark face. He said to the keeper, "You have a little financial arrangement with the two landlords, I gather? Well, more power to you." He reached into his pocket for several more coins and bestowed them on the grinning keeper.

As he and Hilary left the tollhouse, Jon said, "I didn't really think Wilfred would choose to be married at the toll bridge, but I had to ask. We can't overlook any possibility."

"I daresay Wilfred would consider it demeaning to be married by a mere tollkeeper," Hilary agreed.

As they rode into the town, they found its streets virtually deserted now that night had fallen; the only signs of life were the lights from individual houses and the several inns in the main street. Hilary voiced a thought that had begun to trouble her. "Jon, what if we've guessed wrong? What if Wilfred decided to go elsewhere in Scotland? To Gretna Green, perhaps?"

Turning his head to look at her, Jon said bleakly, "Then we've failed, but only temporarily. For my part, I intend to pursue Wilfred Rayner to the Antipodes, if necessary." The venom in his tone sent a chill to Hilary's heart. Jon glanced to his right. "There's the Crown and Anchor. We might as well try there first."

The Crown and Anchor was a disappointment. The landlord had registered no guest named Rayner.

"Perhaps Wilfred gave a false name," Hilary said to Jon in a low voice.

"If you marry under an alias, the ceremony isn't legal," Jon replied. "But I daresay Wilfred might have registered at the inn under a false name to throw us off the scent."

The landlord listened to a physical description of Wilfred and Belinda, and shook his head. "Nay, sir. I havena any sich young pairsons staying wi' me the nicht."

Hilary thought the landlord was telling the truth. So, evidently, did Jon. He thanked the landlord and took his leave.

"Well, we have one more chance," said Hilary as Jon helped her to mount. "The Coldstream Arms. Wasn't that the other inn the tollkeeper mentioned?"

"There must be more than two inns in the town. We'll try them all," Jon replied, but he failed to sound very convincing. And time was passing, Hilary thought. The more time that elapsed until they found Belinda, the more dire the consequences could be.

In the courtyard of the Coldstream Arms, they gave the reins of their horses into the hands of the ostler who bustled out to greet them, and trudged into the inn. As she stepped over the threshold, Hilary suddenly realized that every muscle in her body ached from the long, wearying ride. She longed for a cup of hot tea, a plate of buttered toast, and a comfortable chair beside a roaring fire.

"I wish to see the landlord," Jon curtly informed a manservant.

The stout, genial-looking individual who appeared in the foyer took a long look at Jon's unfashionable garments and at Hilary's serviceable, worn cloak. Some of the geniality faded from his features. "Aye, sir. Be ye wanting a room fer the nicht?" The man's eyes brightened. "Or mayhap ye're wishing tae be married?"

"I am not. However, I'm looking for a man named Rayner, Wilfred Rayner, who may have come to your

331

establishment in the company of a young lady sometime this evening with the intention of being married. It's urgent I find this man."

The landlord shrugged. "I fear I canna help ye. I'm nae acquainted wi' anybody named Rayner. Certainly I've nae married any gentleman o' that name this day, nor any other day. Weel, then, if ye ha' nae more questions—?" The man turned to go.

Hilary grabbed Jon's arm. "I think he's lying," she muttered. "Did you notice how he avoided meeting your eyes?"

"Yes. I think you're right." In two long strides Jon caught up with the landlord and seized him by the shoulder. Jon growled, "You'll give me a straight answer, man, or you'll be sorry you were ever born. Now, then, is Wilfred Rayner here?"

Before the frightened landlord could reply, the sound of thunderous knocking reverberated from the second story of the inn, accompanied by a man's loud, angry voice.

"Jon! That's Wilfred," Hilary exclaimed.

Without a word Jon leaped for the staircase. Taking several treads at a time, he disappeared around the bend of the stairs. Hilary followed behind him as fast as she could.

Near the head of the staircase, Wilfred Rayner stood pounding on a door with both fists, bellowing furiously, "Belinda, open up. If you think you can play me for a fool, you're badly mistaken."

"Go away," came Belinda's tremulous voice from the other side of the door.

"The hell I will. Open this door before I break it down—" Wilfred subsided with a gasp as Jon's sinewy fingers closed around his neck.

As he shook Wilfred's body back and forth like a mastiff preparing his victim for the kill, Jon snarled, "You're the mistaken one, you damned loose fish. Did you really think you could succeed in marrying my sister, turning her into little more than a whore, while you continued to sleep with her mother?"

Rushing to Jon, Hilary tugged at his arm, desperately trying to break his hold on Wilfred's neck. "Jon, stop," she panted. "You're killing him. Can't you see he's turning blue?"

"Good," Jon growled. His face was livid with rage. "He's getting what he deserves."

"Jon, listen to me," Hilary pleaded, tugging even harder at his arm. "Didn't you hear what Wilfred was saying to Belinda? I don't think they're married. There's no need to kill him."

For a moment Jon's hands stilled. "*Are* you married?" he asked Wilfred.

Hilary caught her breath. The tension was almost unbearable.

Close to fainting, unable to speak, Wilfred shook his head from side to side. Jon released his grip and Wilfred staggered away, supporting himself against the wall while he sucked in air in great gulping gasps.

Jon wheeled toward the door of the bedchamber in front of which Wilfred had been standing. "Belinda," he called. "Are you all right?"

"Jon! Is that really you?" In a few moments the key turned in the lock and Belinda peered out through the partially opened door. When she caught sight of Hilary, she dashed into the hallway to throw her arms around the older girl. "Hilary—oh, I'm so glad to see you."

Jon said, "Belinda, did you marry this man?"

Belinda shuddered. "No. Oh, thank God, no."

His slate gray eyes still blazing with anger, Jon turned on Wilfred. "Get out," he barked. "If you ever come near Belinda again, I'll kill you. Is that understood?"

Clutching his throat, Wilfred nodded. He stumbled toward the head of the staircase. Jon made an instinctive move to follow his cousin, and Hilary called out to him sharply, "Jon, don't even think of going after him. He's finished. He can't harm Belinda any more. You'll only hurt yourself if you try to punish him."

Jon stopped in his tracks. Slowly his eyes cleared, and some of the tension left his body.

Gently releasing Belinda's clinging arms, Hilary said to her in a low voice, "Go into your bedchamber, love. I'll join you in a moment." As soon as the girl had gone, Hilary walked over to Jon, who suddenly seemed a little dazed now that the necessity for violent action had passed. She put her hand on his arm. "Go downstairs and wait for me," she urged. "I think Belinda needs to talk to another woman just now. Order some wine and a meal. It's been hours since we had anything to eat."

"Yes. All right," he muttered, and walked slowly toward the staircase. Hilary gazed after him worriedly. His fury had apparently dissipated, leaving him in a strangely altered mood that she couldn't fathom.

"Oh, Hilary, I've been such a fool," Belinda wailed when Hilary entered the bedchamber.

Seating herself beside Belinda on the bed, Hilary hugged the girl, saying, "I'm sure you weren't such a fool as all that. Do you want to talk about it? For instance, how did you come to elope with Mr. Rayner? You didn't love him."

Belinda hung her head. "I was all to pieces when

Matt refused to marry me. I kept to my bedchamber and simply wanted to die. Well, not really, I suppose. I know now I was being very childish. People don't die for love. Anyway, after a while Mama insisted on talking to me, and somehow she wheedled out of me the reason I was so unhappy, and she told Wilfred about Matt. I was angry with Mama at first for betraying my confidence, but Wilfred was *so* sympathetic. He made me feel better almost immediately. So when he suggested we should get married and go live in London, I agreed. Seeing new places and meeting new people, I thought, would help me to forget about Matt."

"Not a very good reason for getting married," Hilary murmured.

"No. I realized what a hideous mistake I'd made about halfway into the elopement when we stopped at an inn for coffee and a bite to eat, and Wilfred kissed me. I couldn't bear the touch of his lips. Feeling that way, I knew I shouldn't marry him, and I told him so. But he just laughed and said all brides are nervous before their weddings, and I thought, well, perhaps I *was* just being nervous."

"And then?" prompted Hilary.

Belinda's voice trembled with remembered anguish as she said, "Well, then we arrived here at the inn, and Wilfred sent me up to this room to rest and to change my clothes for the wedding while he went off to find a clergyman. The landlord of the inn could have married us, of course, but Wilfred said it would be more dignified, more suitable to our rank, if a clergyman performed the ceremony. While Wilfred was gone, I came to my senses at last. I knew I'd rather die than marry him. So I locked myself in this room and refused to

335

open the door for him. Wilfred threatened to break the door down, and I told him I'd hit him over the head with a poker if he set one foot inside the room."

Torn between sympathy and a desire to laugh, Hilary said, "Did you really mean that? You would have hit Wilfred with a poker?"

Belinda nodded her head vigorously. "Oh, yes." She pointed to an object on the floor near the door. "There's the poker. I dropped it when I heard Jon's voice." Suddenly reaction set in, and Belinda began shaking. "Oh, Hilary," she whispered, "I can't bear to think what might have happened if you and Jon hadn't come after me."

Holding Belinda close, Hilary said, "But Jon and I *did* come, love, and you're safe now. We'll bring you back to Wycombe tomorrow." She stood, pulling Belinda up with her. "Here, let me help you undress. You brought a valise? Good. Here's a nightdress. Now get into bed. You're exhausted."

Hilary tucked the coverlets snugly around Belinda. Smiling down at the younger girl, Hilary said, "You'll be all right if I leave you? You need a good night's rest."

Belinda smiled back at her. "I'll be fine now that I know you and Jon are nearby."

"I'll send up a servant with tea and a light supper. Good night, love."

Hilary came down the stairs to find the landlord standing in the foyer, obviously waiting for her. "There ye be, ma'am," he said, bowing deeply. "The gentleman be waiting fer ye in the private parlor juist down the hallway, first door tae yer right."

Hilary smiled to herself. Jon's inborn sense of authority had worked its usual magic with the surly landlord, who now seemed eager to ingratiate himself. "Thank you," she said. "Please send up some tea and a light meal to the young lady."

As she turned to walk down the hallway, the landlord said, "Please tae wait ane moment, ma'am," He cleared his throat. "The gentleman, he signed his name 'Alverly.' Be he an English lord, forbye?"

"Yes, he is." There was no need to be any more explicit, Hilary thought, no need to publicize Jon's rank or Belinda's. The fewer who knew about Belinda's elopement, the better.

The landlord nodded with satisfaction. "Ach, I kenned as much. Weel, noo, ma'am, His Lordship wouldna talk tae me, but I wish tae inform him that I didna realize the ither gentleman was sich a villain, kidnapping the puir young lassie, trying tae force her tae marry him. Will ye tell his lordship that, ma'am? I meant nae harm."

"Yes, of course." Jon must have been more intimidating than usual, Hilary mused, as she walked down the hallway. Why had he refused to accept the landlord's apology? As soon as she entered the private parlor, she understood. A table had been set with a cold supper, but neither the bottle of wine nor the food had been touched. Jon sat on a settee before the fireplace, his shoulders hunched, his face buried in his hands. His body reflected an attitude of despair more eloquently than words could have done.

With a brightness she didn't feel, Hilary said, "I've just left Belinda. She's calm. I think she'll be fine." She added, laughing, "Actually I don't think Belinda really needed to be rescued. She told me she threatened Wilfred with a poker and had every intention of using it."

Slowly Jon straightened and looked up at her. There

337

were deep lines in his face, and his eyes were dull. He didn't respond to her laughter. "I'm glad Belinda is all right," he muttered.

Hilary poured a glass of wine and offered it to him. She said quietly, "What's the matter, Jon? You should be feeling relieved and happy that Belinda is safe and well."

"Happy? God!" Jon drained the wine and hurled the glass into the fireplace. "I nearly committed murder tonight. If you hadn't stopped me, I'd have killed Wilfred Rayner."

"But Jon—you *didn't* kill Wilfred. You're not guilty of anything. Why—?"

He interrupted her. "You don't understand. Wilfred is a conscienceless libertine who tried to use my sister for his own ends, but if he'd been a saint in monk's robes, I'd still have tried to kill him. I went nearly berserk when I thought he'd persuaded Belinda to marry into the Rayner line of succession and contaminate it with our poisoned blood."

"Poisoned blood? What do you mean?"

He hesitated for a moment, and then the anguished words poured out as if emotions repressed for years had finally broken through the dam of stoic reserve he'd built around himself. "Hilary! Belinda isn't my sister. She's my daughter. She's the child of incest."

So profoundly shocked that her knees felt weak, Hilary sank onto the sofa beside Jon. After a moment she recovered herself and reached out to take one of Jon's hands in a warm, comforting grasp.

He gave her an astonished look. "You aren't sickened by me?" he asked.

"Sickened? Oh, no, Jon, never that. But I don't understand . . ."

Now that he'd revealed the damning secret he'd protected so fiercely for so many years, Jon seemed to find relief in telling Hilary the whole story. Staring straight ahead of him into the flames of the fireplace, he spoke haltingly, pausing at intervals when a wave of bitter memories swept over him.

"I never liked Elvira," he began. "I suppose I was jealous that a young and beautiful woman—Elvira is only four years older than I am—had replaced my mother. We rubbed along tolerably well, though, until my father had a stroke about a year after he married Elvira. He was totally paralyzed. He couldn't even speak. Elvira felt nothing but revulsion for Father in his helpless state. She could scarcely bring herself to visit him for a few minutes every day."

Hilary drew a quick breath. "Oh, no. How could she be so unfeeling?"

Jon shrugged. "It's not something you could do, Hilary. But then, you're nothing like Elvira."

He went on. "Well, then, Elvira had always hated Wycombe for its isolation, its lack of the lively social life she'd enjoyed in London. Now that my father was ill, she hated the castle more than ever. So one night, no doubt to relieve her boredom and unhappiness, she came to my bedchamber. I was fifteen. I'd never—I'd never had sexual relations with a woman, and I didn't try very hard to fend Elvira off. God help me, I enjoyed the night of passion we spent together. But the next morning when I fully realized what I'd done, that I'd slept with my own father's wife . . ."

Jon shuddered. "What happened afterwards was infinitely worse. Elvira became pregnant. In the last few months of my father's life, her condition became obvious to him. Although he couldn't speak, couldn't move a muscle, I could read his feelings in his eyes. His mind was as clear as ever. He knew his wife was pregnant by another man. He died knowing Elvira had betrayed him with another man. Thank God, oh, thank God, he never knew I was the man."

After a long pause, Jon continued in a dull, flat voice. "When Father died, I felt so guilty I wanted to kill myself. But Elvira gave birth only a few days after the funeral, and I realized I had responsibilities to the child and also to the estate. I didn't commit suicide. Instead, I vowed never to marry, never to allow my bad blood to continue in the veins of another generation."

Hilary gasped. "Is that why——?" She cut herself short, feeling the heat rising in her cheeks.

Looking steadily into her eyes, he said, "Yes. That's why I never asked you to marry me, Hilary, even though I am madly in love with you. I couldn't risk having children." He flushed "Legitimate children, I mean." Noticing her confused, uncertain look, he said incredulously, "Hilary! You did know I love you? How could you not know?"

"You never told me. I thought you were only interested in sleeping with me."

"Oh, my God! How could you think that? If I'd simply wanted sex, I had other outlets for that."

"Like the farmer's widow in the valley?"

After a single surprised moment, Jon began to laugh so hard that the tears gathered in his eyes. Finally he said, "That's so like you, Hilary. You've always spoken up to me, and devil the consequences, since the first moment we met. It's one of the things I've always loved best about you."

Gradually the laughter faded from his face. His expression became sober. "I never thought I'd tell anyone

340

about Belinda's conception," he said slowly. "Actually I tried not to think about her birth, but the knowledge was always there, festering deep inside me." He gave a great sigh. "I'm glad I told you, Hilary. Now at least you know I'd marry you if I could."

"What makes you think I'd want to marry you?"

He looked at once shaken and crestfallen. "I was sure—that is, I hoped—that you cared for me at least a little," he stammered.

"Of course I love you, you idiot. I love you so much it hurts. I said what I said to shake you up a little. Jon, you've allowed this notion that you have bad blood— 'poisoned blood'—to ruin your life, and now you're about to ruin Belinda's. You don't want her to marry at all, do you? That's why you've kept her cooped up at Wycombe Castle, that's why you don't want her to have a London season. You're afraid she might meet some man who would want to marry her."

"I think it would be better if she doesn't marry, certainly," Jon said in a low voice. "I don't want either of us to pass on this taint in our blood—and it *is* a taint—to another generation."

Drawing a deep breath, Hilary said, "My darling, listen to me. You've been consumed by guilt for years because of a boyhood mistake. A terrible mistake, I grant you, for which Elvira was far more responsible than you were. Think about it. You were a boy of fifteen, little more than a child, when an older, experienced woman seduced you. No doubt she began by offering you comfort and affection at a time when you were overcome with grief over your father's illness. Perhaps a saint might have resisted Elvira, but God knows you've never been a saint!"

341

White to the lips, Jon said, "I *am* guilty. I committed incest. I slept with my father's wife."

Clenching her fists in angry exasperation, Hilary cried, "You did *not* commit incest, whatever the church or the law has to say about 'spiritual consanguinity.' You and Elvira aren't related by blood, and you never had any intention of betraying your father. Jon, you've cut yourself off from a normal life for years because of that boyhood transgression. Haven't you done enough penance for your 'sin'? Can't you put what happened that terrible night behind you and let yourself enjoy a little happiness at last?"

His face twisted with pain and uncertainty, Jon jumped up from the sofa and stumbled over to the fireplace, where he stood tensely in a pose now familiar to her, looking down into the flames.

Hilary sat watching him in helpless silence. She'd done her best, but she had little hope that a few words from her could help Jon erase the guilt that had paralyzed his life since he was fifteen years old.

The seconds passed, and the minutes. The only sound in the room was the occasional crackle of a burning log. At last Jon turned away from the fireplace. His face lit by a radiant smile, a smile Hilary had never seen before, he exclaimed, "My love, will you marry me?"

She rushed to his waiting arms. "Oh, darling, of course I'll marry you," she cried, as he folded her in a crushing embrace. For the first time Hilary allowed herself to respond fully to his hungry lips, to the hard pressure of his body against hers. She made no objection when he lifted her in his arms, muttering, "I've waited for this for so long. I want you so much," and flung himself down beside her on the sofa.

As Jon's seeking lips trailed scorching kisses along her

342

cheeks and the sensitive skin of her throat and his know-ing hands caressed her body, Hilary relaxed in a flood of physical ecstasy she'd never known before. A primeval urge to reciprocate the exquisite sensual pleasure Jon was giving her led her to tear off his cravat and unbut-ton his shirt and glide her fingers over the firm skin of his chest and his hardening nipples. "Darling, oh dar-ling," he gasped, and then, to Hilary's astonishment, he pulled away from her and sat up. "We've got to stop this," he said breathlessly.

Hilary looked up at him, bewildered. "What's the matter?"

"Nothing's the matter. It's just—we can't make love, that's all."

Jerking herself upright, Hilary exclaimed indignantly, "Jonathan Rayner, you've been trying to entice me into your bed for weeks, and now that I've agreed to marry you, you don't want to make love to me?"

Looking a little sheepish, Jon said, "Of course I do. I never wanted anything more in my whole life. But now that we're properly engaged, I want us to be respect-able. I want to wait to make love to you until after we're married."

Hilary shook her head. "If I live to be ninety, I'll never completely understand you."

"I'll make sure you don't," he retorted, with a grin so youthful and lighthearted that Hilary caught a glimpse of the boy he'd been before Elvira fastened her claws into him. He paused, casting a rueful look at his unbut-toned shirt. A glint of passion ignited in his eyes. "I'm not sure how long I can be a gentleman. If you kiss me like that again ... Hilary, I don't think I can wait for the wedding. Let's get married right away by special li-cense."

Hilary threw her arms around Jon's neck. "What a splendid idea," she murmured, nestling her head on his bare chest. "Let's find an accommodating bishop as soon as possible."

Epilogue

"She's such a beautiful bride," Mrs. Trevor remarked fondly as she watched a flushed and smiling Belinda make her way down the line in the country dance. "That coral-colored gown is so becoming, and the little tiara in her hair makes her look like a queen." The vicar's wife fanned herself gently, although the windows and doors of the parish hall were all opened to admit the soft breezes of a balmy August evening.

"Yes, she looks lovely," Hilary agreed. She laughed. "What's more, Belinda's really enjoying her own wedding." Belinda had insisted on inviting the entire village of Wycombe and all the tenants of the Rayner estate to her wedding ball.

From her seat beside Mrs. Trevor on the edge of the dance floor, Hilary looked at Matt, standing next to their brother and his wife. Sir Richard and Lady Vane had come all the way from Suffolk for the wedding. However, although Matt was apparently deep in a conversation with his brother and sister-in-law, his eyes were locked on his bride as she flitted gracefully through the figures of the country dance.

Hilary's mind drifted back to the previous November,

shortly after she and Jon had returned to Wycombe Castle following their hasty marriage ceremony performed by the Bishop of Newcastle and a brief whirlwind honeymoon. Her lips curved in a smile as she remembered the family dinner party celebrating the marriage. With his usual bluntness, Jon had said abruptly to Matt and Belinda, "If you two wish to get married, I have no objection."

Turning pale, Matt looked deep into Belinda's eyes, saying, "I love you with all my heart and soul. If you still love me—"

Belinda interrupted him, her face glowing. "Oh, Matt, of course I still love you."

"Then I'd like very much to marry you next August—after you've had a London season."

"Matt!" wailed Belinda.

He'd been obdurate. If, after Belinda had plunged into London society and had met swarms of eligible men, she still wanted to marry him, well and good. So Jon and Hilary had rented a large, imposing house in Grosvenor Square and launched Belinda on her social career. To everyone's satisfaction, Elvira had claimed no part in her daughter's come-out.

Evicted from Wycombe Castle after Jon discovered her connivance in Belinda's elopement with Wilfred, Elvira had fallen on hard times after her return to London. As Jon had suspected, she had squandered the money left to her by the Earl of Lansdale and had no source of income except for borrowing from her friends and acquaintances, a source that had quickly dried up. However, using her charm and still astonishing beauty, Elvira had succeeded in turning her fortunes around. She'd snared a wealthy, obese, and aged Hungarian diplomat as her third husband and had gone off with him to Vienna.

Belinda had thoroughly enjoyed her season. She adored her wardrobe of dazzling new gowns, she danced until dawn night after night, she fended off scores of suitors with smiling politeness, and in the end she came home to Wycombe and threw herself into Matt's willing arms.

Gazing at Belinda as she came off the dance floor and paused to chat with her new husband and her new brother-in-law and his wife, Mrs. Trevor murmured, "I'm so glad Belinda married your brother, my dear. Last autumn we all thought she would marry Mr. Wilfred Rayner."

"Oh, I don't think that was ever a serious possibility," Hilary replied. She reflected with a grim enjoyment on Wilfred's fate. After his failed attempt to elope with Belinda, Wilfred, like Elvira, had returned to London. His finances were even shakier than Elvira's. Deeply in debt, hounded by his creditors, he'd been forced to flee to the Continent to avoid being clapped into debtors' prison. How he lived in the Netherlands or whether he would ever return to England were matters of indifference to the Rayner family.

Jon came up to Hilary's chair. "This is my dance, I believe," he said. He looked magnificent in his evening clothes from the master hand of the London tailor, Weston. After her marriage, Hilary had finally met Jon's valet, who, it turned out, was named Leonard. She and Leonard, who was deliriously happy to have an ally at last, had ruthlessly taken over Jon's wardrobe. He was still supremely uncaring about his clothes and how he looked in them, but between them Hilary and Leonard had succeeded in winning an accolade from the great

Beau Brummell himself. "The Duke of Alverly," the Beau had pronounced, "is one of the best-dressed gentlemen in the *ton.*"

The fiddlers struck up a waltz, and Jon swept Hilary into his arms and onto the dance floor. Glancing around her, Hilary said with a laugh, "We've debauched the entire population of the Wycombe Valley." Tonight, unlike their experience at the Harvest Ball, she and Jon weren't the only couple performing the waltz. Belinda had mischievously taught the steps to all her former classmates in Hilary's school, and they, obviously, had taught their friends. The dance floor was crowded.

"I'm the border lord, remember," he retorted with a grin. "I can do whatever I like in my own territory."

"Wretch," she said fondly. He swung her around in a sweeping circle, and she remonstrated, "Careful. You'll disturb your heir." She glanced down at the decided bulge in her midriff. "Soon I'll be fat and ugly," she teased. "You won't want to dance with me."

A flame ignited in the slate gray eyes. "You'll never be ugly. You'll always be the most beautiful woman in the world, and I'll adore you until the day I die."

Hilary smiled up at Jon. "I'll hold you to that, love."

WHAT'S LOVE GOT TO DO WITH IT?

Everything . . . Just ask Kathleen Drymon . . . and Zebra Books

PENELOPE NERI'S STORIES WILL WARM YOU THROUGH THE LONGEST, COLDEST NIGHT!

BELOVED SCOUNDREL	(1799, $3.95/$4.95)
CHERISH THE NIGHT	(3654, $5.99/$6.99)
CRIMSON ANGEL	(3359, $4.50/$5.50)
DESERT CAPTIVE	(2447, $3.95/$4.95)
FOREVER AND BEYOND	(3115, $4.95/$5.95)
FOREVER IN HIS ARMS	(3385, $4.95/$5.95)
JASMINE PARADISE	(3062, $4.50/$5.50)
MIDNIGHT CAPTIVE	(2593, $3.95/$4.95)
NO SWEETER PARADISE	(4024, $5.99/$6.99)
PASSION'S BETRAYAL	(3291, $4.50/$5.50)
SEA JEWEL	(3013, $4.50/$5.50)